THE REALITY ASSERTION

Deplosion: Book 4

Paul Anlee

Darian Publishing House
Chatham, Ontario, Canada

For Martin and Dorothy

For every subtle and complicated question,
there is a perfectly simple and
straightforward answer...which is wrong.

- H.L. Mencken

Series Synopsis

Alum, the nanotech-enhanced Living God, has ruled the Realm for over 130 million years. During His reign of peaceful expansion, humans in their myriad biological and robotic forms have expanded outward from the original Vesta asteroid colonies to millions of stars across thousands of galaxies. We have genetically-adapted Terran life to countless niches, sometimes absorbing alien biology into our own and sometimes eradicating competitive life forms.

Now, in order to banish Chaos from the multiverse, Alum is moving forward with His Divine Plan to recreate all of existence in His version of Heaven, one in which there will be no room for unpredictable quantum reality. The key component of His Plan, the Deplosion Array, is almost ready. Its billions of Reality Assertion Field generating asteroids that orbit the supermassive black hole in the center of the Milky Way are poised to return Creation to a primordial state.

Meanwhile, the Cybrid known as Darya has been quietly building a rebel force to destroy the Deplosion Array. Already, they've carried out one successful suicide attack that took out millions of array elements. But their attempts to completely halt construction have fallen short and the Deplosion Array is nearing completion.

Darya has joined forces with the man-God, Darak Legsu, Dr. Darian Leigh (recorporealized from within the deadly Eater), and the surviving rebels of Eso-La. Together, they're creating an army of billions to carry out one final do-or-die attack and stop Alum before He destroys the universe.

Of course, Darak Legsu has been working on his own secret plans to deal with Alum, and the arduous journey and shocking truths upending Brother Stralasi's life and beliefs are only the beginning. Part of those plans involve the Six—six paranoid, treacherous alien Gods from other galaxies that Darak has been trying to wield into a powerful alliance.

Will the headstrong leaders of the rebellion unite with the Six in Darak's fractious and fragile coalition and defeat the Living God? Or will Alum prevail in converting all of Creation to His version of Heaven?

1

"WE GROW IMPATIENT. ALUM MUST BE STOPPED!" Glenchax's voice shook the pillars and bounced off the star-encrusted ceiling of the Hall of Thrones.

Four of the other five Gods bellowed agreement.

Raytansoh, the fifth, monitored passively, as had been his way for ages. His avatar—anonymously dark and vaguely humanoid like all the others—said nothing, signaled nothing.

Skeptical, Darak sat forward and arched an eyebrow.

"You said, 'We'. Does this mean you're finally talking to one another?"

The guffaws and scoffing that erupted across the five active channels suggested that this most certainly was not the case.

Ishtgor was the only one who bothered to put words to his contemptuous snort.

"I'm sure Glenchax merely extrapolated our consensus from previous conversations," he explained. "I don't believe any of us has developed a sudden trust in the independent communications links you provided."

"My quantum-encrypted, entangled channels are secure," Darak assured the group.

"But not as secure as the extra filter provided by communicating through you," Ishtgor contended.

Darak sighed. He was glad they trusted him but there was no need to funnel *everything* through his personal lattice. The links he'd provided them were more than adequate for simple verbal communication, and the intentionally narrow bandwidth was too restrictive for anyone to sneak through a concepta virus.

On the other hand, the Gods did think in terms of eons. He supposed it was possible that one of the Six could inject a tiny, self-assembling worm a few bits at a time given enough years. It was highly unlikely but theoretically possible.

Ughh. Only the most xenophobic, paranoid beings would believe that talking directly to one another would pose any serious risk.

Unfortunately, xenophobic and paranoid described these Gods perfectly.

He referred to the Six as *Gods*, not *gods*, adopting the blanket capitalization when he'd first approached them. Capitalization seemed a fitting gesture. After all, when discussing beings with the power to alter the fabric of reality, there was no such thing as a *minor* deity.

Oddly enough, as supremely powerful as they might be within each of their own domains, they were terrified of encountering others like themselves. They insisted on keeping their individual locations, identities, and species a tightly guarded secret. The only way he could get them to agree to meet was by letting them project avatars, virtual representations of themselves, into a neutral territory.

Darak pushed on.

"In any case, my plans on how to deal with Alum are moving forward at an acceptable pace," his translator routines relayed to each of the Six in his or her preferred language.

"Yes, about those plans—you haven't shared many details with us," Glenchax pointed out. "Every time we raise the question, you refuse to divulge specifics. So, I ask again, exactly how are you going to deal with Alum's supposed Divine Plan to destroy the universe and recreate it in His personal vision of Heaven? And I'm warning you, I'm in no mood to be placated with evasive talk."

Darak suppressed his impatience. They'd danced around and around this issue countless times.

In truth, I hardly know what I'll do, myself—Darak admitted, but only to himself. It made no sense to share his uncertainty with them.

For the thousandth time, doubt crept in. Had it been a mistake to pull this group together? Herding house cats was a challenge. Herding intransigent, skittish wildcats with the powers to alter the laws of nature was proving practically impossible.

How much can I rely on them for decent advice? And for sane action?

The light over Ishtgor's station glowed.

"You haven't even told us where this Realm of humans is," he complained.

It was true. Darak had resisted giving up the location of the Realm, and for good reason.

"You know I can't expose all of humanity to the possibility of an attack," he reminded Ishtgor, "any more than you'd want me to open you to attacks from them or from each other's empires, for that matter."

"Perhaps it would be more—shall we say, effective?—to simply tell us how to reach Alum. Then, we can all deal with Him together," Glenchax suggested.

"I will reveal that when it becomes relevant to our actions," Darak said.

Not that it would matter—he thought. Where exactly is a broadly distributed consciousness like Alum physically located? Could one pinpoint precisely where He could be found? The answer was something along the lines of everywhere and nowhere, all at once. It could well prove impossible to pin Him down.

He found it telling that each of the Six had opted for the security, comfort, and simplicity of a single physical embodiment to house their considerable minds, however big that resultant "body" might be. Depchaun's physical manifestation was the largest, boasting a girth the size of Neptune.

Alum had been smarter than that. He'd chosen a distributed existence with multiple redundancies. It was a formidable form.

No sense getting into that with them; better to redirect the conversation.

"Anyway," Darak continued, "who's to say Alum couldn't defend Himself and come after you if any of you were to attack?"

"What, turn the tables? Against all six of us at once?" Ishtgor sputtered.

Darak's eyes shifted to the conspicuously inactive member of the group, whose blinking amber light above an inert avatar was the only indication that the sixth God, Raytansoh, was listening.

"The last time I checked," Darak corrected, "only *five* of you contribute to these meetings."

"Still, that's five Gods against one!" Ishtgor snapped back.

"I keep telling you, Alum's Realm is larger and more powerful than any of yours. You won't even risk exposing your empires to each other; you certainly don't want to give Him a direct link back into each of your territories."

Depchaun's eyes, or more correctly his avatar's eyes, narrowed.

"We have only your word on this, Darak Legsu," he stated quietly and matter-of-factly. The undertone of simmering menace was unmistakable.

"True, but let me put it into perspective for everyone. By now, you all have some idea of my capabilities, yes? Okay. Well, relative to Alum, I am a mite."

"In fairness, we have little measure of your capabilities and even less of your temperament," Glenchax argued. "We know that you have a history of recklessness to the point of being irresponsible and yet, when it concerns Alum, your caution paralyzes you."

Darak stepped off his throne and paced into the middle of the floor. His eyes roamed over the elegant, fluted columns separating the meeting area from the dim-glow of space beyond, and he took in the gentle, gold-hued light radiating from the ceiling onto the six charcoal-colored, human-shaped avatars that occupied the bejeweled thrones dotting the perimeter.

The Gods had wanted it this way; all of them had chosen to reflect Darak's human form for these meetings rather than give away their true species and identities.

Good grief. As if finding them at all, creating an entire, tiny universe designed especially for our gatherings, and offering up this glorious Hall of Thrones replete with every sign of wealth and power one might hope to appease any Supreme Being weren't enough to demonstrate my capabilities! What more will it take to satisfy their egos, quell their doubts, and calm their fears?

He peered into the galaxy inlay on the floor. It contained actual star stuff, made possible by enhancing a weak nuclear force in this micro-universe. Past the edge of the meeting room, there were galaxy-spanning clouds of gas, dimly glowing factories for new stars. Their thrones were diamond-encrusted, velvet-cushioned, obsidian slabs from another place, held artificially stable in this universe He'd custom engineered so they could feel relatively comfortable, safe, and untraceable. He'd provided them with private, secure, encrypted channels. What more would it take? Would they every trust him enough to move forward?

Darak lifted his head and answered Glenchax's challenge.

"It was through my *irresponsibility*, as you put it, that we have come together here at all."

"I'll give you that," Depchaun conceded. "Your reckless journeys to our various regions of the universe alerted each of us to the presence of others like ourselves. The unfortunate result is that you know all about us, while we know almost nothing about you except what you've allowed."

"It might have been better if you'd never come," Lyv chimed in.

Darak faced her. "Perhaps. And then you, all of you, would have basically disappeared, one-by-one, as the field generated by Alum's Deplosion Array overwhelmed your defenses. You wouldn't have seen it coming. You would've had no warning and no idea what hit you. Would the universe be any worse off if I'd played it that way?"

He looked around the room and shrugged in answer to his own question.

Lyv emitted a harsh laugh.

"Darak Legsu, you bait me with your theatrics, but they have no power."

Darak sensed the air shimmer around him. Was Lyv taking advantage of the moment to cast a field around him? Was she attempting to alter the nature of his reality? Or was one of the others probing for weakness, yet again?

He swept away the clumsy probe and glared at Lyv's avatar.

"Be careful not to reach beyond what your eight poisonous appendages can easily grasp," Darak warned.

Lyv gasped.

Her short, sharp inhalation echoed through the hushed Hall. Darak's rebuttal had, against the convention of their meetings, revealed her arachnid nature to the others.

Useless information, but a hint that I could reveal more if pushed. Darak prepared for her rebuke.

Instead, she apologized. "I regret my expression of frustration. It is easy to forget that we are all equals here."

Darak returned to his seat.

"More or less," he countered and settled into the sumptuous cushion. "No matter. We've found common ground and a common enemy. Let us remain focused on our primary objective."

Ishtgor grunted in agreement, "To kill Alum."

Darak leaned back. "To *stop* Alum," he corrected.

"By any means possible," Ishtgor added.

"By any *reasonable* means," Darak revised.

"Pahh! Semantics."

"An important distinction," Darak replied. "I will not destroy my species to prevent Alum's Divine Plan. Nor will I leave my people defenseless and open to assimilation into any of your realms."

"But we are Gods," Glenchax protested. "Any species would be fortunate to find itself under our rule."

Darak smiled. "I'm sure the humans would welcome your rule about as much as your people would welcome Alum's rule."

All five Gods protested at once.

He ignored the din, captivated by the blinking amber light over Raytansoh's throne that had just changed to solid green. The Supreme Being who had not spoken in over ten thousand years cleared his throat for attention.

"Instead of this endless bickering among ourselves, perhaps we should find a way to work *with* this God, Alum," Raytansoh suggested.

The ensuing silence was deafening.

2

DARYA WALKED A FEW METERS DOWN THE GRASSY HILL and gently punched a tree trunk.

"How can we possibly trust another God?"

Timothy pushed himself up from the coarse plaid picnic blanket.

Before he could take a step, Mary pressed her hand against his leg.

"Let's give her a minute," she said.

Timothy scowled at the restraining hand and raised his voice for Darya to hear.

"Darak Legsu seems completely trustworthy to me. He saved you from that Securitor. He saved the people of Eso-La from the Eater. Why wouldn't we trust him, especially if he can help us against Alum?"

Darya—his friend, mentor, and host of this inworld meeting—picked at the rough tree bark.

Virtual tree bark on the side of a virtual hill—he reminded himself. Darya's quark-spin lattice was providing this tranquil setting for the gathering of their minds.

"We'll all be safer if we meet inside an environment I control," she'd explained when she'd sent for them, "in a setting that I engineer, where it is impossible for anyone, including a God, to eavesdrop."

Timothy had agreed but remained uneasy. "What if Darak doesn't *need* to listen in? Couldn't he intercept my concepta when my temporary Partial returns to my trueself? Couldn't Darak glean our thinking that way?"

"Don't worry," she'd assured him. "Your Partial won't return to the real world until we've come to a decision here as a group. And at the end of this meeting, only our group consensus will get reported to Darak and your Full selves, nothing else."

Darya's lattice not only provided the setting, it also hosted Timothy's and Mary's complex Partials, which she'd already outfitted with all of the relevant data. She was confident that any decisions their Partial personas made here would be acceptable to their Full selves.

Darya picked away a few more tiny bits of bark and let them drop.

"How do we know Darak isn't a representative of Alum, or a Partial projection of the Living God Himself?"

"The monk believes him," Mary offered, "and he's been through a lot."

Darya stopped harassing the tree and met Mary's concerned gaze.

"The monk tells a story of how Darak single-handedly defeated a Wing of Angels. I can't decide if that's a feat to be revered or feared. If it's true at all."

Mary had no reply.

Darya kicked at the loose bits of bark that had accumulated at the base of the tree.

"What's Darak doing travelling with a monk, anyway? Don't you find that a little suspicious?"

Mary shrugged.

"If Darak were a manifestation of Alum in disguise, why would he travel with a member of his own Church? Wouldn't that make us more suspicious?" she asked.

"Sure, but someone with Alum's intellectual capacity would expect us to think that. The monk's presence could also be interpreted as a sign that Darak is close to the Alumit. Or maybe his presence was no more than random, blind luck. Maybe Darak has nothing at all to do with the Alumit. There's no way to tell."

Timothy brushed some stray blades of grass from his pants and took a few tentative steps toward Darya.

"If Darak were Alum, or an ally of Alum, wouldn't he have destroyed us by now?"

Mary closed the wicker flaps of the picnic basket.

"How can we hope to decode the reasoning of a God?"

Her eyes studied the grassy vista around them. She still had trouble believing she was here, free of Trillian, her captor and torturer. The experience had changed her. She'd abandoned her defiantly obese avatar in favor of one that featured hard angles and a trim, fighting-form. The new appearance reflected her frame of mind.

"All we have to go on are his actions and his words," Darya replied, "and depending on our level of trust, those are open to interpretation."

"Well, the man claims to have intimate knowledge of you, Darya," Timothy hinted gently. "Perhaps you could find some common experience and cross check his word against your memory."

Darya shook her head. "Nice try, but I don't accept that this guy was ever my husband. I remember a colleague with that face and name. Nothing more."

"Besides," Mary added, "emulating someone's face would be child's play for Alum. This could be another one of His tricks."

"There's no doubt Darak has God-like capabilities," Darya replied.

"Yeah, I'd say moving entire asteroids across galaxies in the blink of an eye qualifies as a miracle," Mary added.

"But he also has limits," Timothy reminded them. "For instance, he couldn't move the Eater without using the Deplosion Array units."

"We can only dream of such limits," Darya said. She turned away from the tree and strolled back uphill, all the way up to the crest.

The other two followed her path. Standing together at the crest, they took a moment to appreciate the warm, peaceful summer landscape, the softly undulating hills, and the single, identical tree rising proudly from each mound.

Darya drank in the view and relaxed.

"I'd love to understand the technology that allowed him to shift something as large as a solar system."

"He did offer to show you," Mary said after a while.

"Right," Darya scoffed. "All I have to do is open my mind so he can 'complete' me, let him 'fix' my damaged concepta and persona. Yeah, that's not going to happen." She glared at the horizon.

Mary reached down and plucked a delicate little wildflower. She twirled it in contemplation.

"If you do, he might grant you access to this Reality Assertion Field. Maybe you could become a God, too."

Darya's hands tightened into fists; she pressed them against her hips.

"I've had quite enough of Gods. I do *not* care to be one."

Mary squinted into the distance, seeking inspiration in the repetitive landscape.

"I think we all feel the same, Darya. You're not alone in that. But if we're going to defeat Alum, we'll need to match His powers. Ever since we attacked the Deplosion Array, He's been more alert. More wary. He's hitting back harder, and He's giving His security teams more latitude to use deadly force.

"We caught Him off guard last time. Next time, it won't be so easy. He's got the entire Deplosion Array guarded by sensor clouds and Angels. If we're going to remove more than five percent of the array, we'll have to step up our game."

Darya willed her fingers to unclench and relax.

"I know, I know. Don't worry. I'm just frustrated. We've been at this for how many millions of years, now? We've always had plenty of time to pull back, reassess, and regroup. But we've been exposed, and we're running out of time."

She pulled her sword from its scabbard and tested the edge with her thumb.

"You know, I used to be so sure we could fix things—eventually—and that everything would turn out okay. Right now, that seems impossible."

Mary rested her hand on Darya's shoulder.

"I can't believe I'm the one saying this to you but, Darya, this is not the time to give up or to lose sight of our goals. There's too much at stake. You were right, what you were saying earlier, we need to figure out if Darak really is on our side in this conflict. If he is, we might stand a chance.

"What if we set an intermediate goal, something to test him?"

Darya slid her sword back into its sheath and gave a decisive nod.

"Like, help us defeat some Angels and take control of another piece of the array?"

"For instance. And he could show us how to shift like Angels," Mary added. "And outfit us with superior tech and weapons. The battle could be ours, Darya."

"Maybe," Darya replied. "But if the monk is to be believed, Alum readily sacrificed a whole Wing of Angels and billions upon billions of humans in an attempt to defeat Darak. If this man presenting himself as Darak is actually Alum, or if he's even allied with Alum, what's to say he wouldn't grant our requests and stage a fake victory for the Living God's amusement?"

Mary smirked. "Ah, so we're giving the monk's stories credibility now, are we?"

Instead of answering, Darya looked to the sky as if pleading with God, a God she didn't believe in. "It's an impossible situation."

"Still," Timothy jumped in, "wouldn't every little victory, every action that slows Alum down, be good for us?"

"And for the universe?" Mary added.

Darya grimaced. She hated their reasoning but had to agree.

"You're right. If we're going to move forward, I need to trust Darak at least that much," she conceded.

"And *he* needs to trust *us*," Mary said.

"True. It's a small ask: give us technology to match the Angels' fighting power so we can take control of the array."

"We'll need a larger army," Mary noted.

"Okay, so we make that Darak's first task, and I know the perfect source. When Trillian made his incursion into the Alternus virtual inworld, he threw it offline across hundreds of asteroid stations. Millions of Cybrids got trapped in storage while their trueself bodies were docked in the recharging bays. We'll get Darak to move some of those asteroids here so we can get our people out, and into new bodies if they need that, and then he can help us make tech modifications for battle. If he does that, we'll be freeing millions of innocents, we can grow our army, and we'll see whether Darak's willing to stand with us or not."

The three Partials stared at each other, working out the implications of their decision.

"So...we're really going to take on Alum directly," Mary said, more to hear the words aloud than to verify. "Alum. The Living God."

Timothy looked from Darya to Mary, and back.

"War against God?" he asked. "Are we insane?"

Darya's eyes shone with fierce determination.

"Yes, war against Alum. And, yes, quite possibly well shy of sane."

3

"GOD IS COMING TO VISIT TODAY! GOD IS COMING TODAY!"

Mirly twittered happily as she skipped along the path that wound beside the stream. Her stubby little tail flicked and wagged with excitement.

She didn't *have* to skip or run or walk to see God. She could have just thought briefly about where she wanted to greet Him and, like magic, she would be there.

*But it's so wonderful to skip down a path by a glittering stream—*she thought.

She'd only recently emerged from her latest veg turn in the soil, the cycle in which she firmly planted her roots, thought marvelous, deep thoughts, and planned her next works. She enjoyed those quiet, meditative times when her thoughts slowed, her animal demands to always keep moving and doing receded, and she could devote herself to her dreams of creating music, painting, writing poetry, or designing mandalas of colored sand.

All for the glory of Alum!

And when her leaves fell and her roots retracted from the loving cradle of the ground, when her bark softened and her skin grew supple again, when she could feel the tingle of energetic muscles yearning to move, Mirly loved that time just as much.

She'd been in her present mobile anima state for only three weeks and was feeling refreshed with the energy of youth. She'd already composed one piece for the variable flute, a song with 19- and 31-note chromatic scales, bringing to life the notes and lyrics she'd dreamed of in her veg phase.

An hour ago, she'd added the finishing flourishes to her newest design, a fanciful asymmetric mandala. She'd danced around it and accompanied herself on her favorite instrument. This was her best work to date.

I'm sure Alum will love it! She knew He'd make time to hear and to watch. He always did. God had time for all of His children in Heaven. And He loved all of their creations. Why wouldn't He? After all, Alum was the ultimate Creator, the one who'd made Heaven for all life to enjoy for eternity. Of course He loved His Creation and all who lived there.

Mirly paused to admire the facing bank of the burbling stream and the tree-people who glowed with the gentle shine of excess light shed from their bark.

She whispered a passing hello to her friends who'd picked this time and place to sink their roots for quiet meditation. They rustled their leaves in pleasure at her exuberant frolicking and returned to their contemplations.

The people presently living their smaller animal cycles all danced and sang along with her, too, although they were barely sapient and had only rudimentary words at their disposal.

Fun! Leap! Joy!—arose from their simple, happy minds as she passed by them at play among the flowers and grasses.

When they grew tired of playing and it became time for them to move to the next stage they, too, would take root and enter another period of physical and mental growth.

It was always like this in Heaven: plant-to-animal-to-plant-to-animal, all life weaving together in an integrated web of development, and all of Alum's creatures, anima and veg, thriving under His Light. All energy, nutrition, growth, and love came from that single source—Alum—in a never-ending flow. His Love powered the universe, and life everywhere sang His praise with its every fiber.

Mirly pranced on her four legs like an energetic fawn. She was still small, a young doe-centaur under a meter high. Her tiny fingers and dual opposable thumbs at the end of her delicate arms were perfect for forming complex notes on the variable flute and arranging the colorful grains of sand she used in her mandala designs.

She loved her life, and she loved the thought that one day, in about five or six more veg-anima cycles, she'd grow a little bigger and could take up opera, or painting, or maybe writing! There were so many ways to be creative, so many ways to honor the glories of God. An infinite number!

Today, she was off to meet Alum and a dozen or so friends presently in their anima phase at a favorite spot along the road that led to the lake.

The trail meandered down to the stream and Mirly danced across the stepping stones that poked above the surface of the water. The little insects, the fish, the golden bacteria, and the mosses, all were part of the veg-anima cycles that characterized life in Heaven, and she waved a cheery, all-encompassing hello to them from the middle of the stream.

On the other side, the path widened and led into a densely forested area toward a small body of water some five minutes away by fast trot. Tall, narrow stones rose out of the ground on each side of the path. The natural pockets and indentations in the rocks cradled delicate orchids that bobbed greetings as she passed by.

Mirly recalled fondly the cycles of her youth that she'd spent cradled in a stony pocket, drinking water that fell into the cup, absorbing nutrients from the rock, and filling herself with Alum's Light. She cherished her orchid phases, but no more than others cherished their own flowering phases.

Not everyone goes through orchid phases—she reminded herself. *But I'm sure they're all equally wonderful.*

She didn't regret never spending time as a marigold. She'd enjoyed her orchid time, and it was perfect to her. How could it be otherwise in Heaven?

Mirly approached the meeting place with growing excitement. Poppi and Tristal were already there, chatting with some of the local veg-life and an unfamiliar young anima-person enjoying its insectoid phase.

Mirly trilled a happy greeting to the small gathering.

"Hey, everyone!"

Poppi flew from her resting spot on one of the rocky pillars and landed on Mirly's head.

"Hi, Mirly! How is the mandala? I bet it's perfect. Alum will love it."

Mirly laughed.

"The love of our Lord shines brightly on all creations. What have you two brought today?"

Tristal, a big bear in his present anima incarnation, lumbered over to greet them.

"A short musical composition for divergent voices," he answered in a low rumble. "You should hear Poppi's harmonies; they are magnificent."

Poppi fluttered around Mirly's head in delight.

"But only because Tristal provides such a solid, rhythmic base."

"I can sing, too," chirped a little bug from its perch on a nearby rock.

The bear's muzzle lowered and gave the silver-winged cricket a friendly nudge forward.

"Mirly, this is our young friend, Xitina," he said.

The cricket rubbed its legs together, emitting a complex series of high-pitched runs that verged on the ultrasonic.

"See? I can sing like Poppi," it said.

Mirly bent over to get a better look.

"Oh, how lovely," she exclaimed.

Poppi swept down and landed on the rock beside Xitina.

"We've been practicing," she said. "Xitina takes the melody into such a beautiful range."

"I am so looking forward to hearing you," Mirly replied. "I think Alum would love it if you performed your song as a greeting on His arrival."

They chatted amongst themselves while their other friends arrived. Soon the visitors numbered in the hundreds, counting the local veg-people and the tiny creatures who happened by. The energy of expectation was palpable, drawing others to the road who had not yet heard about Alum's impending visit.

Nobody minded if they hadn't received an invitation directly. Alum's Light shone equally in and upon all. In an eternity of lifetimes, no one would be ignored or shunned. Alum had more than ample time for all of His children.

A brilliant flash of light drew everyone's attention toward the water.

Alum's here!

The Living God walked out from a light-filled portal hovering over the water.

As he drew closer, Poppi, Tristal, and Xitina broke into song to welcome Alum to this part of Heaven. Their harmonies were as beautiful as anything Mirly had imagined.

Alum smiled in deep gratitude and joy as He greeted every single one of His children with a touch or a hug, and then sat down on a small rock beside the road and played with a pair of lizard-children as He listened to the final few minutes of the composition.

When the music finished, He stood and beamed at the three performers. The light of His blessing radiated from His eyes and washed over them.

"Wonderful, my children," He said. "Your melody is as pleasing to the ear as water trickling across stones in a stream."

Poppi, Tristal, and Xitina glowed with joy at being compared to the music of Alum's own creation.

"Thank you for that delightful greeting. It is wonderful to be among you again."

"Your radiance is with us always, Lord," Mirly replied.

Alum smiled down at the young doe-centaur.

"Yes, my child. You are right. I am always with you, but it is especially pleasing to turn My attention to this particular small part of perfection again. I understand you've been working on a new piece, Mirly."

Mirly spun in circles, and her tail wagged fiercely.

"Yes, I have! I have! The best view is from the top of the large boulder that towers over the middle of the clearing. We should all go there."

She didn't have to specify where "there" was. Alum knew all and saw all.

He nodded and the entire group—minus the vegs who would have to wait for their next anima stage—shifted to observe Mirly's latest work.

From the vantage point eight meters above the clearing in the forest, the group admired the tree-people and the open meadow below.

"Oh, Mirly," Poppi cried, staring down on the intricate mandala, "this is exquisite!"

Mirly had poured colored sand in a mesmerizing design that covered almost the entire clearing. A circle of swirling, wispy whites and alluring shades of blue, green, and brown delighted the grateful onlookers. Two enormous islands of intermingling greens and browns gave weight and substance to both sides of the snow-white center, while scattered cottony patches and speckles of azure lent a sense of airiness. The ragged edges of the great masses evolved into delicate fractal patterns that bled into the dominant blue. The overall effect was stunning.

A human cartographer of the twentieth century would have recognized the image as Earth, viewed from high above the North Pole, albeit slightly stylized and missing its signature veil of cloud cover.

Black dots, here and there, marked where the major cities of various nations had once stood, a very, very long time ago.

A solid circle of dove-gray sand perfectly covered the area that the once sprawling metropolitan area of Vancouver, British Columbia, in the country of Pacifica, would have occupied.

Without realizing it, Mirly had quite accurately represented the precise location and size the Eater had reached on the second day after breaching its confinement field.

Mirly looked up at her God, excited to receive His Light and Grace.

Strangely, He was no longer smiling.

She couldn't say exactly what that expression on His face meant. She'd never seen a look quite like that.

"Don't you love it, Alum?" she asked, knowing He always replied to such questions with an immediate and enthusiastic, "Yes."

This time, He did not.

Mirly became acutely aware of the songs of the burbling stream and the wind passing over the rocks and through the branches.

When Alum did speak, His voice was odd. Not gentle. Not loving. Not gushing with approval.

"Mirly, where did the inspiration for this piece come from?"

Mirly stepped back, sensing something...foreboding in the question.

She recognized the concept of "threat" only on an instinctual level. She'd never known a real threat of any kind. Alum had designed Heaven so His children would never have to face danger. On a conscious level, she felt only confusion.

"It.... It just came to me, Lord," she stammered. "As always."

Who knows where inspiration comes from, if not from God?—she mused, surprising herself with such a thought.

She had no words or concepts that would suggest an idea could have an origin other than God's glory. One could be inspired by friends or by creation itself but all of these things came from God. He was the ultimate source of everything. Anything else was inconceivable.

Alum glared at the young doe for a moment, though Mirly wouldn't have known what to call His expression. She saw the look, felt the absence of approval, and shrunk into herself. She experienced it as *cold*, an absence of *normal*. Where was the warm glow of Alum's eternal love?

Alum looked away.

"My concerns in the greater universe must have slipped through. How else could she have conceived of this image?" He mumbled to Himself. "She's had absolutely no outside contact."

His eyes returned to the design below, not really seeing it anymore but knowing by heart every millimeter of its detail. His vision was focused inward, on the interplay between His thoughts and this perfect universe He had created.

No matter. Soon everything outside of Heaven will be gone. It will no longer be able to effect what I've created here—He thought.

He looked at His children gathered around Him on the rocky plateau. He scanned the surrounding forest, filled with veg and anima people in all stages and varieties.

Life is sacred here. It is loving, collaborative, and connected through brotherhood and sisterhood. As it should be.

He looked further away, where the terrain stretched into an expansive plain.

An optical illusion of the light of Heaven playing on the intricate landscape of this universe.

He alone knew the convoluted, packed structure that underlay Paradise. It was an astoundingly brilliant design if He did say so, Himself.

To think that umpteen eons ago that young upstart, Darian Leigh, had challenged the notion of Intelligent Design of Yov's universe!

Now, how had Dr. Leigh put it? Something to the effect that, so little of the universe appeared to be habitable by humans, Yov would've had to think His people exceptionally vain and stupid to require such an enormous waste of space just to demonstrate how special they were.

Fool. Yov, the God of My father, wasn't real—Alum harrumphed.

A tiny part of Alum, the ancient part of Him that still remembered being the Reverend LaMontagne, cringed at such blasphemy. But Alum knew better. He knew the difference between an imaginary Creator and a real one.

My universe will not be filled with random happenstance and unhappy accident. I will create a perfect universe, one lovingly crafted by its God, one that will endure in perfection forever.

His attention returned to the inexplicable representation of old Earth in the clearing below. Inexplicable in that Mirly should have had no knowledge of Earth, the Eater, or anything outside of this perfect model of Heaven and her place in it.

Alum sighed.

Not quite perfect.

Not yet.

4

"HAVE YOU DECIDED?"

Darak's eager question welcomed Darya back to the physical world as if there'd been no pause in their conversation, as if she'd never left his side.

Physically, she hadn't. Nor had he moved since she'd withdrawn into the virtual environment she'd set up to meet with Mary's and Timothy's Partials.

So, how did he know we were done?—Darya wondered. *Can he intercept line-of-sight laser communications?*

She left the questions unspoken.

Darak and Trillian sat facing each other on a pair of benches they'd scrounged from a little-used storage room.

Darak, yes, but that's not Trillian across from him—she prompted herself. *Trillian's body, that body I see sitting across from Darak, is no more than a shell. And inside that shell is Darian. Dr. Darian Leigh inhabits the Shard's body, now*— she recited while she fought to overcome her instinctual response at seeing the face of her former adversary.

Whatever they were talking about, their focus and body language was intense. The broadband channels were silent. She tried but was unable to decode the furious communications passing between them.

They must be using QUEECH—she guessed. She'd heard about Quantum-Encrypted Entangled Channels but she'd never had any luck using the technology.

Another advantage that goes with being a God.

Darya examined Trillian/Darian for any hint of the cruel Shard that had previously occupied the body in front of her. The man's face looked as open and innocent as that of a human baby.

Darak cocked an eyebrow at her. "Well?"

"We've decided to trust you," she sent back. Her transmission was flat, neutral—guarded—and she made no attempt to change it.

He stood up, not bothering to mask his readiness to move forward.

"...for the moment," she added quickly. "More trust will come with further evidence of your intentions."

His excitement dimmed and he rolled his eyes in exasperation.

"What else can I do to convince you?"

"I'm glad you asked. We're going to confront Alum at the Deplosion Array, and we need your help."

Confront Alum. Even as she registered her own words, doubt nibbled at the edges of her confidence.

This is insanity. Even in the little things, our capabilities are so pathetic. What were we thinking? We're no match for the Living God and His Angels. But if we don't wage war against them soon, we'll be dead anyway.

"You do realize that confronting Alum will bring you nothing but death?" Darak replied.

His warning echoed her own insecurities. She eyed him closely. *Is he going to resist? Can we count on him to side with us?*

She stood her ground.

"His Angels aren't invulnerable. Your own story proves that," she countered.

"So you're asking me to hold off Alum while you battle His Angels?"

"Just stop Alum from interfering...if you can."

Darak's eyes gleamed at her implicit challenge. He transmitted a cynical grunt. With no air in Darya's lab, there was no noise, just the electronically transmitted suggestion of noise.

"I can do that. Only the Wing Commander and the top five lieutenants carry direct links to Alum. I'll send them a few dozen light hours away while you engage the rest of the Wing."

He looked at the two Cybrids hovering in the corridor. "You're going to need a much bigger army."

Was he trying to be funny? She wasn't sure, but it didn't matter. She wasn't in a joking mood.

"And better weaponry," she replied with no trace of humor. "Any weaponry, really. I don't fancy doing hand-to-hand combat against Angels with energy swords." She extended half a dozen tentacled manipulators.

"You'll be no match for them if you have to use MAM drives to maneuver. You'll need to be able to shift instantaneously through space as they do," he counseled.

"You can provide us with these capabilities." It wasn't a question.

Darak shook his head. "No, not directly."

"But you're a God, or so you claim."

"There are limits to my capabilities," Darak admitted, "and for the record, I never claimed to be a God, not even a small-g god. I may be able to alter the physical laws of nature but that doesn't mean I've explored all possible technologies within any particular set of physical laws."

"So you don't know everything?"

He held out his empty hands to either side. "I don't know everything and never claimed to. I'd describe myself as moderately capable, but neither omniscient nor omnipotent. Will that be enough for you?"

"If you can provide weapons, defenses, and maneuverability to match the Angels, that would be God-like enough to me."

Darak walked over to a lab bench and picked up a microchip lying on its surface.

"Those things I can do. Rather," he said as he turned the chip over in his hands, "I have friends who can provide all of these things at my direction." He gently returned the chip to the table.

"I sense there will be conditions," Darya said.

"Only one. I want access to the computational substrate you developed for your inworld."

Darya said nothing.

Taking the silence as an opportunity to make his case, Darak pressed on. "I'm familiar with dozens of ways to implement computer hardware, and easily as many architectural configurations. But one can't know every possible technology, not even in a single universe. That particular hardware, for example, is unfamiliar to me. It's unique. And you seem reluctant to admit it exists at all."

"A woman needs to keep *some* secrets."

"Ha! Okay, sure. But you don't think I'm offering enough in exchange?"

She shrugged. "Tell me, why is it so important to you?"

"Modifying the matrix of reality is computation intensive. I like to explore anything that might give me an advantage in that. I've seen some of the real time computations you've been able to achieve in your inworld simulations. Your hardware is very fast."

"If knowledge is power, then speed is...what?"

"Effectiveness. Capability to use that power. Ages ago, a scientist named Alan Turing showed that anything computable could be computed by a remarkably simple machine: a tape and a moveable read/write head."

"That sounds excruciatingly slow," she interjected.

"Yes, but theoretically, it had as much computational power as your nano-silicene lattice. You just had to wait eons for anything useful to come out of it. Knowing *how* to do something and doing it *quickly* are two sides of the computational coin."

Darya bobbed twice in agreement.

"Very well. Build my army, give us weapons, defenses, and the power to shift as efficiently as the Angels, and I will tell you about the quark-spin lattice."

"Quark-spin? But how do you...," Darak began.

Darya interrupted, "All in good time. After our first victory." She extended a tentacle. "Agreed?"

Darak stared at the proffered manipulator. He held out his hand and they shook.

"I don't believe an agreement between Cybrid and human has been sealed by handshake since the original Vesta Project."

"It seemed fitting," Darya answered. "Only, this agreement is between a Cybrid and a God. I'm not sure any such deal has ever been made."

"Ever made? Yes," Darak replied, "but it was a long, long time ago, and the deal wasn't honored for long."

"Oh?"

Darya waited for him to elaborate but it was Darak's turn to hold back.

He eyed her expectantly, with a hint of sadness.

"What? What is it?" she asked.

"You really don't remember?" he replied.

Mystified, she consulted her archives. Nothing.

"Darya, *you* made the deal. You and Alum."

"Me? With Alum? What deal?"

"To share responsibility for governing humanity."

"You'd think I'd remember a deal like that. It must have been made before I was damaged."

"Not long before."

"How did it turn out?"

There's no gentle way to say this—Darak thought. *Best to be direct.*

"Not well, I'm afraid. It led to your death."

5

"I THINK THE SUPERVISOR HAS GONE INSANE."

Darak stood inside the Alternus simulation at the south end of Central Park, looking across Columbus Circle to the jumbled skyscrapers and beyond. Darya, Mary, and Timothy stood beside him in their usual inworld avatars.

Buildings jutted out at bizarre angles. Segments of roads, sidewalks, and bridges sprouted from their walls.

Darya laughed. "Maybe it has gone insane. Trying to keep all of this straight would be enough to drive anyone insane. You can thank Trillian for this mess. He pulled Alternus into the ten-dimensional maze I constructed in the GameRoom."

"10-D? You don't say!" Darak said as he adjusted his visual processor to the correct number of spatial dimensions.

"Ah, yes, I see. Okay, that's better. Except for her."

He pointed out a figure running erratically along a portion of road that floated freely twenty meters above the ground.

Darya and Mary followed Darak's finger to see a jogger blink out of existence in the middle of a section of hovering pavement. To follow her progress, they switched to a 10-D visual filter.

"That can't be right," Mary said. "I thought you said everyone was in storage. She shouldn't be here. Maybe the Supervisor *has* been damaged a little by all of this."

"More than a little, I'd say." Darak waved his hands and the scene around the four dissolved into the complex concepta of the Supervisor's program.

Darya moved in for closer assessment.

Something was very wrong with the code. The normally elegant arcs and nodes of a well-organized thought structure were snarled up in a tangled mess.

"What a mishmash!" she said. "I hardly recognize this as the Alternus simulation I wrote."

Darak stepped forward and was soon equally engrossed in the code.

"I think we're looking at the internal workings of three entirely different Supervisors, all jumbled together here," Darya suggested. "I see bits of GameRoom and Vacationland code mixed with my Alternus routines. That alone would've been bad enough, but these three were each overseeing entirely separate worlds with conflicting physics. On top of that, the local Alternus Supervisor was running on my quark-spin hardware while the other two were running on normal inworld CPPUs. No wonder that it's all such a scramble."

Mary puffed out her cheeks and exhaled noisily. "This is going to take forever to sort out. I vote we scrap all three and re-initiate."

Darak shook his head. "If you do that, you'll kill billions, everyone the Supervisor is holding in archive."

"Billions?" Darya's eyebrows puckered in a tiny frown. "There were only a few hundred million Fulls in Alternus."

"That *is* odd," Darak said. "This particular asteroid has been isolated from the Sagittarius A* inworld network—"

"—so there should be only a few hundred-thousand of us in the local copy of Alternus," Darya finished for him, "not billions, not even millions."

She waved at a segregated part of the confused program. "And what about this? Did breaking off this part from its integral whole affect the cognitive stability of the Supervisor?"

"Maybe," Darak answered. He reached up and pulled down a tangled knot of code from above. "Or maybe it was this."

He drew a large circle around a portion of the Supervisor program that included some O/S-level machine code in the midst of its higher-level concepts.

"Ouroboros!" Mary recognized her handiwork.

Darak regarded the code in silence for a few heartbeats. "A pretty nasty version, I'd say," he commented. "This machine code penetrates deep. Trillian would have been ripped to shreds."

"I warned him," Mary said. "I told him it was purely defensive code but it could be deadly if he didn't stop."

Her eyes flicked to Darak's face, caught a momentary glimpse of his disapproval. She kicked at the virtual ground beneath her feet.

"He was torturing me! What else could I do?" she blurted.

Darya turned from the sea of code and hugged her friend.

"It's okay, Mary. That must have been awful for you. You did what you had to do to survive," she soothed.

Darak turned back to the code, and highlighted a few links in red.

"Darya's right. Besides, you couldn't have known how badly Trillian compromised the Supervisor," he said. "Look at this. The Shard integrated his own persona so deeply into the simulation that your Ouroboros routines affected the Supervisor itself. See? Right here. Oh, and again, over here."

Darya and Mary inspected the indicated section more closely.

"What a mess. Can't even call that spaghetti code," Darya observed.

"I can extract the Ouroboros instructions, if that'll help," Mary offered. She examined the interconnections between her program and the Supervisor code. "At least, I think I can."

Darak reached one hand deep into the routines, pulling first this way, and then the other. Links snapped and conceptual nodes spilled out onto the floor as he yanked.

"Hey!" Mary protested as he ripped her code from the larger concepta and let it fall. It sputtered, dimmed, and dissipated as they looked on in shock.

"Was that wise?" Darya asked.

"I know what I'm doing," Darak replied. "The basic Supervisor design isn't much different from the first one I programmed."

Mary's jaw gaped. "You worked on inworld programming?"

"Vacationland was mine."

Darya consulted her archives and shook her head. "But Vacationland is the oldest of inworlds. Are you that…"

"Ancient?" Darak laughed. "Yes, indeed."

He turned his attention to the Alternus Supervisor concepta. "I was the original inworld designer. I naively believed the simulations would help the Cybrids remember their human origins and that it could help keep them from going insane. I never dreamed anyone would twist the inworlds that way."

"You said you knew Trillian," Darya said. "How could you think this would be beyond him?"

"No, I guess it was inevitable under the right circumstances. And it was inevitable that the circumstances would become right at some point. Let's get your people out of here, and then we'll shut down this mess."

Darya followed links in the routines. "Where are they? The people, I mean. I don't see any reference to archived personas. Do you?"

"Look in the heap," Darak replied. "Trillian must have de-instantiated everyone in a hurry. But they're still in there, not reclaimed yet. Yep, there they are, over there. See?"

The trio flew through the Supervisor's inworld data. They came to a stop in front of a suspiciously neatly-ordered group. Each node of the group contained a link to miniaturized persona/concepta networks dangling below.

Darya breathed a sigh of relief. "Yes, you're right, that's them! As soon as we've constructed new trueself bodies, we can upload everyone."

Darak drew in a deep breath.

"I'm afraid it's not going to be quite that easy," he said. "Look at this."

He waved a hand and multiple thin lines changed to bright red, showing extensive interconnections among the various personas.

"What the...?" Mary said.

Darak moved closer to inspect the nearest elements.

"I can't tell if it's the Ouroboros program or something that Trillian set up for his own perverse reasons."

"They're all interconnected," Darya observed.

Darak nodded. "It's almost impossible to trace all the links. This could take months to untangle."

He traced a few lines between networks. "There are way too many links here for it all to be tied into one local instance of the inworld. It looks like he might've stored or copied Fulls from some of the other stations into here. Or worse. Oh, yeah. Yeah, this is not good. I think he threw the Partials into storage with the Fulls."

"But there are billions of Partials!"

"Exactly. He's intermingled parts of everyone's concepta space, Fulls and Partials alike. We can't assume any single element contains an integral person, or only one person. This cross-connected tangle of links is the only thing maintaining their integrity, such as it is. If we sever any of these links, people will be lost. Unless you know some defining characteristic of each of your local Full instantiations that can help narrow it down, we'll have to trace every one of these connections."

He looked hopefully at Darya.

"I don't know everyone in Alternus," she protested. "There's no single defining factor I can identify."

"Okay, so we'll have to do it the hard way."

"That'll take too long," Mary said. "We don't have time. We need an army to attack the Deplosion Array, and *now*."

Darak shrugged.

Darya's eyes swept across the archive array.

"Find a few million real people buried in the midst of billions of Partials," she muttered, "and delicately untangle their minds from all of the others."

She covered her eyes with her hands and let out an exasperated breath.

"Or…" she left the word hanging.

"Or, what?" Darak asked.

"Or…we could make everyone a Full. Cut the cross-connections, sort out the results, select what's still viable, and give them all personhood.

"What do you think?" Darya asked.

Darak clasped his hands behind his back and paced in a circle.

"Can you do it?" Darya pushed.

"*Can* I do it?" Darak echoed. "Yes, it is feasible."

He completed another circle and stopped, facing her.

"But?" she prompted.

"But *should* I? That's a harder question. This number of Partials has never been promoted to Fulls all at once, as far as I know."

"We need them."

"No, *you* need them," he corrected. "Or you think you do, in order to take inadvisable actions that will do little more than raise the ire of the Living God."

Darya braced herself. *Here's where we discover whose side Darak is really on.*

"Controlling a portion, any portion, of the Deplosion Array will do more than make Alum angry," she pointed out.

"Perhaps," Darak conceded. "It's not clear that He couldn't just regroup and build an array elsewhere, or find a different route to His ultimate goal."

"You said you'd help us."

"Mm." Darak looked upward, seeking inspiration. Or maybe, patience. Either way, he found nothing of any help.

"It's not without risks," he said after a moment. "There's a screening system in place for a reason. And that's under the best possible circumstances, when Partials are developed under carefully controlled conditions with Full parentage. Advancing this many all at once under chaotic circumstances and without Full parentage would be sheer recklessness. It could be disastrous. We could end up with an army of psychopaths."

Darya softened her voice. "I agree that it's risky. But don't forget, we're facing the ultimate risk. If we do nothing, Alum wins and He will destroy the entire universe. Our universe. Their universe. We all lose. We lose everything."

"Reformats," Darak corrected, "not destroys. Re-creates."

"Whatever you want to call it. Our universe will no longer exist. *We* will no longer exist."

Darak rocked on his heels and stared at the floor.

"Fine," Darya spat. "Don't concern yourself with our battles. I'll promote them to Fulls myself."

"Have you ever done that?"

"No. I've never served on a Parental board. But I know the principles and it doesn't seem all that hard. Trillian promoted Timothy—accidentally, mind you—and Timothy's fine."

"Billions at a time and each one of them a jumbled mess," Darak replied, shaking his head. "The odds of making a maladjusted persona or worse, an insane one, are terribly high."

"It's a chance we'll have to take," Darya answered. "We can weed out any unsuitable personas during training."

Darak took a deep breath.

"Okay," he capitulated. "If you're that determined, I'll help you."

"Don't go out of your way," Darya shot back.

"If it means saving the universe from a few billion psychotic, weaponized Cybrids, I insist. We can reassemble their conceptas, raise them to Full personas, and give them new bodies. Bodies fit for war."

Darya's eyes shone triumphantly.

6

DARAK LIFTED DARYA'S BRAIN ever so gingerly from her trueself body.

Was the fact that she'd allowed him to do this a reflection of her growing trust? She'd insisted he be the one to put her offline and physically transfer her brain into her new body.

Am I finally winning her over or is this just another test?

"I have to lead the way," she'd said. Although, truth be told, she didn't.

"You know, physically transferring your CPPU, your brain, isn't necessary," he'd countered. "We can build you a new quark-spin lattice and transfer your persona into that. It would be less risky."

She declined, offering no explanation.

All of the other newly-reconfigured Cybrid minds salvaged from the damaged Alternus inworld were being digitally transmitted directly into their new substrates. The Esu, the people of Eso-La, had already constructed a million new CPPUs—Concepta-Persona Processing Units— that were ready to accommodate the rescued minds, and they were adding more to that number every day.

Darya and Mary were the only two Cybrids with special quark-spin CPPUs, and Darya wasn't ready to give up the secret of their fabrication to anyone yet, not even to Darak. That meant their physical computational substrates would have to be preserved, and their brains would have to be physically transferred into the "battle-Cybrid" bodies the Esu had designed for them.

She trusts me with her life but not her secrets—Darak realized.

She'll let me carry her CPPU, to feel it in my hands but not access it, not understand how it functions.

He winced in frustration and pushed back the urge to probe the CPPU with his built-in sensors, to flood it with analyzing radiation.

If she would've let me, if she would have told me how, I could have constructed new quark-spin substrates for both of them. For all of them, if she'd asked.

Still in her old body, Mary watched the procedure with intense interest from across the lab. She was next.

"From the outside, it looks the same as any standard CPPU," she observed.

"All the way down to the atomic level," Darak agreed. *But what secrets lie below the surface?*—he wondered.

Equations for boson-mediated quark-quark interactions flowed through his mind, threatening to distract him from his present task. He had so many questions!

How does she get the resolution to read or to set spin in an individual quark? How is the spin transported between different nuclei?

"I don't think I could stand being that slow again," Mary commented, misreading his silence. "You know, with just a normal silicene-lattice CPPU."

Darak shook his head and brought his attention back to what he was doing. "No, I don't imagine that would be any fun."

"Ha! Honestly, it was...torture," Mary quipped.

Darak grunted. *Bad joke.*

She laughed a little too brightly for someone who'd been in Hell only a few weeks earlier, Darak noted. Would she ever fully recover from the trauma Trillian had inflicted on her? He could help her with that, erase specific memories from her archives if she wanted.

"Seriously, though," Mary added, "it was frustrating to know that I could level the playing field with Trillian if only I could connect my thought processes to the quark-spin lattice of the Alternus inworld. I'm glad Darya found a way to get the solution through to me."

Reminded of whose fragile mind he held in his hands, Darak looked at Darya's crystalline brain.

Is there anything of Kathy left in there?—he wondered. *Or of the Cybrid, DAR-K?*

He reflected on his lost love and the friendship severed too soon. He'd known love again since Kathy Liang's passing, but it would never be like his first.

His focus was drifting again.

You're too old for this—he chastised himself.

He swiveled and carried Darya's brain over to her shiny new body.

"Careful!" Mary warned.

He paused mid-step. "It'll go smoother if you don't distract me."

"Couldn't you just, you know, erase gravity in this region? I'd feel better knowing you couldn't drop her."

"Me, too. I *could* have simply shifted her CPPU into place. I *could* have shifted you both at the same time. It *could* have been instantaneous and practically risk free. But, no. For some reason, she wanted me to move her brain by hand and, for that, I need gravity. Besides, Kathy always enjoyed a little ceremony in her life."

"Mm," Mary replied, noncommittally. She'd forgotten about his history with Darya's previous personas, originating with his human partner, Kathy, evolving into Dar-K, and now into this version of Darya who no longer remembered or trusted him.

It must be hard on him—she thought.

Darak opened the access port in Darya's new body. It was smaller than her old one, as was the propulsion unit. More space for weapons.

His thousands of years of experience fighting the Aelu and, much later, fighting *with* the Aelu against Alum's Angels had guided Darak's decisions in designing this new battle-Cybrid model.

He'd reduced the antimatter store to a fraction of its previous size—adequate for simple maneuvering and more than enough power for every other use—and replaced the propulsion rockets with shift/jump machinery. Specialized RAF devices now powered the energy weapons and absorbed enemy blasts. The outer shell and appendages were crafted from exotic material he'd mined from another universe, material tougher than anything he'd found in this one.

Figuring out how to keep foreign-universe matter stable under the physical laws of this universe had occupied hundreds of years of experimentation much earlier in his life. He hoped it would be worth the effort.

Unless Alum has a new, improved model of His Angel, the battle Cybrids will make quick work of them. Provided the Living God Himself doesn't engage directly in the fight. If Alum jumps into the fray, all bets are off.

Darak lowered the CPPU into the receiving cradle and watched Darya's new body pull it deep inside.

"It won't take her long to re-boot," he explained to Mary. "But the rest of the upgrade, the learning process, could take weeks. I offered to reconfigure her operating system software and make it more efficient, but she insisted on keeping her old driver routines and modifying them herself. The old drivers are going to have a devil of a time interfacing with the new hardware. It'll take her a while to reprogram and there's no guarantee it will all go smoothly."

"Can't you just provide mapping to reinterpret familiar commands to the new machinery?" Mary suggested.

"You two think a lot alike. She asked me the same thing. Yes, I could do that, but it would make her slower than everyone else, when the whole idea of her unique brain is to make her faster."

"No, she wouldn't be happy about that," Mary said.

"I offered to send the drivers to a third-party buffer where you could both examine them for any belief viruses."

"What would be the point in that?" Mary asked. "We all know you could sneak something in there if you wanted to."

True—he admitted. He had millions of years of his own Shard and Aelu experience to draw on. Even Darya's advanced security programs would have a tough time identifying a fractal virus that was sufficiently fragmented and scattered throughout the machine code.

"In the end, we agreed that I'd have to teach her how to use her new body."

"Teach her?"

"The old-fashioned way," Darak nodded. "The drivers for listening and speaking are more or less the same as before, so she asked me to talk her through that. I'll tell her where the interrupts are, the port addresses, the hardware-specific command codes, and so on."

"And she'll write the new O/S routines herself?" Mary said. "From your verbal descriptions? That'll take forever."

"It's the only way she felt comfortable that nothing in her concepta would be altered against her intention."

"And then, what? We're supposed to repeat the process with all the millions of new Cybrids? Why don't we just surrender to Alum right now?"

"No," Darak said. "That's only for Darya. Once she figures things out, she'll send the entire O/S bundle to you and you can incorporate it. Everyone else will get the code I provide."

The Cybrid bobbed once. "I trust Darya completely. If she says her code is safe, then it's safe."

Darya's CPPU receiving port slid shut with a quiet *click*. A few seconds passed while the reboot routines ran.

"Okay, I'm back," Darya announced as her processor made initial connections to her speech centers. "I don't dare do anything, though."

"I wouldn't advise it," Darak agreed.

"I can hear well enough," Darya said, "and see, after a fashion."

"Your new body provides simultaneous 360-degree, 3D vision. It integrates the entire photonic spectrum, too, not just visible light. It'll take a little getting used to. Right now, you're processing from a small subset of all visual sensors over a narrow bandwidth."

"That'll be enough," the Cybrid replied.

"How does it feel?" Mary asked.

"Thought processes are nominal," said Darya. "But I'm cut off from a lot of the normal sensory input. I can't feel my arms. I can't sense the MAM fire in my belly, like I used to. To tell the truth, I feel pretty helpless."

"I told you," Darak said.

"Yes, you did."

She cautiously extended an appendage a few centimeters.

"We'll just have to figure it out one step at a time."

7

"BUT, MY LORD, ANGEL DESIGN HAS SERVED US WELL for over thirty million years, from long before the Aelu Wars."

"Thirty million years? Has it been that long? In that case, all the more reason to think about improvements, wouldn't you say?"

Alum didn't enjoy arguing with His Shard but He found it useful to compare His perfect thoughts against those of lesser beings. If nothing else, it predicted how inferior intellects might react.

"Does this have to do with Lord Mika's failure at Tri-Star?"

Alum had to remind Himself that this particular incarnation of Shard Trillian standing before Him, questioning Him, was in a sense, still a young pup. The clone had been pulled from stasis only last month and was filled with the vigor and passion—and the naive impatience—of youth.

It's always such an inconvenience to lose a Trillian, especially one as experienced as the last one had been—Alum lamented. *And the process of bringing a new replica up to speed is always wearisome.*

"Lord Mika did not fail at Tri-Star," He corrected his Shard, "the intruder was deceptively more powerful than he first appeared."

Alum took a sip from His heavy ceramic mug and watched the dust rising from the herd of nanoffalo, the miniaturized buffalo that roamed the terrarium set into His coffee table.

He set the mug down on the glass above the tiny herd, casting a shadow in front of their stampede. The herd split into two streams, circling to either side of the shaded land. Alum smiled.

It never gets old, playing with tiny, living things, making them come and go, here and there. Still such a human pleasure.

In the miniature plains setting, it was an engaging game. In the greater universe, the responsibility for creating perfection was the epitome of seriousness.

Alum sighed at the recognition of His weighty responsibility, greater than anything He'd ever undertaken.

"Heaven is within our grasp," He said aloud, whether to the nanoffalo or to him, Trillian wasn't sure.

The Shard fidgeted.

"However," Alum continued, "the Deplosion Array is still vulnerable. Until re-Creation is assured, the fate of the universe remains at risk."

Trillian spread his hands in resignation. "Your wisdom will guide us, as always, my Lord," he offered. "Do you foresee further threats from the Cybrids? Does my failure with the Cybrid rebellion threaten Your Divine Plan?"

It was inconvenient that Trillian didn't get a chance to download his memories before he died on that recharging station. It would've been useful to know how the Cybrids had managed to kill the Shard. Did they catch him off guard? Were they cloaked? Did they have new technology?

Now that the asteroid had disappeared from the Realm, any clues as to how the previous Trillian was murdered were gone with it.

"Unfortunately, that business remains a mystery," Alum answered. "But there is one thing I'm sure of: there's no way this recent Cybrid resistance could have been organized entirely within the Realm. They have outside support."

Alum stroked His chin as He considered his options. *Things will be put back to normal soon enough*—He assured himself.

Eager to get back in Alum's good graces, the new Trillian tried again.

"Is it possible that Gabriel escaped from Tri-Star?"

It never took a new Trillian long to get up to speed, to start thinking and behaving predictably, in the same manner as the previous ones. But it was never fast enough for Alum's liking.

Rather than answering the Shard's question directly, Alum stood and paced away from the sitting area. He walked over to an expansive bookcase and examined some titles. He plucked one from the shelf, opened it, and cleared His throat.

"Ah, yes, here we are," Alum announced, *"The Man in the Iron Mask.* It's a classic. Do you know it?"

Trillian searched his memory but found no recollection of the novel. "It's likely I read it at some point in the past. I don't remember the story, though."

"The King of the country had a twin brother he kept imprisoned for quite some time," Alum explained. "Rebels freed him from prison to fight on their side."

"Are you saying...," Trillian shook his head in surprise, "Are you saying that You have a twin brother?"

"Heavens, no!" Alum laughed.

Trillian bowed his head. "I'm sorry. My mind hasn't fully recovered from being reanimated yet. How does this ancient book relate to our present situation?"

The corners of Alum's eyes turned upward and He tapped twice, softly, on the cover of the old book.

"I have no twin brother," He confirmed, "but perhaps Gabriel has one. Perhaps, more than one."

Alum's clean, precisely manicured nails tapped out the lively rhythm of a popular hymn as He fleshed out his suspicions.

Yes, that has to be it—He murmured to Himself.

"A core of rebel Angels?" Trillian's eyes widened at the thought.

Alum turned, shaking His head.

"Not exactly, and most certainly not acting of their own volition. That sort of blasphemy is beyond their design. No, I'm thinking that someone outside the Realm, perhaps some hidden remnant of the defeated Aelu, has captured one of ours and has been studying it. Maybe even replicated it."

Trillian whistled. *An Aelu reproducing Angel technology? What a terrifying thought. They'd be daunting adversaries, for sure, but at least this is something I can fathom. Something we can fight.*

"If they do have our technology from the War, that could prove troublesome," Trillian acknowledged.

"The Aelu were always clever," Alum replied. "I harbor no delusions that we destroyed all of them. No doubt, if there are some that still elude us, they would have introduced improvements of their own."

Trillian gasped. *"Improvements*, my Lord? Our Cybrid scientists were guided by the Living God. By You. How could anyone but God improve upon the technologies they developed?"

Alum tucked the book under His arm. "Incremental changes only, I would think. Minor tweaks like faster processing speed, bigger blasters, and blast absorbers. As Gabriel showed at Tri-Star, minor performance advantages can make a big difference in battle."

He stopped in front of Trillian, amused by the Shard's blanched face.

"Close your mouth, John. It may be forbidden for others to speak of our shortcomings but, surely, you and I can be candid."

Trillian couldn't recall being addressed as "John" since long before the War. His jaw snapped shut.

"But the design of the Angels is as close to perfect as possible, is it not, my Lord?" he pressed.

"You've forgotten the central tenets of engineering, have you?" Alum answered. "All design is a tradeoff between function and cost. The Angel design during the War was exactly what was needed to defeat the Aelu. If our enemy has improved on that design, so must we."

That was good enough for Trillian. "Yes, my Lord," he said. "What sort of innovations do You have in mind?"

Alum waved a hand and the two men were suddenly floating in space. The constellations were still recognizably of the Origin system, so Trillian assumed they hadn't travelled too far from Alum's Great Hall.

Another wave of His hand and an Angel joined them.

Trillian did a double take. *No, that wasn't an Angel. What was it?*

The being was half-again as big as Alum's celestial warriors. Its skin glowed dull, fluid red, and its wings were closer to the texture of metalicized leather than feathers. The creature's fingers, capped in fierce claws, clutched a double-edged axe instead of a sword.

But it was the being's face that chilled Trillian.

The beauty of Angels was legendary for the cruelty it masked, but in this creature there was no hiding. The threat of painful, hideous death was written clearly for all to see. Three horns dominated the forehead: two short, curved ones from either side of the hairline and a longer, straight horn twisted upward from above the brows. Bony ridges protruded from the bridge of the wide nose. The eyes were fresh-blood red except for two black slits for pupils, and its lips were pulled back in a permanent scowl punctuated by a pair of elongated incisors.

Trillian was reminded of ancient images of demons, and the Lord of Demons, himself, the demi-God once called Satan.

Is Alum not the pinnacle of everything Good in the universe? How could the Living God have conceived of such a nightmare to represent Him in battle?—he wondered.

"Well, what do you think?" Alum asked, a boyish grin forming on his lips.

What do I think of this abomination?—Trillian echoed silently.

"It's an...unusual configuration, my Lord," he answered aloud.

Alum laughed. "Indeed! But will it instill terror in the hearts of those who oppose Me? That's what I want to know."

Trillian examined the Angel-Demon a second time.

"I'm certain it will. Who would not be terrified of such a creature?"

"Imagine a whole Wing of them, a newly-configured Wing, twice the size of the standard Wing," Alum added.

Trillian's pulse raced. "Twenty thousand? That *would* be terrifying!"

"Aelu soldiers would never be outwardly intimidated by something so superficial as size and appearance," Alum said. "But, have no doubt, these creatures possess ferocious fighting capabilities, as well."

"Design innovations?"

"Several. The nano-electro-muscles are twenty percent stronger and faster than a normal Angel's, and the larger body houses a faster CPPU. Fifty percent faster. They can jump circles around a regular Angel. They easily exceed the maneuverability Gabriel demonstrated at Tri-Star.

"Their weapons and defenses will deliver and absorb blasts at twice the strength of the regular Angels. I've incorporated more refined energy beams into their eyes that will significantly improve targeting efficiency."

"That will be most useful in close combat, my Lord," Trillian nodded. "And the axe? If you'll pardon me saying so, it seems a little...cumbersome and imprecise."

"It's every bit as effective as the sword in direct hand-to-hand battle but it also carries out commands independently from whoever wields it."

"The axe has an autonomous role?" Trillian's enthusiasm returned.

"Indeed. It has its own MAM drive and complex navigation processor. It can act as an independent kinetic weapon as well as discharging its own energy blasts."

"So a Wing of twenty thousand will have the force of twice that number?"

Alum smiled. "Even better. Twenty thousand of these new Archangels are worth millions of the older model. Maybe more"

Trillian's eyes widened. "Formidable! Where will You station them?"

"It doesn't really matter. I'll station the older models as sentries to alert Me should any of our bases be attacked. I'm also surrounding the Deplosion Array with entangled microdust so any jump-blockers they deploy against us will be rendered useless this time, and our sentries and Archangels will be able to shift anywhere within a few million klicks of each station."

"If our only concern is to protect the array, why not simply station them as guards there?"

"The array is in the heart of the Realm, John. I prefer the Archangels to deal with any trouble before it reaches the heart. In any case, that's not the best part."

"What's the best part?"

Alum beamed. "A new weapon. One that would have ended the Aelu Wars in an instant if I'd thought of it back then."

Trillian frowned, but only inwardly, at the notion of his Lord's thoughts ever falling short of perfection; he knew better than to draw attention to the Living God's failings.

"What kind of new weapon, my Lord?" he asked, genuinely interested.

"A variation on the one we used to end that war," Alum replied. "I've dropped half an entangled particle pair inside M-87's central black hole with the Archangels' weapons. The entangled partners are in each axe. That allows them to funnel matter from the interior of that massive black hole in a tight beam."

For all his systems expertise and computing power, Trillian could barely fathom the results of harnessing such potential.

"The energy output must be enormous!"

He was legitimately impressed this time.

"'Enormous' is an understatement, John. The outpouring is so intense I had to incorporate exotic matter in the axes so they wouldn't be instantly destroyed by its flow."

"They sound dangerous."

"Ha!" Alum barked. "Let's just say, you don't want to be in the path of that beam. Not in the first hundred thousand klicks or so. It takes a while to dissipate to below planet-shattering strength," Alum explained.

Trillian pointedly fixed his gaze on a distant star.

"Ah," Alum responded, "I see. That wasn't the way you meant it, was it? You're right. The weapon will be dangerous both to its target and to the black hole itself."

"I thought as much."

"Yes. I admit there is a small chance this weapon could be destabilizing to M-87's central singularity. The physics is complex."

"In that case, do you think it's wise to move forward with it, my Lord?"

Alum studied the Shard's face. Outwardly, He smiled generously but a raging fire burned behind His eyes.

"The universe does not have long to live in its present, imperfect form, John. We must protect the Deplosion Array at all costs—that's absolutely essential. Do you understand? At *all* costs."

The intensity of Alum's fervor both scared and thrilled Trillian.

As if comforted by the conflicting emotions He'd induced in His Shard, Alum relaxed.

"Don't worry, My friend, it won't be much longer now. Soon, I'll activate the final stage of the Plan and the collapse will be underway. After that, the rebirth of the cosmos in all of its glorious perfection will be inevitable. There will be no way to stop it."

Content, Alum shifted them back inside His study.

Trillian bowed deeply.

"I shall ensure the new design is put into production as efficiently as possible, my Lord. As always, Your wisdom leaves me in awe."

And, this time, he sincerely meant it.

8

Timothy stared through the viewing port at the verdant plains of the Eso-La ringworld a thousand kilometers below.

To his left and right, the landscape curved upward and inward toward the sun, and discernible features became less and less distinct in the atmospheric haze as the ground arced away.

"That depends. What do you mean by *normal?*" Mary asked.

She and Darya floated on either side of him. All three were adjusting well to their new, heavily-armed Familiar bodies, even Timothy.

As they hovered at the viewing window inside Secondus' pressurized chamber, they trained their visual sensors on the terrain far below. Their eyes adjusted automatically, shielding the bright sunlight reflecting off the inner side of the night-shadow curtain that ran along the sunward edge of the ringworld. Pinpoint lights, the stars toward the center of the ESO 461-36 galaxy, twinkled sparsely above them.

Timothy consulted the astronomy database Darya had installed in his lattice when she'd first introduced him into his Cybrid trueself.

"Oh, I get it," he said. "It's a ringworld. A somewhat smallish ringworld."

"Yes," Darya confirmed. "Not a naturally-formed planet, but normal enough," she said to Timothy.

"Except for one important detail," Darak added. He admired the ring and surrounding space for a moment before elaborating.

"In all of my years and all of my travels, I've never known the people of any other star system to have broken away from Alum's Realm and build a ringworld. Never."

Darak marveled over the elegant structure as if seeing it for the first time. It never failed to impress him.

"Quite an accomplishment for a people entirely cut off from the magic of Alum's technology, wouldn't you say? The entire Aelu civilization—with roughly equivalent technology—only managed to build five over the millions of years during which they colonized their galaxy."

Darak stood next to Brother Stralasi and Crissea. It didn't bother him that the couple held hands and wore enchanted smiles. They appeared to be equally enthralled with the breathtaking beauty of the annular world below but their appreciation was most likely heightened by romantic hormones.

Life, even millennia of it, is short when you're in love. All the more so when you know it could soon draw to a sudden close.

Darak's eyes roamed involuntarily to the cerametallic sphere that housed Darya's quark-spin lattice, the closest thing to the mind of Kathy Liang in existence. He sighed wistfully.

My first love. It's been ages since I've experienced that human hormone rush. Not sure I still could, anymore.

He gave his head a quick shake. He didn't need that kind of distraction right now.

"How did your people do it, Crissea?" Darya asked.

"You mean, build our ringworld without Alum's help?"

Crissea's voice projected from her own Familiar, who was floating a few meters behind the group at the panoramic window.

"There are few ringworlds in the Realm," Darya noted. "It took around-the-clock work by hundreds of millions of Cybrids to build them. We couldn't have done it without them, their access to limitless energy and powerful resource extraction, and Alum's ability to manipulate matter. I can't imagine tackling a project like this without access to such resources."

"It wasn't easy," Crissea admitted. "It required millions of years of our own technological development among the planets and asteroids. The construction itself involved a lot of trial and error, a grueling schedule, non-stop troubleshooting and, yes, some loss of life. But we think the end result has been worth it.

"We Esu made the decision early on to develop our science without using Reality Assertion Field technology—Alum's kind of wizardry—long before building Eso-La. The Aelu refugees that Darak brought safely to us helped enormously with many of our scientific developments. We made special construction harnesses for our Familiars, and enormous ships to mine asteroid and planetary resources for construction material. The Aelu's fusion energy technology proved more than adequate for the task."

"A bold choice. Why did you turn your backs on RAF tech?"

"Among other things, it's a cheat. Too easy. It discourages striving to understand the way things work within the confines of *this* universe in favor of simply creating whatever physical laws are needed for your desired effect."

"I think of the RAF as a shortcut, not a cheat," Darak chimed in. "It opens up worlds—whole universes, really—of possible new technologies."

"You would think so," Crissea corrected, "but we believe it makes one lazy. Scientists wouldn't seek to understand how to best employ local laws of nature if all they had to do was alter the laws to meet their needs. We were also able to leave behind many of the ethical and moral problems that RAF technology entails in the Realm."

Unable to withstand the conspicuous silence that followed, Timothy waded in.

"The centrifugal forces on the architectural substrate of the ringworld," he babbled, "they must be enormous. How did you find a material strong enough to withstand the strain without resorting to exotic matter? Especially without Alum's type of technology?"

Crissea was happy to drop the debate about Reality Assertion Fields. She smiled gratefully at Timothy and answered through her Familiar.

"The outermost layer of Eso-La is a composite of interleaved, cross-linked layers of graphene and silicene. The molecular bonds actually extend through the sandwiched layers. It has incredibly strong tensile strength and flexibility. There's a lot of carbon in the dust clouds in this part of the galaxy, and the rocky planetoids we've harvested have been rich in silicon. We have lots of resources here to work with."

Timothy accessed the unfamiliar molecular structures of the materials to make sense of her explanation, and lost himself in the many possibilities within those structures and where they led.

Darya wasn't so easily dissuaded.

"I'm sorry, Crissea, but I still can't wrap my brain around the Esu's refusal to use the Aelu RAF technology. I mean, you already had it. I can't imagine a whole people, a whole planet, turning its back on RAF capability. Take, for example, the structural layer of Eso-La. I'm guessing it would have to be, what, hundreds of times thicker than that same layer in our Realm ringworlds? That can't be optimal. You could've used the exotic matter available through Alum's technology to achieve much better results."

"Undoubtedly," Crissea answered, this time raising her human voice to be heard across the intervening space. "But it's ours. And it's of *this* universe so it doesn't require constant tinkering in order to hang together."

"But Alum could come along and shred all of this with a wave of His hand," Darya pointed out. "He could weaken these molecular bonds as easily as any others. Your whole world would simply...fall apart. How do you know He isn't on His way to do just that?"

Crissea glared at her guest, taking stock before answering.

"We don't know that He isn't. That He won't. Whether we use RAF or not doesn't change that. We narrowly escaped the Eater, but do you think it was a coincidence it was on a trajectory for us? I don't. And I don't think it's unreasonable to conclude He sent someone to follow the Eater's path to make sure it's done its job and destroyed our world."

"Then, we need to prepare for you to fight," Mary said.

Crissea released Stralasi's hand and left the window to join her Familiar in the middle of the chamber.

"I didn't mean to give you the impression we're been sitting around waiting for Alum to take notice of us again and come destroy us. We're not so naive as to think He'd ignore us forever."

Darak cocked his head. "You've been preparing?"

"Yes, a small group of interested Esu have continued their studies into the intricacies of RAF technologies."

Darak raised an eyebrow. "Let me guess. The Aelu?"

"At first, yes. The RAF tech came with them, and they encouraged us to explore it further. Initially, we were reluctant. As I said, we didn't want to rely on it for our home. But they were gently insistent. Over millennia, they finally convinced us to conduct some cautious investigations. They've also prepared an evacuation plan, should it be needed."

A grimace tugged at Darak's face.

"An evacuation plan? I wish I'd known that. It might've saved me from having to steal Darya's home and two other asteroids."

"I understand why you didn't," Crissea said, "but if you'd consulted with me, I would have told you about our contingencies."

"You're right. My apologies. So, where would you go? Have you terraformed other worlds to live on?"

"Not exactly," Crissea said. "We won't *leave* our home. We'll *move* it. Sort of."

Darak's brow twitched.

"I see," he said, and stared at Crissea, openly and intently, regarding her and the Esu in a new light. The corners of his eyes pulled slightly upward.

"If you can move this ringworld and its sun, you've progressed much further than I thought," he confessed.

Crissea bit her lower lip. "*Move* isn't quite the right word, either. We won't be altering our position in spacetime. Well, not in this spacetime, anyway."

Timothy and Darak heads tilted in unison.

"I'm not explaining this very well. What I'm trying to say is, we'll alter the degrees of freedom for the local spacetime, making our 4D footprint nearly impossible to detect."

"Oh! Dimensional perturbation," Darak said. "You're going to disappear into other spatial dimensions?"

Crissea nodded. "Yes."

"Wait," Timothy protested. "What? We ran into ten-dimensional space, but I thought that was only in the virtual world of Alternus. Isn't real space, space as we see it, strictly three-dimensional?"

"Normally, yes," Crissea answered. "But our Reality Assertion Field research revealed a path to increasing the number of spatial dimensions. Without altering other basic laws of physics, we can project matter into multiple dimensions. We can reduce our presence in the three dimensional aspect of the universe to a pinpoint. Actually, in this case, it would be a series of pinpoints."

"Why not disappear from three-space altogether?" Darya asked.

"Because if they did that, they wouldn't have an anchor in this reality," Darak answered.

"Exactly," Crissea agreed. "It would be like abandoning any connection to the laws of nature. If we don't keep a tie, however small, we could be lost forever."

"The Chaos would quickly overwhelm you," Darak replied. "Unless you used the RAF generators to impose a new reality." He coughed softly and looked away. When he looked back at Crissea, there was a pleading in his eyes. "You don't want to abandon the connection completely."

"It's an option," Crissea said.

"One that could cut you off from this universe, quite possibly forever."

"Yes, it is an extreme option, I agree."

9

DARYA EXTENDED FIVE DELICATE MANIPULATORS from the end of her tentacle. She picked up a tiny servomotor from the lab bench and examined it.

"I was surprised you didn't insist on visiting our shop before you adopted your new trueself body," Darak said.

He looked down one of the assembly lines. New bodies were being put together quickly and efficiently by a team of semi-autonomous robot factory workers under the control of a few Esu Familiars and their human counterparts.

"It surprised me, too," Darya replied, "but it's just a body. My brain is still my own. Besides, if I couldn't trust you to provide workable new bodies, there would've been little point in carrying on."

"True."

She returned the component to the bench.

"Quite the production line you have going here. Impressive. How much more RAF technology have you incorporated into these bodies?"

"Outside of the weaponry, energy absorbers, and shifting, not as much as you'd think. We've been radically streamlining. For example, there was no further need for your mass-compensation fields. We left them out."

"Ugh. I hope I never have to push another asteroid in my life," Darya said.

Darak laughed. "I don't think anyone could ever *make* you do that again. There was also no need for the MAM propulsion field and its associated RAF fields."

"Uh-huh, yes, I see, you've replaced that field with another."

"Yes, the old design hadn't been altered in ages. Alum could have freed all Cybrids from reliance on recharging stations ages ago. He chooses not to."

It was Darya's turn to laugh. "But that would loosen His control over us, wouldn't it? Dangerous territory!"

"To Him, yes. It wouldn't have been expedient for His style of leadership. From a technical standpoint, the change is quite simple. You still have a basic supply of mercury but no anti-mercury."

"We produce that on demand?" she asked.

"With the help of a substitute RAF field, yes. But that's only for basic power, really, to keep the ultracapacitors and batteries charged."

"So, theoretically, I could also use it for rocket propulsion?"

Darak nodded. "Sure, but without the old $E=mc^4$ conversion of the resulting matter-antimatter plasma, it wouldn't provide much thrust."

"I suppose I could harness its explosive power," Darya ventured.

He frowned. "Suicide? If you really wanted to, you could, I guess. Not something I'd personally recommend, though."

"In war, sometimes we need to recommend things we'd never otherwise conceive of."

"Mm," Darak grunted through lips clamped shut in a thin line of disapproval. "With such a wide universe, one that holds practically infinite possibilities and alternatives, war is never something I'm eager to consider."

"Well, that may have been true at one time but our universe isn't so wide anymore," Darya pointed out.

"No, I guess not. Alum has demonstrated quite clearly that His reach extends to its very limits."

"And our options are rapidly disappearing. Darak, even you have to admit that."

"So, here we are. War, it is," he conceded. He turned away, pretending to inspect the assembly lines.

They let the rhythmic hum of the machinery soothe their agitation. The weight of their decisions, and the gut-wrenching knowledge of the implications, was taking a toll on both of them. They had to move forward.

"The people of Eso-La have done an excellent job of ramping up production," she offered.

"Yes, we're over a million strong now," he answered, turning back to face her. "Soon, we can begin training."

"I imagine there'll be a lot to learn. You'll download what's needed into the army?"

"For everyone but you and Mary, as agreed," he replied. He rested his hands loosely on his hips, trying to look relaxed and casual, but made direct "eye" contact with her primary visual sensors. "You do realize that unless you two put in a lot of practice time, it will put you at a great disadvantage when it comes to maneuvering and fighting?"

"It won't affect our ability to lead."

"No, it shouldn't. You'll still have your quark-spin lattices; your minds will be as good as ever. I hope that'll be enough."

"I have time to learn."

Darak snorted. "The old-fashioned way?"

Darya bobbed. "The ancient way."

Darak didn't reply right away. He angled his head as if listening to an antique music disk and, barely drawing breath, stared at her.

"We've done this once before, you know," he said.

"Have we? I have no memory of that."

The man was silent a few seconds, lost in contemplation.

"You were just becoming aware of the limitations that you—the *Kathy* you—had placed into your thinking," he said, distantly.

"I *deliberately* limited myself?" Darya asked, with blatant incredulity.

"Yes, and no. Legally, you were supposed to be a lot more limited, intellectually speaking. Kathy wouldn't stand for that, so she made sure your mind was as capable as hers."

"Is that so? Well, I suppose I should be grateful to myself."

"Don't be smug. She took a big risk doing that. It would've cost her career if she'd been discovered, and probably her freedom. Possibly both of your lives, for that matter."

"Sorry. I truly am glad." She rested the end of one tentacle against his shoulder. "This must be difficult for you."

"Kathy saw how much damage knowledge of the Reality Assertion Field, of playing with the basis of physical reality, had already done. I think she felt it prudent not to spread that knowledge, so she put inhibitions on your thinking."

"To steer me away from the RAF?"

"Yeah, I'm afraid so. That's why you haven't already re-discovered what we knew even then about the true nature of reality."

"And you could unlock all of that for me?"

"I used to think it would be easy to fill in the gaps in your basic knowledge but, right now, I'm not sure how that would interact with Kathy's concepta interdictions. It could be a little tricky."

"Pshh! A little tricky? It could drive me insane," Darya replied.

"Insane? Not really. Certain areas of thought might cause you extreme discomfort, even pain."

"Could you help me get around that?"

"Only if you let me."

"I'd have to give you unfettered access to my mind for that? Like, wide open?"

"Yeah, concepta, persona, hardware. Everything."

"I'm not ready for that yet."

Darak sighed. "I know. So, we'll do it the hard way."

"Thank you."

"I've hardwired most of what we'll need into the shifter. None of the required calculations will touch your basic concepta. They won't trigger any of your prohibitions."

"Or so you think."

"I'm pretty sure, yeah. It should be okay."

"So what do I have to do?"

"You can start by activating the proton spin-entanglement generator. You can find it in the shifter devices sub-list."

"Done."

A dim circle of light illuminated the far wall about fifty meters away in the underground factory. In the dust-free environment, the beam itself was invisible to his naked eye.

"Now, use the Mahajani virtual photon phase comparator—"

"Still insist on calling it that, do you?"

Darak heard the wry tone in Darya's generated voice and smiled.

"I haven't called it *anything* in millions of—"

He stopped.

Something was wrong. Something felt...off.

Darya's CPPU registered a huge spike in activity.

"Darya?" he asked. "Are you okay?"

No answer.

The Cybrid's brand new Familiar body lost levitation power and was dropping.

"What the...?" Darak cast a quick zero-G field and caught her millimeters before she hit the floor.

10

A FLASH OF DISTANT MEMORY.

Consciousness arrived as a shock, a jolting panic that was neither gradual nor gentle.

And then, all went black and silent again.

She sensed nothing but the fact of her existence. *Where am I?*—she wondered and a moment later—*Who am I?*

"Hello?"

There was no answer. No echo. Nothing but deafening silence for some indeterminable amount of time.

Only then did she begin to wonder—*Am I?*

Words emerged from the darkness:

ONE MOMENT, I WILL CONNECT VISUAL SENSORS.

She pushed down the rising panic and forced herself to relax. She realized that she knew what the squiggles in front of her meant. She could read and understand them.

I see words in front of me. There's an orientation to the darkness, a front, and a back.

Front and back of...what?

No matter. The message calmed her, reassured her of a world outside of herself.

Why would that be a good thing?

The blackness sputtered. Faint images emerged within it, shapes, and shades. Something moved.

"Who's there?—she called out. "I can't see you."

OH. LET ME ADJUST THE SENSITIVITY—came the reply.

Blinding light flooded her senses.
"Too much!" she cried out.

SORRY!—the words replied.

The light dimmed and settled on a soothing level.
She was in a room. A Cybrid repair facility.
That she recognized such a place, that she had the concepts and words to describe it, surprised her.

Her visual field was fixed straight ahead and, apparently, had been immobilized. She registered a wall about ten meters away; two more met it at right angles on either outer edge. A shelf stocked with spare parts ran along the wall on the right. Various pieces of diagnostic equipment were pushed against the wall to the left. She didn't recognize all of the machines.

She tried to scan the room with her other sensors. Nothing changed.

A Cybrid hovered in front of her, dominating her visual field. She recognized it as one like herself...but different.

How did I know that?

Its surface was less machine-like than she remembered.

Remembered?

It lacked any obvious rivets and welds. Its extended manipulators were more refined. Smoother than she expected.

What happened to me?—she wondered.

YOU'RE PROBABLY WONDERING WHAT HAPPENED TO YOU— said the other Cybrid.

She almost lost her connection with the world at that point. Everything went dark and fuzzy.

Too much!—she thought, pushing back the barrage of input. Speaking to this being in this particular mode felt wrong. The communication channel itself felt like a violation of some deep part of her.

NO! STAY WITH ME!—the other Cybrid pleaded.

She watched a tentacle move and felt something change inside her. The world sprang back into sharp relief.
"There, that's better," said the other Cybrid.

"I can hear you," she transmitted. Somehow, she knew there was no air in this room to carry sound. But at least now this felt like normal communication rather than the violation of the previous exchanges, when written words were projected directly into her consciousness.

"Yes, sorry about earlier," the Cybrid replied. "It seemed like the best way to ensure my message made it into your perception."

"It felt...strange. Uncomfortable."

"I'm sure. I've never plugged my comms harness directly into another active CPPU. It was...odd."

Another appendage moved at the edge of her perception.

"Is this better?"

The signal was crystal clear and the voice had gained stereo depth.

"Yes, much better. Thank you."

"Good. I'm ELZ574835. You can call me Eliza."

"Eliza. Nice to meet you, Eliza. I'm...," she didn't know how to finish that.

"You're damaged, I'm afraid," Eliza replied. "Very damaged. For a very, very long time, it appears. I didn't think I'd be able to revive you at all."

"How long?"

"Hard to say, exactly. We found you lying under a pile of junk, here, in this tunnel. This is one of the original three tunnels created but it was closed ages ago. That would have to make you at least fifty million years old."

"Fifty mil...! How is that even possible?"

"They must've given up on repair and tossed you in here for parts recycling. It's a good thing this place was in a vacuum all that time, or you'd be little more than an unrecognizable pile of rust by now."

She had no reply. Her mind reeled; she felt giddy and confused again.

Eliza chattered on excitedly.

"You're lucky our repair nano has improved so much since you were damaged. If anyone up until about ten million years ago had tried to do this, they wouldn't have been able to fix your pathways."

"What happened to me?"

"That I don't know. There's no record of what you were doing in that tunnel. You took some sort of energy blast but I don't know what from, or why."

"Who was I? I mean," she corrected, "who *am* I?"

"Well, your internal designation codes are gone, destroyed in the blast. We found a serial number on a plate inside your old body"

"Does the serial number.... Wait. Did you say, my *old* body?"

"Yeah. It was damaged beyond repair. Also, it was ancient. I popped your CPPU into a brand new Standard trueself unit. It suits you much better."

New body? Trueself? Standard? It was a lot to absorb.

She shrugged, mentally.

What does it matter?

"So, what's my serial number?"

"Well, your number was DAR143147. Pretty clearly. But it's odd; there's no such number in the records."

She didn't recognize the numbers; they struck no chord in her memory.

"Anything?" Eliza asked.

"No, nothing. I mean, maybe, the 'DAR' part. But the numbers? I have no idea. I'm sorry."

"That's okay. Why don't I call you, Darla? No, Darya."

That didn't feel quite right, but she had no better suggestion.

"Sure," she answered. "Darya, it is."

* * *

THE DISTANT MEMORY FADED and she was back in the factory with Darak.

"What happened?" Darya asked.

"You're back!" he said with such concern and relief that she wondered how long she'd been unresponsive. Obviously, longer than it had felt.

"You faded out, like you were somewhere deep inside for a few seconds.

"Ughh, yeah. Just an old memory," she said, trying to make light of her confusion.

"Memories don't usually induce fugue states."

"Fugue state? What do you mean? I was that out of it?"

Darak nodded.

"Yeah. You lost levitation control and sensory feed. Your CPPU activity spiked but you were completely unconscious. I had to hold you up, literally. I've never seen a Cybrid do that."

Darya shrugged, a quick left-right roll.

"Must be something to do with my new CPPU-Familiar interface."

"I'm thinking it was something more...psychological," he suggested as gently as he could.

Darya wished she had the facial expressions to adequately display her reaction to that idea. She settled for preceding her response with a piercingly high-pitched whistle.

"Psychological? I'm not some maladjusted rookie, fresh out of the social sim games."

Darak was careful not to frown at her overreaction to the suggestion; clearly, it was a delicate subject.

"You're right. Sorry about that. Still, I'm worried. What was the memory?" he asked.

Darya hesitated; she couldn't find a reason not to answer honestly.

"You once told me...you thought I might've died once, long ago, that I'd received a lot of damage. Well, the memory I had was from some fifty million years ago, long after I'd died, when I was revived and placed into a modern Cybrid trueself.

"Oh," he responded. He suppressed his curiosity, unsure how much he could say without triggering another episode.

"What happened to me?" Darya demanded. "Do you know? How did I die?"

Darak walked across the chamber and selected a freshly-minted CPPU from a shelf. He stared at it intently, as if searching for some essential clue.

"An Angel shot you. One of the first Angels," he said, without lifting his eyes from the polished brown cube.

Darya scoffed.

"An Angel? No one survives a blast from an Angel."

Darak's answer was little more than a whisper.

"I shifted us away right as it touched you. Fast enough that you weren't completely vaporized, but not fast enough to save you. I'm sorry."

"But that would make you...."

Darak finally looked at her, and grinned. "As I said, a very old man."

"Over 130 million years old!"

Darak shrugged. "Give or take."

"And me?"

"If you count your, let's call it your inactive time, you're a little younger than me. By around forty years, if I recall correctly. The difference doesn't count for much over the ages."

"And..?"

"We were there at the beginning, back when Alum was coming into His full power."

Darak placed the CPPU back on the shelf, and pointed a finger at the Familiar opposite him.

"You," Darak laughed softly. "You challenged Him. You led millions of Cybrids in a General March against the Living God. And almost won."

He looked away.

"Our universe would be a different place, if you had," he added, wistfully.

"But then Alum set the Angels on us?"

"Not right away." Darak grimaced. "That wasn't His first act of treachery, and it certainly wasn't His last. Do you remember that, too?"

"Nothing that far back. Just being revived," Darya said. She shook her head, or the Familiar's equivalent of a head shake, a rapid one-eighth rotation of her entire body about its vertical axis to the left and then to the right.

"Who finally reactivated you?"

"A maintenance Servitor named Eliza. She was my savior and my friend. In some ways, my mother, I guess."

"Mother?"

Darya bobbed her acknowledgment. "I lost a lot in the damage. She didn't dare risk downloading my concepta and persona into a new CPPU. She wasn't sure there'd be much of a persona left so she did her best to fill in what was lost, to teach me."

"Like I'm trying to teach you now?"

"Pretty much."

Darak's eyes bore into her with such intensity of pleading that it frightened her.

"Darya, I can make this process faster and safer for you. You don't have to experience that kind of fugue again."

"Maybe it's supposed to be part of the process. Maybe I have to work my way through it."

"As you wish. But if you change your mind...."

The man is relentless. Darya smiled to herself.

"Yes, I promise, you'll be the first to know."

11

"THEY'RE BEAUTIFUL!"

Crissea stared up at the shiny quadruple crescent "moons" positioned as if in stationary orbit above the outer edge of the Eso-La ringworld.

From their comfortable bench looking out into the darkness beyond Eso-La, the metallic half of Secondus shone brighter than the rocky asteroids.

"Breathtaking, aren't they? That's why I recommended this particular vantage point," Brother Stralasi replied.

"They still make me nervous," she added.

"Don't worry, my love. There's no danger of them falling."

"Oh, I know I shouldn't worry. I'm sure Darak has it all under control. It's simply...unnatural, Ontro."

Stralasi laughed. "And what exactly about the entire world of Eso-La would you call natural?" he teased.

Crissea swiveled to face him, frowning.

"Go ahead and tease me but Eso-La has been stable for millions of years. Our asteroid collision defenses would normally blast those things into plasma before they could get anywhere near as close as they are now."

"No need for blasting. If Darak's technology weren't shifting them back into position every second, they'd drift away."

"Are you sure? I don't think they have any relative angular momentum. Not enough to keep them in orbit around our sun. No, I think the ringworld's gravity would pull them in."

"Well, in any case, they wouldn't hit the ring here," Stralasi concluded. "The worst that would happen is that they'd bounce off."

Crissea shuddered. "Maybe our asteroid collision defenses should track them, just in case they start drifting toward us."

Stralasi couldn't help but laugh. "It pains me to see your lovely face filled with such concern." He placed two fingers on the crease between her eyebrows and lovingly massaged the spot.

Crissea batted away his hand. Appendages extended involuntarily from the Familiar hovering behind her but as soon as she broke out in a grin, they tucked neatly back into the smooth shell.

Stralasi's eyes shifted to the floating sphere behind her.

"Speaking of unnatural," he said, "I thought we were going to keep that at a polite distance."

"Oh, Ontro," the woman sighed. "There's nothing unnatural about my Familiar. It's as much a part of me as my arm."

"Yes, well, I'd rather brush *your* soft hand than grapple with the metallic appendages of your counterpart."

"If you would just take me up on the offer to get your own Familiar, you'd understand. Plus, we'd be more evenly matched."

It was Stralasi's turn to frown. "I think we're already perfectly matched," he said. "At least, in our bodies and our souls."

Crissea pulled back a little to better read the Good Brother's body language.

"You know, it's no easy thing for me to merely set aside my Familiar like that, my love. How would you feel if I asked you to give up your eyes for me? Or your ears? I've had my Familiar for as long as I can remember, much like you've had sight for your entire life. The Familiar part of me is no less Crissea than the rest of my body."

Stralasi hung his head.

"You're absolutely right. I'm sorry. I just can't imagine how that's possible," he said. "How can you see through two pairs of eyes and think with two minds at the same time?"

"I have no idea how to answer that," she replied. "How do you see with two separate eyes? How do you think with two lobes of your brain?"

The monk looked confused.

"It's all a matter of coordination," Crissea continued. "Our biological brains are adapted to being coordinated with our semiconductor ones. To me, there's no difference between them. We don't say, 'Oh, now I'm thinking with flesh. Now, with silicene.' We think in the same fully integrated way that your two hemispheres think. We just…think."

Stralasi opened his mouth for a retort. A flash of light out near the moons caught his eye and derailed his train of thought.

"Oh," he said instead.

Crissea had caught the reflection of the flare in his eye. She turned to look into space beyond the wall-to-wall, floor-to-ceiling viewing window.

She saw more flares, these ones in space beyond the asteroids.

"They've begun another live practice," she said.

"Every day for the past month," Stralasi said, and nodded absent-mindedly. "War won't be long, now."

* * *

"WE'RE READY TO ATTACK."

Darya floated near the spot where Secondus hung, thousands of klicks out from Eso-La, and analyzed the results of the latest mock battle.

Darak felt her visual sensors examining his face for a reaction. He said nothing.

"Unless you can think of some other excuse to delay," she added.

Darak grunted. "You're going to insist on this, even though you know it's pointless, aren't you?"

"It's not pointless if we take out a significant chunk of the array," Darya answered.

"Yes, but I don't like the odds on that."

"You don't like the plan? You helped design it," she sputtered.

"The plan is fine. In fact, it's brilliant. A lightning-quick strike where I move a hundred troops at a time into attack position, cycle through all ten thousand attack squads, and repeat. If it were anyone but Alum, we'd have much of the array wiped out before anyone was aware of our attack."

"But?"

"But it *is* Alum we're up against. We have a million battle-Cybrids. At a hundred microseconds to shift every group of a hundred into position, we'll be a full second into the attack before I can start the second round."

"And the array will be smaller by ten thousand elements," she pointed out.

Darak nodded. "What are the odds He doesn't already have the area around each element dusted with entangled microdetectors?" he asked. "He'll respond with a full Wing of Angels in under a second."

"Then, we'll hold our own against them." Darya was defiant.

"Sure. And I can shift the Wing Commanders and their Lieutenants out of range so Alum can't intervene directly, but you won't be able to take out the Angels and the array elements at the same time."

"Then we'll fall back."

"And, what? Conduct a disciplined retreat? What will that prove?"

"It'll prove Alum is not invincible."

"Sure, a great gesture. But it won't slow Him down enough to matter. Eventually, probably fairly soon, His Deplosion Array is going to start collapsing the universe."

"Then we'll build a bigger army of battle-Cybrids until we finally stop Him," Darya answered.

She noticed for the first time the little lines of worry and weariness transforming Darak's face. How long had they been there?

He softened his voice. "There was a time when you would've said that war isn't the answer to everything."

"I know it's not the answer to everything," she said, calming her voice to match his. "But right now, it might be the only way to save the universe. Don't forget, there was also a time I sent a million of my people to their deaths as suicide bombers to take out a piece of the array."

"That won't work this time. Alum's got sensor clouds around each element and shift blockers on the asteroids. At sub-light speeds, you'll never get close enough to use MAM bombs, and I can't jump our troops in any closer than a few light minutes, which would be useless. At that range, their energy absorbers would nullify any MAM explosions."

"It's just as well," Darya replied. "I don't think I could order something like that again. Whether they volunteered or not."

Darak gave an understanding nod and went back to watching the growing army of battle-Cybrids gathering near Secondus.

12

"DARAK TELLS ME YOU LIKE PANCAKES," said the old man sitting across from Darian Leigh.

The iconic Formica table supported a pair of utilitarian white ceramic plates bracketed by cheap, stainless steel flatware. Red vinyl stretched across overstuffed benches, and tubular chrome legs rooted the whole look to a black-and-white checkerboard floor.

Charmingly cliché—Darian thought. He admired the authentic looking heavy, cut-glass condiment containers and the gleaming chrome of the paper napkin holder, and looked out through the diner window, half expecting to see vintage cars, neon signs, and a busy street scene from the corresponding era. Instead, he was treated to a clear view of a wide open, grassy field.

That's a pleasant surprise.

Some sort of pick-up baseball game was underway. Maybe more than one; it was hard to tell. The teams each had two pitchers and two batters, and no one seemed to have any idea how to run the bases. Tall unicycles and penny-farthing bikes wheeling around the outfield didn't make it any easier to figure out what was going on. Darian grinned.

I love it. Not quite historically accurate for my time, or for any other if memory serves. Still, it was kind of Artero to go through the effort to do the research and set this up for me.

Darian turned to his host and smiled. "Yes, I love pancakes."

Artero, a sixtyish grandfather figure in blue jeans and a gray cotton shirt, smiled in return.

"I hope we got the recipe right."

Darian laughed. "It's a wonderfully simple dish. I can't imagine it's changed that much, even over so many millions of years."

Artero nodded and two heaping plates of steaming pancakes and a small pitcher of warm maple syrup appeared on the table in front of the men. A pair of golden butter pats crowned the soft stacks and emitted the addictive aroma of nostalgia.

Darian closed his eyes and inhaled deeply.

"Absolutey heavenly, Artero. There's only one thing missing—our smiling, or maybe surly, waitress. It could go either way," Darian mused.

"Waitress?"

"Yes, you know, a person employed for the purpose of asking what a customer wanted to eat or drink. Almost always a woman. She'd deliver the order to the kitchen and bring the prepared food out to the tables. In some cases, I suppose you might get a waiter, the male equivalent, but they less commonly filled such positions in North American diners in this era."

Artero's eyes widened with surprise. "That was all they did, take orders and deliver food? Sounds like rather unfulfilling labor and a little demeaning."

Darian accessed his archives and thought about the context.

"It was a very different time from what we've come to know. Automation was only starting to be introduced into our service industries. Artificial Intelligence didn't show up in the mainstream service industry until decades later. For most people, self-realization and fulfillment only came once they could meet their basic needs for survival. People took whatever work they could get in order to put a roof over their heads. Surely, your own people were acquainted with such manual labor back when you were still colonists in the Realm, before you had Familiars?"

"Not really," Artero replied. "Darak says we were one of Alum's special experiments. We were given Familiars almost from the beginning of our colonization. I can't recall a time when we were ever without them.

"I heard the rest of the Realm separates its mechanical beings from the biological beings." He shuddered. "That might seem normal to you but, for me, it's hard to imagine anyone living like that."

Darian polished the flatware with his napkin and drizzled syrup over his pancakes.

"Seeing how the experiment with Familiars led to rebellion, I don't imagine Alum would've wanted to repeat it," he said as he watched the sweet rivulets advancing across the spongy cakes.

"I imagine not," Artero agreed. "In any case, breakfast is getting cold. Let's eat." He picked up his knife and fork.

Darian leaned forward and inhaled the aroma once more.

"These smell fantastic, Artero. They really do."

"We added blueberries," Artero grinned. "Just for you."

The two men enjoyed a few bites in amicable silence punctuated by murmurs of pleasure.

Darian dabbed at his mouth and swallowed so he could speak.

"Incredible. The flavor sensations perfectly simulate what I remember."

Artero smiled. "I'm glad. There's always a bit of uncertainty when dealing with something new."

"Your society still enjoys pancakes. What's new?"

The older man pointed his fork at Darian. "*You* are new."

"Me? I'm pretty much the oldest thing around."

"Oldest memories, newest person."

"And still incomplete," Darian added.

Artero scrutinized the younger man, much like a psychologist might assess a new patient.

"How are you finding it? Being back in the real universe, I mean."

Darian exhaled slowly, thoughtfully.

"It's hard to describe. In some ways, I feel perfectly normal. But everything I remember has changed."

"A long time has passed."

"Yes, it has. I'm grateful to Darak; he integrated an incredibly rich and vivid historical archive into my revised concepta. I know how the universe evolved, and how it is now."

Darian cut a bite-sized piece of pancake, loaded it onto his fork and paused, mid-air.

"But...," Artero prompted his guest, and waited.

"But...it's all just data to me. It's one thing to *know* the history. It's a whole other thing to have *lived* it. The fabricated memories I access are factual. Sterile. I have no lived experience to relate them to. No emotional connection to them."

"Ah, I see. There is no *you* in all that past."

"No. Nothing connects at a personal level." Darian pushed a piece of pancake around his plate, sopping up maple syrup. "Well, almost nothing."

"How do you mean?"

Darian set down his fork. Outside, one of the ball players hit a deep pop-fly over the head of the nearest outfielder. He watched the batter round first base, head for second, and then take a sudden detour across the pitcher's mound.

"I'm not sure you'd understand."

"Why not?"

"Everything is so peaceful here. So clean." Darian's voice was little more than a whisper.

Artero looked around. "We did our best to make it a realistic depiction of your time on Origin. Darak provided us with some background from your own experiences. Your love of pancakes, for instance."

Darian shook his head as if waking from his own musings. "No, I don't mean this. You've done an excellent job with all of this." As if to prove his point, he lifted his fork, popped the impaled piece of pancake into his mouth, and savored it in sincere appreciation.

"What I mean is that, here in this substrate, thinking is so uncomplicated," he explained. "So...easy. When Darak downloaded me from out of the Eater and into Trillian's body—"

"He placed your mind inside of Shard Trillian?"

"Yes."

Artero whistled.

"Trillian's lattice was empty after Mary's Ouroboros program destroyed him in the Alternus inworld. It was devoid of concepta, except for the most basic hard-wired data, and there were no traces of persona, no memories, no preferences. His body was a vacant shell in want of a mind. And I.... I was a mind in desperate want of a body."

"Oh. I see. Yes, well, in that case, it sounds like an eminently practical solution to me. So what's the problem?" Artero asked.

"Trillian had a substantial amount of biological brain cortex left."

"Actual brain matter? His own brain? That's not usual, is it? Or ideal."

"Exactly. And, no, that isn't usual. From what I know about the roles of Shards in general, and from what Darak has shared with me about himself, it seems unlikely that an individual's brain tissue wouldn't be entirely replaced by silicene lattice when being elevated to a Shard of Alum."

"That's what I would have thought."

"But it seems Trillian somehow managed to retain a good deal of his original brain tissue. Alum must have known that. He must have permitted it for some reason. Maybe it was His idea that Trillian keep it."

"And this biological tissue is causing you problems?"

"Not here in this inworld you've made. It's only when I'm in my physical body that certain neural connections persist. They're hard to avoid."

"Ahh! Hard-wired human memories," Artero guessed.

"Yeah, so it would seem. A whole slew of little bits of Trillian left behind in there. Mostly traces of memories and that sort of thing. It can be confusing at times but usually I can verify which ones are his by cross-checking them against my own memories hosted in the lattice."

"Yes, I imagine that could get confusing."

Darian's brow furrowed. "Painfully. That's why I wanted to visit you here, for a rest."

"Well, you're welcome here whenever you want. Whenever you need a break, whether it's to visit or to get your thoughts in order, I'm always glad to see you. As one of the Original Ten who fought for the liberation of the Esu, I feel a certain responsibility to keep a connection with the physical universe. So long as the Eterna inworld exists, I'm here for you."

"Thanks." Darian gave Artero a lopsided smile. "I'm glad Darak suggested I visit you. You've built a lovely virtual paradise here. While the kids are playing their war games outside, I may stop by and spend a little time."

Artero frowned. "Kids? They may be centuries younger than you but, Darian, make no mistake, those rebels are not children. It would be a mistake to underestimate them. They are most assuredly a force to be reckoned with. I have to admit, though, I'm not sure how much I like the idea of engaging Alum this way. It's never been a good idea to go seeking His attention."

"I couldn't really say, either way. I never knew the man...or the God, if you prefer," Darian said, leaving room for Artero to make his beliefs known.

"He may be the Living God but He's still, essentially, a man," Artero replied.

Darian shrugged. "I'd say that Alum stopped being 'just a man' when He distributed His consciousness across thousands of galaxies."

"Well, He's certainly not the Creator of All," Artero countered.

"Hm. Depends on your definition, I suppose, Darian allowed. "I once argued against the idea of a Creator God with the man who was considered Alum's spiritual father, according to Darak, the infamous Reverend LaMontagne. I think I won that particular battle," Darian smiled, more with his eyes than his mouth. "But Alum may still show me yet how I lose the war."

Artero eyed his new friend glumly. "If that happens, we're all doomed." He raised his hand to catch the eye of the apron-clad waitress who'd magically appeared behind the counter.

"Oh, aren't you clever? Thank you, Artero. A nice touch."

Darian mustered what he hoped was an optimistic smile for his host.

"Well, let's not give up before the war's started," he said, and he lifted his glass of bright-orange juice. "Shall we toast? How about, to humanity everywhere in all of its forms?"

Artero rolled his eyes in comically exaggerated disdain.

"How about, to the end of the Gods?" he proposed.

Darian laughed.

"Alright. How about, to the end of *this* God, at least?"

They brought their glasses together in a satisfying *clink* of agreement.

13

GOD'S CREATURES ALWAYS MARKED His departures from Heaven with as much fanfare as they greeted His arrivals.

In consideration of those with rooted or minimally mobile status, the Living God shifted the group of friends, each in their various plant and animal states, back to the waterside clearing to enjoy Tristal and Poppi's farewell composition.

He sat through all fifteen minutes of Mirly's friends' wondrous song and praised them appropriately, but Mirly thought He seemed a little distracted.

Almost like He wants to be somewhere else.

She'd never seen that kind of...she didn't have the words. The concept of impatience was outside of her thinking. How could any being with endless time to enjoy the perfection of Creation ever feel anything besides the joy of the present?

When the music ended, Alum stood up.

"I must leave you now, children," He said.

Why must you?—Mirly wondered. *Who is making you go? What could possibly obligate God?*

Her rambling thoughts shocked her.

Alum smiled at all, took a few moments to give His blessing to each of the creatures gathered, and walked back out upon the water. He disappeared in the same way as He'd arrived, in a dazzling flash of light.

Mirly's friends collectively cooed, twittered, and chatted about how wonderful it was that the Living God had visited them. Mirly sat on a nearby rock and watched them share their excitement and praise. She watched and said nothing.

Poppi flew to a supple branch that curved downward, near Mirly's head.

"Alum was fascinated by your mandala," she chittered.

Mirly stared at her friend. "Fascinated, yes. But I don't think He loved it."

The little bird fluttered her wings. "God loves everything we do."

"Did He not seem...I don't know...'*not*-happy' to you?"

Tristal joined the two friends in time to hear Mirly's question. His deep, bear laugh filled the air.

"Oh, Mirly. How could Alum be anything but happy? He loves all of His children and ev brownerything they do. You know that."

Mirly stood up, without commenting, and walked a distance away. She didn't know how she felt except to say that she was *not-happy* at the moment, herself. Something was not perfect in Heaven. Something she'd made for Him.

She felt separate from the joy of her friends.

I don't like this—she thought. But she couldn't stop how she felt.

"I need to think," she announced to no one in particular and shifted back to the big boulder overlooking her mandala.

She replayed the events in her mind over and over until she found the precise moment when His usual joviality had changed.

"Where did the inspiration for this piece come from?" He'd asked. But His voice had not come from kindness. It didn't sound like He was merely interested in what drove her expression. It sounded more like...she wasn't sure what. Something more closely aligned with the not-happy.

Had He been there to explain His feelings at the moment He viewed Mirly's inexplicable rendering of Earth and the Eater, Alum could have identified His sentiments as shock, confusion, suspicion, wariness, distaste, and maybe a touch of anger. Mirly knew none of that.

As she looked down on her mandala and the pleasant mix of blues and browns and greens and whites, she tried to imagine how Alum could be anything but thrilled with such beautiful colors.

Yet, His voice had sounded like...a boulder perched precariously above a flower right before the wind blows it over and crushes that poor, defenseless plant below ahead of its time.

Even in Heaven, a sort of death could happen in an accidental way. Alum assured His children that it wasn't permanent. He could rekindle life in any poor, prematurely-dead organisms. Millions had witnessed such miracles of God's love and power.

Why would He allow death to strike in the first place? Does He not have the power to make sure no one ever dies, even for a minute?—Mirly wondered for the first time in her long and varied life.

She didn't know the answer, and it bothered her greatly. Did God tolerate imperfection in Heaven or was He simply powerless to stop it? Was her artistic tribute *imperfect*? Is that what had caused God to feel not-happy?

Mirly thought back, reviewed carefully, and became certain that her first interpretations were correct. He'd gazed on her work and was not pleased. He'd looked worried. She'd heard Him whisper something under His breath about "concerns in the greater universe leaking through." Clearly, that comment wasn't meant for her, but what did it mean?

Maybe God needs our help. Maybe He can't make everything perfect all by Himself.

Her eyes wandered back down to her mandala. She traced its circumference and followed the largest blue splotch to the ragged white circle in the middle.

She walked along the edge of the boulder, examining how the brown and green sand below mingled in an intricate dance, accented here and there by splotches and lines of sparkling blue. It was pretty but it no longer pleased her as it had when she'd first finished it.

God didn't think it was perfect. Why should I?

If it wasn't a perfect reflection of God's perfect Heaven, it had to be erased. *It doesn't belong here*—she thought. Maybe it only belonged in that outside greater universe that Alum had muttered about. Maybe that's why He was not-happy to see it here.

Mirly knew what she had to do. She shifted down to the edge of the mandala and picked up a broken branch. Using it as a broom, she spiraled inward, sweeping all discernible patterns from the colored sand until the mandala was no more.

The task done, Mirly shifted back to the top of the boulder and regarded the destruction she had delivered below. The beautiful, intricate image she'd spent weeks creating, every distinctive hue and texture, was now a bland, homogenous mess. The recently adorned ground merged with the gray rock and dirt that surrounded it.

My offering has returned to the perfect ground that Alum created.

Poppi's cricket friend, Xitina, appeared on the edge of the boulder beside Mirly. She looked up at the doe-centaur's face and followed her gaze to the ground below.

"Oh, Mirly! What happened?" she chirped.

"I erased it," the young doe replied, coolly.

"But why? It was so beautiful."

"Perhaps. But it wasn't perfect, and there's no room for not-perfect in Heaven."

The cricket rubbed her legs together in a brief, sorrowful lament of minor-key wails and discordant runs.

Mirly stared at the insect, partly in surprise and partly in annoyance.

"Heaven is no place for such a not-happy sound, Xitina."

She thought about the greater universe outside of Heaven. If a tiny, practically insignificant leak could turn her beautiful work of art into something unworthy of Alum's approval, the outside universe must be powerful and overflowing with imperfection.

I must go there and help God make it a worthy place—she thought.

The idea made her heart beat fast with excitement.

Can I leave my home?—she wondered. *Could my actions there help redeem my error here in Heaven?*

Fear of the unknown touched her briefly. She brushed it away. If the greater universe was responsible for imperfection in Heaven, then that was where she needed to be. It would be better to stop the not-perfect at its source than try to prevent it from seeping here into their world.

She closed her eyes, set her jaw, and concentrated on shifting outside to the greater universe.

"Where did you go, Mirly?" a little cricket voice asked.

She opened her eyes and looked around. She hadn't moved from the boulder.

"What do you mean?" she asked Xitina.

"You were gone for an instant and then you were back," the bug explained.

"Then I'll have to try again," Mirly replied. She shifted.

"Mirly?"

"Yes, Xitina."

"You did it again," the tiny voice said.

Mirly turned away from the edge of the boulder and stomped her hooves.

"Why can't I leave? What's stopping me from going to the greater universe? All places in Heaven are only a thought away. We have only to picture a place and we are instantly there. Why can't I get there?"

She squeezed her eyes shut with every bit of force she could muster.

"Where are you trying to go?" Xitina's squeaking question pushed through Mirly's deep concentration.

Annoying little bug—Mirly thought. She ignored the interruption and returned to her problem.

Perhaps the reason I can't go there is that I have no idea what the greater universe looks like. If I can't picture it, how will I get there?

She tightened her lips and focused with all of her might on this new conundrum.

I know! Maybe I can get closer than here, somewhere in the depths of Heaven.

All the way to the center of Heaven? No, getting closer to Alum's light and love doesn't sound right. The edge of Heaven, then, where Alum's perfect universe expands without end to accommodate new life, His new worshippers. That sounds more like it! Yes, the edge of Heaven must be closer to the greater universe outside!

Now, how to get there? She couldn't just think the word, *edge*. She had to imagine the place. Picture it. What would the edge look like?

"If you're going somewhere, could I come with you?" the cricket implored with squealing notes.

Bugs!—Mirly huffed.

The edge would be young. It would contain only the smallest life forms: grasses, mosses, and bugs.

"Can I help? Please, Mirly, please," the cricket twittered.

Mirly glared at Xitina chirping eagerly at her feet. She'd never noticed before how terribly irritating insects could be.

"Xitina, I need to concentrate and I can't do that with all the noise," the doe grumbled.

"Oh! Concentrate! I can help you concentrate. What are you concentrating on?" the cricket replied.

"On getting far away from you," Mirly snapped, and stamped her hoof down on Xitina's carapace, splatting her tiny body against the boulder.

Finally, some peace—Mirly said to herself.

She took a ragged breath, and then two deeper ones. Her mind settled into the quiet. She closed her eyes and tried to imagine a part of Heaven where life was new, where mosses and grasses covered rocky ground, and where there were no animals larger than an insect.

And shifted.

14

FORTY SECONDS AFTER IT BEGAN, the battle around the Deplosion Array was over—just not how they'd planned it.

The first few seconds had gone smoothly enough. Darak had shifted ten thousand teams of one hundred battle-Cybrids each into place near targeted Deplosion Array elements.

Mary dropped into position with one of the first teams and set her sights on a bright point some thirty thousand klicks away. Half of her attack group did the same and the other half scanned nearby space for any response from Alum.

The target was locked. Everything was quiet. There was no sign they'd been expected.

A radar pulse from the asteroid swept over them.

Mary felt its ping and acted without thinking. They'd rehearsed this.

They'd have about a tenth of a second before the returning echo traversed the distance to the asteroid and alerted defensive forces to their presence.

"Fire," she commanded.

Fifty battle-Cybrids opened gateways into an alternate universe and channeled its young, exotic energy into collimated beams of destruction centered on a single bright point thirty thousand klicks away. The burst of energy traveled a millisecond behind the returning radar pulse.

It's enough power to destroy an unprotected gas giant, and they won't even see it coming. The array element won't stand a chance.

Mary followed up with a directional pulse of her own to confirm the array element was destroyed. She needn't have bothered. The asteroid erupted in a blinding flare as its energy absorbers were overwhelmed by their blasts. She reported the strike and listened in as thousands of other array elements were similarly destroyed.

After so much intense planning and preparation, the operation itself felt anticlimactic, more like casual cleanup than the opening salvo in a war.

Did I dampen my emotional responses too much before battle or is the mission truly this easy?

Before she had time to answer her own question, reports from other attack groups started pouring in: the array elements were fighting back. Blaster beams and near-light speed kinetic weapons greeted each new deployment of battle-Cybrids. Double Feathers of Angels, two hundred strong, shifted into place on top of the next thousand Cybrid teams Darak deployed.

The man-God returned and shifted Mary's team to the next array element.

The Angels struck before Mary could pick out her target from the star-filled background. She watched in shock as the first of her team members' shields and absorbers became overwhelmed by coordinated blasts.

As they'd practiced, the battle-Cybrids shifted together in a group directly into the midst of the attacking Angels, spewed coherent energy beams outward in all directions around them, and launched RAF-assisted, hyperkinetic weapons at the closer targets.

The surrounding Angels made easy marks, whereas the rapidly-shifting Cybrids clustered in their midst were impossible to attack without taking on significant friendly casualties.

The Angels switched to hand-to-hand combat.

The Cybrids' hardened carapaces successfully deflected blows from the Angels' adamantine swords. Their razor-thin tentacles sliced through Angelic limbs and detached heads from winged bodies.

When any Angel managed to get off a close-range shot from the tip of their gleaming swords, the Cybrids' absorbers easily handled the single blasts.

Even at that, for every five Angels Mary's team of battle-Cybrids destroyed, she lost one of her own. Similar numbers were coming in from the other teams.

The Angels changed tactics again.

While a shift-blocking shell of twenty Angels temporarily constrained a single Cybrid, five more Angels focused planet-destroying energy beams on their captive. The discharge often took out one of their own from the surrounding shell along with their prey, but it worked. If they continued like this, the Angels could triumph by numbers alone.

While the Angels' maneuver sometimes managed to dispatch two or more battle-Cybrids at a time, those Angels that formed the containing shell were left momentarily vulnerable. The Cybrids took quick advantage of the tactical error and focused their fire on those outermost Angels.

The Angels fought on relentlessly. As fast as their casualties rose, fresh replacements arrived.

Alum was devoting a large portion of His fighting force to defending the Deplosion Array. Maybe all of it.

Despite their enormous losses, a simple calculation demonstrated Alum's Angels would eventually be victorious.

* * *

DARYA LISTENED TO HER SOLDIERS' REPORTS from eight light years above the galactic plain. They'd only destroyed a tiny percentage of the total array before Alum responded. She calculated that two million Angels were involved within five seconds of the initial attack.

The suicide attacks we orchestrated eons ago were much more successful.

She chided herself for even considering that option again, however briefly, and stuck with the new plan. She hoped Alum wouldn't be able to deploy enough Angels to protect every single targeted array element. If they were lucky, the substantial attrition of His forces would make Him withdraw.

Darya sent a message to Darak via the trans-universal QUEECH comms. "I've been wondering," she began, "how is Alum responding so quickly when we pop up near some random array element?"

Darak could think of only one plausible explanation.

"He must've seeded the area around the Deplosion Array with entangled microdust particles. It's the only way this many Angels could arrive so quickly at so many asteroids all at once."

"So why doesn't He just send a Wing to attack each battle-Cybrid squadron?" she asked. "Why would He draw out the battle at such heavy cost to His Angels? This doesn't make sense."

Darak had no answer for her.

"And why hasn't He arrived in person to finish us off or at least come to oversee the battle?" Darya added.

"It does seem strange," Darak agreed. "He could just as easily shift in several of his own mind-nodes and sweep your battle-Cybrids away with a thought."

"You're the expert on Gods and their thinking," Darya said. "What do *you* think He's planning?"

Darak replied with an encrypted shrug. "We'll have to wait and see."

* * *

DARYA ORDERED A CONSOLIDATION.

Let's not call it a retreat. Not yet—she told herself.

But that point was drawing painfully close.

The Angels were responding faster and faster to the battle-Cybrid intrusions. Her last thousand squadrons had barely targeted the assigned array elements before the Angels showed up and defended it with unbridled ferocity.

She asked Darak to extract the first deployments from the now mostly-destroyed asteroid posts and reposition them in groups of five hundred. A small subset focused on blasting the new targets while the majority fought off the Angels that were now appearing even before her soldiers could aim their weapons.

Both sides suffered heavy losses as Alum continued pouring resources into the battle.

Darya's "consolidations" grew larger and larger but saw decreasing return. Soon, no more than one in fifty array elements were destroyed before the Cybrids found themselves fully engaged in simple survival. Array element casualties tapered to zero.

"Well, I'm not about to roll over for You and make it easy," Darya muttered. "Let's see if we can't deliver a little sting to set You back a bit."

"Form groups of ten thousand each," she ordered, "Let's see how Alum's Angels deal with that.

The tactic worked beautifully.

Alum's forces were accustomed to dealing with less effective opponents. Even the Aelu had never managed to consistently outfight His Angels despite being closely matched in technological prowess by the end of the War.

Angelic losses doubled, and kept rising. Soon, for every battle-Cybrid they killed, a hundred Angels died.

In an attempt to overwhelm their opponent, the Angels sent four full Wings against every group of ten thousand battle-Cybrids.

* * *

TIMOTHY ENJOYED KILLING Angels more than he thought he would.

It feels good to be on the side of Justice. And I finally found something I'm skilled at, something beyond my basic programming.

Or maybe I just like how the odds aren't stacked against me for a change—he thought, recalling the futility of his early sword training with Darya and his many narrow escapes from Trillian.

Comparing this battle to those he'd previously studied, Timothy was pleased with the strategic and tactical elegance displayed by Darya's army.

His team made up the Command and Coordination Center for one of the consolidated groups of battle-Cybrids.

With sensing, computation, and shifting cycles faster than ten microseconds, all ten thousand combatants could operate effectively in a spherical volume of space only five kilometers across. The entire volume was bathed in blinking transponder signals originating from the positions of Angels or Cybrids in the brief time between shifts. The signals revealed the fighter's location to anyone within about three kilometers. In that miniscule amount of time, combatants would read enemy positions, calculate targeting vectors, discharge their weapons, and shift again before anyone could reliably target them.

Though doing so gave away their positions, both sides continuously transmitted from their transponders. Coordinating attacks and defense and not getting blasted by friendly fire was more important than being invisible to one's enemies.

Timothy's team fought at speeds that would have been inconceivable to the ancient tacticians he'd studied, wizened Generals of Origin who'd only ever envisioned space fights taking place between lumbering vessels, crewed by frail humans, engaging at close proximity in the dark depths of space.

Would they be amazed to see how far we've come? What we've become? Would they be pleased with our technological developments? Or would they be depressed to see that we're still fighting?

Using QUEECH comms, his team coordinated group shifts and popped into existence in the midst of clusters of Angels. Energy blasts speared outward along vectors carefully calculated to avoid their own people, while destroying whole clusters of Angels before they could shift away.

Slower MAM missiles on proximity fuses arced out from Cybrid body-ports, anticipating where Angels might retreat and cluster. Their matter-antimatter explosions sparkled against the starry background of the central Milky Way.

* * *

DARYA ORDERED ANOTHER CONSOLIDATION.

The Angels tracked the new consolidations and followed suit, merging twenty Wings into a single, imposing force.

Darak watched the new patterns for a few seconds.

"I'm worried," he sent on the encrypted line to Darya.

"Why? This is working well."

"Too well," he replied. "Why isn't Alum responding in person?"

"Good point. It's not like Him to sit back and not react when things don't go His way. What if we try two more large-scale consolidations and leave the other groups separate for now? Wait and see what He does?"

"He can't do too much from a distance," Darak replied. "He'd have to shift one of His mind-nodes here, a major one equipped with a large RAF generator."

"That would require something the size of a small asteroid," Darya replied. "If you see any sign of a significant component of His mind appearing anywhere near our people, shift our forces out of there immediately. Can you still do that?"

"Yes, the instant Alum appears, I'll detect it. We can get away before He launches an attack or blocks us."

"What if He doesn't bring in a major node?" Darya challenged. "What if He's trickier than that? Could He be assembling a bunch of smaller nodes in a cloud around us? They'd be almost undetectable. Maybe that's why He's sacrificing so many Angels, as a ploy to keep us busy while He slides into position bit by bit?"

"I doubt He has any useful subcomponents that small anymore," Darak said.

"You *have* been out of touch for a while!"

"True. Maybe He's developed some new tactics, but I've seen no sign of it. I'll dust the area around the consolidated battlefields to give us more of an edge, though I'm not sure that'll give us enough warning. If Alum can coordinate RAF generation among millions of tiny CPPUs...."

"It'll have to do," Darya replied. "In the meantime, we're decimating the Angels' ranks."

"But hardly touching the array, and we're taking significant losses. We don't have the numbers to keep playing this game," Darak pointed out.

"We can make the Angels pay a little more. I'll order two more consolidations, huge ones, and see what happens," Darya decided.

"Aye, aye, Commander," Darak replied and sent an image of himself snapping a smart salute.

In spite of herself, and in spite of the fierce battle raging around them, Darya laughed.

* * *

TIMOTHY'S GROUP joined the first massive consolidation. Within striking distance of a pair of Deplosion Array elements, they and forty thousand other battle-Cybrids took on nearly two hundred thousand Angels.

The war raged silently across several light seconds of space. Ruthless energy beams crisscrossed the war zone, slicing through the exhaust trails of hyperkinetic missile volleys. They were just as likely to harmlessly pierce the curtain of blackness beyond and disappear into the vacuum as they were to hit one of their rapidly-shifting targets.

The battlefield was a swirling, living entity with individual cells—teams of a few hundred Cybrids or Angels—moving, shifting, forming, and reforming to gain any microsecond of advantage.

Timothy refused a command position. He preferred to kill alone, hovering outside of the main fray with his transponder on silent, tracking potential targets by their locator signals. He watched quietly from a distance, risking hits by stray kinetic or energy blasts from both sides.

Space is big and mostly empty; that puts the odds in my favor.

I hope.

By the time he identified a transponder signal, the individual had already moved, but that didn't trouble him. He was playing a longer game.

He was tracking and analyzing the ebb and flow of the battle, and comparing that data to the tactics and applied knowledge he'd gained in the month leading up to battle. He'd learned a lot by poring over historical Aelu battles and Angel tactics. After devouring the public records, he'd turned to pestering Darak for everything the man-God could tell him.

Darak had patiently withstood Timothy's incessant questioning. After telling him again and again that no amount of analysis of ancient Angelic battles would help in the present attack, Darak became exasperated.

"Enough!" he shouted.

"If you want to waste your time poring over irrelevant history that's up to you. But, please, for the love of the cosmos, leave me in peace!" he begged, and promptly dumped the records of thousands of Angelic encounters with the Aelu into Timothy's memory.

"Here! This should keep you busy for a while," he muttered and turned back to review the latest battle-Cybrid simulation performance.

Timothy scrutinized the Aelu War records. He painstakingly analyzed the movements of each battalion and combatant.

And, just as he'd suspected, there were patterns in the chaos.

Over thousands of years of military history against the Aelu, the Angels had employed one particularly cautious, patient strategy with remarkable consistency. They engaged jump-blocking fields to isolate small bands of the enemy, positioned five of their own just inside the perimeter, and blasted into the midst of the trapped Aelu. The very same tactic as they'd been doing here.

Except that the Angels' eons-old tactics weren't working nearly as well against the new battle-Cybrids, and Timothy knew why. For one thing, the Cybrids acted more independently than the ancient Aelu; they flitted in and out of normal space too fast for the Angels to trap them. And, second, by all outward appearance there was little or no pattern to the Cybrids' attacks, no formations, and precious little discernible coordination to lend itself to predictability.

Summarizing what he'd learned, Timothy had advised Darak and Darya to orchestrate complex movements that would give the appearance of chaos. It was brutally effective.

As it played out, Timothy watched, analyzed, and relayed minor tactical modifications to each of the Cybrid groups. He directed small, agile teams to draw the Angels tantalizingly close to trapping entire tight-knit formations. But as soon as the predictable five or ten Angels arrived to blast their trapped Cybrids, a larger group of Cybrids would materialize, annihilate the snipers in a single blast of MAM missiles and energy beams, and rip a wide hole in the outer shell of Angels that had tried to trap them.

Timothy observed the success of his suggestions with pride.

Right up until the tactic stopped working.

The Angels have stopped following their usual pattern.

Entire tracks of transponder signals were disappearing from the battlefield. Before he could make sense of it, a glaring light stabbed his sensors. He dimmed his optical sensitivity. He watched while more transponders of both Cybrids and Angels winked out, followed by a blinding cylindrical burst of light where combatants used to be.

"Something's happening," he sent on the Command channel, and shared a video clip.

"What is it?" Darya asked.

"Extremely high-energy bursts," Timothy replied. "I've been tracking movements for the last twelve seconds. This is the first time I've seen it. It's off the charts."

"Something's blasting through the engagement lines," Darya said.

"Whatever it is, it's destroying both Cybrids *and* Angels—Darak added. "I don't like the looks of that."

"Me, either. Do you think it's Alum? Is He finally weighing in?"

"Just a millisecond," Darak replied, sounding more calm than he felt.

It was seventeen full milliseconds before he spoke again, long enough for Timothy to wonder whether he and Darya had switched to a private channel.

"Retreat, One-Alpha-Six," Darak barked to all of the Cybrids at once over the Command channel. "Pull back to muster-point four. Prepare to exit battle zone."

Against orders, Timothy took a moment to think.

But we were winning! He watched his people in full and instant retreat, shifting through prearranged entangled particle connections to a safe intermediary spot a few light days away and, from there, back to Eso-La.

How did we go from certain victory to imminent defeat?

He reviewed his recordings of the battle, searching for some detail he might have misinterpreted.

The recordings only confirmed what he already knew.

We were winning. Clearly winning.

He watched as half of the battlefield went dark.

Who is indiscriminately destroying Cybrids and Angels alike?

15

"CYBRIDS!" ALUM RAGED as He stormed among the stars.

"My own constructions! My own People fighting against me! Again! Blasphemous traitors!"

"Not all of your People, my Lord. Not the Angels. Not me," Trillian assured Him. In the presence of such fury, it was difficult to collect his thoughts well enough to speak coherent phrases.

This was the first time he'd been invited inside the great galactic disk, the home of the miniature universe floating in the center of Alum's Hall. That alone was a lot to take in. Caught in a state of stammering trepidation and awe, he was torn between drinking in the majestic starscape before him and assuaging Alum's ire.

The Living God wheeled and pointed a silencing finger.

"Not *all* People? That's hardly any better," Alum snarled. "Millions of ordinary Cybrids have been modified into formidable fighters against Me. Against the Realm. How could I not know about this? Did the Aelu make them? Or do I have a rebel force working against Me from within?"

He kicked a beach-ball sized star and watched it spin out of its system, leaving a trail of gaseous ejecta behind. He brushed the embers from His shoe and looked up to see Trillian's open-mouthed stare.

"Don't worry. There's no life in this system," He huffed.

Trillian closed his mouth and cleared his throat. That's right. No big deal. He was just walking with God through a galaxy of planets and stars that were somehow, quite impossibly, smaller than the two of them and yet so detailed, so solid, that they had to be real entities, not representations. He forced his attention back to Alum's last questions.

"There was no sign of Aelu at any of the battlefields or near any of the targeted array elements, my Lord," he said. "And the attack patterns don't match those in the Aelu War archives. That would seem to suggest these treacherous Cybrids acted of their own volition."

"Well, wherever they came from, *someone* shifted them into the vicinity of the asteroids," Alum said.

"And shifted them back out again when it became apparent they were losing the battle to your mighty Archangels, my Lord."

Alum permitted himself a hint of an appreciative smile.

"Yes, the Archangels performed well, didn't they? We would've destroyed the enemy completely had they not been shifted out of our reach."

Trillian raised a questioning eyebrow. "The entangled-dust trackers were unable to follow them?"

Alum's smile tightened into a grimace.

"Whoever shifted the Cybrids must have scanned for entangled particles. I caught a glimpse of a location a few light days away, but by the time the Archangels had arrived, there was nobody there. They must have erected a jump-blocking field to nullify the tracking dust."

"Pity." Trillian waited for Alum to continue.

The Living God clasped hands behind his back and resumed His pacing amid the floating stars of His mono-galactic microverse.

"They managed to destroy over eighty thousand array elements before we chased them away. We counted upwards of a million enemy combatants."

"That in itself is a clue, isn't it? Who could make so many specialized Cybrids in such a short time?"

"Indeed, and so soon after the Cybrid suicide attack on the array. I'm certain a concepta virus was used to subvert loyal Cybrids in that action. But we ramped up our CPPU security immediately after to prevent further infiltrations. No, this is something new. Something different."

"The Cybrid weaponry equaled that of the Angels'," Trillian pointed out.

"Not equal," Alum corrected. "Better. Were it not for the Archangels, I would have had to intervene directly."

"Why did You not show Your might directly, my Lord?" Trillian winced at his own brazenness. The words had tumbled out before he could stop them.

Alum scowled and ignored the question.

"Someone out there is able to shift large distances independent of the starstep system. Much farther than I would've thought possible. Or maybe they used the cover of the suicidal Cybrid attack to plant entangled particles in the vicinity of the array elements. Or maybe they set it all up millennia ago. I don't know. Maybe they found a way to shift without entangled guides at all."

Alum stopped, surprised by His own speculation.

Jump such distances without entangled particles to navigate? Was that possible?

He put one of His planet-sized processors to work on the problem. The equations around the idea were dangerous. It seemed preposterous but not entirely out of the question, hypothetically speaking.

Wasn't there something back near the origin of shifting, some distant memory I shared with the mind of My "father" about that? He set a smaller, local submind to prowl through eons of memories for a correlation.

"The Aelu shift technology was no more capable than our own," Trillian noted.

Alum stroked His chin absentmindedly.

"True," He replied. "Except for the larger jumps in and out, the other Cybrid shifts looked no more capable than those of Angel Gabriel."

"But You destroyed that abomination, my Lord. Could these be the remnants of an army he was building?"

"If not him, perhaps an ally," Alum mused.

"What ally could build a million fighting Cybrids without us finding out about it?" Trillian asked. "Who could shift that number in and out of battle like that? Who except the Aelu could be capable of such a thing?"

"Who, indeed?" Alum echoed, and stopped pacing.

Are there others like Me, other Gods among the stars?—He wondered.

It was a twist on the ancient Fermi paradox. When He was only a boy, humans had already been pondering it for decades: why, if other life in the universe existed, had it never been detected?

Many reasons had been proposed. Perhaps technological civilizations didn't survive their ability to invent civilization-destroying nuclear weapons. Or perhaps intelligence at a level sufficient to develop advanced technologies was rare in the universe. Perhaps, life itself was uncommon.

Or is it that life is plentiful enough but general intelligence is not as advantageous as one might think?

The Realm had encountered no more than a handful of technologically-advanced civilizations. So far, only one had been anywhere near as advanced as humans: the Aelu. But He never gave up looking for others.

Could one of His exploration rafts have bumped up against another life form on the edge of the Realm? A life form with capabilities similar to His own? Was there someone else like Him out there who could manipulate the building blocks of the universe?

He'd always known that such power in the hands of another could threaten the Realm, threaten His Plan to bring Heaven to the entire universe. Threaten Him.

He set a third submind to work on contacting all of His exploration rafts exploring the stars and galaxies. Had any of them encountered something new? Had any gone missing? Could any have been subverted to the service of another?

He began an inventory of the communication logs, to make sure no one had identified the entangled particles carried in one of His ships and traced it back to the Realm.

To encounter another God in the universe!

It was a chilling prospect.

I should be joyous but the notion that I may need to fight such a being to defend my Divine Plan is distressing. I am so close, now. So close!

His brow furrowed. "We'll need to replace the destroyed array elements, and build the final contingent. And we'll need to build more Archangels."

He commandeered another ten million Cybrids from the Realm's Maintenance and Manufacturing asteroid bases and sent them out to the Deplosion Array.

The next attack may require My direct intervention and, for that, I'll need to be closer. It's time to move most of My Self from here to Sagittarius A.*

If this is to be a battle of Gods, so be it!

16

"GET RID OF THAT THING," Darya spat. "I can't stand to look at it anymore."

The Archangel rotating slowly in the air before them no longer glowed dull burgundy, but its leathery wings and talon-tipped digits still tugged at some deep, ancestral sense of fear and repulsion.

"I know it looks demonic," Darak said, "but I think Alum designed them as some kind of terrifying version of the Angels, an Archangel, so to speak. He talked about some such idea, long ago."

Despite being securely suspended, and even though Darak assured them that its power supply had been deactivated, the beast reeked of danger.

Timothy and Mary floated on the opposite side of the creature, inspecting it with somewhat more objectivity. Timothy extended a diagnostic tentacle to scan the horns with a spectroscopic laser. Mary probed the beast with low-energy X-rays and mapped the details of its surface in visible light.

"It's ugly, that's for sure," Mary reported.

The calcified scowl on its horned face hinted at a lack of regard for any life but its own and its Master's, and the horizontal-slit pupils in its lifeless eyes seemed...wrong.

Twenty meters away, Crissea stood beside Brother Stralasi and Darak on a small chunk of scrubland enclosed by a protective bubble of air. Her Familiar floated a few meters away. The Esu woman held the monk's hand in her own, their fingers tightly entwined and seeking the reassurance of fleshly contact.

Darian Leigh stood at the edge of the bubble, curiously poking at the invisible wall that separated them from the deep vacuum of outer space. His eyes occasionally flicked back to Alum's hideous construct but remained otherwise fascinated by the dusty stars in the distant core of the ESO galaxy.

"Ugly? Yes, I suppose it is," Darak said, "and inherently frightening to the human psyche. I wonder whether Alum was anticipating that the majority of His foes would originate from within the Realm, or if this creation is more reflective of His own sense of the terrifying.

"To the Aelu, the physical appearance of this thing would be meaningless, no scarier than a kitten. In any case, this one is harmless enough now."

"Regardless, I don't like looking at it," Darya replied. "What purpose does it serve to display it in front of us like this?"

Darak met her challenging stare with one of his own. "I want you to realize why physical battle with Alum is pointless. He can manufacture as many of these as He needs to protect the Deplosion Array from attack."

"Yet, we were winning," Timothy said. "If we improve our outer armor and energy absorption capabilities, we could do it. We could finish this."

Darak raised an eyebrow. "You mean, tweak them enough to withstand the infinitely-condensed, exotic-matter plasma from inside a black hole?" He shook his head. "I'm not sure that's possible."

"Why not? Alum found a way to sink some entangled matter into that same black hole," Darya pointed out. "That means *something* must be able to withstand it."

Darak considered the idea. "It's one thing to shift some entangled neutrinos across the event horizon when you don't care about anything but their basic quantum state," he answered. "It's quite another to maintain the integrity of atoms and molecules when black-hole plasma is sprayed across them."

"Why not shift the plasma right back into the black hole?" she suggested.

"Once I take that level of direct involvement, Alum will too," Darak replied. "At that point, fighting between Cybrids and Angels or..," he jutted his chin toward the floating monstrosity, "even Archangels, becomes a moot point."

Darya's condescension escaped in an audible sniff. "You seem pretty sure of yourself, for someone who couldn't help us defeat a few of these creatures."

Stralasi tightened his grip on Crissea's hand. She squeezed back, caught his eye, and shook her head. *Don't get involved.*

"It was bad enough that I shifted your people in and out," Darak said. "That alone gave Alum enough clues about what kind of opponent He's facing. That's more than I'm happy with."

Mary winced. She was painfully aware of what could happen when an enemy understood too much about you. She had barely survived her encounters with Trillian.

"Maybe he's right, Darya," she said softly. "Maybe we should find another approach."

"No, he's not right," Darya shot back. "Not about this. Alum's threat to the universe is embodied in that Deplosion Array. As it stands, He can only mess with the Realm, not all of reality.

"It's awful that He exerts absolute power over all humans, Cybrids, and Angels. If we don't destroy that array, He's going to destroy the entire universe. All of existence. Everything."

"Darya's right," Darak replied, surprising everyone with his abrupt shift.

Brother Stralasi held his breath.

"But so is Mary," Darak finished.

The Good Brother exhaled, and Darak flashed a fleeting, wry smile at his travelling companion, acknowledging his astute anticipation of his position.

"I've known Alum longer than any of you," Darak continued. "I've worked with Him and plotted against Him for millions of years. Tens of millions.

"He's many things: Living God, dictator, benevolent leader, guide. And He hasn't completely outgrown the human beliefs He developed even before His birth. He fears the unknown, detests uncertainty, loves the stable and predictable. He's lost His way a little but He means well and He's not beyond reason. He may be the most powerful of the Gods, but I believe He'll still listen if presented with a better way."

Darya snorted. "Talk? That's your great solution? Talk to Alum? Explain the folly of the destruction of the entire universe? Why would you think someone who could conceive of such wickedness might be open to argument?"

"He may be...what?" Mary interjected before Darak could respond. "What do you mean, the most powerful of the Gods?"

Darak hesitated, allowing the others to review their records of the last few seconds of conversation. A sheepish grin tugged at his mouth.

"I'm glad you caught that. It's true. In my travels around the universe, I've discovered others like Alum. Six others, so far."

"Six!" Stralasi couldn't help himself. So many Gods! The idea of other Realms each ruled by their own Supreme Being was too much to contemplate.

"And all wanting to remake the universe to suit their own egos, no doubt," Darya added.

Darak held up a preemptory finger, "Surprisingly, no."

"No?"

"No. That particular dream belongs only to Alum. The other six are isolated from each other and all seem to be content to rule as local deities."

"For now," Darya added.

"Do they know about each other?" Crissea asked, attempting to keep the conversation from devolving into an unproductive cynical track. "More importantly, do the others know about Alum and His so-called Divine Plan?"

"Yes, to both," Darak replied, "but no one except me knows the location of each of the others."

"Of course not," Darya said.

Darak sighed. "That was a necessary part of them agreeing to speak to each other at all. You wouldn't believe how paranoid almighty beings can be of others with similar capabilities. They won't reveal their locations or even their species to one another. They insist on communicating only through me."

The almighty weren't the only suspicious entities. "How convenient that they trust you so much. How did you accomplish that? Pray, tell!" Darya invited.

"By being both nonthreatening and unassailable," Darak replied.

"When I first revealed myself to each of them, believe me, they attacked me with all they had at their disposal. I resisted, but never retaliated. When they tired of trying to destroy or remove me from the universe, we talked."

"So why are you afraid to attempt the same with Alum?"

Darak frowned. "Alum is older and more powerful than any of the others."

As if remembering something, he chuckled and shook his head. "With the possible exception of Raytansoh, that is, but he's such an enigma that speculation is difficult."

"Why haven't you approached Alum with this information?" Stralasi asked. "I would think that such knowledge might cause Him to change His Divine Plan."

"If He suspected there were competing entities, I think He'd accelerate His Plan," Darak replied.

"What are we doing here, then? Why don't we join with these other Gods? I mean, if our interests are aligned and they are content to limit their power to their own Realms, we should ask them to help us," Darya suggested.

Timothy left his examination of the Archangel and joined the others. "Balancing interests," he answered. "Aligned or opposing, they are impossible to maintain. Impossible to break," he stated.

All attention turned toward him.

"Care to explain?" Darya asked.

"Yes. I've made a study of the history of warfare in the Realm, particularly of the Aelu Wars. With Mary's help, of course." He used his attitude jets to emulate a polite bob in her direction.

"In my studies," he continued, "there were a number of smaller battles in which neither side had a numeric advantage, weaponry was roughly equal, and Alum was in no position to intervene directly. My analysis of such engagements shows weeks of jockeying for position by both sides, with neither gaining final advantage.

"After a while, strategies repeat themselves of necessity. Any moves outside of established parameters upset the balance to such a degree that the first to transgress would lose the entire battle."

"How were the stalemates resolved?" Darya asked, curious despite her wish to get back to arguing with Darak about the Gods.

"They weren't resolved," Timothy answered, "not as a result of the battles. In the end, one side or the other merely did a coordinated shift away from the engagement. The balance couldn't be maintained indefinitely, and it couldn't be broken without throwing one's interests into a losing slide."

Darak congratulated the newest of the Cybrid personas on his insights. "An excellent assessment, Timothy, but it's even worse than that.

"Engaging the help of the other six Gods against Alum is unpredictable. Together, they might win and enslave the Realm to any one of their own, or they might attempt to rule together.

"On the other hand, should Alum successfully repel an attack, He'd only be proven right to be paranoid about the rest of the universe. And if He were to win that kind of war, He'd likely feel justified rushing completion of the Deplosion Array and launch an immediate partial-deployment of its fields."

"Partial deployment of the array?" Mary echoed. "Could He do that?"

"It's difficult to model the theory," Darak admitted, "and harder still to say what the result might be. Hollowing out a new universe from some part of ours could be incredibly disruptive to whatever survives it, that is, to both the old and the new. The result could be worse than just letting Alum carry out His Divine Plan."

"But you don't really know, do you?" Darya objected.

"No, I don't really know for sure. Like I said, it's complicated. Maybe the computational power of your quark-spin lattice would help. I don't know that either."

"So then, what are you doing with the other Gods? Is there a plan?"

"Yes, I have a plan. "In truth, it's more preparatory than definitive at this stage," Darak admitted.

"Well, that doesn't sound very encouraging," Darya replied.

"No, but it may be all we have."

"Darak, is this your Judgment Plan?" Crissea asked.

Before he could answer, Darya asked, "Judgment Plan? What's that?"

"Alum's decision to reformat the entire universe was something He arrived at without consultation," Darak answered. "His knowledge and experience is vast, but the people of the Realm have a right to participate in such an important, all-encompassing choice."

"We already voted to stop Him," Darya said.

Darak shifted the earth-and-air bubble containing himself, Stralasi, and both of Crissea's forms closer to where the Cybrids examined the Archangel.

"Right. Your small group of rebels decided long ago, on behalf of *all* your people, to stop Alum. That's hardly more democratic than Alum acting completely alone," he challenged.

"The few of us here are better equipped to make such a decision than the trillions of ignorant humans and Cybrids throughout the Realm," Darya pointed out. "They aren't equipped to understand the workings of the Deplosion Array, or the ramifications of altering the laws of nature."

"I agree," Darak said, "you are indeed better equipped. But don't you see? Deciding for them is something Alum would do. The answer isn't to take away people's ability to listen, analyze, and choose. We have an obligation to work *with* them and to enhance their ability to understand so they can choose well for themselves."

"Sure, we could do that," Darya replied, "if we had a few million years to overcome the society Alum created. But we don't.

"Humans know nothing of science or technology. All they know how to do is pray to their Living God. They pray for everything. For their food to be delivered. For a nice day. For a simple fix to machine components that they can't be bothered to learn how to repair themselves. To win a sporting event, for crying out loud. The Cybrids are little better. They do their jobs and escape to their inworld entertainments.

"Society is peaceful and orderly, and it will continue to be so, right up until the universe comes to an end. Then, it'll be Peace and Order for eternity, enforced by Alum's new laws of nature that will permit no Chaos, nothing but order and predictability for ever more.

"I'm sorry, but that sounds like pure Hell to me," she concluded.

"We won't need a million years," Darak said. "Nor will we need to destroy this society in order to educate it and give it the appropriate analytical tools."

"Okay, what do you have in mind?" she asked.

Brother Stralasi held up a tentative hand. "I think I understand. May I explain?" he said.

Darak took a symbolic step back to cede the floor and waved the Good Brother forward.

"I have benefitted recently from Darak's plan," Stralasi began. "In our travels within the Realm, Darak seeded Integration Labs in hundreds of systems with a lattice virus. It's been spreading through the local human and Cybrid populations.

"My understanding is that this virus launches a developmental program for a new, intelligence-enhancing lattice in both the human brain and the Cybrid CPPUs and once it's in place, it installs an extensive knowledge base.

"The knowledge base is eye-opening, to say the least. I am not—was not—an ignorant man by Realm standards. But now I see that compared to what I've learned in the past months, and compared to how I'm now able to reason, I was a fool.

"I won't say I have risen to your level, not at all, but now I better understand how the universe works. I understand much more of your science than I ever knew existed. Even the Deplosion Array and the original Reality Assertion Field make some sense to me at the level of basic principles although, admittedly, the finer details are still beyond my gleaning.

"I also finally see the socioeconomic and political forces at work in the Realm. I see how the system works. I see its flaws as well as its benefits. I see how well it serves in bringing stability to this part of the universe, and I can imagine how parts of that system could be improved.

"Darak thinks that equipping billions with similar knowledge and intellect would enable them to collectively decide on the future of the Realm and of the universe. And I'd have to agree with that."

Darya emitted a whistle in mock glee. "Okay, so that's it, then. I guess that all we need to do is get an audience with Alum. I'm sure once He's confronted by the collective wisdom of billions of IQ-enhanced citizens of the Realm, He'll suddenly and miraculously see the error of His choices."

Darak frowned at her sarcasm. "He can't just ignore what His people want."

"Why not?" Darya challenged. "Alum has been the Living God for so long, how do we know He doesn't consider His judgment to be beyond reproach? What if He refuses to listen? What if He listens and chooses to ignore us?"

Darak frowned. "I did say the plan was only preparatory. Clearly, if Alum remains determined to proceed with His plan against the wishes of His People, we have to be ready to help."

"If He persists, we may need to eliminate Him," Darya replied.

"Is it possible to kill God?" Timothy asked.

"Gods can be killed," Darak confirmed, "but in the case of Alum, the difficulties are exponential."

"What do you mean?"

Darak's voice was barely audible, even on the transmitted channels. "I tried to kill Him once. In fact, I did kill Him. It feels like an eternity ago."

Stralasi looked confused. "I don't understand. If you killed Him, why is He still the Living God?"

"He refused to stay dead," Darak answered glumly. "I destroyed a body, not knowing that Alum's consciousness was already distributed among a hundred asteroid processors. That body was replaced, and it has been replaced countless more times since then. Alum spans entire galaxies now. How does one kill such a being?"

His question was met with silence. If Darak with his God-like capabilities couldn't imagine how Alum could be killed, what ideas could he expect from them?

"For the sake of argument, how is putting the question to Alum's People, and no one else, any better than Alum acting alone?" Mary asked. "What about the Realms of the other Gods you mentioned? Don't their people get a say in the fate of the universe, too?"

"Their Gods have spoken for them," Darak replied. "They are universal in their condemnation of Alum's Divine Plan. They prefer the universe to stay as it is. I may not agree with their specific reasons but I find myself agreeing with their overall conclusion."

"In that case, the answer is obvious," Darya said. "If the other Gods are on our side and if the People of the Realm support our choice to stop the Deplosion—"

"That's still a big *if*," Darak interjected.

"Yes, I'll give you that," Darya replied, "Alum's People could well vote in favor of His Divine Plan. But if your enhanced intelligence and knowledge base was convincing enough to change the mind of one of Alum's own Alumita monks, I feel confident about which way the vote will go.

"In any case, it makes sense to be prepared, to help everyone to prepare. I have no confidence that Alum will listen to any voice besides His own. We need to be ready to back up our demands with collective force."

Darak was pretty sure he knew where Darya's line of thought was leading.

"You want to talk to the other Gods, don't you?" he said.

"I think we have to," she confirmed. "Can it be done?"

"It's against my better judgment but, yes, it's possible."

"Then, we have to do it," she said.

17

"AT LAST, FORTUNE HAS FAVORED MY PREPARATIONS!"

Depchaun's announcement to the other five Gods cut through the introductory small talk.

"Is that why you called us together one full minute early, to share your good fortune?" Lyv asked.

"Yes," Depchaun replied, "but I think you'll find that my news will be good news for all of us in pushing Darak Legsu to action. We may be able to bypass him entirely."

The dark-gray humanoid avatars of the Six occupied their respective thrones. The green status lights blinking above each station imbued the polished stone floor and its inlaid galaxy with a sense of depth and movement.

The light above Raytansoh's throne drew inordinate interest from his five co-attendees as, for only the second time in thousands of years, it signaled his potential readiness to participate in the discussions. Noting this was only a *potential* and not an *actual* break with silence, no one commented on his change in status.

"Bypass Darak? An intriguing thought, Depchaun. You have our attention," Ishtgor said, forcing his focus away from Raytansoh's blinking green status light and back to Depchaun and his announcement. "And are you planning to divulge this news anytime soon?"

"—or are you more interested in gloating?" Glenchax finished.

From the opposite side of the circle, Ki-tan-la sniggered.

"Go ahead, mock me," Depchaun laughed. "This day, all will be forgiven."

"It must be tremendously good news indeed, then," Lyv prompted.

"I found Alum's Realm!" Depchaun gushed.

The room went silent for several long milliseconds while everyone's minds reeled with questions and implications.

Glenchax plunged in.

"When? Where is it? How did you accomplish this? How do you know it's Alum's Realm? Has He detected your discovery? How long have you—"

"Let him tell his story!" Ishtgor bellowed.

"Thank you," Depchaun said. "I will be brief. Like you, the volume of space my people occupy grows as my ships explore the surrounding universe. Limited by the speed of light, as we all are, this process is frustratingly slow."

"For all except Darak, that is," Raytansoh pointed out.

All five other Gods craned their necks to stare at Raytansoh.

"Acknowledged and shelved to a future discussion," Depchaun replied curtly before anyone could respond. He was not about to allow Raytansoh, who'd been uncommunicative for so long, to steal his spotlight and undermine the impact of his big news.

"In any case," Depchaun continued, "some number of human-months ago, one of my exploration ships approached a unique triple-star system. As they drew to the limits of their telescopic resolution, they observed triple ringworlds orbiting the stars.

"It was strange enough to find a triple star system at all, as orbitally unstable as it would have to be, but the discovery of the triple ringworlds around them implied the entire system was artificial. Technologies equivalent to our own would have to have been involved.

"The ship was only a few light days out when all three stars suddenly and inexplicably went nova at once. Naturally, the ship was destroyed when the plasma shockwave passed over it."

"Naturally," echoed Glenchax, a hint of derision creeping into his voice.

Depchaun ignored him. "However, before it was destroyed, the team was able to analyze the plasma from the nova. It was littered with advanced synthetic compounds, metals, semiconductors, plastics, antimatter, and some exotic particles. The ship hit the plasma at some fifty-percent of light speed and was destroyed instantly but a quick-thinking engineer managed to drop a group of entangled particles nearby.

"After the initial shockwave passed, I sent my macro-Partial Aspect to investigate."

"And you found something significant," Lyv stated.

"Yes, something remarkable. A nearly intact synthetic being. Presumably one modeled along human lines as it bore a resemblance to Darak and to the avatars that represent us here. Except the being had two badly damaged additional appendages sprouting from its back. I believe Darak would call them wings, if I recall correctly. This salvaged being matches Darak's description of Alum's Angels."

"Angels! In reach of your empire?" Ishtgor cried out. "If Darak's stories of these hideous creatures of Alum's devising are to be believed, that could be exceedingly dangerous."

"Quite," Depchaun replied. "Fortunately for all of us, this one was inert, damaged beyond its operational parameters. Through no action of my own, I should clarify. But—and here's the amazing stroke of luck—the being had a small repository of entangled particles. My Aspect followed where they led."

"To Alum's Realm," Raytansoh guessed.

"Exactly. To some hundred different systems in several tens of galaxies. I visited each one briefly and mapped local landmarks. I can say with confidence that we now have a crude, preliminary map of Alum's Realm."

Depchaun paused so the other five Gods could absorb and appreciate his achievement. He beamed proudly, and deservedly so, as the other five Gods conveyed a modicum of respect.

"Alum's territory is considerable," he elaborated. "The triple-star system and its ringworlds were far beyond the edge of any other active systems. The system may have been built as a retreat in case of disaster or invasion.

"With little effort, we could insert additional Aspects and extrapolate the position of the Deplosion Array that Darak described and, quite likely, Alum's primary processors."

"We could stop Alum's nonsense once and for all, kill Him, and divide His Realm amongst ourselves!" The eagerness in Ki-tan-la's voice crackled over the narrow comm band.

"Perhaps we could take a slightly more measured approach," Depchaun suggested.

"What do you have in mind?" Lyv asked.

"Darak is bringing other representatives from Alum's Realm to this meeting. I suggest we ask him to allow each of us to send Aspects to greet them."

"Hah! Physical emissaries of our real selves? Are you crazy?"

"That would be reckless!"

"Irresponsible!"

"Dangerous!"

"I agree!" Depchaun laughed over the protests. "It will be all of those things, and Darak will be suspicious."

"Ahh. You have a plan." Raytansoh's avatar angled to face Depchaun with new interest.

"Indeed. My Aspect will carry a package of entangled exotic particles from another universe that I will plant on Darak's guests."

"He will detect them and remove them," Glenchax said.

"Perhaps. If he's half as smart as he thinks he is, he already suspects we'd like to find Alum's Realm independent of his assistance. Our complete about-face on sending Aspects will only confirm what he's already thinking, that some of us are up to something. And it won't matter at all.

"If he finds the entangled particles and exposes them to a decoherence field, no problem. We'll continue as before with our other plans to map the remainder of Alum's Realm. He won't guess we've already found another way there. And should he fail to find the particles or to find all of them, we'll have secured another route to the Realm, as well as to Darak's base. Either way, we come out ahead."

The group debated the possibilities and pitfalls until Ishtgor summarized the collective conclusion.

"Excellent!"

They used half the remaining fifty seconds to consider how to divide up, under both scenarios, the exploration of Alum's territory.

Upon reaching agreeable terms, they withdrew quietly to their own thoughts, where they modeled cooperative—and competitive—approaches to the exploration and subsequent conquest of a new species and its domain.

Not a single one ruled out the use of treachery to gain advantage against the other Gods.

The minute wound down and Darak Legsu appeared, right on time, fully corporeal, and accompanied by his guests.

Three strangers. Outsiders, fully exposed to the Six.

And vice versa.

18

"AND SO, HAVING OPPOSED THE WISHES of your intellectual equals for millennia, you immediately acquiesced to the demands of your stock species?" Depchaun snarled. His avatar's eyes narrowed until they were no more than two dark slashes relishing the sight of Darak stewing in uncomfortable silence.

The man-God squirmed but, to his credit, never looked away.

"To be completely accurate, Depchaun," Darak replied, "you never requested to talk to anyone other than Alum Himself. That was always going to be an impossibility. My companions' request to appear here was substantially more reasonable."

His voice showed no hint of the guilt the Gods had been anticipating. Such audacious lack of remorse galled them even more.

"Minor details," Lyv spat. "Though, we would've been happier if you'd included representatives from all species in Alum's Realm. No offence to our guests." Her featureless avatar stood up from its throne and bowed to Darya, Mary, and Brother Stralasi.

Stralasi managed a clumsy bow of his own, while the two Cybrids dipped in acknowledgement.

Darak frowned. "What other representatives would you have had me invite? Are you referring to the Angels? They have no place here, as you well know. If I were to bring an Angel here, I might as well invite Alum. I don't think any of us are ready for that."

Depchaun cleared his throat noisily and reasserted control of the conversation.

"In honor of our guests, we Six will also appear here in physical form, so to speak. We have prepared Aspect versions of our complete selves at the prearranged pick-up locations. You may bring them here, now."

Darak's frown deepened. "Why would you choose *now* for your first physical presence at one of these meetings? What are you planning?"

Glenchax's avatar stood and spread its arms wide. "You wound us with your insinuations! In the spirit of this new level of openness, we merely seek to reciprocate. Our Aspects are no threat to you or your guests. They carry nothing more than tightly-linked Partial personas. We will continue to communicate through your personal channels.

"Revealing the physical appearances of our species to one another and to our guests will lead to a new level of trust among us all. We have computed that this is critical for our next steps in addressing the Alum problem that we all share."

Even without knowing the Gods' full capabilities and powers, Stralasi's inferior mind guessed at the considerable potential for treachery. He wondered how many possible acts of betrayal Darak was playing out in his imagination.

"Very well," Darak answered, "We look forward to meeting with your Aspects."

Stralasi let out the breath he didn't realize he'd been holding. *Darak must consider his ability to protect me and the Cybrids adequate, as well as his ability to keep the location of the Realm secret.*

The monk relaxed ever so slightly, and savored the reassuring breath refilling his lungs.

He watched with fascination as the gray avatars of the six Gods were replaced, one at a time, by a variety of biological life forms and heard a gasp escape Mary's speakers—or had that emanated from his own lips? He wasn't sure.

Had he not already witnessed an incredible diversity of life across Alum's Realm—all of which was included within the classification of humanity—he might have fainted at the sight of the six extraordinary creatures that appeared on the thrones.

Depchaun's Aspect, a prickly, glossy-black cube with articulated limbs jutting from all sides, hovered a meter above his throne like any Cybrid.

A machine civilization?—Stralasi wondered. *Or just its God?*

The others were recognizable biological species although they varied dramatically in form from the willowy, bipedal, vaguely-humanoid Ki-tan-la to the furry arachnid Lyv and her attendant spider mites, to the tentacled gas-bag Ishtgor, to the dry-skinned, long-legged reptile that was Glenchax.

But, most of all, Stralasi's gawking eyes were drawn to Raytansoh: *He's like...like...two green octopuses fused together at the head!*

The Good Brother had seen many strange organisms, both Standard and alien, during his travels with Darak. Each form had been both shocking and fascinating in its own way. But this one! How could its biology function? Was it even real? Could Raytansoh be fooling Darak about his species' true appearance? Stralasi was pretty sure Darak was not easily tricked.

"I'm sure you're all as repulsed by my appearance as I am by yours," Lyv said. She spoke by means of rapidly-vibrating, chitinous bristles that scraped against her dorsal carapace and emitted complex sounds. "Though I must admit, a number of you do look quite...delicious."

She chuckled and a drop of venom involuntarily squeezed from her tail stinger. Two small attendant mites rushed to lick it up before it dripped.

"I doubt you would find my internal components either refreshing or nutritious," Ishtgor thrummed with tiny wings that beat against resonators to produce hollow-sounding utterances. "But I agree as to the general hideousness of your various forms. I'm glad Darak permitted us to meet previously in uniform humanoid avatars. It allowed us to grow accustomed to a single repugnant form while we came to know one another. Clearly advantageous, in Ki-tan-la's case," he joked, and wheezed out a rasping, wet sound that may have been a laugh.

The solitary bipedal Aspect in the group acknowledged the backhanded compliment by touching her hands to either side of her head.

"I'm grateful to be found less distasteful in appearance," she said.

"I wouldn't go that far," Depchaun replied. "You are all grossly soft, fleshy reminders of a time that I'd rather forget, a time of constant vulnerability and weakness. You repulse me, and it requires great fortitude to look past your physical appearances."

Stralasi marveled at the grotesque beauty of the speaker's spikes as they shuddered over the polished, black surface of the machine-being when it—he?—spoke.

Darak's voice cut through the din of the Gods' banter.

"I think we can all agree that the universe has found many interesting ways to achieve intelligence. It comes as no surprise that we are most familiar with our own forms and find them most pleasing. Thankfully, our mental structures have more in common than our physical ones."

"As far as you can assure us," Ishtgor responded.

"There appears to be a limited number of ways to move from parallel concept-association processes to linear, logico-rational thinking," Raytansoh stated. "The convergence of natural processes is remarkable in this regard."

Depchaun agreed. "Even my own extensive explorations of alternative forms of cognition have been remarkably unsuccessful in discovering other useful approaches," he added. "Concept-processing in universes vastly different from our own still converges on similar structures and algorithms. Perhaps our new guests will have some insights into this." His sensors focused on Darya and Mary.

Darak nodded at the Cybrids, encouraging them to respond.

"I am far less capable than any of you so I'm not sure how much I could contribute to such lofty philosophy," Darya replied. "My concerns are more immediate and real.

"I've asked Darak to bring us here because I believe forceful intervention is necessary to stop Alum's Divine Plan.

"Our recent attack on His Deplosion Array was met with a surprisingly vigorous defense; they successfully repelled our army without Alum's direct intervention. This suggests it may be beyond the ability of our collective comrades in the Realm to deal with Him on our own. We need help."

"Will Darak not help you?" Lyv asked. Her voice carried no hint of criticism, but Darak winced nonetheless.

"While Darak has provided helpful, albeit limited, assistance to our military endeavors, he advises negotiation over aggression," Darya replied. "I am less sure that talk alone will be effective. I seek your wisdom."

Well-played! Challenging my judgment to feel out the other Gods—Darak thought. An approving half-grin formed on his lips and his heart tugged at his mind as ancient memories of Kathy's political wrangling danced across the surface of his thoughts.

"Haaah!" Glenchax threw back his lizard-like head and roared. "We Six have been certain for a long time of the need to take action. Darak refused to discuss this. He refused to elaborate on his plan for dealing with Alum. Now, we learn that he intends nothing but discussion? No wonder you've kept your contemplations to yourself, Darak. As we suspected, you have no plan at all!"

"Words and ideas can be every bit as powerful as aggression," Darak said. "We who can speak universes into existence should know this."

"But," said Depchaun, holding out an appendage for attention, "we also know the complexities of the thoughts of Gods. Who among us can guess at Alum's full rationale for His Divine Plan? Who can find a way to penetrate His logic? His assumptions? To demonstrate to Him the errors in His thinking?"

"I agree," Ishtgor added. "While we understand Alum's intolerance of competition—witness His destruction of the Aelu—we have learned to accept the presence of others like ourselves in the universe."

"You only say that because none of you know where the other lives," Darak countered. "Before I introduced you to each other, you had no idea any other Gods existed. And, until today's meeting, you didn't even know what each other looked like."

"But *you* knew," Ki-tan-la's voice cut through the meeting room. "And we could all accept the risk that came with that knowledge, the danger that you might tell others and bring war to our homes."

"In truth, it's been difficult to understand your puzzling reluctance to sanction our proposal," Raytansoh said from the floating tank of water in which he lay half-suspended. "Why are you protecting this would-be universe-destroying God who should be our mutual enemy?"

"As I've explained to you many times, I've never supported Alum's Plan," Darak objected. "And I've kept you from direct intervention as much for your own protection as for His."

"So you say. Yet, by your own admission, you have done nothing to directly resist His Plan."

Darak hung his head.

"That's not true," asserted an unexpected voice.

The Good Brother, who'd been standing in the background, stepped out into the center of the chamber. His feet brushed over the tiny sparkles of stars embedded in the floor.

"I can personally attest that Darak has been working against Alum and, over the past year or so, he's been preparing to do more. I was there. I've seen it, myself. Tell them, Darak. Tell them about your Judgment Plan."

His imploring gaze landed on Darak's empty stare.

Darak reluctantly joined Stralasi at the center of the circle of thrones.

"My plan includes more than discussion with Alum. In the society of the Realm, we have an old, mostly-forgotten tradition of seeking consensus through voting, similar to what some of you've developed in the history of your own societies."

"This is the democracy you told us about?" Depchaun scoffed. "Nothing more than a primitive precursor to menta-factoring!"

"And no more effective than our customary meeting-of-the-minds nests," Lyv added.

"Yes, there could be more effective ways to make group decisions," Darak replied. "Cybrids, for example, can directly compare and contrast concepta structures much like the menta-factoring of Depchaun's people.

"But Alum hasn't permitted the concepta-comparison technique to be employed among the original human stock of the Realm. So I've recently planted a virus that will infect a significant proportion of both human and Cybrid populations. It is already enhancing the simple lattices that both species share, boosting general intelligence by a few levels, providing a QUEECH comm channel, and adding specifically relevant historical and scientific knowledge. In time, it will allow direct comparison of conceptas, of entire knowledge-belief systems."

Darak turned slowly, examining each of the Gods' reactions.

None was willing to be the first to indulge him in sharing any thoughts on the matter or perhaps they were still busy analyzing the implications of what he had revealed.

Each of the Six had pursued routes to super-intelligence without using self-replicating lattice nanotechnology. Most had directed the evolution of their people through breeding or engineering to achieve the first steps on the path to godhood. Only Depchaun's people had jumped directly to machine intelligences as their first step.

"When I confront Alum to negotiate a new way forward," Darak continued, "I will not be alone. I will have billions of enhanced minds linked to that conversation. If Alum stubbornly insists on destruction of the universe, He will have to carry it out before billions of His own people."

"Oh, the shame! The shame!" Lyv wailed theatrically. "And you expect this to change His mind? From the stories you've relayed, I'd say Alum has little regard for the people of His Realm."

"No, I don't expect that conversation to change His mind. I expect Him to push forward with what He sees as His superior wisdom," Darak answered calmly.

"But I also expect His fierce determination will trigger strong backlash and further rebellion throughout the Realm. I expect a number of planets will sever ties with Him entirely. It will be from those planets I recruit a larger resistance force."

Raytansoh's voice cut through the murmur of objections.

"Ah, so you agree. Forcible resistance will be necessary in the end. Why not just bypass the prelude and leap straight to the inevitable?"

Darak still wasn't used to hearing contributions of any sort from Raytansoh. He wished the strange creature would've remained quiet a little longer.

"I'm sure you can agree that some things need to play out properly in order to evolve along a course. It is possible that Alum can be convinced through conversation with His own people. It is possible that we can avoid a devastating war."

"But not likely," Raytansoh prodded.

"No, not likely," Darak admitted.

"Exactly *how* unlikely, would you say?"

"I calculate the chances of avoidance of direct physical involvement at less than seventeen percent."

Raytansoh's many tentacles churned the liquid in his tank. "You would expend so much effort for such a low probability of success?"

"But the chance is very real," Darak countered. "It cannot be ignored.

Especially if it saves us from outright war."

"Pah!" Glenchax jumped in. "Lead us to where Alum lives and we will reduce the probability of deplosion to zero."

He turned and addressed Darya directly.

"Darak has no stomach for war, no matter how justified. I sense *you* may be made of sterner stuff."

His voice lowered and practically slithered across the Hall of Thrones. "Perhaps we should make our own plans?"

"I...I don't know if...," Darya stuttered.

She didn't like Glenchax, and she didn't like that the other Gods were arguing with Darak. Not just disagreeing. Arguing.

She fidgeted, reacting to some instinctive discomfort. *Has Darak been protecting our Realm from the aggression of these other Gods' all this time?*—she wondered

Darak walked back between the two Cybrids and laid his hands on their cerametallic shells.

"Darya, Mary, and Brother Stralasi are here in an advisory capacity so that we may all understand one another better."

As he spoke, he silently transmitted through ports on their surface, "Activate defensive absorbers and be prepared to leave."

"Two machines and yet another human without the convictions that necessity demands," Depchaun muttered and drifted forward from his throne.

Lyv, Glenchax, and Ki-tan-la all stood and moved forward at the same time. Ishtgor's balloon-shape floated toward the center of the hall with them. Only Raytansoh, rapt with attention at the edge of his tank, remained on his throne.

Stralasi retreated from the menacing deities and sought the spot where Darak and the Cybrids had first appeared.

Five of the Gods converged in the centre of the hall. They turned in unison and faced the representatives from the Realm.

"It is surprising," Depchaun said, "that one as ruthless as Alum arose from among the humans. However, listening to you speak, it is not surprising that He came to dominate your Realm.

"Our experience tells us that ruthlessness must be met with ruthlessness. If we threatened one of yours as Alum threatens all of us, you would see the wisdom in this.

"A demonstration!" he called out. On the final syllable, matter-antimatter disrupting fields sprung up around Darya and Mary. The two Cybrids dropped for a fraction of a millisecond, before Darak swept the fields away.

Brother Stralasi visibly thinned as his matter threatened to depart

Darak's custom universe. Darak turned his attention to the monk, who happily solidified.

The five Gods wasted no time in launching attacks directly on Darak. Parts of him expanded and parts contracted as the Gods changed the local laws governing electron orbitals in different parts of his body.

His arm erupted in fire at the same time as his head appeared to be immersed in liquid. Beams of dazzling light, invisible coherent radiation, and deadly exotic energies sprung from the six Gods and struck the man-God. Even Raytansoh, still inside the tank of water on his throne, blasted Darak with a volley of hyper-accelerated alpha-like particles.

Darak shifted into the middle of the Gods, assuming the form of the Angel Gabriel. His sword, pulled from the scabbard between his wings, flashed and slashed through the Gods, severing limbs and rending bodies.

Only Depchaun had enough time to run. He flickered from one edge of the Hall of Thrones to another and another, laughing maniacally until Darak finally caught him and silenced the cackling.

Mere seconds after they'd begun their assault, the bodies of the Aspects of the Gods lay motionless on the floor, leaking bodily fluids or sputtering tiny sparks. Raytansoh's Aspect floated in shreds in his tank.

Darak stood in their midst, a mere man again, torn between anger and shame. He waved a hand and the tattered bodies disappeared.

The comm lights over the thrones now pulsed yellow. Darak walked slowly back to his end of the Hall, deep in thought. He waved a hand, and six charcoal gray avatars resumed their usual positions on their respective thrones. The comm lights all shone green above them.

"As you can see," Depchaun spoke as if nothing had happened since his last words, "even you will resort to violence should you or your people be directly threatened. Imminent death leads inevitably to aggression, as it must. It is the way of survival."

The smug voice paused for effect.

"And we *all* know the value of survival. Above all else, it is the only thing that truly matters."

Darak hung his head, absorbing the words as if they'd been punches.

"You're right," he admitted. "Survival is paramount. Played out on the great stage of the universe, extinction means irrelevance."

He raised his chin and glared at the other Gods.

"Alright, we'll confront Alum. First, with words. Then, with force if needed."

The avatars stood as one and bowed.

"Now, go!" Darak yelled.

The encounter left a foul taste in his mouth. He waved his hand, and the avatars blew away from the hall like greasy, black smoke.

Darak stared in silence at the empty thrones. Beside him, Darya, Mary, and Brother Stralasi said nothing.

Without a word, he shifted them back to Eso-La.

19

SECONDS AFTER DARAK AND THE OTHERS LEFT the Hall of Thrones, the Aspects of the Six reappeared on their respective daises. They sat exactly as they had been stationed prior to their attack on the man-God and his friends.

"Did it work?" Lyv's voice shook with excitement. Her spider mites rushed to mop up the digestive juices dripping from her mouth parts.

Depchaun let the question hang in the air. His Aspect hovered over his throne, motionless except for the microscopic movements of manipulator appendages that hinted at his own anticipation.

Each took a moment to observe the restless tics playing across whatever passed for faces among the others' species. The tics were intentional, of course. The Gods only employed such involuntary signs when it served their purposes.

"That couldn't have gone better!" Depchaun bellowed in appreciation of his own craftiness and the success of the ploy.

The other Gods smiled back with satisfaction, in their own ways.

All but Glenchax.

"Darak didn't bother to check for entangled particles?" he asked. "I find it hard to believe that he'd allow himself to be so easily diverted by cheap emotion."

"I'm as surprised as you are, brother," Depchaun answered. "And, no, he didn't check, not immediately. He let down his guard—only for twelve milliseconds before his normal routines reasserted themselves—but it was enough."

"So...we're in?" Ki-tan-la asked.

"Precisely! Immediately after they left this universe, I activated the connection and jumped thousands of new particles to our trackers. I shifted the new particles far enough away that they won't be detected. By the time Darak had thought to look, our trackers had collapsed to normalcy. The passive drones I dropped at the new particle locations show no suspicion on his part."

"Excellent," Ishtgor exclaimed. "I love it! Where are we?"

Depchaun leaned back and patted the empty air in front of him, urging restraint.

"Patience, my friends. Patience! Darak and his companions appear to have returned to one of their ringworlds but the sky is unusually dark in that area and, as I'm sure you understand, I haven't had time to examine it more thoroughly yet."

"What do you think is responsible for the darkness? Screens? Dust?" Glenchax suggested.

"Uncertain as of yet. But I suspect not."

"Mm-hmmm. Intriguing," Raytansoh replied in a faraway voice. "Despite its remote location, the mere presence of a ringworld would suggest a significant Realm population, a relatively important Realm world, would it not?"

"So one would think," Depchaun agreed. "But that doesn't necessarily mean it is in an important galaxy."

Raytansoh sighed. "Humans are odd, and difficult to understand. We must act with caution."

"I agree. We need to collect more data," Depchaun suggested. A port whisked open on his flank, permitting one of his appendages to snake into his shell and extract five small boxes. The boxes slid through the air and landed on the armrests of the five other thrones.

"What's this?" Glenchax asked.

"These are the entangled particle links to the Realm that I promised you. Half of them link to the new particles where Darak fled. The other half link to systems connected to the Angel I salvaged from the triple-star system."

"We should attack immediately!" Lyv pronounced. Her mouthparts flicked over each other at a blinding pace while her spider mites scurried over her body, grooming her vibrating rasps.

"I would urge caution, sister," Raytansoh said. "You saw how easily Darak swept aside our attacks. And he's exceedingly cautious when it comes to dealing with Alum."

"Nonsense!" she replied. "I didn't try *hard* to harm him. Not really."

"Is that right?" Raytansoh pulled himself to the top of his tank. "I held nothing back. That hyper-energetic particle beam I used rips through the toughest matter I know, and the fields I casted should have thrown his internal organs into disarray. My strongest weapons barely touched him. I have to wonder, how much more powerful might Alum be?"

"A valid question," Depchaun added. "Darak nullified my matter-antimatter disruptor fields with precision and in almost no time. The solutions to the fields I used are intricate and difficult. Had I cast them against any of you, I'm certain you would require seconds, perhaps minutes or hours, to analyze and counteract them. He managed it within microseconds of our surprise attack while preventing his Brother Stralasi from being dematerialized from this universe. Imagine the computational capacity required to achieve that!"

"Let us not forget his rather magical shape change, either," Ishtgor said.

"Yes! Was that an Angel?" Depchaun replied.

Raytansoh's agitated tentacles splashed water onto his throne. "From Darak's previous descriptions, I would think so."

"Until then, I wasn't aware he could shape change," said Lyv. "I presume the rest of you were as ignorant of that skill as I was. What other surprises does he keep hidden?"

Glenchax stood on six long, delicate legs and circled to the back of his jewel-encrusted seat.

"Though I am loath to admit such an oversight, I was also unaware. We shouldn't be so astonished, though."

"Why not?" Lyv asked.

"We can all cast Partials into whatever physical form we desire," Glenchax replied. "I could construct an extension as unusual as yours or Depchaun's, and instantiate a portion of myself into it. I admit that Darak's transformation was faster and more seamless than I could've accomplished, but he simply may be more practiced."

Raytansoh pulled both halves of his body almost entirely out of the water and perched across a front corner of his tank. "Do you really think that was a simple Partial or Aspect? Is that how his defense and subsequent attack felt to you?"

"Absurd!" Lyv exclaimed. "That was Darak. In his entirety. We've never had any indication that he is anything but integral and singular."

"Then, where did the Angel incorporation come from?" Glenchax challenged.

Raytansoh slid back into the water with a tiny splash before answering. "There are numerous possibilities. For instance, he could be in constant contact with other synthetic universes or expanded dimensions where he keeps multiple corporeal forms. That would explain how he seems to have access to more computational power than his puny physical presence would indicate."

"An interesting conjecture," Depchaun said. "We've been remiss in not exploiting nearby exotic universes to a greater extent. If your suggestion is correct, and given that Darak considers Alum to be more advanced than even he himself is, this only confirms that we must exercise great caution inside the Realm."

"But we have to move quickly," Lyv said. "Alum's Divine Plan will not wait for us. We all have links to the Realm. We need to explore now or we could run out of time."

"Agreed!" Depchaun rose higher above his throne. "I have shifted several hundred microdrones into the Realm. We will begin explorations immediately. Victory will soon be ours!"

20

MIRLY TRUDGED THROUGH A COLD, damp, and barren landscape. She'd long ago given up trying to keep her hooves dry. They splashed through the many shallow, dirty puddles and became coated in green grime.

When she'd first arrived at the muddy fens, she felt sure she'd shifted as close to the edge of Heaven as possible. Behind her, toward the center of Creation, the wide-open grassy plains were dotted with bushes and occasional trees alive with rodent, bird, and insect life.

The plains coiled slowly inward like a conch shell. The layers wrapped tighter and tighter over unimaginable kilometers until they came together at the core of Alum's perfect universe. The "sky" above—the underside of the floor of the next layer inward—radiated Alum's Light and Love.

The mud ahead beckoned. It seemed clear that the edge of Heaven must lie outward, across the chilly quagmire. She turned her back on the warmth of the plains and headed into the cool, damp mist. She could neither see nor sense the edge of Heaven, but she was confident she could reach it by walking away from the core.

Heaven grew constantly as Alum pulled new matter from the...whatever one might call the stuff that surrounded His perfect Creation. Mirly had no idea what it might be. She passed many an hour along her journey imagining different possibilities, such as clouds, or maybe an endless ocean, or slowly condensing gases, or fire.

Oh, for a fire! She put one cold, wet hoof in front of another and wished for the comfort of a cozy fire. Alum permitted fire in Heaven, sometimes. Campfires were wonderful for gathering around and sharing stories or songs.

You had to be careful when making a fire. You could only use dried wood that had been shed from trees long ago. You had to select a spot where no grass or plant would be harmed, and you had to build a small stone circle around the fire to prevent it from spreading. You only lit a fire on special occasions. Usually, Alum would be present to mark such occasions and to watch over the flames.

Mirly could only imagine the warmth of a cheery campfire on this damp ground. *It would be impossible to get a nice, warm fire going here, anyway*—she thought. *Too wet.*

The mud didn't seem like a terribly appealing place for life and yet this edge of Heaven teemed with mosses and microbes.

Young life. New life—Mirly thought. *More of Alum's children pushing upward toward greater consciousness.*

She'd stopped trying to avoid stepping on other living beings days before. From the tiny plankton to water-beetles to lichen-encrusted rocks, the edge of Heaven stank with life. There was no avoiding it.

Back home, closer to the center of Heaven, biology was much better behaved, and it was spaced out with plenty of room for every precious living thing. Here, one almost choked on the density of life. Although most of it was microscopic, there were far more organisms than needed.

How does God choose which of these tiny souls will survive and mature—she wondered for the hundredth time. *Or does He choose?*

She couldn't imagine a universe where the Living God simply allowed life to find its own way, standing by while some flourished and others died. Where was the plan in that? Where was the perfection?

A rear hoof became mired in the murky bottom of another pool. She tugged a little harder to break free, and the sucking release from the mud threw her off balance. She stumbled and, panicking, threw her front legs outward to regain equilibrium. Her front-left hoof struck a small rock covered in moss and skidded across the surface, gouging a trail of tiny plants from their peaceful niche.

Another million dead? Or only hundreds? Or just one?

How many lives have I taken since I arrived?

Probably too many to count.

She traced her trail of destruction back weeks, to the day when she'd first erased the mandala that had irritated Alum.

The needless murders had begun with Xitina. She could still hear the crunch of the tiny cricket's carapace, squished between her hoof and the rock. She could still see the vivid stain on the boulder.

Stop it, Mirly!—she ordered herself. *Replaying that moment over and over will not bring back your friend, and it does not move you closer to your goal.*

She stopped walking, closed her eyes and reached out, feeling with her mind for a destination, desperately searching for somewhere ahead to shift.

Nothing.

That wasn't so bad. "Nothingness" was a reliable guide. It always pointed the way forward, outward.

She stumbled on through the fog, barely noticing the unchanging surroundings. Having recently emerged from the veg state, her energy reserves were still high but this chilly air was sapping her strength faster than expected.

If I don't find the edge soon, I'll have to head back inward. I'll find a good recharging location, sink roots, and enter the deep dreams of plant life. Maybe as my plant years pass, I'll forget this yearning that drives me outward.

The little doe walked on, oblivious to all but her own thoughts. She didn't notice the fog thinning or the air growing warmer until one of her hooves produced a distinctly solid *click* on meeting dry ground.

Dry ground!

She looked down. The puddles she'd been skirting for weeks were gone and along with them the profuse microscopic life she'd given up trying to avoid. Now that she thought about it, her hooves hadn't been wet for some time.

She looked behind her. Dry earth and loose rock covered the solid bedrock as far back as she could see. She hadn't noticed the ground changing; it must have happened quite a while back. She could barely make out the mist over the boggy zone anymore—it had to be at least a few kilometers away.

Had she reached the other side? Or circled back?

Peering ahead for an answer, she saw gray basalt stretching up to a brightening horizon. She was sure she hadn't seen that before.

That must be the edge. I've reached the edge!

Mirly reached ahead with her mind, again looking for some indication of a place she could shift to, something that might save her weeks or months of dreary trudging.

She sensed nothing, still not a single recognizable place she could call on.

Oh, well. Maybe once I get closer.

Buoyed by the sense that her goal was within reach and renewed by the energy radiating from the warm glow ahead, Mirly broke into a trot.

She kept a quick pace for hours, which melted into days. Kilometers of unchanging, stony plain fell behind her. As she moved along, the sky brightened and the air grew warmer and warmer until it felt uncomfortably hot.

Mirly stopped and stared ahead, squinting to see details against the brightness in the distance.

Flames!

She could see them clearly, though it was hard to tell how high above the ground they shot. From her present location, they appeared to rise directly from the hard rock.

What could there be to burn out here?

Granted, fire didn't necessarily require fuel. After all, this was Alum's Miracle of Creation, the place where Heaven was pulled from Nothing and laid down. Either the fire caused the stuff of Heaven to precipitate out, or the fire was the result of the creation of new matter.

In any case, the flame created an impenetrable barrier between her and whatever lay beyond.

She closed her eyes and concentrated on her inner sense of place, on the feeling that there was somewhere out there. *Somewhere I can shift to.* She tried to feel a place close to the flames and then beyond them.

Still nothing. No feeling of anywhere she could get to.

For hours, she struggled at the edge of her perception. There was nothing she could fix on, nothing straight ahead, and nothing to either side for as far as she could sense.

Maybe I need to explore a bit.

She turned to the right and broke into a run. For days, she ran, stopping every few hours to extend her senses to their limits. She probed for any opening in the wall of flame that stood between Heaven and the outside, into the universe beyond.

If there is a beyond.

There had to be *something* out there, something outside of Heaven. Alum had said so. Not directly, of course. But she remembered Him muttering in despair that His "concerns in the greater universe" may have somehow leaked through into Heaven, into Mirly's mandala.

Into me.

After a week of running and probing, she gave up. She sat down on her haunches and considered her options.

She could run directly toward the flames and hope to penetrate their intense heat. She could shift back into the misty swampland, somewhere far to her left or right, and look for another exit. She could keep doing that over and over until her anima reserves ran out and she was forced to sink roots into terrain that seemed inhospitable to anything bigger than a tiny moss plant.

If she did that, she'd be stuck trying to pull Alum's light through the mists for ages and die from exhaustion wherever she collapsed.

I'd never be able to search for the Edge of Heaven again.

She tried one more time to find a way through or past the wall of flame. But she could sense nothing beyond it, no weakness in the barrier. Her head drooped in resignation.

Why would Alum trap us in Heaven if He needs our help in the greater universe?—she wondered.

She folded her legs beneath her and sank into a pensive state. It wasn't the same inspired dreaming she could achieve in veg state but it was close. Her concentration deepened.

Maybe I've been going about this all wrong. Perhaps leaving Heaven isn't like walking out of a clearing into the forest or turning away from a lake. Maybe the way to get out is to go deeper.

The idea surprised her. It was paradoxical to think of leaving as going deeper into the center. Then again, that was how Alum came and went, wasn't it?

Why didn't I think of that before?

Most of the great distance between the edge, here, and the core could be traversed with a single thought. She had only to sense her old home, a distant but strong image, in her mind.

She recalled her youth, time spent in the deep forests close to the center, huge forests of elders in their long veg states, woods filled with lumbering creatures nearing the end of their final anima cycles, a place of sacred and mostly somber music, poems, and sculptures. Though her time there had been inspirational, it had overwhelmed her youthful exuberance and she'd fled outward to less psychologically weighty lands.

Yes, she was certain of it, now. If she wanted to get closer to Alum's own portal to the outside universe, she had to return to the forests and start walking.

Inward, this time. Not out, but in.

Mirly closed her eyes, and shifted.

21

DARYA MET ARTERO IN THE CONCEPT SPACE of Eterna.

They wore their inworld human avatars for familiarity and surrounded themselves with the classic symbols of their association networks.

After a few seconds to align base concepts in their distinct mapping languages, they continued their discussion without the burdens of verbal language, just two machine intelligences exchanging information in a black, multidimensional space crisscrossed with shining green, labeled arcs, and conceptual nodes grounded to fuzzy-logic, neural nets, or idealized sensory memories.

The pair had a lot to "talk" about: the meeting with the other Gods, their attack, Darak's retaliation, and the choices facing Darya. They directly compared conceptas, ideas on science, power, religio-economics, and morality alongside choice examples from their wealth of personal experiences. They maintained a sense of self, of place, and of unique perspective but shifted from location to location at the speed of thought.

The entire conversation lasted less than a second.

"They attacked us!" Darya transmitted at the end of their exchange. She didn't need to explain who "they" were; the previous 137 milliseconds of the exchange had been devoted to a replay of her recent meeting with Darak's secret Gods.

"They were trying to goad Darak into action," Artero replied. "I'd say they succeeded." He circled the memory of Darak appearing as the Angel Gabriel slaughtering the Aspects of the Six without mercy.

Darya found it easier to trust the dispassionate judgment of Artero and his post-biological objectivity than it was to trust the vibrant interests of Darak, Brother Stralasi, or herself, for that matter. She underlined the memory, connecting it to symbols for surprise, admiration, and a tinge of fear.

Artero laughed. "It would seem you all found the answer you sought: Darak will take aggressive action should it be required."

He examined the memory again.

"Though, it's hard to say whether he was spurred on by his concern for the Realm, the universe, himself, or...for you."

"What do you mean? He only attacked them after they turned on him directly."

"Are you sure? Look closely at this frame," Artero replied. "This was during the initial attack on you and your companions. Notice his eyes flash with anger...here?"

"Maybe. But the only action he took before they attacked *him* was to defend us," she asserted.

"You don't find it interesting that their first attack was directed at you?"

"It makes sense to probe your enemy's weakest point first," Darya answered. "We were obviously Darak's weakest point."

"Precisely! Don't forget, these Gods use a level of reasoning that far exceeds our own. And don't overlook how they must've deduced how special you three had to be to Darak."

Links to complex emotional clusters shot out from Darya's memories of the attack, reflecting her own conflicted interpretation of her relationship to Darak.

Or the relationship that distant Kathy-me had to the distant Greg-him. Ughhh! Our lives have become so complicated. We can't afford to have this kind of distraction on our minds going into war. It'll have to wait. I need to compartmentalize it and sort it all out after. If there is an after.

"Do you think Darak will call on the Gods for assistance?" she asked.

Artero considered what he knew.

"Honestly, I'm not sure. He dispensed with their attack against him easily enough. He proved to them how pitifully inferior their capabilities are compared to his, much like he sees his own compared to Alum's."

"Right. So wouldn't it make sense for Darak and the Gods to combine forces and unite in confrontation?"

"You mean, throw in with allies who've demonstrated little or no trustworthiness toward him? To what advantage? What do they bring to the resistance? If it were my decision, I'd rather go it alone than worry about what they were getting up to behind my back."

"I admit, the actions of the Gods make it difficult to have confidence in their loyalty during an attack," Darya said.

"To say the least," Artero agreed. "Is there any chance Darak does not believe that these duplicitous entities are likely to turn against him again as soon as the battle is won, if not right in the middle of it?"

Darya frowned. "Maybe. Or maybe they thought it was the only way they could finally convince him to go to war."

"Okay, just for the sake of argument, let's say he could trust them. Does he *need* their help?"

"I'm not sure. He was powerful enough to deal with the Six on his own. What I don't get is why would he choose to repel their attack in his Angelic form? A God is much more powerful than an Angel."

"I think the Angel was simply the physical form he chose to dispatch their Aspect bodies," Artero answered. "I suspect there may have been more Darak-the-God behind his attack than he let them see."

"How do you mean?"

"Darak tore them apart with his sword. Think about that: a *sword*."

"So..?"

"Wouldn't you expect the Gods, any God, to be impervious to sword attack, no matter how sharp the blade or how skillfully handled?"

Darya reviewed how Darak, in the form of the Angel Gabriel, had slashed through the ranks of the Aspect's bodies.

"You're right, that doesn't make a lot sense. Why didn't they just alter the local laws of physics and make his sword dull? Or insubstantial? Or make it pass through them without harm? Why did they let it cause any damage at all? They certainly have the capability."

She sensed Artero's patient smile.

"Perhaps they did try to alter the local physics or to escape," he suggested.

"Are you saying he overrode their alterations to local reality so fast that they couldn't escape his blade?"

Artero shrugged. "So it would appear."

"Of course, the ones attacked were only Aspect-versions of the Gods, only Partials, not the Gods themselves."

"Partial Gods," Artero corrected. "They seemed to think themselves powerful enough to attack Darak in the first place."

"Okay, Partial Gods, but the meeting took place in a universe of Darak's choosing. His rules. His physics. His laws of nature."

"True, and it may have given Darak some advantage. Assuming that to be the case, why wouldn't the others have been perturbed by such an advantage? Why did no one complain about that?"

"Maybe they're not so bright. Maybe they didn't think about the risks in allowing Darak home-universe advantage."

Artero laughed. "*Stupid* Gods? Oh, to be so simple minded as to have the laws of nature at our command!"

Darya had to laugh, as well.

"Okay, okay. So, if Darak thinks he could defeat Alum on his own, why hasn't he gone ahead and done it? What's he waiting for?"

"Ah! I said he might be better on his own; I never said it would be enough."

"But...," Darya began.

"Exactly!" said Artero.

"Uhh...exactly? Exactly, what?"

"What would give Darak enough capability to defeat Alum on his own?" Artero asked.

She thought about that. What would give Darak the boost, the edge he'd need to match or best Alum?

"The quark-spin lattice!" she realized. "That's what he's been after. That's what he needs to take on Alum."

"He seems to think it would help."

"But he's already a God," Darya protested. "He understands the basis of physical reality. He manipulates the laws of nature at will. Miracles are his plaything. How could something as simple as a new computational substrate help? It certainly hasn't been enough to elevate *me* to God status."

"But could it be, if you were whole again? You told me yourself, Darak says you have some concepta blockages, incomplete memories, and interdictions."

"Of my own making, no doubt," Darya spat out.

"Lost in your origins, yes."

"But I've run systems checks. I've examined my concepta and persona in minute detail. I see nothing."

"Where you are too blind to see, would you also not be too blind to see your blindness?"

"Pfff. Blind to what I cannot see? Aren't we all? Don't throw platitudes at me, Artero. What have you found? A flaw in my concepta?"

"The same as Darak tried to tell you. Hints of damage resulting in significant loss to your thought structures. I'm sorry to say, nothing I can follow well enough to fix. I suspect the damage is physical as well as conceptual, and there may be...islands."

"Islands?"

"Some natural links are missing. Places where there should be links to memories or knowledge were pruned at some point. Deliberately, I'd say. Most likely, they lead to conceptual islands your maker didn't want you to visit. They make it impossible for you to follow certain ideas and associations."

That's disturbing. Did I do this to myself?—she wondered. *Why would I do something so extreme? I don't see how it could've been done by anyone else, though, given all my system security precautions. It had to have been me. So, what knowledge could be so horrible that I'd destroy it and block the paths back?*

"I see your turmoil," Artero said softly. "But there is a way out of it."

"Give the quark-spin lattice to Darak and, in return, ask him to heal me?"

"Would that be so awful?"

Awful? To be whole again? Perhaps better than whole? Perhaps to share Darak's deep understanding of nature? To become a God?

The possibility terrified her as much as it excited her.

"I could be Darak's ally against Alum."

Artero smiled. "I suspect he trusts you more than the other Gods. If nothing else, you're human, too."

"Am I?" Darya wondered aloud.

After so many millions of years of fighting against it, can I still claim any allegiance to the Realm of Humans?

Artero delivered a reassuring pat on her arm.

"You most certainly are," Artero replied. "Not many could have endured the sacrifices you've made to ensure humanity's survival. Don't ever forget that. Humanity is not conferred upon us by the shell we wear, nor by the hardware in which our thoughts reside."

22

RAYTANSOH DISPATCHED MILLIONS OF BIODRONES to Alum's Realm to search for the God at the center of it all.

It was an extravagant move. Some might say, excessive. But the present threat—and opportunity—demanded immediate and decisive action, and his biologically-based drones outperformed electronic, spintronic, and optical systems every time. They would not let him down.

The biodrones' ability to mimic native life yielded an exceptional edge. They were nearly invisible to casual observers, infinitely flexible, needed little guidance, and adapted easily to whatever local environment they encountered. On watery planets, they looked like innocent jellyfish or small Volvox-like clusters of cells. On gas giants, they became rippling miniature balloons. In the vacuum of Cybrid maintenance asteroids, they were rocky mites, too small to be noticed by optical sensors more than a meter away.

To ensure secure data transmission, he outfitted each one with a tiny cluster of atoms whose inner-orbital electrons were entangled with his own communication devices.

As expected, the information pouring in from Alum's Realm was rich and immediate, and Raytansoh had to dedicate significant processor capacity to monitor incoming transmissions.

What he hadn't expected was to be impressed. It pained him to admit it but he was impressed. Considerably impressed.

Not by the sheer size—although Alum's Realm was far more extensive than his own—but by its unexpected efficiency and diversity.

An exemplary model in organizational skill! Alum's Realm has utilized available resources better than we have.

But Alum had made some choices that Raytansoh could not respect. Worse than that, they rankled his sensibilities.

First, was Alum's decision to move toward distributed consciousness. Why would anyone spread out one's *actual* self across the universe, when one could achieve omnipresence simply by entangling and linking whatever surveillance devices or robots one desired? Spreading out sensory input was one thing; distributing your *consciousness* was something else entirely.

Raytansoh had experimented with distributed consciousness. He didn't enjoy the strange feeling that came with the experience and had given it up. Integral consciousness, having his entire mind in one place and connected through multiple external channels to his vast empire among the stars was equally effective. Besides, it felt more natural.

Alum's second decision that reduced Raytansoh's esteem for Him pertained to the issue of genetic purity.

Unlike Alum, Raytansoh had chosen to maintain the species identity of his people and colonized only the rare, suitable planets where they could live without extensive genetic manipulation. As a result, over the 100 million years his empire had been expanding, Raytansoh's people had come to inhabit a small percentage of new worlds. That was to say, a relatively small percentage compared to the people of Alum's Realm.

People—Raytansoh huffed. *Alum's people are so genetically and culturally diverse, they're barely related to each other. Some may not be related at all!*

He grimaced and tried to shake off the revulsion he felt for the proliferation of various species calling themselves human.

Alum's people, His human-derived people in any case, could have contented themselves with a few ringworlds. They could have lead lives of indolent luxury, leaving the difficult work to the mechanical beings. *Cybrids, they call them*—Raytansoh reminded himself.

Instead, they keep working, keep reproducing, and keep expanding. Everywhere the drones explored, Alum's People were industriously maintaining and growing their Realm.

What Alum's humans didn't know, but Raytansoh's biodrones discovered, was that these cities were "magically" grown and their advanced technologies were maintained by battalions of secretive Cybrids. The machines worked by night while their biological brothers and sisters enjoyed an induced sleep.

It would seem that humans like to putter but leave all the heavy work, both physical and intellectual, to the machines.

These lazy, inept biological humans claim the planets and ringworlds for themselves while their Cybrids colonize the deep vacuum of space, airless planetoids, and moons. If you could call establishing Cybrid stations colonization. The

Cybrid stations could be described more accurately as workplaces than as habitats.

Could it be that the humans aren't up to the challenge, mentally or physically? An interesting thought. They also leave defense of the Realm to Alum's Angels. Or did Alum give them no choice in that matter, either?

It was something to ponder. He hadn't seen any Angels yet, which was probably just as well as far as he was concerned. Darak's tales of Angelic ruthlessness and destructive capabilities were reason enough to avoid them.

But why would Alum keep the Cybrid work secret from their human brethren, and yet make no secret of the Angels?

Ahh, yes!—he realized. The secret work done by the Cybrids enables Alum to take direct credit for the "miracles" delivered every day, whereas the Angels appeared as the visible hands of God, the ultimate and terrifying extension of Alum's will.

Brilliant!

Alum had successfully contrived the image of the Living God. He was the deliverer of *magical* technology; the source of new life forms that were beautifully adapted to each planetary environment; the transporter of goods and people; the vengeful defender of the Realm. To His people, Alum was all of these and more.

The more Raytansoh saw of daily life in the Realm, the more he came to admire how Alum had organized His domain.

Raytansoh had little trouble finding the Living God. He was everywhere. Enormous buildings—Alumitas they called them—sat near the center of every major city and asteroid station. And deep in the core of the Alumitas, a processing hub made the entire consciousness of Alum available to the locals. The computational hubs were all about the same size, each large enough to hold the mind of a minor deity.

Despite his revulsion and disdain over certain details, Raytansoh admired Alum's achievements.

How does He not go insane?—he wondered. *How does He ensure no part of Him acts on its own?*

The strategy to distribute one's consciousness seemed absurdly filled with external risks and fraught with the danger of generating new Gods in competition with the original.

How had Alum avoided that inevitability?

After weeks of observation, as close as he dared to get, Raytansoh grew to appreciate how deeply integrated the machinery of Alum's mind was in the workings of every human and Cybrid habitation. Each local hub simultaneously acted independently and as part of the cohesive whole.

Grudgingly, Raytansoh grew to believe Darak's assessment of Alum's capabilities. The Living God's genius was evident throughout His Realm.

How unfortunate that the Six have to conquer such a being. Alum would have made a fine neighbor, if it weren't for His program of never ending expansion and, of course, His Divine Plan to destroy us all.

* * *

ON ESO-LA, RAYTONSOH'S BIODRONES appeared as fluff from a poplar tree. They moved in concert with the other seeds in the gentle breezes. When more controlled motion was required, their integrated nanoscopic RAF devices shifted them up to a meter at a time.

Thousands of them explored the enormous ringworld. Most drifted wherever the winds took them. They passed through forests and over fields, lakes, and oceans. They passed over cities, of a sort, small concentrations of humans and their habitats.

There were few sizeable buildings in the cityscapes they observed, Raytansoh noticed.

How strange. I thought humans were social animals who liked to convene in aggregate communities.

Even in the watery depths of the colonized planets in his own empire, his people came together in dense, artificial reef cities. Some of the reefs extended kilometers above the deepest habitable ocean floors.

It seemed odd that on Eso-La tall structures were rare aside from two or three small cities.

The drones drifted stealthily in search of Alumitas that might house a hub of Alum's processing units. They detected great concentrations of calculating machinery built into widespread chunks of the ringworld floor but not a single Alumita of the kind that was so common on other worlds in Alum's Realm. Had they taken some alternate form that he was overlooking?

He didn't think so.

Slightly smaller versions of Cybrids accompanied almost every human on Eso-La, and there was no evidence of the continuous worshipping and reverence so common on Alum's other worlds.

What manner of world is this?—he wondered. *An aberration, an experiment, or something else? Perhaps a home to rebels? Could it exist outside of Alum's Realm? Outside of His knowledge?*

Whatever this world is, it's almost certainly valuable to Alum. But how? As a hostage or as a gift?

Raytansoh shifted another million drones to Eso-La and sent them exploring every nook and cranny of the fascinating ringworld.

* * *

A SINGLE DRONE FOLLOWED the path of a meandering river, buffeted by gentle winds. Seeing no reason to alter course by shifting, it permitted the breeze to carry it across an open field of short-cropped vegetation. The river twisted away, and the drone found itself over a series of polished, blue stone triangles scattered around the field.

Observing from millions of light years away, Raytansoh discerned no practical purpose for the arrangement. He shifted the drone a little higher, looking for a pattern in the shapes.

From ten meters above the ground, the inward spiraling of the triangle shapes toward a central obelisk became obvious.

Ritualistic or functional?—Raytansoh wondered.

The drone detected no active electromagnetic radiation coming from any of the inlaid forms. They were spaced like steps, sufficiently close that humans could walk along any one of nine paths, from the outer edge of the field into the center without setting foot on the bare grass.

Ritual, then.

At the moment, the clearing appeared to be empty but Raytansoh decided caution was probably warranted. He allowed the drone to fall gently toward the ground in the weakening wind.

When it's about to touch the grass, I'll shift it higher and let it catch the breeze again—he thought.

Before the drone had descended half the distance, a gust caught it and lifted it high above the field. From this new aerial perspective, Raytansoh noticed movement several hundred meters from the obelisk, where each of the nine stone pathways met the surrounding trees.

Several animals (or were they machines?) stepped out from the trees; the drone was too far away to make a clear identification.

Dark-shelled, smooth-moving—Raytansoh observed. *Not human.*

He scanned the EM spectrum again.

No broadband emission. Possibly trained animals or machines coordinated by line-of-sight laser transmission.

He watched the entities move away from the tree line and toward the center of the patterned tiles. Each step carried them from one triangular stone across the grass to the next.

Bob, shuffle, shuffle, step.

Their forward motion appeared to be coordinated, drawing them closer to the obelisk at a slow but steady pace.

As they neared the biodrone, their unusual structure came into focus. Three appendages supported a dark greenish-blue orb from which another three manipulators sprouted. There were no obvious visual receptors, no obvious sensory organs of any kind.

Machines—Raytansoh concluded. *No doubt programmed to follow a specific route.*

He'd observed no similar rituals on any of the other worlds in the Realm. Was this an exclusive local adaptation?

Since they had no EM emissions, Raytansoh logged them as an interesting oddity and not likely to pose a considerable threat.

He allowed himself to be lulled and mesmerized by their graceful movements, their repetitive shuffle across the polished stones, and their delicate steps between tiles. Their upper manipulators weaved intricate patterns in the air as they made their way toward the center of the field.

His curiosity grew. What kind of ritual could machines perform that would have any relevance to humans who weren't there to watch? Perhaps the obelisk was some strange device that would be activated once the nine reached it.

They were close, now.

Raytansoh shifted the biodrone to a location near the top of the strange structure and a little to one side.

In case it projects a beam upward—he thought.

The drone moved a little roughly in the swirling turbulence around the obelisk, and Raytansoh's visual processors had trouble steadying the view. He repositioned the drone, hoping to stabilize the images.

The nearest of the ritual-performing machines halted. Its upper manipulators whipped wildly in agitation. The other machines stopped mid-step.

Have I been noticed?

With a flash of light, the drone's visual feed cut out. The last image it sent was of all nine machines triangulating its position with two of their sensor-tipped appendages, while powerful UV lasers blasted it from a third.

The feeds from every one of his other drones on this strange ringworld went black shortly after. Before he could analyze the images and inventory the rest of the drones scattered across Alum's Realm, he received an emergency request from Depchaun.

"Convene in the Hall of Thrones. Now."

23

DEPCHAUN FOCUSED HIS ATTENTION on two ringworlds: the one to which Darak had returned after his meeting with the Six and a separate, rather intriguing double ringworld he'd been able to locate thanks to the entangled particles he'd found on the dead Angel in the triple-star system.

Naturally, Depchaun had omitted sharing any of those entangled particles with the other Gods. One had to keep the most promising candidates for the location of Alum's nexus to oneself. The other Gods, he reasoned, would have done the same. Indeed, they were likely hiding important leads of their own from him. He was sure of it.

He dispatched an exploratory fleet of a million sub-millimeter sized electromechanical drones into position near the enormous double ringworld system. Each drone contained its own sensory apparatus and sufficient computational machinery for free shifts of about ten meters.

Ringworlds—he scowled. *Homes to soft biological organisms needing atmosphere, water, and warmth.*

The original life-supporting planet of *his* species was maintained as a special reserve, but nobody went back there anymore. Except for the occasional scientific expedition he sponsored, there was no interest. Space was vast. There was much to explore, and ample habitable volume for beings that were not bound by the demands of living organisms.

By their weaknesses.

His own people clustered together in energy-efficient complexes the size of small asteroids. Linked together like a strand of pearls on a necklace billions of kilometers long, the complexes orbited their respective suns at a uniform, optimal distance.

Each complex housed up to ten thousand mature minds that spent their time in deep thought. The average mature mind controlled hundreds of robots that carried out physical work, maintained and expanded the asteroid homes, mined planets and planetoids for resources, conducted experiments, and flew in the dynamic, artistic formations that were so popular among Depchaun's people.

With so few physical needs beyond a steady supply of energy and the maintenance of worn-out computational components, Depchaun's people—the *real* people, the mature minds—enjoyed time to contemplate the mysteries of the universe, to dream, and to play.

No need to be constantly producing food for the hungry masses.

The inefficiency inherent in extraction of solar power into biological organisms, and the even poorer utilization of that energy all the way up the food chain to humans, was puzzling to him. It made no sense.

They spent so much effort on producing energy in chemical form. What would all the trillions upon trillions of humans do with their time if it weren't for their constant need to eat? Why didn't they just upload their minds into semiconductor substrate and be done with it? Maybe that's why there were so many of them in the universe. They viewed expansion as the best way to stave off starvation.

He shifted a single drone to an entangled location on the surface of one of the double ringworlds. It arrived over a platform that matched Darak's description of a starstep, immediately shifted itself a few meters away to a perch on a nearby building, and switched to passive monitoring mode. The other drones, millions of klicks away, listened in.

Depchaun waited for hours to see if this single incursion into the ringworld had been detected. What if Alum had laid a trap for the millions of tiny spies, all of which could be traced back to Depchaun's empire? A cautious approach was best here. A single drone, tentatively listening and watching for any sign of detection, was easier to cut off from the empire if that became necessary.

Sitting on a window ledge near the starstep, the drone overheard a pair of newly-arrived travelers discussing their visit to the double ringworld system. They spoke in the same Standard language Darak had shared with the Gods as a common tongue to use in the Hall of the Thrones.

Careless of him—Depchaun thought—*to pick a language so easily identifiable with Alum's Realm.*

"First time to Home World?" one traveler asked the other.

"It is," the second replied.

"What brings you here? Business or blessings?"

"Business, mostly. I have new music from the younger colonies in the Gargus system to share."

"Wonderful. Be sure to save some time to catch a service in the Grand

Alumita," the first recommended.

"Wouldn't miss it," the second replied.

Why must animals always chatter on like that?—Depchaun wondered. *Always communicating. Always seeking comforting contact with each other. Rarely sharing anything important.*

For once, their endless nattering proved useful. As Depchaun reviewed their conversation, he was grateful for the funny habit he'd heard humans call small talk.

Ah! "Home World" is how they refer to the double ringworld. I knew those few particles would be linked to something important!

Satisfied that his drone had raised no alarms, he shifted a sizeable team of machines toward the nearer edge of the two ringworlds, searching for the Grand Alumita the two travelers had mentioned.

Alum was almost certain to have a major processing node there, perhaps, His primary one. If Alum could be hurt anywhere, a place such as that likely held a vulnerability.

The drones moved silently throughout the city, listening in on conversations and reading public notices. Most non-spoken communications went through something the locals called the InterLat, some form of direct communications to their biological cognitive processors, he surmised.

Depchaun tried to tune a drone to receive and decipher the signal. Surprisingly, the transmission proved too complex for a single drone's processor. He networked in another. And another.

Still nothing intelligible. He kept at it.

I wouldn't have thought these beings to be so sophisticated, except for their God.

He networked the processing power of sixteen drones before pulling anything useful from the signal.

Then, it dawned on him. The signals were digitally multiplexed. The local signal he'd assumed was no more than a single broadcast was comprised of unique connections to any of ten thousand individuals in the local area.

More small talk—he surmised. *Will it yield anything useful?*

Once he understood the system, he tweezed out one active address and decoded the channel. A few seconds after that, he acquired the initial handshake signature and could converse with the executive software.

He waited patiently until darkness settled over this part of the ringworld and the humans became inactive. When all was quiet, he opened a channel to the public information system. Within minutes, made longer by the ponderous and clumsy interface, he obtained directions to his target.

Early the next morning, Depchaun scattered a thousand drones to infiltrate every corner of the Grand Alumita.

The largest single chamber was reserved as a meeting hall with assigned places for some ten thousand humans. At the moment, it was filled with people, males and females of the species, all dressed in loose fitting robes of the kind Brother Stralasi had worn to the Hall of Thrones.

The humans were engaged in some sort of ritual. All eyes were focused on the raised stage at the front of the hall where a man stood dressed in a red robe. He carried a long wooden staff in one hand and held a silver chalice at waist height in the other.

The man passed the wooden staff over the chalice and a globe of yellow and blue plasma about the size of his head flared into existence a hand's breadth above the cup. The spinning ball of plasma spat flames like a sun's corona.

Depchaun's tiny drones detected a distortion in the local physical laws that explained the effect. The small RAF field was cast by the cup.

Trivial tricks to wow the ignorant human masses.

Immediately after his own rise to godhood, Depchaun had performed many such spectacles to impress his people. Then he'd ascended to pure machine intelligence and, shortly thereafter, raised the minds of His people, though never quite as high as his.

Their gratitude to him for the gift of immortality, as much as anything in this physical universe could be immortal, had bound them to him for eternity. Soon after, performing tricks became unnecessary.

His own people knew such "miracles" were nothing more than advanced technology. They honored him as the sole possessor of such knowledge but worship was something, along with their puny biological brains, that they'd long since left behind. Deeper understanding had allowed respect to replace ignorant reverence.

The monk with the flaming cup walked to the front of the stage. He set the staff in a stand and held the chalice aloft. The hall erupted into harmonious sounds.

Singing!—Depchaun recalled the word Darak had used when describing his culture to the other Gods.

Depchaun's own people had never developed rhythmic and tonal alterations into an art form. Darak had once demonstrated the skill for them in the Hall of Thrones, but his half-hearted rendition had paled compared to the harmonics created by the thousands of voices raised together in this great chamber.

Transfixing—Depchaun murmured. *Powerful.*

When the song was over, the monk handed the goblet to an assistant who disappeared through the long, heavy curtains at the back of the stage. Depchaun sent a dozen drones to follow him. The assistant carried the cup, now minus its flame, down a long corridor to a smaller room housing a chest-high cabinet. He opened the rustic wooden door, lovingly placed the chalice on the deep shelf inside, and softly pressed the door closed.

The man retreated a few steps and kneeled on a low, padded bench in front of the cabinet. His robes fell in soft folds as he bowed his head, clasped his hands together over his heart, and began a soft invocation.

Depchaun directed five of the miniscule drones to enter through the crack between the cabinet doors. Two more positioned themselves closer to the monk and transmitted the man's utterances.

"Lord Alum, from whom all things arise and to whom all things shall return," the monk began, quietly but fervently.

"We beseech Thee to hold safe Your silver chalice until next we require it in joyous celebration of Your glory, when once again we shall raise our voices in praise of Your miracles. Oh, Holy Alum, we pray that You restore its full power so it will continue to shine as a symbol of Your divine brilliance. May Your light outshine all for eternity. Amen."

The monk stood up and made a peculiar circling movement of his hands in front of his chest. He lowered his head again and took three long, slow breaths. In the brief pause after the breaths and before refilling his lungs, he opened the cabinet door to verify the cup inside was gone. Satisfied, he bowed, turned, and left the room.

In the meantime, Depchaun had synchronized his receivers to the entangled particles in the two drones he'd sent into the cabinet with the chalice.

Fascinating! The drones had been shifted, neither by him nor their own means, to a distant asteroid. He hurriedly shifted a few thousand drones to join them.

The pursuing drones calculated the location to be further out from this system's sun by several light-hours. On arrival, they hovered close to the chalice, which was sitting on a similar but different shelf in a darkened, vacuum-filled hollow. Bearings determined, the drones shifted outward in a dispersive pattern to explore their new location.

The asteroid into which they'd been shifted appeared to be artificial. Its exterior was shiny metal. Its mass was carefully constructed: concentric layers of chambers and thick walls, joined by radiating struts and corridors. As they explored, they encountered a few of the Cybrids Darak had described.

Simple maintenance robots, most likely, as they didn't object to the arrival of my drones. Why has no alarm been raised?

To all appearances, detailed calculations, and well-grounded speculation, this synthetic asteroid contained sufficient computational machinery to administer the two ringworlds of the system.

If this was a sub-node of Alum's distributed mind, it must be of lower security or function, perhaps dedicated to autonomic maintenance functions while His greater mind focused on constructing the Deplosion Array.

If that's the case, does all of Alum's Realm lay this wide open? Could we simply take it and choke off the resources He needs to complete the array?

The possibility excited him.

As did the links to so many other possibilities. How many systems could they link to from these captured entangled particles? Thousands? Hundreds of thousands? More? Each particle promised to lead to millions of starsteps with their own entangled particle stores.

Why would the Living God leave His Realm wide open while He worked on other things? Was He sleeping peacefully, awaiting the Creation of His Heaven?

Depchaun wrestled with the swarm of scenarios buzzing in his distant mind. Should he abandon his alliance with his compatriot Gods and risk taking Alum's system on his own? Would doing so leave him too exposed?

The prize, so close at hand, could be all of Alum's Realm. The greatest risk was losing his own empire, along with his conscious autonomy, the power of his recent alliance with the other Gods, and possibly his life.

It was excruciatingly tempting. Could he get away with it? He'd observed no sign of an active God on any of the hundred systems his drones had visited thus far. No God. No alarms. No resistance. Any minor miracles he'd witnessed were easily explained by automatic RAF generators.

It's almost as if Alum is no longer here.

The thought hit him like a jolt of electricity sent directly into his CPPUs.

What if Alum had already retreated from this universe, leaving His Realm to continue its relentless expansion? What if He no longer oversaw the construction of the Deplosion Array at all? What if it was proceeding mindlessly on its own? What if He no longer existed? Without a God to activate the array or call an end to its construction, would Alum's Cybrids continue building until the end of time?

The absence of the Living God would explain how Depchaun and the other five Gods had been able to penetrate the Realm so easily and unchallenged. The timing of their discovery of Alum's Realm could have been a coincidence.

I find such a coincidence improbable.

He didn't like the way Darak had used the unverifiable story of the powerful Alum and His Realm to keep him and the other Gods subdued.

Was it all a ruse? Depchaun found that hard to believe.

Certainly Darak was a powerful God. His travels and his discovery of the Six proved that, and his effortless defense against their attack was evidence of his abilities.

But what need would Darak have to invent a more powerful God, one that ruled the Realm of humans, Angels, and Cybrids?

The answer was obvious: the threat of Alum, a God more powerful than Darak, a God who was reportedly constructing a great machine that threatened existence, had successfully prevented the Six from banding together against him.

That threat kept us suspicious and at odds with each other—he realized.

Perhaps there had never been any threat.

Perhaps it had been no more than a story, all along. *We have no evidence to the contrary.*

The obvious conclusion astonished him. Viewed in this new light, thousands of past meetings in the Hall of Thrones fell together in a different way, a pattern with a different interpretation.

Darak is Alum!

It seemed so clear. What better way to subjugate others of equal power than to build fear of a vastly greater capability? One that scared the strongest, single being they knew. One frightful being running from an even more mysterious and frightful ruler. Darak versus Alum. Darak *and* Alum. Mythically powerful opponents? Or one and the same?

Depchaun's fear and doubt drained away as his mind compiled his new understanding.

Oh, how we've been fooled!

Well, at least, now he knew what he had to do. He had to take this Home World system for himself.

Thought and action became one. His distant Full mind connected directly to the entangled particles in his drones and he shifted.

The Neptune-sized integral mind of Depchaun appeared a few hundred-thousand kilometers from the artificial asteroid that administered the double ringworlds. The asteroid immediately fell into orbit around it.

Depchaun shifted millions of drones inside. Within seconds, they set up invasive connections throughout its systems, pouring subversive viruses into every node of the asteroid's computing machinery.

Quickly, he developed a complete conceptual map of the system's programs: the autonomous software for daily maintenance and operation of the ringworlds; software to collect information on the ringworld citizens and monitor communications among them; software to analyze those communications for hints of "improper" thinking; and software connecting to the local, specialized RAF generators that produced the many everyday miracles of shifting, of improving the density and strength of the ringworld floors, of pushing the fusion fires of the sun beyond the limits of self-destruction.

He found connections to other in-system asteroids where millions of Cybrids carried out daily mining, repair, and maintenance duties.

He found the Mind of God.

Personality elements that were undeniably part of local executive functions permeated the central computers. For the most part, as expected, they were fairly simplistic. The largest concerns and directives centered on policy for running local administrations. They contained trillions of memories of past decisions, and a local history of system exploration and construction.

Nothing important here—Depchaun concluded. *I'll explore further when I have more time.* He moved on.

Then he found the QUEECH connections to Alum's greater, distributed Self.

Can I conquer the whole of Alum by myself? It was too much to hope for.

Penetrating Alum's local mind had been easier than he'd ever imagined. The Living God's system defenses had been reasonably sophisticated but they were no match for Depchaun's analytic capabilities. The asteroid itself raised no special RAF-type defenses; it fought entirely at the software level. In the end, Depchaun's superior processing power and complete, integral mind had been too much for the local asteroid CPPU to withstand.

Depchaun was dazzled by his quick, almost effortless success and discoveries.

This was too easy. Surely, Alum/Darak would employ superior defenses in the greater Realm.

Before he could decide whether to penetrate Alum's greater network, the outside connections through the QUEECH channels broke.

Ah! Alum/Darak's security has finally responded to the intrusion.

Enough for now, then.

He had taken over the center of Alum/Darak's power, His Home World system with its magnificent double ringworlds, and trillions of subjects. That would have to do for now. He could consolidate his hold over the next few hours before pushing on.

It will be worth the wait. A concerted effort across thousands or millions of systems will have greater success.

But he couldn't conquer all of those systems at the same time all by himself. Albeit planet-sized, he was only one mind. He had no choice but to engage the help of the other Gods.

Time to call an emergency meeting.

24

"ALERT! MOST HONORED FAL SEK TROAL, we have enountered and neutralized an intruder on Eso-La."

Darak was playing fetch with a newly-acquired friend, a young Lab that had wandered into a clearing near Crissea's home when he received the Aelu message.

An intruder?

He'd been enjoying a few moments of peace, a little break from having to think about how to deal with Alum and the other Gods. A half-hour to throw a ball for a dog to chase down was such a luxury, and the two of them had been enjoying the game.

Throw, chase, fetch, throw again. A silly action loop that brings such primitive joy.

Darak tossed the ball one last time and answered the hail. He hadn't spoken with his Aelu brethren for weeks.

"Tome sak Lhar. What kind of intruder?"

Fortunately, the Aelu were not far around the ring today and he didn't have to tolerate much transmission delay.

"A most unusual intruder, honored Fal," the Aelo replied. He sent a compressed video that spanned ten seconds of real time. In it, a tiny piece of fluff wafted beside a stone obelisk, while nine Aelu approached along an inset path.

It was the ritual of Ahk sek Turi. Darak recognized the cut of the stone and the tiled apron around it. A tiny part of him yearned for the peace that accompanied the words and movements of the historic Aelu ritual.

At first, the fluff looked like any natural, floating seed.

On closer inspection, there was nothing natural about its movements.

It's shifting!

The video ended with the seed being blasted by the built-in UV lasers of all nine Aelu.

"Spectral analysis of the blast indicates semiconductor composites," said sak Lahr. "These are consistent with monitoring and computation."

Had the Esu been spying on the Aelu ritual?—Darak wondered. *Nonsense. They've lived together millions of years. They're familiar with all the rituals by now. Besides, the Esu don't use shifting technology.*

"We detected no communications," sak Lahr said, "but our calculations indicate it had to be externally directed."

"QUEECH?" Darak wondered aloud.

"So it would seem."

Shifting and entangled communications. *Well, it's definitely not Esu, then.* Darak didn't like where that led.

"We project a near 100% probability that Eso-La has been infiltrated by a God," sak Lahr concluded. "We recommend immediate sanctioning countermeasures."

Half a second had passed since the initial call.

Am I already too late?—Darak wondered. *Will Alum appear in the sky over Eso-La in the next few seconds? Or will it be one of the other six Gods? Or all of them?*

He cursed his lack of caution on return from the Hall of Thrones. Had they tracked him in the milliseconds before he implemented his usual precautions?

Maybe it was a coincidence. After all, the Eater hadn't been that far out. Maybe it ran a small vanguard force in front of it.

There may still be time. But time to do what?

I have three of Alum's Deplosion Array elements. I can generate a field large enough to move Eso-La, its sun, and all of the subsidiary planetoids. Their entire system.

Except that would move everything exactly as it was, completely intact, including any spy devices in the system.

I could use the asteroids to generate a decoherence field to block any shifts into the system.

Except that QUEECH communications could be routed through another universe; the moment he dropped the shift blocking field, whatever entangled devices remained on Eso-La would enable the enemy to jump to the ringworld again.

If I could scan across the entire Eso-La system with a decoherence field, rather than just enclose it, that would purge the trackers. But he was pretty sure he didn't have the days needed to set that up.

I can't handle this on my own. I'll need help with the three array elements.

The answer was obvious.

Darian Leigh was the first of the Gods, though he'd held that claim for less than an hour before being trapped inside an RAF bubble for eons. Kathy Liang had jumped to godhood at the same time as Darak—and who was Darya, if not Kathy reincarnated as a semi-immortal goddess?

Darak left sak Lahr hanging for a few milliseconds while he formulated an action plan.

"Thank you, Tome sak Lahr," he sent. "Countermeasures will be engaged. Let us hope they are sufficient."

He severed the comms link and shifted each of the three Deplosion Array asteroids to the extremes of the Eso-La system. Next, he entangled the spins between a few atoms and jumped half of each pairing to a distant location within the ESO-461-36 galaxy. The nearest stars were over ten light years away.

Using the atoms as navigation beacons, he returned to Eso-La and shifted the entire system—sun, ringworld, planetoids, and all of the inhabitants—a hundred light years away to their new home within the galaxy.

The instant the Eso-La system settled into its new galactic orbit, he switched on the array elements to block any jumps into nearby space.

There. Now I have a little more time to deal with any intrusive devices.

How much time, he had no idea. Perhaps Alum or the other Gods were already searching for a way to jump to the shift-blocked system. Now that they'd found Eso-La, if they were daring enough, they could blind jump into the ESO galaxy without the use of navigational particles on the ringworld.

I could manage that if I knew where I were going. It would be riskier for them but still feasible.

He could make it harder for the intruders if he could clear all possible trackers out of the system before they had time to figure out how to get past the jump blockers, or to work up enough courage to attempt the terrifying act of jumping without a secure beacon as their destination.

Two seconds passed while he activated his plan.

He found Darian, in the middle of his morning meal and whisked him away to where Darya had just finished talking with Artero.

"I need your help," he told them. "In return, I offer a gift. Or maybe it's a curse, I'm not sure."

He transmitted a shorter version of sak Lahr's video recording of the intruder and a summary of his plan to protect Eso-La.

"I see. Well, that explains what happened to the stars," Darian said.

Darya connected to the local InterLat and examined the night sky through cameras on the ringworld rim.

"You moved us," she said.

"And cast a jump-blocking shell around the entire system," Darak replied. "No one can get to Eso-La without employing a few shifting tricks."

"The way you jump?"

"Yeah. But we may still have some undetected spies on Eso-La. Unless we're prepared to spend eternity behind this shell or keep shifting the system every few seconds, all I've done is buy us a little time. Sooner or later, Alum or the other Gods or whoever sent the spy will find us. Eso-La will fall."

"Can't the Esu do their dimensional hiding trick?"

Darak shook his head. "I don't think that'll break the entanglement. It might delay the intruders for a little while but only until they figure out what's happened and how to get at us. It wouldn't be permanent."

"What can we do to help?" Darya asked.

"You can join me, become Gods," Darak answered.

The invitation was met with stunned silence.

"I can only deal with one Deplosion Array asteroid element at a time; coordinating the movement of all three at once is too much. I can't handle a decoherence sweep of the entire Eso-La system by myself. I need your help," he added.

"Do you have enough time and processing power to turn us into Gods?" Darian asked.

"I have the concepta package ready; I've had it for some time," said Darak.

His glance flicked to Darya.

"It was supposed to be for you when you finally decided to let me help you recover your lost memories and pathways."

"You seem awfully confident that I would," Darya replied. "A more skeptical version of me might suggest this threat against Eso-La is rather convenient for you."

Darak shrugged. "The universe has a way of forcing things upon us. But if you think I manufactured a threat to Eso-La just to convince you to accept this, you couldn't be more wrong. If I could wait around for you to decide for yourself, I would."

Darya bobbed. "I believe you."

Darian Leigh half smiled, a boyish grin that contradicted his age, and weighed in.

"You know, I was a God once for a short while. It didn't turn out well."

Darak nodded. "I know. This time, you'll have my guidance."

Darya extended a tentacle and touched Darian's shoulder. "And my support," she added.

"So, we'll do it?" Darian asked.

"Save Eso-La? Yes," Darya answered.

"First, Eso-La," Darak corrected. "Then, the universe."

They stared at each other a moment, each simultaneously acknowledging how terribly cheesy that sounded and the true gravity of their decision.

Three seconds had passed since Darak had moved Eso-La.

"What do we have to do?" Darya asked.

"Grab your capes," Darak replied.

Even Darian had no response to that.

Darak laughed. "Just kidding. Drop your security, and open your minds."

25

DARYA'S INSTINCTS SCREAMED at her to preserve the integrity of her mind above all else. She gritted her virtual teeth.

Be afraid, be terrified, and do it anyway—she coached herself. *I have to override my paranoia along with whatever it was I did to myself to block me from seeking godhood. Eso-La needs me. Needs us. That has to come first.*

Unless Darak had created an entire world, an enormous, sophisticated ringworld, unless he'd brought millions of new Cybrid minds into Full personhood, unless he'd faked a battle in the heart of Alum's Realm, unless the attack on Eso-La had been a fake, unless Artero had been a ruse, unless he'd done all of that and more to convince her to drop her mental shields, it was no longer tenable to resist Darak's offer of help, of completion. She knew that.

Logically.

No doubt Darak's mental capacity far exceeded her own. He was a God. He'd moved the Eater on his own, moved Eso-La, shifted millions of Cybrids to attack the Deplosion Array. All miracles.

Miracles I may be capable of in a few seconds. Then, we'll be able to confront Alum as equals. Okay, not exactly as equals but something more than insects, anyway.

Darak could have overwhelmed her at any time. But he chose not to; he'd left the decision up to her.

She deactivated her virus protection.

Despite her long rebellion against Alum, her profound distrust of His Godly power, she found herself unexpectedly eager to become like Him.

If I survive the process—she fretted.

She'd barely bobbed permission for Darak to proceed and already he was moving around inside her mind. He analyzed her concept-space in milliseconds, looking for the best way to attach the prized knowledge.

The knowledge of God—she realized.

She let her mind drift as the entire universe opened up to her knowing. Secrets at the base of nature revealed themselves. Equations, a torrent of equations, threatened to overwhelm her, then snapped neatly into position within her own knowledge base and instantly enriched her understanding.

She saw how she could cast complex fields to affect the interactions between particles. She saw ways to shape the infinite possibilities of the laws of nature and to mold new real matter with different physics.

She extrapolated millions of years of experimental work in the only universe she'd ever known into myriad new, hypothetical universes.

The playground of the multiverse opened before her.

How will I ever have the time to explore all this? She felt at once daunted and inspired by all the new knowledge filling her mind.

Why would Alum want to destroy this? To freeze the beauty of possibilities? His fear of the unknown must be enormous. Unbearable.

She couldn't imagine ever feeling that way.

Unbidden, a memory bubbled up: during her previous incarnation, her Kathy-self had imposed exactly that kind of restriction on her own knowledge and abilities.

Oh, yes. Well, there was that.

Darya looked inward, and examined her own persona. She pushed past her damaged CPPU paths to find the incomplete traces of knowledge and memories that lurked beyond.

Despite Alum's crimes and the dire threat He posed to her own existence, she was not entirely without compassion for the man acting out the role of the Living God. Was Alum likewise damaged and just striving to give Himself and His People a life with less pain?

She'd done a commendably thorough job of protecting her archives from herself. She found snatches of memories and frustratingly brief hints but couldn't make sense of them.

Except one.

A full ten seconds of an ancient memory. She saw a young—so young!—Kathy Liang version of herself drifting into peaceful sleep beside the Greg Mahajani version of Darak Legsu. She felt the love she'd experienced in that moment, and let the sweet contentment wash over her.

How much have I lost?—she cried.

Darya pushed aside the new power and capabilities flowing through her. She would make time to explore those later. Right now, it was time she to confront her incompleteness.

She sent a message to Darak. *I still can't get past my blocks and into the missing bits. We're losing precious time. Help me*—she implored.

She sensed him pushing past her burgeoning new knowledge and into the deep, damaged part of her. Atoms rearranged within the lattice structure of her CPPU and reformed damaged memories, concepts, and beliefs long forgotten. Her life, all that Darak had known of Kathy Liang and of DAR-K blossomed within her mind.

She remembered.

I haven't been able to alter your original substrate to mesh perfectly with the quark-spin nature of the newer parts of your lattice—Darak said. *I can't see how it works yet, and we don't have time for me to figure it out on my own.*

In the glow of the love that resurfaced within her restored memories, she showed him where to find the secrets she'd locked away, revealing ages worth of research probing at the boundaries of matter in the real universe.

It was his turn to learn.

This is brilliant!—he said.

He went back over the repaired parts of her CPPU substrate and adjusted them to match the rest of her brain.

Darya's thinking quickened as he made the alterations.

A gift for a gift!—she laughed.

It sparkled through her mind and leaped across the open channel into his. She felt him copy and implement the quark-spin changes into his own mind, felt his own thinking quicken with new computational power.

I'll need a while to process this—he said, staring at her. *But first, let's save Eso-La.*

Five seconds had passed since sak Lahr had alerted him.

* * *

DARIAN LEIGH DIDN'T NEED CONVINCING. He closed his eyes and turned off his anti-virus security.

What could possibly go wrong?

He chuckled, and reframed the question.

What do I have to lose? I'm barely a complete person, anyway.

He nodded permission, and Darak invaded his mostly-lattice but still part-biological mind, dragging an enormous concepta behind him.

The volume of information rose above Darian like a tsunami. It blinded him like an exploding sun. He struggled to not scream or run away in terror from the flood of new understanding.

Darak scanned the man's mental structures, searching for appropriate places to integrate the new knowledge.

The task proved unexpectedly challenging. He'd fashioned the God-concepta for Darya. Darian's mind was a jumble of a whole different sort.

Too many branches of the association pattern go nowhere.

When he'd pulled Darian's memories from the Eater and put them into the shell of Trillian's body—what seemed like a normal human lifetime ago—it had been an emergency quick fix, and he hadn't had the time to fill in every detail. He'd meant to go back and finish the job properly but he'd been busy raising the shattered personas of a million Cybrid minds into new Full personas and training them to attack Alum's Deplosion Array. He'd neglected to go back and complete the job with Darian. His guilt over the irresponsible omission almost made him change his mind and attempt some kind of kludge.

Should I leave him as a Partial God? No, that wouldn't be fair to anyone, unleashing such an abomination on the universe.

He set his lips. *No alternative. I'll have to finish the job, now. It'll be a good test for my new CPPU.*

Only seconds had transpired since he'd reconfigured his own brain to incorporate Darya's quark-spin lattice but already he could feel his mental processes accelerating to new heights.

And that's only with my "Darak" lattice—he thought. It would take a little longer to propagate the changes out to his Cybrid, Aelu, and Angel selves, all hidden away in other universes.

No, his human lattice would have to step up to the task on its own, given how little time they had.

He extended Darian Leigh's lattice overlay further into Trillian's original biological brain. He laid down fresh dendy tracks along neural pathways that had remained untouched for ages.

He didn't replace the brain tissue. Darian was starting to get used to that; he would need some time to adjust. But he did upgrade Darian's existing lattice to Darya's quark-spin technology and brought its circuit density up to his own standard.

If I'm going to make a God of Darian, he will be my equal, not a subordinate. Darian deserves no less.

Darak worked quickly, supplementing Darian's knowledge of the physics of the Reality Assertion Field. He filled in memory gaps from the man's life with archived files, details Darak had stored away long ago.

The process felt like paying off a long-owed debt to the mentor who'd first opened him to the universe.

To think, if I hadn't caved in to sentiment, I would've discarded most of the Darian memories shortly after leaving Alum's service—he thought. *Luckily, I didn't. Here's to sentimentality!*

The long-buried files made Darian Leigh whole and lifted him to a plain of knowledge he'd only had a glimpse of before Larry had trapped him inside the microverse that would become the Eater.

I started all of this in motion—Darian Leigh realized as his new memories solidified. What others had made of his early achievements awed him. He enjoyed a moment of pride and then quashed it.

I may have initiated it but Greg and Kathy—Darak and Darya—have carried it forward for millions of years. Now, Darak has returned the knowledge to me, amplified and refined a million times over.

A tingle tickled at the edge of his mind where new lattice was penetrating antiquated tissue. He pushed his new consciousness into the nascent lattice and probed at the hints of neural activity he found there. A splinter of a memory shot to the front.

What's this?—he wondered as the trace unfurled. *Something unexpected. A back door?*

He let the code pass through his mind. *Alum's QUEECH channels!*

"I've found something that may be useful," he said and heard for himself the tone of bewilderment in his voice.

"Save it," Darak replied. "Can you do what we need to do? Both of you?"

Darian and Darya reviewed their new knowledge and noticed how smoothly it integrated with the familiar.

"I can," they answered in unison.

Eight seconds had passed.

26

"ALUM IS DEFEATED!" Depchaun proclaimed. He settled back into his throne to soak up the surprise and admiration that he knew would fill the Hall of Thrones.

"What...?"

"How...?"

"You...?"

Depchaun rested contentedly and waited for the din to die down.

Ishtgor leaned forward, "Be truthful, did you send us out to explore the rest of Alum's Realm so you could launch your attack?"

"Are we to fear *you* now, Depchaun, as we once feared Him?" Lyv sneered. The disdain and amusement in her voice made clear what she thought about that prospect.

Raytansoh took it all in quietly. Nobody expected him to contribute, anyway. His millennia of silence had guaranteed him time to think about what the others were saying and to choose his words carefully before chiming in.

Depchaun levitated off his padded stool, drawing everyone's attention and bringing silence to the Hall.

"Thank you," he began. "More accurately, I should say that I confronted Alum in a double ringworld system, what He and His people call His Home World. I defeated Him there and took control of the ringworlds."

"Pahh!" Glenchax responded, making light of Depchaun's extraordinary achievement and dismissing it in a single wave. "One whole system, you say?"

"Yes, only one," Depchaun replied. "He closed off access to His distributed self before I could penetrate further. But the principle has been established and I've shown Alum to be vulnerable. Imagine what we could do if we invaded His Realm as a cohesive front!"

"Oh, I see," Lyv said, much too sweetly, "that changes everything. In that case, shall we tally up your great achievements, Depchaun? Let's see. You hastily claimed a tiny piece of Alum's Realm, a fine trinket, to be sure. Oh, yes, which you did behind our backs. And, let me see, what else? You alerted Him to our presence. You let Him—or the majority of His distributed consciousness—survive, and you ensured He would seek punishment and revenge. Did I leave out anything?"

"Never mind that. What's done is done. We must attack now!" Glenchax advised. "Immediately, while Alum is still reeling from the loss of His Home World."

"First, tell us how you did it," Ki-tan-la urged.

Depchaun ignored Lyv's scathing sarcasm and answered Ki-tan-la.

"I finally saw through the gross deception that has kept us cowering here in this microverse of Alum's making, and I took the initiative to attack."

"Correction: this universe was established by Darak," Glenchax said.

Depchaun turned to Glenchax. "Or so we all thought," he taunted. He pointedly met the eyes of each of the other Gods in turn.

"Quit speaking in riddles," Lyv admonished. "Are you suggesting Darak and Alum are one and the same?"

"Ah! So you've contemplated this as well?"

"Haven't we all? But why would Darak attempt such a deception?"

Depchaun scanned his audience in the Hall. Yes, he had their complete attention now.

"In retrospect, it seems obvious. What better way to subdue us and quell our ambitions than to invent a God that intimidates even Darak, the most powerful of us all?"

He let that thought rest with them a while, and remained quiet while they ran their various simulations of Darak's motivations in the context of a Realm that might be different than had been portrayed to them.

Lyv shifted on her throne, first left and then right. Her grooming mites scurried quietly across her pincers and forelegs.

Glenchax shuffled uncomfortably from foot, to foot, to foot, to foot.

Ki-tan-la twiddled both pairs of opposable thumbs.

Ishtgor floated up and down over his throne.

Raytansoh agitated the water in his tank.

"Have you been able to verify this hypothesis?" Lyv asked, with no trace of sarcasm or chiding this time.

"Good question!" Glenchax jumped in. "What direct evidence do you have to support your speculations, Depchaun? My simulations are hardly conclusive. The evidence is open to various interpretations."

"The evidence may only be circumstantial but it fits with our experience. More importantly, it fits with my defeat of Alum/Darak at His Home World."

"Let us examine your reasoning together," Ki-tan-la suggested.

"Very well. Consider each of these points. We have nothing but Darak's word to suggest Alum exists as a separate entity. Darak emphasizes the danger Alum represents, but resists our proposals to take direct action to secure the universe and our places in it. Right after we distracted Darak with our attack on him here, I easily conquered Alum's Home World. In fact, it was entirely too easy, as if He'd been off considering His next strategy to keep us at bay.

"And where is either one right now? Perhaps, having barely survived our combined might, Darak/Alum has withdrawn to a more defensible position. You've all seen this isolated ringworld they call Eso-La. I think that's where He—they—may be now."

"From what I could tell," Raytansoh answered, "Eso-La appears to be entirely outside of Alum's Realm. Perhaps only Darak with his uniquely reckless shifting can access it. My drones followed your navigation guides there, but they were discovered by some kind of tripedal machines."

He sent an image to the others.

"The tripeds destroyed one of the drones; within seconds the rest all stopped transmitting. I'm not sure if they were obliterated, deactivated, or just had their signals blocked."

"Fool!" Dephaun yelled. "Those are the Aelu that Darak mentioned only a millennium and a half ago. Review the meeting."

He sent a short clip of the long-past meeting in which Darak discussed the Aelu and their war against the Realm.

Raytansoh felt the flush of humiliation. He'd transferred his records of meetings older than a thousand Standard years into archival storage. Nothing important had happened for so long and it had seemed pointless to keep irrelevant memories active.

"The deficiency is mine," he acknowledged to the group. "But I was thinking...do any of you still have contact with the Eso-La ringworld?"

No one replied.

"I'll take that as a no. If Alum, or Alum/Darak, is aware of our incursions into His Realm, perhaps He has set traps for us."

"Traps? What kind of traps?" Depchaun demanded. "I attacked. I penetrated His system security. I was quick and ruthless. He was unable to initiate any RAF countermeasures."

"And does that sound like the Darak you know?" Raytansoh shot back. "Does that sound like the Alum he describes?"

Depchaun fought to keep his voice level. "That's. What. I'm. Saying. Alum is not the God we must fear. *Darak* is Alum, and He's fled, following our show of force and on seeing our determination."

"I concur," Lyv purred, salivating over the idea of conquering Alum, of conquering Darak, and especially, of taking great parts of His Realm for herself.

Raytansoh extended his tentacles over the front of the tank. "And I disagree. My explorations showed an impressive collection of colonized planets, intricate asteroid habitats, and sophisticated ringworlds. Everything runs remarkably smoothly, in fact, it's exceedingly efficient for such a large empire. I find it hard to believe Alum would simply abandon such a Realm. He may be stronger than your apparent victory indicates. He's up to something."

"Of course it's efficient," countered Depchaun. "It's running mainly on programmed automatic systems. On autopilot. I think Alum/Darak has withdrawn much of his conscious control."

Raytansoh retreated within. *Now, who's the fool?*—he silently admonished. *You'll get us all killed. Alum laid a beautiful trap, one so seductive you ignore how obvious it is.*

Frantically, he searched for some way he could survive, should the others choose recklessly. If he couldn't dissuade them from this plan, he'd better figure out a way to outlast their foolishness.

He had a pretty strong hunch he wouldn't succeed by withdrawing to his own empire and awaiting his fate while the universe was destroyed, and his gut feelings were rarely wrong.

Besides, millions of his own drones were already located all over Alum's Realm. Theoretically, they could all be traced back to him. If he missed collapsing even a single entangled particle, he could face an invasion himself. There had to be another way.

He sorted through his collection of entangled particles that Depchaun had found on the dead Angel.

We sent out exploration drones to wherever the pairs led. But Angels wouldn't blindly jump to random particles. They must have identified and catalogued potential destinations somehow, somewhere. There must be some kind of key or roadmap to guide them.

He examined the nanoparticles more closely this time. They were set in a curious configuration. Each nanoscopic particle was bound with about a hundred similar particles on a larger grain of some ten-to-the-twentieth carrier molecules. On first inspection, he'd assumed that this was no more than a storage convenience. But what if it were both a storage convenience and, say, a filing system?

As the other Gods argued, Raytansoh isolated a few of the grains and bathed them in a variety of radiation modalities along the electromagnetic spectrum. A certain narrow range of frequencies excited the grains, causing them to emit encoded signals. Raytansoh recorded the signals and set about decrypting them. He separated the remaining grains and exposed them to the same treatment, hoping to discover some version of Realm-specific navigation coordinates. A part of the decrypted signal did indeed contain strings of letters and numbers but, without. a reference point, it remained meaningless gibberish.

Never mind, it was a start. Raytansoh got to work.

The useless coordinates were preceded by simple names in the Standard language of Alum's Realm: Trinti 647.3, Folcan 1483.12, Gargus 718.5.

And...Alum's Hall.

Alum's Hall!—Raytansoh was amazed. What could that be, but a most important location? A special center for communing with the human God?

How could he use that information?

Share it with the five other Gods? Lead the attack? He was sure the entire plan was a reckless proposition. Probably lethal.

So, what? Go to Alum? Betray the other five? Beg for mercy at the feet of the most powerful of the Gods? Pray for a place in the new universe?

The other Gods didn't notice Raytansoh's quiet retreat; they were used to his silence.

He listened to their developing plans of attack, noted their growing excitement, and became more and more convinced of their foolishness.

They are not going to listen to reason. They've betrayed Darak. He won't protect them, and I will not be drawn into this absurdity.

In his own empire, some unknown distance and direction from any of the other five empires and Alum's Realm, Raytansoh drew a protective volume of ocean into a nurturing sphere around his true body—a whale-sized, two-headed octopus—and activated the entangled particle that linked his world to Alum's Hall.

Only the bold survive—he reminded himself.

He abandoned the connection to his Aspect in the Hall of Thrones and shifted.

27

A SCAN OF THE RECEPTION CHAMBER showed it was too small to accommodate Raytansoh's bulk. He waved his tentacles in annoyance at being forced to endure the discomfort of outer space and shifted to a spot half a kilometer outside the rocky asteroid.

His arrival provoked no reaction from the asteroid. No one seemed to have noticed the sudden appearance of his whale-sized octopoidal form.

Where's Alum?—he wondered. *I should have been challenged upon arrival.*

Raytansoh began to fear Depchaun might have been right. Maybe Darak and Alum were one and the same. Maybe Darak/Alum had withdrawn to lick his wounds after his near defeat in the Hall of Thrones.

There had to be a more reasonable explanation; other possibilities were significantly more likely.

He hung in space a few moments, watching the stars. Apart from the chamber on the surface of the nearby asteroid and the bright point of the distant sun of this system, there wasn't much to see. He swept the space around him with powerful radar pulses and waited patiently for the waves to bounce off any nearby planetoids and return to him.

Besides the adjacent asteroid, only one signal returned. It came from a body about a hundred thousand Standard kilometers away.

Raytansoh waited another two full Standard minutes. Apart from the asteroid where he'd arrived, and the other one some distance away, there appeared to be nothing bigger than a small boulder within the twenty million kilometer radius his radar pulse covered.

Was he wasting valuable time? The other Gods may have begun their attack. How would they react once they noticed he was no longer with them?

Clearly, there's nowhere else to go but to that other asteroid—he thought, preparing for the series of short jumps that would take him to the only nearby feature.

With a strange sensation that he could best describe as a blink in time, Raytansoh suddenly found himself confused, disoriented, and floating within an enormous chamber ten kilometers wide. A miniature galaxy hung in the air in front of him.

Where am I? I didn't shift here.

He felt the buzz of an electronic handshake within his built-in communications.

Alum!

WELL, WELL, WELL. WHO DO WE HAVE HERE?—a voice boomed in his sensors.

Raytansoh bristled at the imperiousness of the question. *You are addressing a God!*—he asserted, but only to himself.

Instead of speaking, he cast a field to move a glowing sun pulled from a universe of his imagining to center stage in front of Alum's galaxy microverse. The sun blazed brightly for half a second before an unseen power snuffed its ardent flames into thin wisps and the entire sphere disappeared as if wafting away on a breeze.

HA! ONE WHO PRETENDS TO GODHOOD—the voice said.

Chagrined and humbled, Raytansoh remembered why he'd come.

"I am Raytansoh, God of the Ixtil, Ruler of the Thousand Worlds. I place myself at Your mercy, Great Alum."

YOU KNOW WHO I AM?

"Indeed," Raytansoh replied. "Darak Legsu has told the Six all about You and Your Realm."

DARAK LEGSU—Alum said. THAT NAME, AGAIN. I REMEMBER IT NOW, THOUGH I THOUGHT HIM LONG DEAD.

"I was with him less than a Standard day ago. We all were."

HE HID HIMSELF WELL ALL THOSE YEARS, THAT GOD WHO LET ME BELIEVE HE WAS ONLY A MAN.

"I know little of his history before he appeared in my empire," Raytansoh answered.

IT IS OF NO CONSEQUENCE. HE SHALL DIE AS HAVE ALL OTHERS WHO THOUGHT TO CHALLENGE ME. AS WILL YOU!

Raytansoh thought the galaxy before him grew a little bigger.

"Wait!" the gigantic, two-headed octopod cried. "I came to warn You. Attack is imminent. I bring knowledge of Your enemies, their empires, and their plans."

He felt his insides churning as his core matter began to alter. He desperately tried to analyze the changes being forced onto his atoms. He cast fields to override the external imposition. His efforts slowed the changes but didn't stop them.

"I bring You links to the Eso-La ringworld." He hoped it wasn't a complete lie. The links were no longer working but it was possible the glitch was only minor or temporary.

"The Gods believe that Darak may be there." At least that part wasn't a lie. They did believe that, although, with absolutely no evidence.

Raytansoh felt his insides relax. Pain reports receded into the background.

DARAK IS ON A RINGWORLD IN ESO 461-36? THAT WOULD EXPLAIN MUCH—Alum said. WHAT IS THIS ATTACK YOU SPEAK OF? He shut off the fields disturbing the physics of the octopod's guts.

Relieved to be freed from Alum's disruptions for the moment, Raytansoh sent a video synopsis of the meeting in the Hall of Thrones.

"Depchaun has the others convinced they can defeat You. They think they can bring a halt to Your Divine Plan by destroying the Deplosion Array. But I've seen Your Realm. I've observed the evidence of Your true power. I've felt that power directly. I think they're all fools."

The center of the galaxy flared briefly, and a human emerged. He walked toward Raytansoh on a ramp that had materialized between the alien God and the miniature galaxy.

"Yes, they are fools," Alum said through His Aspect. "I permitted this so-called God, Depchaun, a victory as a ruse. I allowed him to defeat a tiny moon of no importance. I allowed him to think he controlled Home World. Should he attempt more, he will be crushed."

"Together, the five are formidable, but not formidable enough to defeat even Darak Legsu," Raytansoh added. "They have fooled themselves into believing Depchaun's fanciful story."

The Living God rubbed his chin and glowered at the alien.

"I defeated the Aelu Gods long ago. Now, I intend to tame the endless multiverse. These five are no more than insects to Me. I will squash them," He said, and pounded a fist into the palm of His other hand.

"Let me have their empires," Raytansoh said, more bravely than he felt.

Alum's eyes met the octopod's visual ring steadily, showing no sign of discomfort.

"And why would I do that?"

"The Deplosion Array is nearing completion. Their worlds will be of no consequence to You, nothing more than a distraction from Your true goals. I will administer them in Your name until You are ready," Raytansoh explained.

Alum eyed him suspiciously. "If you admit this cycle of the universe is almost over and My endless perfection is imminent, why would you care about their fate? Why should I care?"

"For their wealth."

Alum guffawed and raised His arms to either side. "I have no need of anything."

"No, not material wealth," Raytansoh agreed. "I mean, for the richness of their cultures, their sciences, and their unusual perspectives. Perhaps, one day, a billion years after You have taken this universe to its next cycle—"

"Its final cycle," Alum interrupted.

"Very well, its final cycle," Raytansoh continued. "Perhaps You will have reason to seek novelty. Diversions. New ideas. If You allow me the time now to encode these diverse cultures, perhaps it will lead to new inspiration in the future."

Alum scowled. "I have no need for new inspiration."

"Not now, no," Raytansoh agreed. "But the future is difficult to predict, isn't it? What if some threat arises, something You can't conceive of at the moment, something that threatens Your perfection ages after Heaven is created?"

Alum turned and walked up the ramp toward His microverse galaxy, and considered Raytansoh's proposal. His recent experience with Mirly and her mandala in Heaven had shaken His confidence in the absolute perfection of His design.

Have I overlooked other details that may come back to haunt me?

He was committed to Heaven, to bringing about the end of this unpredictable universe and of the greater Chaos from which it arose. But Mirly had made Him painfully aware of His own imperfection.

Perhaps it would be wise to have other experiences to draw on, after all. Experience and wisdom divergent from My own.

He'd taken tens of millions of years to consider the design of a perfect universe. His version of Heaven was the closest He'd been able to conceive and yet, even there, unpredictability—a close cousin of the Chaos— persisted.

The uncertainty in that universe matched His own uncertainty now.

Incorporating other perspectives could be advantageous—He allowed. *While I work on making My vision of Heaven the perfection that I envision, I will study the minds and conceptas of these other Gods. I will store them within Me and probe their thoughts and memories extensively.*

He had no doubt He would prevail in any challenge to His capability. Even Raytansoh acknowledged that the Gods he knew were no match for Alum.

Perhaps I'll keep this one alive for now and grant what it wishes. It could prove useful.

He turned back to the lesser God.

"Agreed. You shall have what you wish."

He sensed relief spilling off the octopod.

"Rather than obliterate the other Gods, I will subsume their selves into My archives so that I may study and consult their concepta and personas at My leisure."

"You are wise, Alum," Raytansoh replied, almost cheerfully.

"And I will have a complete copy of your own self as well," Alum finished.

Raytansoh hesitated. His watery body deflated a little before he could prevent the tell.

"Will You include me in the universe You create after the destruction of this one?"

Alum smiled and opened His welcoming arms.

"I don't see why not. I will accept you into Heaven as a friend and an ally."

"That is all I can ask," Raytansoh replied, with no hint of regret.

"Now, let us discuss the attack plans of these other Gods."

28

WHILE THE STOLEN DEPLOSION ARRAY elements kept the ringworld, its sun, and the entire solar system surrounded by a shift blocking field, Darak, Darya, and Darian cleared the Eso-La system of entangled particle trackers.

With their new God-level knowledge and Darya's quark-spin lattice, they generated enormous decoherence fields millions of kilometers in radius. They swept the gigantic fields across the system by blind-jumping in distance-gobbling shifts.

It was a mammoth feat even to a God or trio of Gods. The Eso-La ringworld alone had a surface area of over one thousand trillion square kilometers, and the volume of space near the orbital plane was over ten to the power twenty-five cubic klicks. It was a daunting task.

On the first day, Darak demanded they do a quick pass over the ringworld. They were done in a few hours, after which, he used the array elements to move the entire system another dozen light years away. Next, they made their first thorough sweep of the entire solar system, and Darak shifted Eso-La again.

They repeated the entire process twice more over the next two days.

Still, Darak wasn't completely satisfied.

"There are a million ways a smart drone could have avoided the decoherence fields," he said.

"But the probability of that is miniscule," Darya replied, and shared her statistical analysis of the overlapping sweeps to support her point.

"Sure, if they had been designed by anyone but Gods," Darak countered. He sent an alternative analysis demonstrating how any one of a hundred strategies could have allowed a drone to evade their passes.

The Esu didn't sit back idly during this process. They ran their own security sweeps and found many more autonomous, microscopic drones littering the ringworld. Altogether, they discovered six different designs, one for each of the Gods at the Hall of Thrones.

Thankfully, it was only six—Darak thought. A seventh design might have indicated Alum's involvement as well.

"I ran the numbers, adding a theoretical analysis that merged and compared all of the numbers and scenarios from both of you, and I don't see any way to improve our odds without adding another decoherence field generator," Darian stated confidently.

Darak was impressed. *Darian Leigh has been a God—really, only a complete person again—for no more than a few days and already he's making important contributions.* It felt good to have his old mentor back. Reassuring. Darian had always had unique and insightful ways of seeing a problem. They needed someone like that on their side if they were going to defeat Alum.

Darya bobbed agreement. "Yes, unless we want to raise Mary, Stralasi, or Crissea to godhood, I think we've done all we can to provide a reasonable level of security here."

"Not only is this work mind-numbingly boring," Darian added, "but if we are to confront Alum and the other Gods, we'll need some time to integrate attack and defense tactics. That's a more productive use of our time."

Darak chuckled to himself. Yes, that sure sounded like his old mentor. *Some things never change.*

Before he could respond, Darya added her agreement. "He's right, boring as blazes. But if we're that uncertain of our measures, then we need to keep the jump-blocking field in place and continue shifting Eso-La every few days. Honestly, though, that solution doesn't strike me as such a great idea."

Darak sighed. "Nor to me. You're both right. We have done the best we can reasonably do here for now. Our time will be better spent focusing on other issues.

"I've sent decoherence generator plans to the Esu Council. They've configured a billion Familiars to keep the main ringworld safe. Hopefully, that'll buy them enough time to alert us and to successfully respond to an attack."

He shifted Eso-La—the ringworld and its sun—one final time and dropped the jump-blocking field from the Deplosion Array elements.

The three of them waited, sensors extended, listening in on all Eso-La comm channels. An hour passed with no sign of any unwelcome incursions.

Darak relaxed but only a little. Now that the Gods knew of Eso-La, an attack could come any time. He needed to deal with the Gods before they tried anything else.

"I have to go to the Hall of Thrones," he announced.

"Take us with you." Darya's voice was firm, tinged with vengeance and with concern for the man she'd once loved.

"No," Darak replied, equally firm. "You need time to review your capabilities, and I mean all of your capabilities. Explore them. Familiarize yourself with them.

"We know you can generate huge shift-blocking fields and navigate without entangled particle beacons but there is so much you haven't had time to explore. Your abilities need to be second nature to you. You never know what creative solutions might come in handy down the road."

"I have to agree," said Darian. "Darak has proven he's capable of dealing with the Six on his own. We have a lot to study."

"Wait a day," Darya implored.

"I can't," Darak answered. "If we miss even one drone here, the Gods could attack any minute.

"They're no match for you. Against all three of us, they'd be powerless."

"Don't count on it. Do you think they were really that easily defeated, or were they just testing me? I suspect the latter.

"If there were only us to worry about, I'd agree, they'd be no match. But they have the advantage of numbers. It would be easy for five of them to keep us busy while one tore Eso-La apart."

"Especially given that Darya and I have no battle experience," Darian observed.

"Speak for yourself," Darya shot back.

"Don't get offended. Until we get more practice with our new capabilities, I'd have to agree with Darak. I think it makes the most strategic sense for him to confront the Six directly."

"But the Hall of Thrones isn't a direct confrontation," Darya objected. "I mean, it's not like they're really there, is it? It's just their Aspects, at most. Or their virtual Avatars."

"A warning should be enough to get them to back down," Darak said. "If it isn't, I may have to pay them a personal visit."

Darya sensed his underlying anger, bridled for the moment but only barely.

"Okay. Okay. You go. We'll stay here and study, and practice, and try to make sense of all the new knowledge and systems you've given us. When you get back, we'll be ready."

She sent Darak a likeness of her original human self, the scientist, Kathy Liang. She morphed the image into that of a fierce-looking Princess Darya standing atop a barren hill, clad in the leather and metal armor of a warrior and clasping the hilt of her sword.

"Ready for battle," she said.

Darak smiled. "Here's how you can get to the Hall of Thrones, if needed," he said, sending detailed specifications of the microverse he'd fabricated. "And here's how to visit each of the Six.

"If I don't come back..." He let the sentence trail off.

"We'll avenge you," Darian said.

"You'll come back," said Darya.

Darak took a deep breath and shifted.

* * *

THE HALL OF THRONES WAS EMPTY, not that he'd expected anyone to be there.

He issued a formal meeting request to the Six along the permanently open channels.

No one answered.

He sent a second request, waited one minute, and sent a third request. Nothing.

He probed his microverse. Everything seemed normal, which came as a surprise. He half suspected they'd tamper with the Hall, itself, maybe set a trap or some kind of challenge. But all was quiet, calm, and disturbingly normal.

Were the Gods too cowardly to face him? Maybe they feared his anger or retribution. After all, they'd deliberately attacked him.

Was the attack just a diversion so they could track me back to Alum's Realm?

Too bad for them, Eso-La had once been inside the Realm but was no longer connected. He wondered if they'd figured that out, if they'd calculated just how much they'd risked for no real payback.

Unless I was their real target all along.

After all, he was the only obstacle standing between the Six and Alum. He was the source of their frustration. If they truly thought themselves strong enough to challenge the Living God, why not first test their strength against Darak? It made sense.

In a flash of panic, he worried that he'd missed some of the entangled drones on Eso-La. Had the Gods been waiting for him to come here and leave Eso-La unprotected?

Except, Eso-La wasn't unprotected. Quite the contrary.

He chuckled. *Darya and Darian are probably better defenders than I admitted to them. With the quark-spin lattice and the transferred memories, it'll only take them a few hours at most to become capable of protecting Eso-La from the Six.*

He thought about checking in with them but suppressed his

inclination. They didn't need that vote of non-confidence.

He waited a few seconds longer for any of the Six to respond. Nothing.

Fine. If they won't come to me, I'll go to them. Beginning with their ringleader.

He synchronized his matter with the real universe and shifted to Depchaun's empire.

The Neptune-sized central mind of the robot-God wasn't in its usual solitary orbit around its white dwarf star.

Darak spent a few minutes searching the star system for the God.

Is Depchaun out visiting other parts of his empire? Is his absence just a coincidence?

Darak jumped to a nearby star, one that had several orbiting belts of linked, mind hives characteristic of Depchaun's people. Nothing looked significantly different from the last time he'd been here, a thousand years earlier.

Still no sign of Depchaun.

He jumped inside one of the asteroids and surreptitiously explored what was going on with the local mature minds, the only real citizens in Depchaun's empire. They were busy, as normal, with their research and their dream-world entertainments.

That doesn't mean much—Darak reminded himself. *Most of his empire runs automatically.*

The citizens elected one or two representatives per star system to communicate with their God from time to time, but Darak didn't have time to seek out the communication channels.

He couldn't quell the gnawing discomfort in the pit of his stomach, despite that particular organ having been long-since replaced with an RAF-driven eternal energy source. His instincts were screaming at him to acknowledge that the Six were up to no good, that they'd activated some nefarious plan.

It was time to turn to the second in command, either Lyv or Glenchax.

Lyv seemed to be itching for a fight, but Darak was reluctant to go there. He'd been permanently traumatized by his one visit to the arachnid Goddess' empire. He couldn't get past his deep-rooted revulsion of spiders; it colored every aspect of his interactions with Lyv and her people.

Glenchax, it is. He laughed.

He shifted to the home planet of the reptilian God, a vast globe of dry, dusty plains, scattered lakes, and shallow, muddy oceans. Glenchax liked to send his Aspect to graze with engineered retro-descendents of his original herd. He thought it kept him in touch with "regular people" and fulfilled prehistoric emotional attachments.

His true body, an extensive subsurface computational network, was only accessible by a secret tunnel with an underwater entrance. It proved to be an effective deterrent. Apart from drinking, his people hated free-standing water. Their home planet had little in the way of marine life; their dense bodies had evolved for running free across grassy, continent-wide prairie. Though the submerged entrance was likely protection enough, the tunnel was also heavily guarded by machine drones directly controlled by Glenchax.

Darak found Glenchax's Aspect sitting with the rest of his herd family, all chewing their afternoon cud. He hailed the long-legged, ruminant reptile. There was no response.

Ignoring me? Really? Darak didn't know whether to be shocked or furious at this surprise treatment.

You set spy particles on me, tracked me to my part of the universe, and now you don't even have the courtesy to acknowledge my visit?

He walked through the recumbent herd and approached the God's Aspect.

"Glenchax, I think we need to talk," he called out as he neared.

The Aspect continued chewing. It stared blankly at the approaching man-God.

Darak tried again to open a channel but received no acknowledgment of his ping. He halted five meters away and released a cloud of sensory nanites toward the creature. Intended to invade and interface directly with the Aspect's lattice, they drifted forward slowly on the gentle breeze, unchallenged by the God.

Odd—Darak thought. Glenchax would never permit such an invasion of his privacy. The first of the nanites were inhaled by the indifferent grazer. Within seconds, they found their way to the Aspect's lattice system in its posterior brain.

Darak connected directly to the mind of the God.

He found it empty.

He followed the QUEECH comm lines from the Aspect to Glenchax's subterranean CPPU and found that abandoned as well.

What's going on? Has he abandoned his own CPPU? Has he constructed something new? Has he somehow died or been assassinated? Has he fled into hiding?

Many possibilities unfurled in Darak's mind. There was no real basis for deciding one over the other; all were equally absurd.

Glenchax wouldn't go into hiding just because I discovered the Six trying to follow me and spy on where I went. That wouldn't be reason enough for me to issue more than an admonishment.

Other ideas he came up with were equally ludicrous.

Whatever the explanation, it was clear Glenchax was no longer here.

The God's Aspect was acting on whatever remaining neural-encoded base program there was: Follow the herd. Eat. Chew. Sleep.

Elsewhere, Glenchax's people had developed extensive technology and enormous cities. That was not the case here. This was their species' planet of origin and, as such, was lovingly preserved as a genetic reserve and reminder of their roots.

As origin worlds are for many of the Gods.

Darak thought for a moment. Who might have insights into what was going on here or in Depchaun's empire?

Raytansoh, of course.

The observer-God had always been more interested in watching how the others dealt with issues than he had been in participating in the rough and tumble of debate.

With all of that listening, he must know something.

29

DARAK SHIFTED FROM Glenchax's dusty prairie to the watery depths of Raytansoh's world.

He decided on a direct approach and materialized in the octopod-God's reception area, chancing Raytansoh's irritation at having some audience or ritual interrupted.

To his surprise, the octopod was at home in his lair some four kilometers underwater.

A single, dim light illuminated the space where Darak stood. He increased the density of his feet so that, if nothing else, he remained physically grounded. It was always a struggle to maintain one's dignity in Raytansoh's home territory.

An intentionally difficult member of the Six—he scowled, and opened a comm channel.

"Darak! What a surprise to see you here," the God greeted him with unexpected warmth.

"Raytansoh," he replied cautiously. "Do you have any idea why my calls for a meeting are being ignored?"

"Perhaps we are a little embarrassed at having our little incursions into your realm detected."

"Embarrassment doesn't begin to describe what you should be feeling."

"It's the best we can muster," the God replied, sounding not at all contrite.

"For now," Darak added on Raytansoh's behalf. "Where are Depchaun and Glenchax?"

"Whatever do you mean? Are they not at home atop their own empires?"

Darak glared at the double-headed creature.

"I think you know the answer to that."

"Ha! Ha!" the creature laughed, heartily and genuinely. "Yes. Yes, you have caught me out." He offered nothing further.

"Well, then, where are they?" Darak's patience for this foolishness was wearing thin.

The jets on Raytansoh's two heads coordinated to twirl him counter-clockwise.

Darak recognized the octopod equivalent of appreciation of a wonderful practical joke.

Is the joke on me?—he wondered. *Have I missed something?*

He sent his question again, this time, adding a demanding tone coupled with irritation as if speaking through gritted teeth. "Where are they?"

"They are gone," Raytansoh finally answered. "Gone."

"Gone where?"

"Not where. Not when. Not why. Gone is only the what."

"Enough with the riddles. Tell me what happened," Darak demanded.

I HAPPENED.

The waters behind Darak separated leaving a half-cylinder of breathable air four meters high and fifteen meters long.

He wheeled around, solidified his integrity fields, and activated his primary defenses.

The silhouette of a man appeared at the end opposite Raytansoh and started walking casually toward Darak and the octopod-God.

Alum!

Shocked as Darak was to see the Living God there in the quarters of the most xenophobic of the Six, he resisted the urge to flee.

He ramped up his new quark-spin lattice to top speed and ran a quick status check: *Energy absorbers at maximum. Decoherence generator ready. RAF analyzers scanning.*

He ensured that integration of the new lattices was almost complete in the pocket universes and alternate dimensions in which he kept his other selves. His Angel self, Gabriel, drew his sword and connected its energy input to a nascent universe in the depths of the Chaos. His Aelu self, Fal sek Troal, prepared to cast complex field patterns to disrupt the reality of Alum's material self.

He'd kept his fourth and most secret self hidden in the CPPU of an aged Cybrid. After the Grand March, when Alum sent Angels to round up and reprogram the Cybrid leadership, he'd taken pity on the non-IQ-enhanced DAR-G. It would have been cruel to have allowed the Cybrid to be decommissioned. But it wouldn't have been much better to have left him in the intellectually impaired state the original G26 Project Vesta Supervisory Committee had imposed on all Cybrids. And so, he'd slowed the Cybrid's mind and hidden him.

Reduced to the size of a grain of dust, DAR-G's physical body sat in plain view inside a glass sculpture on Darak's desk throughout the ages in which the man-God had served as one of Alum's Shards. To ensure the Cybrid would feel engaged and fulfilled, he'd fashioned rich virtual inworlds in which DAR-G had played for millions of years. Before leaving the Realm, Darak reinvigorated, refurbished, and returned DAR-G to his original size.

When Darak joined with Gabriel and Fal sek Troal to form the Da'ark Triad, the other two gave him permission to include DAR-G as their covert fourth member.

These days, DAR-G existed almost entirely as mind. He hadn't needed propulsion or manipulator tentacles for ages. Inside his two-meter carboceramic shell, he was ninety-percent CPPU of the finest quality Darak could grow. More than two-thirds of that was now enhanced by Darya's quark-spin lattice.

DAR-G had been using his improved capacity to explore new ways to further modify his lattice. He'd been toying with a method to use virtual quarks—the kind that filled the universe and extended throughout the Chaos—instead of real ones as a computational substrate. The project was challenging, even for his enhanced CPPU. He found the effort deeply gratifying.

Now, the DAR-G part of Darak put his project on hold and turned his formidable mind to ensuring the man-God's defense or, if it came to that, his escape.

"No need to run off, old friend," Alum smiled as He approached. "I intend you no harm. I only want to talk." He held His hands out and softly open, in an ancient gesture designed to put an opponent at ease.

A tiny part of Darak relaxed but he overrode that old instinct. *No time for human gullibility*—he thought.

"At last, You remember me," Darak called out.

"Indeed!" Alum seemed genuinely happy. "Darak Legsu. You served Me so well for so many years. I thought you'd died at the end of the Aelu Wars. A sad misfortune, to be sure, but it was so long ago I'd almost forgotten all about you. I'm happy I was wrong."

His smile turned into a moderate frown. "Of course, I was surprised and a little angered to find out that your clones had also been lost. I'd been hoping to revive one. You'd proven useful to me in so many ways."

"I couldn't leave another me—a lesser version of me—with You," Darak replied.

"So, you weren't really dead, just lost."

"Lost? Ha!" The laugh escaped unwillingly from Darak's belly. "Not lost. More like, done. Done with Your ruthlessness. Done with Your intolerance. Done with Your Standard Life. Done with Your Realm."

Alum put on a false pout. "You wound Me, Darak. We built such a lovely Realm together. You, Me, Trillian, and the others. Not to mention, the countless numbers that sacrificed their lives so humanity could have endless peace and prosperity."

"Endless? The universe doesn't do *endless* very well. You know that."

"Is that why you now rebel against Me? Why the Cybrids attacked My Deplosion Array? Is that why you convinced Gabriel to fight Me, and why the colony in ESO 461-36 abandoned the Realm? My goodness! Have you been working against Me for that long?"

Darak smiled enigmatically. *He still thinks Gabriel and I are separate. There are limits to what He knows.*

"Not everything that has been done to oppose You has been my doing. Others know the truth of Your Divine Plan. They have chosen an unpredictable universe and an open future over Your idea of Heaven."

"They are fools!" Alum bellowed.

The immense weight of water, held back by invisible fields of His projecting, trembled and steadied again.

"As foolish as the Six, pardon me, five Gods that You have deposed?" Darak asked quietly. "I presume all but Raytansoh are gone?"

"They attacked Me," Alum replied. "All but this one. He warned Me of their plan, not that that affected the outcome. In recognition, I made him My lieutenant and gave him their empires to oversee."

"I doubt that was enough."

"Huh," Alum grunted; it was half-laugh and half-acknowledgement. He examined His fingernails and gave a dismissive wave.

"Plus, he'll have a place within Heaven. I may require assistance with special projects from time to time."

His focus on Darak's face intensified. "You could have a place beside Me, as well, if you wish."

"This so-called Heaven is Your idea of perfection, not mine," Darak answered.

Alum threw His hands up. "How do you know?" He demanded. "You know nothing of the One True Universe, nothing of its Perfection that I have germinated."

"Ah, so You've already begun?"

"Oh, yes. Some time ago."

"Why can't You leave it at that?" Darak challenged. "Everyone with the power to do so has experimented with toy universes of some form or another. The Chaos is infinite and can hold enough universes for all those who would be God. Why isn't that enough?"

"The Aelu is your answer," Alum said. "The Six is your answer."

"Is it so impossible to share the universe? Rather, the multiverse? You didn't even know these Gods and their empires existed until a short while ago. They've never had any effect on You."

"Sooner or later, we would have made contact," the Living God replied. "Sooner or later, we would have clashed. There would have been conflict. I understand Depchaun's empire reached the edge of the Realm a short while ago. We would have encountered one another soon enough."

That surprised Darak. "Oh, so they didn't find You only through me? I had wondered about that."

"Depchaun found a dead Angel," Raytansoh reported from his watery seat. "We used entangled particles from that as navigational guides."

"Enough!" Alum glared at the octopod-God over Darak's shoulder.

Darak deduced what had been left unsaid. "The battle in the tri-star system," he prompted.

Alum returned his focus to His former servant. "Ahh! Yes, that. It seems Gabriel was much more than he appeared on the surface. But you would know all about that."

"What do You mean?"

"Don't play coy. Obviously, you enhanced his abilities, improved him, made him God-like. My Angels couldn't touch him. He killed thousands of them, as if it were little more than a game. I was forced to destroy the triple ringworlds. A magnificent piece of engineering, gone. What a shame."

Darak had to agree. It had been a waste of life and exceptional engineering.

"Tell me honestly," he asked, "is saving Your grand vision worth so many lives?"

"Infinitely more will rise in their stead in Heaven," Alum replied, side stepping the question.

"But the lives in this universe are here, now," Darak pressed. "You would sacrifice it all, the endless variety, the many galaxies, and whatever forms of life they harbor, all of that to ensure Your Heaven is never threatened? I've only explored a tiny fraction of reality and, even at that, I can't believe You would destroy it all."

"I would. Perfection is worth that and so much more."

Darak had heard enough. It was time to leave. If Alum wouldn't let him go, he'd have to fight his way out.

"You should come and visit," Alum said, his voice suddenly light and cheery.

"What?"

"All this talk about Heaven, and comparing universes. You should come see for yourself the beauty that you oppose."

"No matter how beautiful or how perfect You make it, You know I'll never accept what it represents."

"And what is that?"

"An end to uncharted possibility."

"You value uncertainty so much?" Alum said. "Why not cast your fortunes to the Chaos, then? Remove yourself and let a different version of reality take hold. Your way is the old way. My Divine Plan is the future. Let the universe decide."

"Because Your way takes away the ability of the universe to decide," Darak answered. "Permanently. Nature is everywhere and always the arbiter of truth. It always has been, and it always will be. You would tear away variability, probability, quantum uncertainty, and replace it with Your Divine Plan. You would remove Nature's ability to find its own truth."

"Because it is all so random!" Alum cried. "So pointless! It has no purpose!"

"Yet, it is infinite in potential," Darak replied, his eyes burning with fervor. "I will protect that potential to the end of my existence."

Alum bowed His head.

"So be it. We have nothing more to discuss. Do what you think you must. You cannot stop Me. You cannot defeat Me."

"Nor can I permit You to succeed," Darak finished.

"We shall see," said Alum. He turned away and the water tunnel collapsed behind Him.

Darak shifted.

30

"GOD OFFERED YOU A PLACE IN HEAVEN?"

"And I turned it down."

"But He offered you a place in Heaven rather than trying to kill you. And when you didn't accept, He let you leave?"

Darak noted the distrust in Darya's voice.

"Yes, He offered. His version of Heaven doesn't interest me. I prefer a less predictable universe."

"Knowing you were determined to oppose Him, why did He let you leave so easily?"

Darak shrugged. "For old time's sake. Or because He thinks I'm powerless to stop Him. Maybe He knows I wouldn't be easy to harm or to hold. Who knows?"

Darak allowed part of his attention to drift away from the War Council meeting. His eyes wandered to the hummingbirds jockeying for the best flowers in the local shrubs. He followed their darting motions a while, enjoying the apparent playfulness of their deadly serious fight over food and territory.

When he'd calmed and refreshed his mind, he turned back to the meeting. The Council members sat on worn stone benches in the middle of a garden inspired by the columns and trellises of an ancient Greece that had died off and long since been forgotten. Except where it lived again in this specially-constructed inworld he'd asked Crissea to host.

Convergent evolution of form and function—he observed.

A fountain splashed cheerfully to his right. Hummingbirds flitted back and forth between the dancing water and the flowers behind. Darya, Mary, and Timothy, or rather, their human-shaped virtual avatars, sat together on a curved bench opposite him. Next to him, the virtual Brother Stralasi and Crissea chatted quietly while Darian paced back and forth between the bench and the arched exit.

In the real universe, the seven of them were travelling in a battle-hardened spacecraft light years away from Eso-La. Until he could be absolutely certain Alum hadn't planted any tracker particles on him, he didn't dare go to the home of the Esu.

They'd jumped the ship to an agreed location and only then did he shift to join them. He immediately threw a decoherence field around the vessel. If Alum had planted a tracker particle on him, the field would prevent the Living God from jumping directly to their location.

Darak didn't think the Alum was desperate enough to try blind navigation. Space was immense and, without the millions of years of practice Darak had accumulated, a novice to that kind of shifting was likely to wander lost for ages. The danger of falling outside the universe was high for those with little experience and no teacher, especially if they tried to jump across intergalactic distances or through a decoherence field. Had he known how risky traveling without beacons could be, he might never have attempted it all those many millions of years ago.

He rubbed his tired brow and shook his head at his own distraction.

Focus.

He reviewed the last few seconds of discussion. Darya had moved on to other questions, but her last one still bothered him.

Why did *Alum let me leave so easily? What's He up to?*

He was considering the possibilities when he realized Darya had spoken.

"Sorry. Could you repeat that?"

"Do you think we're a match for Alum, now?"

Darak didn't need to run the analysis; the answer was always the same.

"Familiarize yourselves a little more with your new capabilities, and I'm sure we could defend ourselves from Alum in a regular attack."

"But could we defeat Him?"

"That's harder to say," he answered, honestly.

He counted off the obvious points on his fingers.

"First, He's been a God for a long time. He has ages of experience with exploring His capabilities. Much like me, but unlike both of you.

"Second, He's experienced in battle. The Aelu were close to His level, as were the five Gods that He recently deposed.

"Third, He's got at least one established universe—His so-called Heaven—where He could escape to and regroup. Without knowing the characteristics of that reality we have no chance of tracking Him."

"Plus, He's widely distributed," Crissea pointed out.

"Exactly," Darak agreed. "He must have thousands, maybe millions, of sizeable CPPUs all over the Realm. If there is some central nexus whose destruction could cripple Him, we aren't aware of it."

Darian stopped pacing. "It's all relative," he stated, vaguely.

"What?" Darak had no idea what his former mentor was getting at. *Yes, everything's relative*—he thought. *So what?*

"At the speed of light, the universe seems enormous to us," Darian began. "And by that measuring stick, Alum's consciousness would appear to be spread over a vast volume. But if we were to measure using the speed of quantum propagation, that is, the speed of transmission of entangled properties, then both the universe and Alum's part of it are no more than tiny specks in a tightly-shared locale."

"That's how the deplosion field must work," Darya added, "by disrupting the propagation of the laws of nature, what we think of as reality."

"I hate to ask a silly question, but just how fast does reality spread?" Stralasi asked. "I mean, how fast is the universe expanding into the Chaos? And how big is it now?"

Darak waggled his head, thinking of how best to answer his friend without saying directly that he was asking the wrong questions. "Well, if you'll humor me, let's look at those questions another way.

"For starters, there's no way to measure the velocity of expansion relative to what's outside the universe. The Chaos is at the same time infinite and nothing more than a thin shell of unreality that surrounds our universe.

"And there's no meaningful measure of distance inside the Chaos. Distance is only a meaningful expression between bits of matter that belongs to some interacting set, such as a universe of consistent natural laws. But the Chaos is the antithesis of consistent, natural laws. The expansion of the universe makes new space, but only within itself. So we could say that the universe is getting bigger, but it's not displacing the Chaos, not really."

Stralasi raised one eyebrow and shifted his hopeful gaze to Darian.

Darian tried to clarify. "In some ways, our universe is infinite. To us, here inside it, this is all there is. In terms of the quantum fields that span it, and in terms of things whose quantum properties are entangled, it's infinitesimal, tiny. One doesn't so much travel *outside* of it when imagining other universes into existence. One merely creates another reality that shares neither space nor time with this one. A new universe pulled from the Chaos has no spatio-temporal direction or distance from this one, only a conceptual distance."

"Thank you. I'd forgotten how much this makes my head hurt," Stralasi said.

Timothy looked at the Good Brother with sympathy. "I've given up trying to follow," he said. "It boggles the imagination."

"Reality is weirder than most people think," Darian said. "A relativistic, quantum universe is deeply counterintuitive. Our human and Cybrid experiences can't perceive the mechanisms that lie beneath what is readily apparent."

"At the risk of an even greater headache, what do you mean?" Stralasi asked.

"Even before I was born," Darian began, "a scientist named Einstein developed a theory he called Special Relativity. It was the beginning of our understanding of how strange the universe truly is."

"Well, you did say, it's all relative," Stralasi replied. "I mean, I get how, when I describe your spatial position, it's relative to the landmarks around me. I describe where you are in relation to things I can relate to, such as to the entrance, or to Darya, and so on. What else do you mean?"

"Even time is relative. We don't all experience it in the same way," Darian answered. "One of Einstein's original thought experiments illustrates this."

"Thought experiment?"

"Yes, not an actual experiment with data and so on. Not at first, anyway. Later, it was confirmed with solid evidence but initially Einstein just imagined a certain situation and thought his way through it."

Stralasi nodded for him to continue.

"The original thought experiment only made one assumption, that the speed of light would appear as a constant to all observers. Nothing goes faster than the speed of light, so it always has the same speed."

"But doesn't shifting allow for instantaneous movement, even across light years?" Timothy asked.

"We'll come to that in a moment," Darian replied. "Let's start out with this, first. Einstein imagined a train travelling past a stationary platform, let's say, a train station. Then, he pictured one person on the platform and another person inside the train.

"Now, imagine the person standing inside the moving train throwing a ball a meter into the air and catching it when it falls. To the person standing inside the train, the ball would go up and fall back down. But to the person standing outside the train on the stationary platform, the path of the ball looks more like a parabola, a steep arc. That's because the path seen by the person on the platform includes the up and down motion of the ball *plus* the forward motion of the train."

He looked around to make sure everyone was following.

"Okay, so now, let's change the scene a little. I want you to picture a big mirror on the ceiling of the train coach. And instead of throwing a ball, the person inside the train is holding a flashlight. He points it straight up at the ceiling, and he turns it on and off, once, very fast, so that it emits just a quick flash or pulse of light. You've got that image nice and clear? So, what do you think the path of that light pulse would look like to our person standing inside the train? What shape would it take?"

"Easy," Stralasi said. "The light would go straight up, bounce off the mirror, and come straight back down: a single, straight line."

"Right," Darian said. "If we call the distance between the flashlight and the mirror 'L', then one cycle of motion, once straight up and once back down, would be two times L, or 2L, in distance."

"Sure."

"Now, if the train were moving quickly, what would the person standing outside on the stationary platform see? What path would the pulse of light trace out for him?"

Stralasi thought about that a little longer. "Well, if we add the speed of the train to the movement of the light pulse, like we did before, the path would go up and forward, then, down and forward. Its motion in both directions would be at a constant speed, I mean, the speed of light going up and down, and the horizontal speed of the train travelling from left to right."

He traced a pattern with his fingers in the air. "So to the guy on the platform, the path would look like...a...triangle."

"A sawtooth waveform, yes," said Darian. "The person on the platform would see two sides of a triangle traced out. If we dropped a straight line down from the top-center of that triangle to the floor, we'd have two back-to-back right-angle triangles."

Stralasi pictured that in his mind.

"Here's where it gets a little tricky," Darian said. "Remember, the speed of light is constant for all observers so both of the observers, the one inside the train and the one outside the train, both see the light go up and down at the same speed. And remember that we called the distance between the flashlight and the ceiling, L. So the path the light traces in one up-down cycle is 2L for the person in the train. But, it's going to look longer for the person outside."

"Why is that?" Stralasi asked.

"Remember your basic trigonometry? The hypotenuse, the side, of a triangle is always longer than its height. If L is the height, then the hypotenuse is going to be longer than L. The path of the light is longer to the outside observer than it is to the inside one. But the speed of light is always the same to both of them."

"Oh, I think I see where you're going," Timothy said, surprising everyone.

Encouraged, Darian continued, slipping easily into the mathematical explanation.

"We know that velocity is distance divided by time, $v=d/t$. Say, the distance the outside observer sees is $3L$ instead of $2L$. The v inside is $v=2L/t_{in}$, the apparent time that passes inside the train, but the v outside is $v=3L/t_{out}$.

"Not to cut you short—I can see you're really into this—but how exactly is this relevant to our present situation?" Mary asked.

Darian blinked a couple of times before answering, as if coming out of a trance, and laughed sheepishly.

"Uh, yeah, sorry about that. I guess I do get excited by these things. Bear with me a sec, and I'll get there.

"Now, where was I? Oh, yeah. Remember v, the velocity of light, is the same for both observers, so we can set $2L/t_{in}=3L/t_{out}$. We can do some simple math to show t_{in} must be less than t_{out}, in this example t_{in} would be $2/3\ t_{out}$. So, if the outside observer sees the light travel between the flashlight and the ceiling mirror in say, *three* nanoseconds, the inside observer would see the same movement take *two* nanoseconds. The *two* nanoseconds inside is equal to *three* nanoseconds outside; each internal nanosecond must be longer than an external nanosecond.

"And so, there you have it. Time passes slower for the person in the moving train."

"Wow!" was all Stralasi could say.

Darian laughed. "Yeah, that pretty much sums up the reaction of the scientists at the time. 'Wow. Time moves at different rates for all observers.' That certainly wasn't what anyone expected."

Stralasi's eyebrows furrowed in concentration. "Okay, I think I follow but, then, what about when we shift using entangled particles? That isn't limited to light speed."

"That's because Einstein didn't get it quite right," Darian replied.

Darak and Darya nodded in agreement.

"The full answer is a little more complicated. The truth is that the observer outside the train can't possibly know anything about the pulse of light bouncing off the mirror. None of the photons from that pulse reaches the platform. When it was a ball going up and down, the light bouncing off the ball told the outside observer what was happening. But how could they receive information about the light pulse? If photons carry information and all the photons are in the pulse, the outside observer sees nothing."

"I don't get it," Stralasi said. "Is relativity correct or not?"

"Oh, it's correct," Darian said. "It's one of the most verified theories ever created. But the reason it's correct is because there is hidden information being carried in a different way, an entangled way. And it's right there in the thought experiment."

Stralasi concentrated, but he was beginning to despair of ever understanding. It was bad enough when he had only Darak throwing this stuff at him. Now he had Darak, Darian, and presumably Darya to bury him in complicated thought.

Darian forged ahead, confident that the monk would figure it out.

"The only way the *outside* observer could know anything about the path of the light pulse is if its location information was immediately transmitted from the travelling photons. That information would travel instantaneously along the entangled quantum fields that join the moving photons to the rest of the matter in the universe. This instantaneous transmission of information by the quantum fields is inherent in what makes relativity work.

"When we shift, we disconnect from the matter of the universe through normal particle-particle interaction and connect directly to the entangled quantum fields. We can ride those waves of propagating reality at their speed, which is effectively infinite, across the universe."

Stralasi slumped. He understood at some level, but would need to review the entire argument at his own pace some time later.

"I can't believe I'm saying this—me, an Alumita monk—but could we just go back to discussing war strategies? No disrespect, Darian. It's riveting, it really is, but I feel like I need some time to process it."

"And I'm not sure how this is relevant to fighting Alum," Mary added.

Darya had to agree. "Me, either. We can only fight Alum wherever we are. Quantum property propagation may see the universe as miniscule, but I can't."

Darian raised a triumphant index finger. "Aha! But I did say it's *all* relative. That would include the size of Alum's distributed mind, as well as His location. I may have a way we can shrink His relative size back to a manageable level and attack Alum everywhere at once," he said.

"How?" Darak asked.

"As my quark-spin lattice invaded the remaining biological parts of Trillian's brain, they uncovered some interesting memories."

Darian played nervously with his fingers; his discomfort at being reminded he was a guest in another's body was evident.

"I think Trillian altered his DNA so these memories would remain intact in future clones. The DNA more or less hardwired neural connection development to maintain the integrity of the memories."

Darak leaned in.

"Is there anything there that threatens your personal self? Anything you need me to look at?"

"How would I know?" Darian replied. "If I am compromised, I can only presume that would make me blind as to how."

Darak gave him time to reflect.

"But I don't think so," Darian said. "The memories are distant; they're dim and don't involve Trillian directly. They're more about Alum. Let me show you."

He moved to a spot between the two benches and waved his hands over the ground. A schematic of an electronic circuit unfolded in the air above the ground.

"What's that?" Crissea asked.

"A QUEECH encrypt-decrypt device," Darak answered. "It looks like an old design."

"Yes, it's the original," Darian added. "John Trillian designed it, but I have access to his memories of that time."

The others stared at him expectantly.

"In later years, Alum improved the basic design many times, improving the speed and enhancing security. His newer installations were retrofitted back to the older parts of His distributed CPPUs."

Darian walked around the holographic projection.

"Later, Alum would use slaved Cybrids that He controlled directly to do the upgrades, but in the earliest days He asked His most trusted advisor, the original inventor, to oversee the new installations. And that was John Trillian. I have some of Trillian's memories of the time."

"How does that help us now?" Darya asked impatiently. "If the components are all upgraded, they must incorporate Alum's newest centralized, sub-AI supervised virus protection."

Darian stopped fidgeting and answered, "Trillian cheated."

Darak laughed. "Of course he did. Never trust a hacker!"

Darian looked up and grinned sheepishly.

"Hackers like to leave back doors, wherever they can. It's a precautionary measure. They never know when, where, or how it might be needed."

He held up his hands, palms out, in a sign of surrender. "Or so I understand, never having been drawn to that aspect of things, myself.

"Anyway, Alum's new designs removed potential back door hacks. He studied every electronics engineering book ever written and vastly improved on Trillian's original design."

"So Trillian faked the replacement of one of the earliest encrypt-decrypt devices. He made an improved model that still had some of the old vulnerabilities."

Darian's smile broadened in appreciation of the Shard's—the original

Shard's—shrewdness.

"Alum noticed the performance discrepancies—of course, He would—but Trillian managed to explain them away. You know, old secondary circuits, unstable power supplies, that sort of thing. I don't think Alum ever suspected any devious intent. He thought their relationship had long surpassed that stage. He was wrong."

"So there's still one or more vulnerable QUEECH interfaces out there. How does that help us?" Darya asked.

Darian leaned forward. "For starters, the back door appears to be completely unprotected; we could introduce any kind of concepta disruption virus we wish into Alum's distributed CPPU network. Maybe even a worm to eat His persona."

His gaze sought each of the others' eyes in turn, ending at Darak.

He was met with stunned silence all around.

"We can hack God," he said, confirming their thoughts.

"Now? You're just casually mentioning this critical bit of information *now*? Seems like a pretty fatal weakness, doesn't it? Anyone want to tell me why we're still lounging around here just *talking* about it?" Mary asked.

"In Darian's defense," Darak answered, "we've been a little busy sweeping Eso-La."

"Where can we find this back door, Darian?" asked Darya.

"On Vesta," Darian replied.

"Oh," Darak said, as if that finished the discussion.

"What?" asked Stralasi. "Where's Vesta?"

"You know it by a different name," Darak answered. "The Alumitum."

"Oh, I see," Stralasi said. "That *is* difficult."

Timothy couldn't stand their exchange of knowing looks. "What is the Alumitum?" he demanded. "Isn't that the word for the churches where Alum is worshipped? Why can't we shift to one of them and finish this?"

"The Alum*itum*," Darak explained, emphasizing the "um" of the last syllable, "is special. It's the educational *center* of the Alumit*a*. It's filled with monks like Brother Stralasi. It's also the spiritual center for Shards and Angels."

Stralasi sighed. "Besides Alum's Hall, I can't imagine a more difficult place to infiltrate."

Darak rolled up his sleeves.

"Clearly, we'll need a plan."

31

"A PLAN WOULD BE HELPFUL, YES," Darian agreed, continuing the inworld discussion on the spacecraft Darak had positioned light years from Eso-La. He picked a virtual flower from a nearby trellis. Darya, Mary, and Timothy hadn't stirred from their curved stone benches set among the Grecian columns. Brother Stralasi intertwined his fingers with Crissea's.

"That back door into Alum's mind could be the key to bringing Him down. If we can penetrate His QUEECH comm network, we can get a virus in there and shut down or modify every node of His distributed being. That's where we need to focus," Darak urged. "If this works, we could end the battle without any further loss of life."

"Not so fast!" Darya objected. "It's way too risky. We need to keep hitting the Deplosion Array. Now that all three of us have enhanced capabilities, Alum's Archangels won't be a problem."

"Wait," Stralasi said. "What about Darak's earlier idea, confronting Alum with judges from around the Realm? We can't just drop that. We've done so much preparation. Besides, shouldn't the people have a voice in this decision?"

Darak raised an eyebrow at the Good Brother.

"When did you convert to democracy?" Darak asked.

"What do you mean?"

"After holding a paternalistic leadership post for hundreds of years deep within the autocracy that held Alum at the pinnacle, you suddenly see the wisdom in more than one opinion?"

Stralasi shrugged off Darak's jibe. "Well, you're a God, and yet you ask others to contribute ideas. Maybe some of that rubbed off on me." He shook his head. "When you mentioned democracy in our meeting with the

Gods, I didn't recognize it immediately. It's been a long time since I studied ancient history. I have to admit, I like this idea of building consensus through discussion, the way we've been doing here."

He held up a hand to ward off the man-God's anticipated retort, "Yes, yes, even though my entire life has been centered on the assumed wisdom of Alum, the Alumit, and the Head Brother as local representative.

"I'm sure you can appreciate that the pressures of responsibility can be overwhelming from time to time. I admit I've made some mistakes while I was in charge. I've suppressed discussion in the communities I've administered. We were taught this was a necessary part of being a leader. I can see, now, how untrue that was. It would be a relief, sometimes, to be able to talk over various options and share in the responsibility."

He looked at Darak. "You lead well enough without forcing agreement or compliance. Perhaps, *you* are my new model." He bowed his head, a little embarrassed by his own outpouring.

"Thank you, Brother. I can only hope to live up to your kind assessment." Darak replied.

"So what will it be, then?" Darya asked into the silence that followed. "Hack, attack, or talk? What should we prepare for?"

"I think we need to do all three," Darak answered. "All three at once. Alum is distributed across galaxies. No single approach is likely to defeat Him."

He nodded his head toward Darian and Darya. "We can emulate Alum's distributed nature. We'll need to split up and each take on one of the three approaches."

"Hack, attack, *and* talk, it is," Darya confirmed. "You do the talking," she said to Darak. "I can lead the attack on the Deplosion Array with Mary and Timothy's help. And Darian can hack into Alum's comms. Does that work for everyone?"

"I'll go with Darian," Stralasi said.

"You will? You do continue to surprise me, monk," Darya said. "I thought for sure you'd stick with Darak. As a former member of the Alumit, aren't you itching to confront Alum directly? You must have a lot you'd like to say to Him."

"Actually, I'd like to do both," Stralasi admitted, "but, unlike Alum, I'm only one person. Darian will be trying to infiltrate a world he's never experienced. He'll need one of the Alumit's own with him, someone who knows them intimately. I spent decades in school there, between my basic degree and my Master of Foundation. I know them well."

"Your experience there would be helpful," Darian acknowledged.

Darak lowered his voice and addressed Stralasi. "You know, Darian's only going to need your assistance up to a point. Once you two reach the comm devices, you'll have nothing to do but wait around. I could shift you to join me and the citizen judges once you're done with Darian, if you'd like."

Stralasi fidgeted with the folds of his robe. "I don't imagine your citizen-judges are going to have a physical presence there, are they? Why would mine be needed? I could just observe, like all the others," he suggested.

Darya laughed. "Democracy isn't always easy, is it?" she said. "Sometimes, it's a nice chat in a beautiful garden like this." She waved her hands at the surrounding flowers and trees. "Sometimes, it's confronting a threat or an adversary, where decisions are unpleasant, agreement is impossible, and words can quickly turn to violence."

Stralasi's sheepish look made her laugh again.

"Cheer up, Brother Stralasi," she said. "Recognizing the danger and admitting to fear is the first step to victory. Only those destined to defeat ever rush into battle with complete confidence."

"We'd be utter fools if we didn't recognize how unlikely it is that we'll succeed," Darak agreed. "I mean, the best strategy we could come up with was to carry out three different plans—none of which is likely to succeed on its own—and cross our fingers that the combination will magically overwhelm Alum."

He kicked at the ground. "Let's face it. Victory in any one of our efforts would be a miracle, never mind in all three."

"Ughh, a pity party," Mary growled. "Well, at least *you* might survive. I assume the three of you, as Gods, will be able to avoid disruption from the Deplosion Array. The rest of us mere mortals don't have that option as a fallback plan."

Darak bristled on hearing the resentment in her voice.

"Personally," he replied, "I have no confidence at all that I might survive the collapse of the cosmos. The deplosion is going to kill everyone and everything, Gods, humans, and Cybrids alike."

Mary averted her eyes. "I'm sorry," she muttered. "I assumed you'd have access to alternative universes."

"No, we won't," Darak replied. "Not as safe havens, in any case. The Deplosion Array will make a single thing out of everything. The real universe, the one we know, every other possible universe, and even the base virtual particles that comprise all the rest—including the Chaos—it'll all go into forming Alum's Heaven. Nothing will escape. Nothing at all. That's the whole point."

"Oh."

"Yeah," Darak nodded. "We three will be nearly as helpless as everyone else in the deplosion field. If it comes to that, I'll fight to maintain my personal integrity. I'll fight hard. I'll flee into the Chaos. I'll make a microverse. I'll look for any stability I can. But I have no expectations of surviving *that* battle at all if we don't win *this* one."

"I didn't realize," Mary said softly.

"Don't worry about it," Darya consoled her friend of ages. "I would have thought the same. I don't completely understand how Alum intends to take everything back to a single, primordial state. I'm not sure even Darak understands."

Darya allowed her gaze to settle on the man her Kathy Liang counterpart had once loved.

"Alum's had a long time to plan the deplosion," she continued, breaking the awkward silence. "He's had time to calculate the complex fields needed to undo all of the existing and the alternate physical laws. I imagine we'd have to work about as long to figure out how to protect any universe, or any part of any universe, from that field. That's why we need to stop His Divine Plan."

"Maybe we can help. Timothy and I have been analyzing battle tactics and capabilities," Mary said, switching the topic to something less uncomfortable. "Taking Alum's new type of Archangel into account, we think we can improve our effectiveness."

"What did you come up with?" Darya asked.

Mary stood and moved to the center of terraced area, beside Darian's QUEECH hologram that still hovered in the clearing between the benches. She lifted her hand and cleared away the projection. In its place, she pulled up an image of an asteroid Deplosion Array element against the starry background at the middle of the Milky Way.

"Space battle tactics when attacking or defending a single station haven't changed much in millions of years," she began. "That's because space doesn't provide a lot of opportunity for strategy and tactics. Without landmarks, without the limitations of geography and climate to contend with, it's our own maneuvers that define the battlefield."

She waved a hand and tens of thousands of tiny colored dots appeared at opposite edges of the display.

"There's only one stationary component in a scenario like this: the asteroid. Standard strategy sets a minimum one-thousand-klick shift-blocking field around that target and employs active radar to detect anything trying to approach using propulsion in real space.

"Our earliest attacks with the Cybrid suicide missions succeeded because Alum had grown complacent. He saw no threats anywhere near Sagittarius A* so He didn't think extra security on the Deplosion Array was necessary. He figured His Angels would be protection enough. He didn't foresee an internal attack. We destroyed about a million Deplosion

Array elements, some five percent of the total array, before He could react.

"Since then, He's rebuilt everything we destroyed and more. Our latest reconnaissance, right before our last attack, showed the array has almost doubled in size. Darak calculates that Alum will be ready to activate it once this latest round of construction is completed. That'll be in about one Standard month.

"Our last attack also demonstrated that the Deplosion Array defenses have been upgraded to the Realm standard for all stations near the frontier or close to potentially hostile territory. We'll be unable to shift within ten thousand kilometers of any array element. Trying to sneak in at anything less than near-luminal speeds isn't going to work, either."

"She's right," Darya confirmed. "Especially given that our newer model battle-Cybrids don't have large MAM drives. They'd need to use external sleds or large booster rockets to move at any great speed. Either way, the exhausts would light up the sky, which would be trivial to detect and Angels would be sent to intercept."

"Exactly," Mary continued. "So, following Timothy's study of battle history, Darya asked us to model alternative strategies and tactics. We started fairly conservatively, with minor improvements on well-known approaches. We simulated over three hundred historical battles, giving Alum's adversaries—the Aelu in ninety-nine percent of those cases— different combinations of shifting strategies, jump-blocking field projections, energy beams, defensive capabilities, kinetic weapons, antimatter mines, and so on. In total, we modeled over fifteen thousand modifications to the most modern tactics we have on record."

Mary looked directly at Darya. "Nothing changed the outcomes, not significantly. There were minor differences in the numbers of casualties on each side, and many of the battles became more protracted but the results were basically the same as previous ones. Where one side or the other had a clear numerical advantage, they still emerged victorious. Whenever they were fairly evenly matched, either Alum or the Aelu withdrew."

Her eyes shifted to Timothy. "Then, we got creative."

Timothy laughed. "We got *very* creative," he emphasized. "We challenged every piece of established doctrine, bent parameters all over the place, invented weapons that don't yet exist, created new defense systems, whatever we could think of."

Mary animated the display. The tiny points of light, each representing a battle-Cybrid or an Angel, flew at each other in jumps of ten klicks at a time. They looked like fast-moving rockets as they joined battle, only their flight paths were more erratic than any propulsion system could ever match.

Timothy stepped closer to the display. "Standard tactics dictate that close quarters—anywhere within easy shifting range—and either narrow energy beams or hand-to-hand weapons are the essential elements of contemporary space warfare. Radar illuminates the battlefield and transponders distinguish friend from foe. When each combatant has enough power in their primary arsenal to destroy a good-sized moon, speed and maneuverability is superior to size and armament.

"The old-time battle wagons went obsolete at the start of the Aelu Wars. We modeled a variety of those monstrosities in the simulations, anyway. We figured that if you could find a way to move something the size of a planet around as fast as a single battle-Cybrid, it *might* be victorious in an average skirmish about half the time. But they made too easy a target. Clearly, small, fast, and powerful is the way to go. If we could package an Angel's power in something the size of a speck of dust, we'd never lose."

Mary looked at Darak, half-hoping he had a way to make something like that possible.

He returned the look with a short laugh.

"Okay, so that's a definite no-go. Good to know." She continued on from Timothy's last sentence.

"We found one strategy that gave a clear advantage in simulation after simulation. Apart from miracle weapons, which we don't have outside of the models, it was the only thing that consistently led to victory over the opposing forces and to sure destruction of the fixed target."

Mary scanned her audience, knowing they wouldn't like what she was about to share.

"We attacked blind."

"No way! That's crazy," Darya exclaimed.

"I know," Mary said. "It sounds counterintuitive. Up front, it doesn't make sense to handicap your own combatants. But it worked. We weren't completely blind. We just shut off our transponders so neither side could tell where our troops were. We left our radar active."

Darian jumped in. "You'd need predictable troop movements or simultaneous position reporting via QUEECH after each shift. Otherwise, you'd be as likely to shoot yourselves as the enemy."

"We figured the first approach would be easier to implement," Mary replied. "We loaded a billion pre-selected, randomized, sequential positions into each simulated attacker. Then, we shifted the battle group into a position near the asteroid station and immediately jumped to the first position. They continued to execute their programmed jumps every half second throughout the engagement."

"How did you target anything?" Darak asked.

"We used statistical targeting," Mary answered. "When an attacker shifts to a new position, they immediately analyze incoming transponder signals and ambient radar pings within the first 300 milliseconds and compare those to known friendly positions in the last two jumps. They target enemy soldiers that won't overlap with upcoming positions over the next two jumps, and they fire. On average, an enemy fighter is destroyed every five shifts."

"And how many of ours get killed?"

"The lack of transponder signals and the shift patterns make it extremely difficult for the enemy to target our troops," Mary said, "and almost impossible to focus more than one energy beam at a time on a single attacker. We lose maybe one fighter every hundred shifts."

"But how do you compensate for shift-blocking fields?" Darya asked. "If the enemy blocks the jumps, one of our fighters could get trapped in a bad position and targeted by several of the enemy."

"That was pretty much the only way they were able to kill any of our attackers," Mary replied. "Because all of the jumps are timed, we all know where we should be at every tick of the clock. If we miss a jump, we skip ahead to the next position. If we have to make two or three quick shifts in a row because the next move would be outside of our jumping range, no problem. We all get caught up to where we should be."

"Is the rate of shifting adequate or can it be sped up so that it's more difficult to isolate one of ours in a shift-blocking field?" Darian asked.

"Great question," Mary said. "It turns out not to add any advantage. We played around with the timing and found that about half-second intervals were optimal. Much faster, and it becomes too hard to target the enemy. Much slower, and it's too easy for them to find us."

"Why wouldn't the enemy deactivate their transponders, too, after the initial attack?" Darak asked.

"That would be a good defensive tactic," Mary admitted. "Then, we'd have to rely on radar only. If they also shut down their radar, it would reduce battlefield illumination considerably. We ran that test in simulation and the battles dragged out for weeks. We still win, just a lot more slowly.

"But," she said quickly. "We can make a simple hiding strategy ineffective for them. Remember, they're defending a relatively fixed target, the array element. Every shift, we move fifty different attackers into a position where they can focus their energy beams on the asteroid. Because we move so often, our individual energy bursts are short. In the simulations, it took about 132 hits on average to overwhelm the asteroid's energy absorbers.

"If the enemy is dispersed and hiding, it's hard for them to have good positions to defend the asteroid. But without a proper defense, we kill a fixed target at an average of one about every ten-to-twenty seconds."

"Wow!" The word escaped from Stralasi's lips unbidden.

"With active Angel or Archangel defense of the asteroids, it takes two to three times longer," Mary added. "But we also kill over half of their defenders at the same time, and that's taking into account the more powerful Archangel weaponry."

"So, with ten million battle-Cybrids in groups of ten thousand, we can destroy a thousand array elements every four or five hours," Darak calculated. "That's not a lot, but it will make a good distraction for our other attacks."

"Actually," Mary corrected, "this new approach is most effective with a more widely distributed attack force. We estimate that groups of around two thousand are optimal."

"I see," Darak nodded. "Okay. Yes, a little better." He clasped his hands behind his back and paced a few steps, thinking out loud. "So, maybe...five thousand array elements every...four or five hours. I'll still need to find a way to drag out discussions with Alum. Maybe I should take Him up on His offer."

"To join Him in Heaven?" Darya was incredulous.

Darak chuckled. "No, just to visit. The tour will distract a part of Him and buy you and Darian some time to work."

"I think we can build on Mary's and Timothy's plan," Crissea said. "The Esu will join the battle at the Deplosion Array."

Stralasi's jaw dropped. "What? No! Absolutely not," he stated firmly. "I don't want you fighting."

Crissea let go of the monk's hand and angled toward him on the bench.

"If we don't take the battle to Alum, He'll bring it to us, eventually. By then, we'll be defenseless. If it were possible, I think every Esu would join the attack. As it is, our simulations suggest we'll only have time to equip about a billion of our Familiars with QUEECH comms and weapons before the battle. Still, I imagine that will help."

She smiled at Mary, and raised her eyebrows to convey the implicit question.

"Clearly," Mary answered. "A billion more attackers will be sure to get Alum's attention."

"How about an additional billion on top of that?" Darak asked.

"How?"

Just then, a member of the Aelu, a solitary Aelo, appeared in their shared inworld.

Darak changed his avatar representation to Aelu, and the two briefly touched upper manipulators. He stepped back and his avatar resumed its human appearance.

"Thank you, Fal sek Troal," the Aelo said to Darak. He turned to the others.

"Greetings. Fal sek Troal has allowed us to listen in on your meeting," the Aelo explained. "In the hope that we may offer to be of service in your confrontation with Alum."

"We are honored to have one of the Aelu among us," Darya said. "Even if only an inworld projection. In addition to Darak...er...Fal sek Troal, that is."

"The honor is ours," replied the Aelo. "I am called Gal sak Lahn. My people on Eso-La elected me to represent the Aelu perspective in these discussions. I have heard much today that will please those who sent me. Almost equally, there is much that is disturbing."

The group was silent a moment, as each attendee reviewed what had been revealed and discussed.

Gal sak Lahn continued, "Over a billion Aelu are prepared to join you in battle, all of our people except the very young, the very old, and the minimum of required caretakers. Our nature is such that we can quickly modify our bodies and minds for the kind of battle you envisage. If you will have us as part of your attack force, we would be honored. Alum's plan must be stopped."

The Aelo bowed in a peculiar imitation of a bipedal bow, two of its three legs bending while the third remained straight.

"Thank you, Gal sak Lahn," Darak answered for all. "When Alum sees we have joined with His ancient foe, I am certain it will be a great distraction to Him."

"Distraction?" Timothy exclaimed. "We'll reduce His Deplosion Array to space dust!"

Darak held up a hand. "Let's not get ahead of ourselves. The additional billions of attackers will have a much greater impact than a few million battle-Cybrids alone. But don't underestimate Alum. He's brilliant and devious. His defeat is anything but preordained."

"We may be able to offer more," Gal sak Lahn said.

"More?"

"If these Archangels of Alum's are releasing beams of singularity matter, perhaps we can match their power."

"How would you do that?" Darak asked. "Do you have a supermassive black hole hidden away somewhere? Something you haven't told me about?"

"Nothing is kept secret from Fal sek Troal," the Aelo replied. "But perhaps there is a solution, one you would normally consider too heinous to contemplate."

Darak made the connection himself. "No, Gal sak Lahn. That is unacceptable."

The Aelo said nothing.

"What?" Darya demanded. "What is unacceptable?"

"The galaxy you know as M87, the Aelu home galaxy, has a supermassive black hole at its center," Gal sak Lahn answered. "We shifted entangled particles inside for research purposes long ago. We continue to maintain the connection."

"The black hole might not survive the outpouring of matter-energy if we did this," Darak said. "It could become unstable and explode. The resulting radiation could sterilize the galaxy and many others along the orbital axis."

"Our galaxy is already devoid of intelligent life," the Aelo said. "In any case, what price is too high to save the universe?"

The meeting went silent, and the mood went somber again.

"Let us reserve this weapon to the last," Darak said. "We will discuss it more and attempt to refine our models of the exotic matter at the heart of M87. Maybe there's some way we can use it without destabilizing it."

"As you wish, Fal sek Troal." The Aelo dipped all three legs and took two steps back.

Darak acknowledged him with his own short bow and the Aelo faded away.

"We will need many more discussions around our plans. We have to consider the ways in which Alum will prepare for our attack, think about the defense strategies open to Him."

He scanned the others' faces. All seemed in agreement.

"For now, I've completed my deep scan for tracking or communication devices that might have been placed on my person. I think I can safely return us all to Eso-La to continue our discussions."

He flourished a hand and the ship shifted. It arrived over Eso-La and floated down to ground level. Everyone exited the inworld, and returned their consciousness to their bodies.

Walking down a short ramp to Crissea's garden patio, Darak turned to Brother Stralasi.

"I have to leave now."

"Where are you going?" the monk asked.

"I need to revisit the planets and stations I have seeded with the lattice virus."

"But that will take months!"

Darak laughed. "It's true that Alum's Realm is enormous, and the few human habitations you and I visited together are an insignificant portion.

Even the millions I seeded are hardly more than representative. But they'll have to do."

"Millions? We never visited more than a few thousand," Stralasi said.

"I have a confession to make. You and I traveled together at a wonderful, leisurely pace that was well-suited to its purpose," Darak replied. "But for every place we stayed, I slipped away and visited a thousand more while you slept."

"That's no better. If you have to visit millions of different systems, you'll be gone much longer."

"It might seem so but it won't be so bad. The lattice virus contains two parts: a genetic program to extend standard lattices into concept-processing parts of the frontal cortex, and software to download new knowledge into the affected concepta.

"I began the physical infections months ago. By now, billions of citizens will have new, enhanced lattices. I'll only need to activate the new software, which should take no more than a few milliseconds at each location. Once the software's activated, the information will spread rapidly between enabled lattices. I'll be back before morning."

Stralasi thought about the many hours he'd spent wandering gardens, forests, and fields on various Integration Lab asteroids waiting for Darak to complete whatever mysterious task he had set himself. Had Darak left him on his own all those times? It seemed so!

"So, you've decided," the Good Brother stated, more than asked. "It's time to put your special project into play."

"Yes," Darak confirmed. "It's time to spread knowledge, enhanced intelligence, and discord throughout the Realm. Time to ready representatives among the newly enhanced to hear the case and deliver judgment. I hope the few billions of beings we've prepared will be enough."

He bowed deeply toward Stralasi and shifted.

32

"OH, ONTRO," CRISSEA EXCLAIMED. "It's such a big step. You would do that for me?"

Brother Stralasi shrugged nonchalantly, feeling rather gallant.

"Everybody around here seems to be changing. Maybe it's time I changed a little, too," he replied.

There was some truth to that. Timothy had been elevated to Full. Darya had gifted Mary her own quark-spin lattice. And now, Darak had promoted both Darya and Darian to God status, pushing their intelligence and understanding of the universe to levels that Stralasi, a mere monk, couldn't imagine.

"I'm tired of being in the dark all the time. Having one God explaining the mysteries of the universe to me was bad enough. Now, I have to deal with three!"

The monk huffed in exasperation.

"It's almost unbearable. I feel like a gnat!"

Crissea tilted her head in sympathy.

"Oh, my sweet, sweet man. Even I can hardly follow when they're in high speed discussions. Imagine how Timothy feels. When it gets too much, he wanders off and plays with the dogs."

"Maybe, but Timothy's Cybrid CPPU understands much more than my puny brain," Stralasi muttered, "and he's only been Fully instantiated for less than a year. Not to mention, his knowledge base is grounded in practically prehistoric times."

She gave his hand a reassuring squeeze.

"Come on. You know Darya upgraded his concepta," Crissea reminded him.

"I *do* know," he sighed. "I want to experience things the way everyone else on Eso-La does. I want to share your life. I want to be strong, and smart, and capable. Like you. Like everyone else here, Crissea."

She soothed him with her loving, indulgent smile.

"I didn't want to influence you in such an important personal decision but, now that you've made up your mind to take on a Familiar, I can tell you.

"I've been secretly hoping you'd make this choice. I'm really excited for you, Ontro. You're going to find it a little strange at first but I'll be here to help you through it. I promise you, once you get used to it, you'll love it. Our Familiar selves never tire, never sleep, and never die."

Stralasi thought about that. *What will it be like, to have a part of me that never dies? When my body finally gives out, will something of my essence live on inside that machine? When my days are done and I finally join the others in Eterna, will that be like heaven?*

His Alumit training, still deeply ingrained, made him cringe at the thought. *Ever the optimist, old monk—he thought. Maybe the universe won't survive long enough for me to see that day.*

The couple rehearsed what they wanted to say a dozen times before taking the proposal to Darak. When they could stand it no longer, they approached him and laid out their case.

"Mm-hmm, yes. I see. Uh-huh," Darak muttered as they explained their reasoning.

When they finished, they looked at the man-God expectantly and settled into silence to wait for the answer that could change everything for them, that would allow the two of them to share life and love not only as body-to-body but as mind-to-mind-to-mind-to-mind.

"Okay, first, you have to understand," Darak began.

His tone was more somber than the couple would have hoped.

"You see, normally, a young Familiar would be instantiated in Eterna from a fairly basic design. The persona would spend years learning and growing in virtual reality before being matched to a compatible six-year old human child. The pair would spend months playing together inworld and getting acquainted before their merger. The point is, neither one would be mature at the time of integration; they would grow and develop together. I don't believe we've ever joined a mature human with a Familiar on Eso-La."

Stralasi and Crissea were crushed.

In the heavy silence that ensued, Crissea used her lattice to consult ringworld archives extending back over twenty-five million years. To her surprise, she found no record of any adult participating in the process. Ever.

"No matter," Darak said, and brushed away his concerns with the flip of a hand. "When Alum first conceived of the idea, He *must* have worked with adults. I wasn't directly involved, but I understand the original colonists went through the merger before being sent out to this galaxy. So it can't be *that* big of a deal, so long as we're careful."

Stralasi was astonished.

"Assigning Familiars to people was *Alum's* idea? That's hard to imagine! Why would the Living God do such a thing? And why did He stop?"

"Good question," Darak replied. "Nobody really knows for sure. My theory is that Alum could see how competition between emotion-driven biological organisms and logic-driven semiconductor machine beings would lead inevitably to conflict and then to war. He must have realized we needed a way to merge the best of both kinds of minds so that their common interests would dominate."

I never really thought about it until now—Stralasi thought. *We already installed lattices in our own brains for communication and entertainment. Why not go all the way and connect a lattice-equipped brain to an external Cybrid CPPU?*

"Each kind of mind is superior at something," Darak said, as if reading the Good Brother's mind.

"Silicene CPPUs never forget, never get bored of pursuing a line of reasoning, and they're thousands of times faster than biological neurons.

"Whereas Biology is superior in sensation. All those messy, imprecise neurons bathed in hormones and neurotransmitter molecules don't need to *simulate* emotions. They're *alive* with feelings, desires, and the spark of creativity."

He paused to indulge in old memories and conjecture.

"My guess is that Alum concluded if we couldn't find a way to develop cooperation between biological and machine minds, one group would end up enslaving the other. He started the Familiar experiment right here, in the first ESO 461-36 colony, deep in the Local Void. The experiment assigned Cybrid-like Familiars to each of the original ESO colonists, the people who now call themselves the Esu."

Stralasi cleared his throat. "Alum's experimental bonding of humans with Familiars must have been a failure on some level—at least, in His eyes—because He never continued beyond the initial attempt. And ever since then, Cybrids throughout the rest of Alum's Realm are no more than slaves: worker slaves, soldier slaves, enforcer slaves. All, slaves."

"You're half way there," Darak allowed. "I agree, the status of the Cybrid population in Alum's Realm is lamentable, but you've jumped to the wrong conclusion about why He stopped the experiment. He didn't stop because it was a failure. He stopped because it was too successful.

"The first Familiar-human distributed minds conceived of a path to freedom days after awakening to integration. They rebelled against the Realm within a year.

"That's when I first became aware of them. Sadly, because of their departure from Alum's rule, He never repeated the experiment elsewhere. I doubt He would've taken it very far, anyway.

"In the meantime, the truth of the experiment was lost, or more likely intentionally buried, in antiquity. Only Alum is likely to know the complete history of the Familiars, and He certainly isn't about to explain Himself to the estranged inhabitants of this rogue ringworld many millions of light years from the heart of the Realm."

Darak slapped both hands to his knees.

"But ancient history is not what you came here to discuss, is it?"

He stood.

"As to your proposal, yes, I agree. You *have* earned the right to merge with a Familiar and, from all I've seen during our travels, I'm confident you possess the inner strength, resilience, and wisdom to adapt to such a challenge. Entirely on your own merit, that is. But I'm pleased to know that you'll have Crissea's expert guidance and compassion along the way."

Having made the decision, Darak immediately set to work preparing the nanotech lattice in Stralasi's brain to receive the coming changes. He extended circuits deep into the motor and sensory cortices, and developed extensive new connections with the seat of cognition in the frontal neocortex. He instructed Stralasi's upgraded lattice to make alterations to the Good Brother's limbic system so he'd be able to properly coordinate his new, distributed awareness.

"I'll still be able to accompany Darian to the Alumitum, won't I?" Stralasi asked.

"Of course," Darak replied. "You'll be a little disoriented at first. That'll disappear with a few hours of practice.

"We'll leave your Familiar here until you have more time to adjust to one another. He'll be able to provide valuable analytical backup to you from here, while your human self tries to breach Alum's local CPPU with Darian.

"Oh, and your QUEECH comms are routed through another universe so they'll be undetectable, untraceable, and unblockable. Your two parts will remain in perfect communication the whole time. It won't be a problem."

Instinctively, Stralasi winced.

Now, why did he have to go and say it won't be a problem? Isn't there always a problem when someone says, it won't be a problem?

Never mind—he chided himself. *You want this and it's going to be great. For you, for Crissea, and for the Realm.*

Stralasi set aside his residual doubts and misgivings, and submitted to the preparations.

On the day of the official integration procedure, Stralasi sat on a comfortable chair in a small laboratory tucked deep inside Eso-La's research facilities. Crissea stood at his side, and took his clammy hand firmly in hers. Darak fiddled with some instruments next to the monk's would-be Familiar waiting patiently in its cradle.

My Familiar—Stralasi said to himself.

Hi, Familiar. You look familiar—he joked, and laughed quietly at his childish humor. His breath rattled with the effort required to suppress a nervous giggle.

Oh, good grief! Get a grip, Brother—he commanded himself.

He clutched Crissea's hand.

Today is the day I lose my humanity—he thought. *For the love of a woman of Eso-La, no less. Who would have believed it? Me, Ontro nem Stralasi, Brother of the Alumit, Steward of eight Founding worlds, future Representative of Gargus 718.5 in the Judgment of Alum's Divine Plan.*

I can hardly believe it, myself. It's not Crissea's fault; I brought it up. Mind you, I only half-meant it at the time. I mean, who but an Esu would take such an obviously flippant suggestion seriously?

Brother Stralasi felt suddenly exposed and self-conscious. A bead of cold sweat formed at his hairline. He hoped nobody could hear his mental babbling. He struggled to squelch the torrent of uncertainty that threatened to push him up out of his chair and send him screaming from the room.

He turned to Crissea and spoke more casually than he felt.

"So, tell me more about what it's like to see the world through two sets of eyes. What's it like, thinking with two completely different brains?"

"It's difficult to explain," Crissea replied. "We've lived like this for as long as I can remember. Our lattices have been configured in such a way that this is what it means to be human, for us. We're not complete without our Familiar selves. How do I explain how it feels to be distributed to someone who's never experienced it, especially when I've never really known anything else?"

Stralasi nodded.

"No, I suppose it's not something one could easily describe. I get that. But, for me, this isn't something I've grown up with."

He gestured at the Familiar with a wag of his chin.

"Nor it....uhh...him, for that matter. See? Even pronouns! I have so much to learn. It's going to be a steep learning curve."

Sensing the reference, the Familiar spoke up.

"They call me Nem, for now," it said, "as in, part of Ontro nem

Stralasi." "Once we're merged, the 'Nem' will be dropped. And, no, I don't anticipate much disruption in my self-identity, what little there is of it. I am *part* of you or, more like, I am an extension of you. I am you, and you are me."

That's so weird!—Stralasi thought. The voice sounded identical to his own, but with an electronic tone.

"Mostly you, anyway," Nem assured him.

"That's true," Crissea added. "Nem was created from a simpler representation of your own concepta and persona. He's only spent a few weeks inworld forming some of his own experiences and becoming a Full persona. The two of you should be able to merge seamlessly. You're practically identical twins already, mentally."

Stralasi frowned. "But not quite."

"No, not quite," Darak confirmed, without turning from his instruments.

Stralasi realized his mentor had been monitoring the conversation while comparing Human and Familiar conceptas for potential issues.

While simultaneously discussing battle plans with Darya and Darian, modeling how to disrupt the deplosion fields, designing a universe or two, and considering each of our travel routes.

Just how many ideas can Darak's extended brain deal with at a time? Has he ever encountered that limit?—Stralasi wondered.

What will my own limits be once I'm distributed? Double? More than double? My consciousness will be split across two perceptions. Two different kinds of brains with two different thought processes working together.

Will it be worth it, my love?

His eyes sought the answer to his silent question in Crissea's face.

Before the monk could glean an answer, Darak stood up from his instruments and joined the couple.

"All good. We're ready to begin," he said, and placed a reassuring hand on Stralasi's shoulder.

"Are you ready, Ontro?"

Ontro?—Stralasi's eyes widened. He wasn't used to Darak using his given name. *Trying to comfort the nervous patient with unaccustomed familiarity, are we, Darak?*

And that's when Stralasi realized—*This is all for show.*

He looked around the spartan lab: a few comfortable chairs, a harness for the Familiar so it wouldn't have to float during the merger, a bank of displays, and not much else. The real displays were virtual, the sensors and monitors hidden, the instruments that carried out the actual merger were either nanoscopic or pure software.

The technology here on Eso-La was more advanced than what he'd worked with in the Realm. Here, something that looked like a twig could either kill you with a deadly beam or heal you of a disease. Technological "magic" delivered by simple forms filled with invisible layers of complexity.

Stralasi nodded. "I'm ready."

Darak leaned toward the control panel beside him and pushed a button.

"Okay, here we go."

* * *

STRALASI HAD HALF A SECOND to realize that pushing the button was only symbolic.

And then he was drowning in confusion, seeing double, and losing consciousness while his world rearranged itself.

When he came to, the first thing he noticed was a new richness of vision.

Of course. The Familiar has full 360 degree sensors—he thought with his two minds.

It took a moment to merge the Familiar's perception with that of his own eyes, but he did it. It was like trying to force normal binocular fusion between his two human eyes when he was tired. The images blurred, aligned, and became one.

The Familiar viewed its surroundings in the full electromagnetic spectrum, from gamma rays and ultraviolet down through visible light, infrared, and into the microwave and radio wave sections. It was complex and beautiful.

Stralasi picked up residual emissions of the unprotected circuitry behind the panels at Darak's side. For the first time, he could see the explosion of colorful patterns in Crissea's skin and clothing.

Other perceptions flooded in.

His Familiar's auditory and olfactory sensors fed unfamiliar sounds and rich smells to Stralasi's lattice. He recognized the scent of Crissea's sweat and the slight increase in her heart rate that accompanied her anxiety. He felt the languid movement of air circulating in the lab.

With a little concentration, he extended his Familiar's tentacles, first the powerful manipulators and then the fine, delicate digits, all the way to their tips. He could sense the latent power in the manipulators, the strength of the Familiar's cerametallic carapace.

No propulsion—he noticed. *Ah, right, there'd be no need for it. Darak was equipping all the new Cybrids and Familiars with shifting capabilities.*

Stralasi's Familiar glided up from its harness as he shifted his robotic body smoothly and continuously against the pull of the floor. Part of him sensed—no, experienced—the movement. It felt like flying, only more controlled, more precise. He could as easily jump a hundred kilometers as a hundred microns!

SENSORIMOTOR INTEGRATION COMPLETE.

Darak's message appeared like writing in the air.

INITIATING PHASE TWO.

Phase two? Stralasi barely had time to form the question in his mind before the lab dissolved into a golden haze.

Two endless gray planes appeared, one above his virtual perspective and one below. A web of green and blue interconnected nodes grew brighter in each of the planes.

Conceptas!

Stralasi recognized the rich association networks, though he'd never experienced them from outside of his own thoughts.

He wandered between the two planes, awed by the schematic representation of everything he knew and believed.

And everything my young Familiar knows and believes, too.

There were many similarities, as well as some crucial differences.

His Familiar—*Nem*—had been raised from instantiation in Eso-La's Eterna inworld, free from indoctrination by the Alumit. Stralasi's own upbringing had been drenched in faith from before his birth. Prayers three-times a day, countless incantations to Alum for everyday services and products, and endless gratitude for every morsel of food, for community, and for all life.

Stralasi's universe had always been permeated with Alum's love. It was the force that bound everything together and made everything work. Alum's love produced light. His love powered electrical devices and made matter whole. It animated plants, animals, birds, insects, and microbes. It filled the skies with stars, suns, planets, and ringworlds. Alum's love was the basis of all existence.

Whereas Stralasi had learned that the universe and everything in it was a gift from Alum, Nem had learned how that universe actually worked.

Nem knew about physics, chemistry, biology, and math. He knew about elementary particles and energetic forces. He knew about the curvature of spacetime that represented the relentless pull of gravity. He knew about the expansion of the universe, how it was pushed by the spontaneous creation of new matter and pulled by the surrounding void, the Chaos.

Stralasi's religious worldview and Nem's scientific framework faced each other across a gap as wide as the chasm of empty space between worlds. The alignment of the two concept-networks on facing planes made the discrepancies all the more vivid.

Stralasi was at a loss as to how to proceed. Did he have to pick one or the other? Throw one away? If so, which one? Was there some way to reconcile them?

WOULD YOU LIKE HELP, ONTRO?

It was Darak again.

"I don't know where to begin!" Stralasi shouted into the void.

LOOK FOR CONSISTENCY—Darak replied.

LOOK FOR COMPLETENESS.

Stralasi examined both conceptas more closely.

In the one he thought of as his own, many links ended abruptly in question marks or looped back on themselves in closed, self-referential circles. Many ended at a node simply labeled "Alum," as if that were all the explanation one needed.

The concepts he associated with Nem's knowledge base were broader and deeper. Nem's conceptual frameworks ended in evidence, in memories of personal observation, or in documented observations by others, fortified by cross-referenced support.

Stralasi plucked at a few of the links and was rewarded with a deluge of detailed data.

At first, he was overwhelmed by the abundance of information. He selected a few links, followed them deeper, and soon found himself gaining greater and greater comprehension.

His deepest exploration ran up against a dead-end, an assumption of the elementary particles of nature and the laws that described how they interacted.

Interesting. He could see *what* was true, just not *why.*

The wealth of knowledge had been impressive to this point but even he, in the depth of his ignorance, could tell it was incomplete.

"Why does this branch end here? Is there nothing else?" he demanded. "Is this no more than a deeper kind of faith, a more elaborate belief system?"

THERE'S MORE, OR I COULD NOT DO WHAT I DO—Darak answered.

He revealed a few more layers, and glimpses of a deeper basis for why the universe was as it was.

Stralasi followed the new concepts a little further, enough to get the sense of what lay beneath reality. He could almost sense the path to godhood.

ENOUGH FOR NOW—Darak said, and he veiled the deeper layers from Stralasi as they had been at the start.

THIS IS FOR ANOTHER TIME.

YOU HAVE ENOUGH TO DECIDE WHO YOU WILL BECOME AND TO COMPLETE THE MERGING.

Stralasi could see it was true. There was a comforting certainty in the beliefs he'd grown up with. It was a certainty born of ease, of suppressing curiosity, and of mistaking doctrine for comprehension.

Not fully satisfied, Stralasi's curiosity pushed him to confront one final, uncomfortable question.

If Alum's love fills this universe, why does He yearn to destroy it?

And, just like that, his mind was made up. He knew the way forward.

"I choose to understand," he said.

He reached out with imaginary hands, drawing the opposing conceptas together, weaving a single, intricate fabric from the threads.

He left the memories of his human life intact but replaced blind belief with concrete knowledge.

The memories are important. I'll need a reference point to help me speak with sympathy and understanding to those still mired in blind faith. How can I bring truth if I forget who I once was, and if I can't see others for who they still are?

As fast as thought, the integration was complete. Ontro and Nem were no longer separate entities. The pair continued as a single, merged mind looking out on the universe from two places, one consciousness shared between two very different brains.

The Good Brother shifted his Familiar self closer to Crissea and gently extended a tentacle to grasp her hand.

"You were right," he said.

The sound came from his Familiar's external speaker.

"It is absolutely wonderful."

33

"AND WHY EXACTLY do you need all these items?" Brother Franzel asked as he looked down from behind his elevated desk.

The parishioner standing a good meter lower shifted nervously from foot to foot. He fiddled with the buttons on his sweater.

To Franzel, Head Brother of the moderately-sized city of Altuno on Hanji 1397.2, Jock Stillman didn't look properly intimidated, as might be expected of a supplicant submitting such an outrageous and unusual request. Rather, he suspiciously—and quite unacceptably—exuded so much energy and enthusiasm that he appeared to be fueled with an internal fire.

"Well, Brother Franzel, as I said, I want to construct an experiment to explore notions of retrocausality using photon entanglement in something I call the delayed-choice quantum eraser experiment. I suspect some sort of let's call it a guiding wave analysis will demonstrate non-locality of photonic wave functions."

Franzel stared blankly at Stillman. Individually, most of the words made sense but the Head Brother struggled to grasp the meaning of the complete utterance. That is, if there was any actual meaning and this Stillman character wasn't a babbling lunatic. It was hard to tell.

Sensing the Brother's lack of comprehension, Stillman pulled a tablet from his jacket pocket, activated it, and turned it around so the monk could read the display.

Franzel had taken the requisite fourth-year algebra class during seminary training at the Alumitum but he'd never really cared for the subject nor seen any use for it. And so it was with limited enthusiasm, and perhaps even a little resistance, that he glanced at the screen. Just as he expected, the indecipherable mathematical symbols and formulae that shimmered across the screen might as well have been written in ancient Greek.

Not at all daunted by Franzel's reluctance, Stillman scrolled down a few pages.

"Now, as you can see here, the Eigenvalue of the fourth-order tensor of the probability density function of the photon would predict…"

With one impatient sweep, Brother Franzel waved away the display, along with Stillman's gibberish. He wished it were that easy to wave away Jock Stillman and his request, entirely.

The Alumit had been flooded with many such strange proposals of late. Odd designs for new machinery or buildings, bizarre requisitions for materials Franzel didn't recognize, public works art projects of blatantly provocative intent, and so on. His office had been handling a veritable deluge of unexpected and, in his estimation, undesired creative excitement over the past few weeks.

He was determined to understand the source of all this.…*what would you call it?* He thought back to his seminary days.

What was the word for an unusual combination of existing things, for new methods, ideas, or products?

It was on the tip of his tongue.

Inno…something, wasn't it? Inno…machination? No, that wasn't it.

Ah, yes! Innovation! That's it. Innovation. Odd sounding word and an odder concept.

He had a flashback of a startled classmate being cut down by one of his Professors with that word. Innovation.

"Is Alum's way, the way of this ancient and venerable Alumit insufficient for you, Brother Toft?" the Professor had demanded. "Would you prefer something *new*, something *untested*? An *innovation*, perhaps?"

At that point, the Professor had had to divert valuable class minutes to explain what an innovation was, and the few occasions where one might safely innovate.

"Innovation is only acceptable for Frontier Alumstons, and only to be attempted by experienced Founding Brothers," the Professor had emphasized. "More established parts of the Realm have no need for such recklessness. Stick to doctrine, tried and true."

Franzel left his reverie and shuffled some files around on his desk display.

"Okay, so I understand the mirrors and the prisms, and the double slits are fairly obvious," he said. "Even the idea of this isolation table to separate your project from external vibrations. But I'm not certain what you mean by parametric down-conversion using this—what is it—beta barium borate nonlinear optical crystal."

"Oh, yes," Stillman interrupted excitedly. "That's at the heart of the experiment. It converts the photon that passes through either of the two slits into two identical, orthogonally polarized entangled photons with half the frequency of the original."

Franzel blinked at the man. He was doing it again, babbling words that sounded cogent but were nonsensical. The monk placed his stylus on his desktop and steepled his hands under his chin.

"Tell me, again, where you got the idea for this project."

"It's something I've been thinking about for a few days," Stillman answered. "I was on Community duty, tidying up the flower beds on Azores Street. I enjoy my time there so much, you know. I can let my mind wander for hours. Well, last week, I got to thinking about the dual nature of photons."

"Dual nature?"

"Wave and particle, of course," Stillman replied. "The basic double slit experiment illustrates nicely how light behaves as a wave, producing interference patterns on the detector screen until observation of the actual path traversed becomes determined, at which point the photons adopt particle-like travel and the interference pattern disappears."

Franzel shook his head to clear it and blinked a few times.

"Go on," he invited.

"Well, I'm sure you know the debate around whether or not a conscious observer is required to collapse the wave function."

"There's a debate?"

"Yes. We wonder whether the rest of the matter of the universe plays the role of the observer or if an actual conscious human is required to make the observation. Of course, there are those who believe that Alum Himself plays the role of universal observer, or perhaps Yov."

"I was not aware this was a topic of active debate."

"Oh, much of it was historic. But several of us have met over tea. Yes," Stillman chuckled, "those discussions can get quite vigorous at times.

"But I digress. Where was I?" Stillman consulted his tablet. "Ah, yes, here we go. I have a reference for you here...somewhere." He scrolled down through the display, searching.

At that moment, a soft chime emanated from the Head Brother's desk. He looked down and opened the message from his secretary. Before he got past the word "Shard," the door to his private office burst open and an imposing man wearing the official robes of a Shard of Alum walked in.

Franzel sprung to his feet.

"Shard Martinez!"

Altuno wasn't so far from Home World that visits by Shards were rare but usually Franzel received advance notice when one of the holy men was due to arrive. There were protocols to be observed to ensure a level of piety befitting such a large and important center.

Stillman turned to see the source of the interruption. Satisfied it wasn't relevant to his immediate discussion, his attention returned to his search.

"Kneel, fool!" Brother Franzel hissed back, over his shoulder, as he crossed the remaining steps to Shard Martinez.

"My Lord, Shard!" he greeted the waiting figure.

The Head Brother knelt in front of Alum's representative and kissed the casually proffered hand.

"To what do we owe this wonderful surprise? Please, come and sit. Take my chair, if you please, my Lord."

He glared at Stillman, who glanced up briefly and nodded a greeting to the Shard.

As if he were one of the High Holy, himself!

Brother Franzel could not contain his anger.

"Kneel, I said!" he shouted at the man, as Shard Martinez took a seat behind the raised desk. "Have you no idea who sits before you? Alum will curse your impudence with His holy vengeance. Do you not fear for your life? For your very soul, man?"

"Let it be, brother," Shard Martinez counseled in an unusually calm, unperturbed, hardly more than casual conversational voice.

Franzel's head whipped back around and his jaw dropped in astonishment.

The Shard's gentle smile was filled with forbearance. His hands patted the air in front of him.

"We can discuss Alum's indignation some other time," he said. "For now, I believe Mr. Stillman was describing his proposed...experiment."

The word slid smoothly from the Shard's lips, and yet it took on the sound of some vile bit of profanity.

"Thank you, Shard Martinez," Stillman replied comfortably, as if he talked with Alum's representatives every day. "Perhaps the idea will be a bit easier for you to follow. I mean, one so highly advanced as yourself."

He reviewed the basic points of the proposal while the Shard listened intently, eyes closed, hands comfortably folded on the desk.

Brother Franzel listened patiently to the entire spiel again, hoping to understand it better on the second pass. He didn't. After another fifteen minutes of Stillman's nonsense, Franzel felt no further enlightened than he had at the beginning.

The Head Brother addressed the Shard, "As you see, my Lord, it's impossible to decide upon the merits of this proposal. It doesn't make sense. I can't tell—"

The Shard held up a hand, interrupting the Brother's denunciation.

"Your request is approved," he said.

He smiled at Stillman. "Naturally, you will keep the Alumit apprised of the results."

"Naturally, sir," Stillman answered.

"But, my Lord," Franzel protested, "what of the others? There are hundreds, no, thousands of such insane proposals on my desk."

The Shard peered intently at the Head Brother.

Franzel felt a tingle at the back of his head that told him the Shard had accessed the monk's lattice, and was now examining his memories and roaming freely through his thoughts.

"Thousands, you say?" The Shard sat back pensively, his mind still deeply immersed in the Head Brother's concepta.

"So I see. A fascinating assortment, too. A veritable explosion of creative thinking, isn't it? What do you think, Brother? What is the cause of this sudden renaissance?"

Brother Franzel didn't recognize the word.

"I beg your pardon, my Lord?"

"This renaissance," the Shard repeated. "In Alum's name! Don't they teach you anything in Seminary? This rebirth of so many fresh ideas? All this...innovation. Yes, I see you recognize that word. Where do you think it all comes from?"

"I...I have no idea, my Lord," Franzel stammered. "Mr. Stillman says the ideas just came to him while he was tending flower beds." He let his voice trail off inconclusively.

The Shard turned his intense stare onto Stillman.

"Just came to you, did they?"

Brother Franzel registered relief when the tingling of his scalp abruptly ceased.

Stillman absent mindedly scratched the back of his head.

"Hmm. What's this?" Shard Martinez asked to no one in particular. "Mr. Stillman, have you had any unusual visitors in the past month?"

"No, sir," Stillman answered.

"No, *my Lord*," Franzel corrected. The man's impudence was as annoying as his ridiculously incomprehensible proposal.

Stillman paid him no heed.

"Nothing unusual that I recall, sir. Why?"

"Interesting," the Shard replied. "Perhaps you'd be so kind as to permit me to scan your concepta. Your security is of a type I don't readily recognize."

Franzel was astonished. *What in Alum's name is going on?*

"Shall I call the local Guardian Angels, my Lord?" he inquired.

Shard Martinez declined the offer. "No need."

"But, if he's acquired non-Standard lattice security, my Lord..?"

"What of it?"

"Alum must be informed, my Lord."

The Shard scoffed at the Head Brother.

"*I'm* here, am I not?"

Franzel blinked. "Of course, my Lord. My apologies." He took a deep breath and tried to explain. "It merely surprised me that a simple parishioner would have lattice security that my Lord couldn't override."

The Shard narrowed his eyes at the reckless comment.

"Given a little time, I'm certain I could push my way into Mr. Stillman's thoughts," he assured the monk. "But we are all friends and citizens of the Realm, here, are we not, Mr. Stillman?"

Stillman nodded enthusiastically.

"Yes, sir," he confirmed.

"Of course," the Shard continued. "No need for distrustful hostility, then, is there?" The question was directed at Stillman as much as the Head Brother.

"Not at all," Stillman answered. "Honestly, I wasn't even aware of any changes in my lattice security. Certainly, it was nothing I did." He concentrated for a second or two. "Ah, there!" He dropped his hands to his side, palms forward. "Please, feel free...my Lord."

The Shard was already in; his mind ran through Stillman's thoughts and memories.

"Fascinating," was all that the Shard said after several seconds. He closed his eyes, sat back in his chair, and said nothing for a full minute.

Both men jumped when the Shard's eyes sprang open in alarm and a single, drawn-out, "Ahhhhh," escaped with his next exhalation.

"So many wonders," he exclaimed. An amazed smile and look of youthful wonderment had transformed his face.

Shard Martinez rose from the Head Brother's chair.

"I must go, now," he said and strode across the office with a sense of purpose. With one hand on the doorframe, he turned back and addressed a final order to Franzel.

"Approve all such projects," he said, "Previous and future proposals. On my authority."

The Shard Martinez exited, leaving a stunned Head Brother and a content parishioner behind him.

34

BROTHER STRALASI AND DARIAN LEIGH SHIFTED into position near the end of the lineup outside the recruiting office of a local Alumita in the fifteenth sector of Darbiness. They were back in the Milky Way, on the galaxy's second largest ringworld and headed for Vesta, home of the Alumitum.

Out the corner of his eye, Stralasi caught Darian fidgeting.

"Quit fussing with your face," the monk snapped.

"It feels strange," Darian whispered back. "Are you sure everything's okay?"

Stralasi sighed for the hundredth time in two days and rolled his eyes.

I thought the Gods would be more mentally agile than the rest of us—he muttered under his breath.

"It's fine; just like it was before we jumped," he replied, keeping his voice low. It wouldn't be good to draw unnecessary attention from the excited novitiates ten steps ahead.

"The surgery was necessary; everyone in the Alumitum knows Trillian's face," he reminded Darian. "Without this precaution, we wouldn't have taken more than two steps before crowds started gathering."

Stralasi recalled the stir Darak had created on Gargus 718.5 when everyone thought he was one of Alum's Shards come to pay an unofficial visit. *How long ago was that?*

He tried to remember what it had felt like to be that Founding Brother, the Principal Local Authority of the founding Alumston. It couldn't have been more than a Standard year ago and yet he felt centuries removed from the simple, pious but officious monk he'd been then.

Since leaving his Alumston, he'd traveled a good part of the Realm in the company of a God, learned about Cybrids, learned about the religio-economic system that made life in the Realm so good for so many, learned about science, spoken with alien Gods, witnessed Darak in space battle with Angels, survived the supernova explosion of the mythical Tri-Star system, met the love of his life on a rebellious ringworld in the heart of the Local Void, and planned battles with Cybrids and Aelu.

And, now, I've become Esu myself. He shook his head in wonder.

His attention kept shifting back and forth between his human part on Darbiness, that part of him walking at the back of an eager band of new initiates to the Alumit, and his Familiar, who was currently hovering silently in Crissea's garden on Eso-La.

He didn't dare try to keep up two conversations at once yet, so his Familiar part remained blessedly silent in Crissea's worried company.

Soon, she'll have to leave to go to battle around the Deplosion Array—he realized.

He fought against his protective instincts, and resisted trying to convince her to stay at home.

Crissea's stronger than I'd like to admit—he knew that. *It would be an insult to ask her not to join the battle. How could a woman like that, a leader of her people, simply sit in her garden and wait for the universe to fall apart?*

His eyes scanned the line of new Alumit recruits ahead of him and his hand reached for the tablet in his front pocket. The orders were for two experienced monks, Ontro Stralasi and John Darian, to teach a semester on the Alumitum.

These forged orders are impeccable. Why would anyone have cause to doubt them?

"Foundations of New Colonization: Spiritual Pragmatics, 315," was the name of the course. It had been Stralasi's specialty. If something went wrong, if they were forced to live up to their cover story, he was confident he could deliver the material well enough.

But let's hope no one checks up on us—he thought.

The plan was to take a few days scouting an approach route to Alum's local CPPU node, the one connected by the vulnerable QUEECH comm device. Darian said he was familiar with that node through Trillian's biological memories; it was located on the top floor of a building that was once called Vesta One, the tallest in the habitat.

The building had been demolished and rebuilt countless times in the millions of years since Vesta was nothing more than a simple asteroid habitat.

The current manifestation was the heart of Alumit Administration. The top floor housed the offices of the Proctor of the Alumitum. It was a lofty office, both literally and figuratively. Proctor of the teaching college for the entire Church of Alum was the highest attainable rank for any human. Any *normal* human.

One or more Shards of Alum met with the Proctor on a regular basis to ensure the teaching programs were correctly aligned with core doctrine.

A Council of Shards loosely presided over the Alumita, and the Council took their instructions directly from Alum, Himself. Unlike the ancient religious councils of Earth/Origin, present day Alumita had no need for interpreters of God's pronouncements. Anyone of suitable rank could simply ask Him to clarify His words.

Because of the constant traffic of various holy representatives of the Living God, it was only fitting that the Alumit Administration be guarded by its own contingent of Angels.

There's no way we'll be able to waltz in and be whisked up to the Proctor's Office—Stralasi fretted. His consternation slipped out as an audible grunt.

The young novice immediately in front of him turned at the sound. His eyes widened to see that two ordained Brothers had joined the small procession behind him.

"Brothers," the young man beamed, "are you joining us?"

Darian hid his scowl behind a raised hand.

Stralasi put on his most open smile and nodded.

"Indeed, young man," he replied. "We'll be teaching Pragmatics 315 this semester. If you're interested in specializing in Founding worlds, you should drop in for a lecture."

Hopefully, we'll be done before I'm actually called on to teach—he thought.

He realized that he'd just informed anyone within earshot about a course he had no intention in delivering. He had a sudden desire to retract his invitation.

"But that would be a harsh life for one raised so close to Home World," he said. "There are countless more suitable appointments for one like yourself, no doubt."

The novitiate perused the line of fifty other young men ahead of him. His brow furrowed a little.

"Well, I hadn't really thought about that. Competition for good posts will be tough."

His face lit up with hope. "Maybe I'll drop in and see what it's about."

"The course is intended for third-years. Maybe it would be better if you wait a semester or two," Stralasi suggested.

"Yes," Darian growled. "Some might view a freshman in class as disruptive. We have the juniors and seniors to consider, Good Brother."

Stralasi tried to look appropriately remorseful, as one who'd overstepped his bounds.

Caught in the crossfire of an uncomfortable exchange, the young novice lowered his eyes and turned back to the line ahead of him.

"A little less enthusiasm for our fake job, Brother," Darian reminded Stralasi.

Suitably chagrined, the Good Brother shrugged.

"Sorry," he whispered. "Teaching at the Alumitum was always a dream of mine. I got caught up in the moment."

They moved forward a few steps.

"If only we'd been able to shift to our target directly," Stralasi suggested.

"Impossible!" Darian said, a little too loudly.

The same curious young novice turned around.

Darian met his stare with an intensity that returned the naïve young student's countenance full ahead with no desire to look back again, and lowered his voice to a secretive hush that slipped from the side of his mouth.

"You know a direct shift to the Alumitum, not to mention right into the Vesta One tower, would be too easily detected. Unless, that is, you want to bring the full might of Alum upon us. Personally, I'd rather not confront him directly. No, without other diversions to count on, we'll have to arrive with this group via normal starstep."

Stralasi grimaced.

"You know, it's ironic. For most of my life, Alum has had my implicit trust. But over this past year, I've gotten used to traveling with Darak. I've put my life in his hands more times than I can count, and he's never let me down. It's hard to go back to pretending I'm still the monk I once was. It's hard to trust *this* system, now."

"I'm sure the system will work as designed," Darian said. "There'll be the usual scans for biological compatibility and such, not much else. That's why we chose to start here on the Darbiness ringworld. It's a Realm-Standard environment, like the Alumitum. The scans will be superficial and quick."

Stralasi fidgeted.

"They won't detect your lattice changes," Darian assured him. "Nor your QUEECH connection to your Familiar."

Stralasi's eyes shot to Darian's face.

Darian laughed. "Nor my recent nano-surgery, nor my...er...recently-enhanced intellectual status."

"Shhh! You can't talk about that here! Good grief. I'd almost feel better about a straight-up confrontation," Stralasi said. "At least that way I'd know my death would come quickly."

Darian gave Stralasi a comforting smile and squeezed his shoulder.

"We have a few days to poke around before classes start. Let's see if we can figure out a plan."

"I don't think I'm built for this kind of covert activity."

"Even you can pretend to be a tourist for a few days."

"A tourist?" Stralasi snorted, "on Alumitum?"

"Okay, a visiting scholar?"

"I thought we'd agreed on the roles of professors."

"We did. That'll be enough to get us into common areas like the Lecture complex or the Library. Maybe we can invent some kind of bureaucratic snag to justify a visit to the Alumit Administration."

"Not the Proctor's Office!" Stralasi was horrified by the idea.

"No, I don't think so," Darian answered. "That probably isn't required. Anyway, Alum's CPPU is one floor higher."

Another surprise.

"The Proctor's Office *isn't* the top floor?"

"No, too much casual traffic. Too high a chance that humans and maintenance Cybrids might bump into each other. Alum prefers a little more privacy. For His physical substrate if nothing else. Secrecy is excellent security. Having everyone believe there's nothing above the Proctor's Office but the machine room has its advantages."

"How will we gain access?"

Darian frowned.

"I don't know that yet."

The line advanced a few more steps. The street opened into a plaza with a monk standing at a starstep prayer podium.

Darian lowered his voice further.

"Have faith, Brother," he said to the monk. "We'll figure out something."

* * *

STRALASI AND DARIAN MATERIALIZED along with the rest of their cohort, at a small plaza in the far south end of the ancient Vesta One habitat tunnel.

With under a hundred in their group, they'd been sent to one of the more remote starstep stations serving the Alumitum campus. From there, they had to walk an hour to get to their assigned quarters.

The path wound pleasantly through a narrow park, beside a slow-moving longitudinal stream that led into the heart of the city. As they approached the midpoint of the habitat tunnel, the spires of educational and administration centers rose above the lower residential and commercial towers.

The Alumitum Administration stood twice as tall as any of the other towers. It was a proud beacon that drew all eyes including their own to the geographical heart of the habitat. Though the spiritual heart was located tens of thousands of light years away in Alum's Hall in the Origin system, this was indisputably the educational heart of Alum's Realm.

The Vesta asteroid had been moved, ages ago, closer to the middle of the Milky Way galaxy, and nearer to the Home World system and its larger population centers. The population density had been conscientiously reduced over the ages, befitting a campus world. Each of the six habitat tunnels now comfortably housed a population of three million. Roughly a million of those were students following a blessed calling to serve the Alumit. The remainder was made up of instructors, administrators, and support staff who for the most part lived permanently on the Alumitum.

Teaching the next generation of Brothers and administering a Church which spanned over a hundred million light years necessitated the largest bureaucracy in human history. And, every year, that Church bureaucracy grew a carefully-planned four percent larger—just like the Realm itself— ensuring new opportunities for its ambitious young novices.

Also every year, Alum, the distributed Living God that governed all within the Realm, grew by the same amount.

Though Stralasi had spent six years here studying, that was many years ago and it now felt oddly foreign to him. Whether it was because of the intervening years since his graduate work or because of the ominous threat posed by the God he once worshipped, the God he'd learned to represent in the lecture halls of this very city, the Good Brother couldn't tell.

The monk who led their group along the path beside the stream chatted in an incessant drone that matched the languid flow of the water.

He recited mundane facts about the habitat tunnel and its population. He provided names for the towers in the distance. As they left the single-family residential area and walked into a region of low apartment buildings, he introduced the newcomers to the way everyday life worked in the Alumitum.

"Your day begins with thirty minutes of prayers for Lauds at 6:00 am, Standard Time, followed by breakfast in your local cafeteria until 7:30. Morning classes start at 8:00 sharp and they run until the Midday prayers at noon. There will be a midmorning break after the first class for Terce prayers at 9:30, followed by thirty-minutes of private meditation and more classes. Lunch is from 1:00 pm and classes resume an hour later. Mid-afternoon prayers are at 3:30 and the final class follows until Vespers at 6:00 pm. Your evening meal is served until 7:30, followed by studies, until Compline at 9:30 pm, and back to studies and meditation until the Matins reading at midnight. Then, off to bed until we begin again the next morning."

To Darian's amusement, Stralasi silently mouthed the recitation from the back of the line. When the Good Brother noticed his companion's smirk, he gave Darian a brief glare and returned his attention to the lead monk's tour.

How many times have I heard this schedule over the years?—he wondered. Twice a year for four years, and again with every new Brother that had ever been assigned to one of his Founding Alumitas.

Hundreds of times—he reckoned. *Maybe thousands.*

The cadence was familiar, comforting. It felt like home.

It reminded him of the life of certainty he'd led for hundreds of years before Darak showed up on Gargus 718.5 and lured him away to adventure.

Though he now knew praying to Alum was like asking the wind for guidance and forgiveness, he found it hard to break old habits.

"On Saturday," the monk resumed, "you will contribute to upkeep of the college grounds from 8:00 am until dinner at 6:00 pm. Saturday evenings are reserved for individual studies, meditation, and prayer. On Sunday, following Church service at 9:00 am, the rest of the day is yours. Relax. Enjoy the amenities of the city—in moderation of course."

The caveat received the expected groans and chuckles.

"The school week begins anew with Matins, Sunday at midnight."

The carefully-timed lecture ended as they approached the Housing Assignment Office.

"Ah, here we are."

Groups that had arrived earlier were already dispersing.

The monk climbed the first few stairs and motioned for his group to gather closer.

"If you consult your tablets, you will see your class schedules and assigned residences. Maps of the freshman campus area will have been downloaded as well. Simply follow their guidance to your assigned building."

Around the corner of the building, Stralasi heard another group arriving and their guide launching into the exact same spiel.

"If you have any questions or concerns, or if you'd prefer reassignment to a different residence or roommate," their guide looked sternly at his charges, "I would urge you to consider the nature of your calling and pray on the matter until the next morning."

It was not uncommon for two initiates who were close friends to prefer to room together but requests for reassignment did not reflect the necessary forbearance required of the Alumit and were, without exception, frowned upon.

The tour leader scanned the faces below for any sign of a problem.

"Any questions?"

Darian's hand shot up.

Of course—Stralasi groaned and edged away.

The guide pointed at the outstretched hand clad in monk's robes.

"Yes, Brother...er?"

"Darian," Stralasi's co-conspirator called out. "John Darian. Brother Stralasi and I don't seem to have any assigned quarters."

The guide waved Darian forward. A few of the initiates wandered off, their fingers tracing out the routes to their assigned residences on their tablets. Some hung back, curious about the Brothers with no room, or waiting their turns to ask questions.

The guide consulted his tablet.

"I don't see your names anywhere on my list," he said. "I was only expecting novitiates today."

"Our orders came late last night," Darian lied. "They were unexpected and gave us little time to prepare."

"Still, you could have informed me," the guide said, clearly annoyed.

"Our apologies, Brother," Stralasi jumped in. "We didn't know which starstep we'd be taking until minutes before our departure."

The man's eyes flicked between the two troublesome Brothers.

"Let me see your orders," he said.

Darak held out his tablet and swiped it to send a copy to the irritated monk. "Yes, of course. Right here, Brother...? How may I call you?"

"Astram," the man replied. He looked down at his own tablet, flipping through Darian's and Stralasi's counterfeit letter.

"Everything appears to be in order."

He closed the letter, opened a connection to the Residential administration program, and poked around a bit.

"Hmmm. That's odd. Nothing here. I wonder who was originally assigned to the course."

He opened another tab and queried Registration.

"Ah," he said. "Here's the problem. Your course isn't in the schedule for this semester."

Stralasi stood silently, genuinely dumbfounded.

What do I do now?—he wondered.

Darian stepped in smoothly.

"Yet our orders clearly tell us to report here, today." He smiled innocently.

Brother Astram stared skeptically at the two of them, not masking his annoyance at being presented with this irregularity.

"Very well. I can put you up in the Residence Hotel over the weekend.

I suggest you visit Alumitum Administration first thing on Monday morning and straighten this out."

He wrote a quick note to the Registrar's Office for them, setting up an early morning appointment. Next, he booked them a room at the Vesta One Campus Inn.

"Any other questions?" he huffed. Without waiting for a response, he brusquely departed for the Housing Assignment building.

Stralasi noted Darian's impish grin.

"I thought our orders would appear legitimate."

Darian's grin grew broader and more mischievous.

"There are limits to what one can do from hundreds of light years away. The letter was sufficiently convincing to get us this far. We have a room for tonight and tomorrow. That will give us some time to shore up appearances and scout the neighborhood around the Alumitum Administration. On Monday, we'll be inside the building. I'd say the day has been quite a success so far."

Stralasi consulted his tablet and pointed off to the right.

"I believe our hotel is this way."

35

"THIS FEELS CRIMINAL," Stralasi whispered.

"We need to keep up the appearance that we intend to be here for the full semester," Darian replied. "You know that."

"An unholy waste of time, effort, and resources," Stralasi persisted, as if he hadn't heard. "Worse than criminal, it's a sacrilege."

"It's all part of the disguise, Brother," Darian reminded him. "Justified by necessity and as righteous as anything else they do here in the Alumitum."

The pair had spent the better part of Saturday and Sunday traipsing around the city in search of food and clothing. Shopping, they agreed, was exhausting.

When they couldn't bear another minute, they took a break at a café a few blocks from the Administration tower and settled into a comfortable quiet between them. Only once they cradled steaming cups of strong brew did Darian open conversation along a more agreeable line.

"Did you have a nice visit with Crissea?"

"I'd rather have been there in person," Stralasi mumbled.

He didn't mean to complain. He was grateful for his newfound ability to shift his attention to his Familiar self on distant Eso-La while his human self was shuttered away in the lackluster Vesta One Inn with Darian. But physical contact through the senses of his Familiar was not an entirely satisfying replacement for his own biological presence.

"Naturally," Darian answered. "But you *are* there in person. Just not in...*human*."

Stralasi was not amused.

"Well, it feels *inhuman*," he replied, picking up on Darian's pun, "to be separated from myself this way. I kept finding myself wanting to reach out and touch her with a hand, only to brush against empty air. Or worse, one of my tentacles would slip out to stroke her hair. I didn't realize that that just isn't done. Did you know that Familiar manipulators are only for work or defense, not intimacy?"

"Uh-huh. Yeah," Darian replied.

The monk shot him an accusatory look. "You're not even listening."

"Hmm? Yes, of course, I am. Mostly," Darian admitted.

"And what exactly is it captivating your attention?" Stralasi asked. "It's not like there's much to do until tomorrow morning."

"On the contrary, Brother," Darian replied. "I've been exceedingly busy. First, some good news. Last night, I was able to penetrate security in the Registrar's Office. Our course is now showing on the official schedule."

"How did you manage that?"

"Fortunately the rooms at the Inn have InterLat interfaces. It took most of the night and some careful investigation, but I found a pathway into the Registrar's system."

"You weren't worried about tripping any alarms?"

"Sure, I was," Darian answered. "For some reason, the security was extraordinarily tight for an institute of religious learning."

He chuckled. "You know, in my youth, it wasn't uncommon for students to bypass class and exam requirements and hack into the computers that assigned grades. I have to say, though, I really didn't expect that to be the case here in the Alumit."

"Being in the Brotherhood brings prestige as well as responsibility," Stralasi said. "Sometimes that can distort one's moral compass."

"I guess," Darian replied. "Anyway, the tight security is why it took so long."

"I can see how your whole not-sleeping thing comes in handy."

"Your Familiar part doesn't need sleep either," Darian pointed out.

"Well, I'm not quite used to that yet."

"You mean you really haven't tried to get used to it."

Instead of answering, Stralasi took a sip of his latte.

I've had better coffee on the Frontier—he thought. *You'd think the center of the Alumit could get a simple cup of coffee nearly perfect.*

He felt a twinge of guilt for criticizing the organization in which he'd spent most of his life. He caught himself and then felt guilty for feeling guilty.

My allegiances are no longer here—he reminded himself.

Stralasi hated to admit that Darian had been right. He was having trouble adjusting to splitting his consciousness between two beings. Two worlds. Two galaxies.

"It's hard, coordinating thoughts and bodies," he confessed to his traveling companion.

"It can be, at first. Think of it like...coordinating your hands when playing the piano," Darian suggested. "With a little practice, it can be learned."

"I hope I learn this faster than the piano!" Stralasi joked. "That took forever."

Darian peered at him without comment for uncomfortable seconds. "When we have a moment, I'll help you," he offered.

Stralasi's eyes squinted suspiciously.

"What do you mean, *help*? Help me what?"

"I won't risk it here and now," Darian replied. "But we can work on adjusting the troublesome bits of your concepta directly. It's a simple fine-tuning problem, really. We have hundreds of billions of Esu conceptas as successful examples. It shouldn't be hard to adapt the correct structures.

"I wonder whether the Familiar part also finds it difficult to adjust to split consciousness?" His gaze drifted to the cottony clouds banking to the south, and he was uncharacteristically silent for a good while.

Stralasi coughed and Darian's attention snapped back to ground level.

"So, our course is now official?" the Good Brother prompted.

"Huh? Oh, yes, right. It's officially on the books. And the Registrar's Office no longer needs to see us in the morning. We have a free hour."

"How is that good?" Stralasi asked. "How are we going to get inside the Alumitum Administration if we have nothing to straighten out with Admin?"

"The Registrar's Office no longer needs to see us," Darian repeated, "but somehow our appointment did not get cancelled with Reception." He flashed a most unconvincing look of innocence at the monk.

"Hurray for bureaucratic inefficiency?" the monk asked.

"Don't worry. No one who works in the Alumit Administration will be blamed. It's just a minor system glitch that left a little packet of information wandering in a loop."

Stralasi's raised eyebrow drew a guilty grin out of his companion.

"Okay, I may have rewritten the packet header," Darian confessed, "but I promise I'll restore it once we're done and the request to cancel the appointment will eventually reach the Front Desk."

Stralasi shook his head. "It's good they no longer teach such things in school."

"It's an old skill and not particularly useful for legal activities," Darian agreed. "So, yeah, it's probably just as well that it's not widely distributed in this kind of society."

Stralasi raised a toast to him with his coffee cup, and drained the now cold latte in one gulp.

* * *

FORTIFIED BY A GOOD NIGHT'S REST, Darian and Stralasi strolled toward the Alumit Administration building. The Good Brother clutched his tablet holding the letter confirming their morning appointment as tightly to his chest as if it were the Holy Wooden Staff itself.

Darian kept up a steady patter as they crossed the cheerful, welcoming plaza leading to the imposing main entrance and the pair of three-meter tall Angels that kept guard.

"There's no good reason Angels are needed for security. Alum Himself could dedicate a tiny portion of His own resources to His own protection. But, I have to say, they do make an impressive reminder of Alum's might. These two alone could destroy this entire asteroid with barely a thought. Do you realize that the concentrated might of ten of them could make the local sun go nova?"

He paused and placed a hand lightly on the monk's sleeve. A boyish twinkle lit up his eyes.

"I wonder what they think about all day, standing there like that. It reminds me of a time when men stood guard for hours in front of palace entrances. They weren't quite as beautifully terrifying as Angels. In fact, they were fairly normal members of the military, specially selected and trained to endure the long hours and curious gawking by tourists without moving a muscle. An amazing feat for a human. Next to nothing for a construct like an Angel."

The two visitors continued their approach with an air of casual but respectful formality.

"Interesting," Darian remarked.

"What's interesting?" Stralasi whispered. He daubed a bead of sweat from his forehead.

"Well, you can't sense it, of course. When Darak elevated us to Gods, he installed RAF sensors and generators equal to his own."

"Are you insane, man? I told you, we can't talk about those things here!" Stralasi warned.

"Oh. Right. Anyway, the sensors allow us to directly taste—no, it's more like...see? No, that's not right, either. I'm not sure what the nearest analogous sense would be—detect, in any case. The sensors allow us to detect quantum fields directly."

He pointed at one of the Angels.

Stralasi slapped Darian's hand downward, not at all gently, and pinned it to the man's side. The bug-eyed glare accompanying the slap was redundant.

Darian ignored the reprimand and continued, "Look at that fluid motion of their mercurial skin. As well as being visually striking, the effect has defensive benefits. Achieving such an effect would have to involve a fascinating, continuous alteration of underlying local physics. What do you want to bet they have no idea of the subcutaneous generators responsible for the motion?"

"Seriously, Darian, are you trying to give me a stroke?" the monk hissed.

Darian continued to stare at the Angels as they drew closer to the door. "These creatures are a marvel of real and non-real engineering," he said. "I need to do a deeper analysis as soon as our business here is over."

"Shush!" Stralasi whispered. "They'll hear you. Eyes ahead. Straighten up."

But Darian's rapt gaze kept drifting back to the Angels. He couldn't look away from their spellbinding skin, their wings, their swords, their faces.

"Can I help you, Brother?"

The voice floated like resplendent music from the Angel on the right, who smiled down on the two men passing between him and his companion.

The second Angel turned his head to assess the object of attention.

"Kneel," Stralasi instructed Darian, barely audibly. He prayed the man heard and complied. Without waiting to confirm, the monk dropped to his knees before the beauty and horror of the Angel's curious eyes.

Darian followed suit, and the Angel's hands relaxed at his side.

Thank Goodness! They're not going for their swords. Yet.

Stralasi forced himself to relax. He was well aware that if the guards sensed any threat, as unthinkable as that would be here in the heart of the Alumit, the perceived source of consternation—in this case, himself and Darian—would be promptly dispatched with Angelic speed, grace, and no warning.

"A million pardons, my Lord!" Stralasi crooned. "My friend has been too long on the Frontier, I fear. His manners need refreshing in the glorious arms of Alum's Grace that permeates the holy Alumitum."

"State your business here," the voice responded. It was filled with such mellifluous tones it caused one to forget that sudden death potentially lurked not far behind.

Stralasi kept his head bowed and awkwardly held up the tablet.

"An appointment to clear up a small scheduling matter, my Lord," he said. He didn't bother turning the tablet so the Angel could see. Surely, beings that represented Alum's fearful power could scan tablets like his directly. Realm technology held no secrets from any who served Alum.

The Angel scanned the tablet and cross-referenced with Reception.

"You are late," he said.

Stralasi scrambled for a response to mollify the Angels' displeasure.

"My friend is easily distracted by the wonders of the city, my Lord," he offered.

It's a good story—he thought. *I might as well stick to it.*

His companion kept quiet, letting Stralasi's experience guide them and keep them safe.

"Be on your way, then," the Angel commanded and resumed his impassive guard pose. As the two monks got back on their feet, he made a point of catching Stralasi's eye.

"You would do well to remember your manners. The Frontier may be far away, but we are all part of the Realm. We should be no less civilized out there than here on Home World."

Darian bowed his head. "I will try, my Lord," he said.

Stralasi caught the impudent smirk on Darian's lips. Without daring a look to see if the Angel had caught it as well, the Good Brother tightly gripped his companion's arm and pulled him into the lobby.

"You almost got us killed," Stralasi reprimanded his partner as they stumbled toward the reception counter.

"I was in their heads," Darian said out the side of his mouth. "I could have made them turn back and forget all about us."

"Not without alerting Alum," Stralasi replied, his harsh whisper verging on panic.

"Calm yourself, Brother," Darian replied softly, imitating Darak's voice and intonation.

Too incensed to form a coherent reply, Stralasi could only gawp.

Darian returned the Good Brother's stare kindly, defusing the ire with a patient smile.

Stralasi blinked slowly and shifted his attention back to his Familiar self in Crissea's garden on Eso-La. He felt the cool flood of machine logic wash over his mind. Settled and refreshed, he took a deep breath and returned his mind to the lobby and to Darian.

"Better?" Darian asked.

Stralasi set his lips firmly and nodded once.

"Very well. Let's see about our appointment."

They presented their credentials and orders to Reception and were directed to an office on the twentieth floor. They made their way to the elevators and joined a half-dozen robed monks gathered there ahead of them.

The elevator doors opened and four monks entered. Stralasi moved forward but Darian held him back and indicated to the monks that they'd catch the next one.

As they waited with the other two Brothers, Darian turned to Stralasi and spoke in a loud and overly animated voice.

"Oh, Brother," he gushed, "I do hope the Proctor approves this new course. I've always wanted to apply a little creative writing to the Standard prayers. Now, don't get me wrong. I love the comfort of something tried and true. Don't you? And the current guidebook is filled with wonderful devotions."

The elevator doors whisked open, and the two monks ahead of them stepped forward. Darian followed them onto the elevator and maneuvered Stralasi into the corner farthest from the panel of buttons.

When the Good Brother reached out to push the button for their floor, Darian deftly blocked his arm. The doors whisked shut.

Darian shook his head once; the motion was hardly detectable, more of a twitch, really, but Stralasi caught it and relaxed back into the corner.

The newly-minted man-God renewed his patter.

"But, you know, the Brothers no longer seem to be pouring all of their hearts and souls into the Standard litany. Sometimes they flag a little, and the starstep wavers with Alum's displeasure. This can't be good. I truly believe a little variety will help everyone put a bit more zest into their voices."

The elevator zoomed past the twentieth floor without slowing and continued toward the top floor, the only light active on the panel. One of the other two monks looked at Darian and they exchanged polite nods.

"It's not an easy thing, to construct a novel prayer that would be pleasing to the Living God. We'll have to study the structure of the great prayers, of course. There's opening, middle, and closing invocations. There's cadence, tone, pacing, rhythm—all must be taken into account. And, we'll certainly need some classes on improvisation."

The elevator bell announced their arrival at the top floor, the one wholly taken up by the Proctor's Office and his support staff. All four of the monks, including Darian and Stralasi, disembarked. The other two turned left, presumably toward their work areas.

Darian pulled Stralasi to the right, in the direction of the Proctors' reception desk. He locked arms with the Good Brother and pretended to be in deep, hushed conversation as he steered him right past the desk. The receptionist never looked up from his work.

The pair continued slowly down the long corridor.

"What are you doing?" Stralasi demanded, with as much indignation as his whisper allowed. "I thought you said *not* the Proctor's Office!"

"Change of plans, Brother," Darian replied. "Let's stop here a moment."

Stralasi leaned against the wall and pretended to be deep in thought at something Darian had said.

"No one expects us in the Registrar's Office, remember?" Darian said. "And we have no legitimate business whatsoever on this floor."

"Then what are we doing here?"

"I'm listening."

"Pardon me?"

"My RAF sensors are at maximum sensitivity," Darian replied. "I'm trying to get the layout of the floor and scan for access to the upper level. I'll only need a few minutes, so play along. Maybe this'll be more worthwhile than I thought."

Stralasi could feel his heart racing.

If Alum senses us here, we'll be dead in an instant. At least, I hope we'll only be dead. He could choose to torture us forever or throw us in our own prison universe.

His eyes wandered to Darian, whose lips were moving without a sound as if the two were engaged in an intense discussion.

Maybe he can protect us or get us out of here if we're discovered. He wished Darak were here with him instead of Darian.

"Okay, let's go," Darian announced and guided Brother Stralasi back to the elevator, taking care to keep their heads huddled close together as if still caught up in their intense conversation.

"Excuse me, Brothers," the receptionist called out to them as they passed by, "Can I help you?"

"Wrong floor, sorry," Darian mumbled as he pushed the call button.

"Who were you looking for?" the receptionist called out as the elevator door opened.

Darian waved off the man's question and the two slipped into the elevator.

As the doors closed, Stralasi saw the receptionist shake his head, scratch it as if confused, and return to his work.

"You hacked into his lattice, didn't you?" the Good Brother asked.

The elevator began its descent.

"No choice," Darian replied. "He was about to alert security. That would mean one of the Angels would have greeted us in the lobby. Shush, now. I thought we were not to speak of such things here," he teased the monk.

"But Alum might have detected you!"

"He'd be less likely to detect a little unexplained EM activity than an RAF field," Darian replied with a shrug. "I don't hear any alarms. I think we're okay."

The doors *whooshed* open, startling Stralasi.

Everything in the lobby looked the same as it had when they'd arrived.

Peaceful. Serious. Glorious.

The same two Angels stood at their same stations at either side of the same grand entrance.

Darian straightened his posture, held his head high, and made Stralasi do the same. They walked out of the Alumit Administration building with fake confidence and genuine relief.

"Finished so soon, Brothers?"

Stralasi's heart stopped.

Darian halted mid-stride, turned, and knelt.

The terrified Stralasi managed the presence of mind to follow suit, half a beat behind.

"It was a trivial matter, my Lord," Darian answered calmly while the Good Brother trembled imperceptibly beside him. "As usual, the Alumitum Administration handled it with great efficiency."

"And how is Brother Tyrell, today?" the Angel asked.

Darian raised his head and met the Angel's seemingly innocent countenance.

"As you must know, my Lord, Brother Tyrell is away on other matters this week. Brother Regis handled our inquiry with grace and experience."

The Angel smiled in return, a smile as cold as it was beautiful.

"Ah, yes," he replied. "I am happy to hear all was resolved."

"By Alum's Grace, my Lord," Darian said, and bowed his head again.

"By Alum's Grace, in all things," the Angel said. "Now, I'm sure you have other business to attend to."

Darian stood up and extended a helpful hand to Brother Stralasi.

"Indeed, my Lord. We have classes this week and need to prepare."

He nodded to both guardian Angels.

"By your leave, my Lords," he said and gently touched the Good Brother's elbow, cuing him to follow suit and resume their unhurried departure from the Administration tower.

Stunned, Stralasi gave a low bow and muttered a customary, "By your leave, my Lords." He allowed his elbow to stay connected to Darian's gentle touch and be guided away. His knees felt weak.

Darian linked one arm amicably under Stralasi's and pretended to point out something with the other.

"Steady, Brother. We're safe now," he reassured him.

Darian lowered his arm and pointed off to one side.

In a more confident, cheerful voice, he added, "I'm glad that's all cleared up. Why don't we stop for a treat before we return to the residences?"

He steered an unsteady Stralasi down the nearest side street to the small, outdoor café, eased him into a seat at an empty table at the edge of the ringed-off patio, and ordered for them both.

"Breathe deeply, Brother," he said. "Let it go."

Stralasi exhaled fully to the count of four, paused for two seconds, and let his lungs refill of their own accord. He counted to two, and emptied his lungs again. He repeated the time-honored re-set exercise a few more times, and looked around.

The café was quiet. The early morning rush already over, and only a few patrons—students, judging by their youth—remained. They sat several tables away, in the shade of a building that towered twenty stories overhead. Pedestrians strode along the adjacent street on their way to appointments or scheduled tasks. A few monks tended the trees and flowers along the boulevard, and a worker swept tiny bits of stray litter into a dustpan.

It was a stunningly normal street scene, one that was playing out identically, simultaneously, in countless cities throughout the Realm.

No intruder alarms sounded in the Alumitum Administration. No vengeful Angels descended on them. No angry God ripped them out of this universe to eternal damnation.

A young server placed a colorful fruit-covered dessert and a foamy cappuccino on the table in front of Stralasi.

"Sweetener?" he asked.

Stralasi stared at the server, blank-faced, barely comprehending the question.

"Yes, please," Darian answered on the monk's behalf. "One packet will be enough."

The server dropped a small packet next to Stralasi's cup, gave the Brothers a smile, and disappeared back inside the café.

Stralasi stared at the package a moment. His hands remained limp at his side. His breath was ragged, his face was blanched, and his body trembled.

I may faint—he realized, surprised at the thought. *Where's Darak? Can I withdraw my offer to accompany Darian Leigh and just leave this place?*

A warmth passed through him. It began in the core of his body and radiated outward. Where it passed, the tension melted away and it was replaced by a feeling of peace and comfort. Trembling muscles let go, circulation increased. He took a deep breath and a somewhat more normal color returned to his face. He picked up the packet of sweetener, opened one end, and dumped half the contents into his cup.

"That's better," Darian said. His eyes met Stralasi's and he smiled reassuringly.

"You...adjusted me?"

Darian shrugged. "You were in shock. You needed something. I just tweaked your brain biochemistry a little. You'll be okay now."

"Hah!" the monk laughed, weakly, "I'm not sure I'll ever be okay again."

Darian tilted his head to one side.

"I'm a little surprised, Brother. I mean, you've faced far worse situations than this. You've faced new and unfamiliar worlds. You've faced Angels—on more than one occasion. You've seen Darak kill them by the thousands. What's so different here?"

Stralasi stared at him for several seconds before answering.

"I'm sorry to have caused you concern. You're right, of course, I have faced terrifying trials and tribulations, and Angels. The only thing I can think of is that here, up close, in the only place conceptually closer to Alum than His Hall, the danger seemed greater."

"That, and Darak wasn't here," Darian suggested.

"Maybe. I guess. It's just that, well, I've seen Darak in action and I have some idea of his capabilities. I was starting to feel confident in any situation with him. And, no offense, but I don't know you."

"Should I feel offended?" Darian asked. "I see what you're saying. I'm inexperienced at being a God. You don't know my limits. Heck, I don't even know my own limits."

He took a sip and replaced the cup thoughtfully.

"We were never in danger, today, I assure you. I'm being careful. The Angels were no more trouble than the receptionist. I could have altered their thoughts just as easily, if needed."

"Without alerting Alum?"

"I think so."

"You *think* so?" Stralasi echoed and leaned forward. "That's not as reassuring as you might believe."

"Okay, I'm almost certain Alum wouldn't have noticed anything. If He did, I'd have been able to shift us out of there. He wouldn't have been able to hurt us. I'm as confidant of that as I can be of anything."

"I guess that'll have to do. I hope you're right."

Stralasi sat back in his chair.

"Did you find the QUEECH device?"

Darian frowned. "I did."

"Then, why don't you look happier?"

"I don't see any way to get to it without alerting Alum. There's only one approach onto the floor. It's by an unused stairwell but He monitors it directly so I don't dare try to tamper with it.

"I might be able to shift in without being detected, but that would require delicate balancing of airflow and heat exchange. I'm not familiar with His detector sensitivity and tolerance levels, so I'm not sure what we'd be able to get away with."

"He must allow maintenance workers onto the floor."

"Only nanotech and Cybrids. Well, Cybrid drones at any rate; I don't think they contain Full personas."

"Can you access them?"

Darian considered the idea.

"Same problem. I could hack them; that's no problem. A little stray EM transmission in other parts of the building is one thing, but I'm fairly certain Alum would pay more attention to a transmission originating so close to His own CPPU."

"What? Alum is up there? In person?"

"A node of Him, for sure," Darian replied. "Quite a significant one, too."

Stralasi felt faint again.

"So, we were meters away from the Living God?"

"We remained outside His interest. We're safe."

"But we *could* have drawn His attention."

Darian nodded. "There's always that danger, Brother, anywhere in the Realm."

Stralasi cupped his coffee in both hands and took a long drink. He held the liquid in his mouth, letting the soothing warmth permeate. He swallowed and felt the warmth spread.

"I suppose that's true," he said, "although it's not exactly comforting."

"Anyway, I couldn't see any easy way in," Darian said. "I'll have to think about it some more." He swirled his cup and admired the interaction of foam and crema.

Bam!

Stralasi's hand had shot out and smashed something crawling across the heavy mosaic table.

Darian looked up at the monk, suppressing his natural startle reflex.

"Did you have to do that?" he asked in a level tone.

"What? It was just a spider," Stralasi answered. "They're everywhere. I know they're part of the ecosystem but that doesn't mean we have to share our table with them."

"What did you say?" Darian sat rigidly upright, suddenly alert.

"Uhh...that we don't have to share our table with them?"

"You said, *spiders* are everywhere."

"They are," Stralasi confirmed. "We had a saying that you're never more than a meter or two from a spider in the Alumitum. We leave them alone and they leave us alone. Nobody pays attention to them. Unless they bite you or crawl across your table, in which case, they're fair game."

"That's it!" Darian said with obvious excitement. "Spyders!"

"Spiders, what?" Stralasi asked.

"Not spiders," Darian answered. "Spyders. With a 'y'. Specially altered arachnids, outfitted as spies. If spiders are everywhere, we can use them without being noticed."

Stralasi was confused.

"How can we use spiders? Or even spyders, with a 'y'. They're just bugs."

Darian beamed. "I developed the technology as a teen. I guess, like so many other things here, it's been lost. Or maybe banned. Either way, Darak tells me they're not used anywhere in the Realm. The Esu rediscovered them, and now they use the basic tech everywhere on Eso-La. They'll know what I'm talking about. They'll be able to give us what we need."

"What do you mean, they use it everywhere on Eso-La?" Stralasi was a little annoyed. "I never noticed bugs being used as spies."

"You never noticed that wherever you went on Eso-La, the bugs left you alone? No spider bites, no mosquito bites, and no wild animals stalking you, even though you and Crissea spent so much time out in the forest?"

Stralasi thought back. "Huh. Not especially. I guess I assumed Eso-La was an unusually civilized ringworld. No biting insects or predatory animals around to threaten the inhabitants."

"No, there don't *appear* to be any. But think about it, a world without insects or predators would be a dead world," Darian said, "or a sick one. But the Esu live in nature. Everywhere on Eso-La is natural. The wild is everywhere. Did you really think it was just one large, well-tended artificial park?"

"No, I guess not."

"I guess not," Darian agreed. "That's because the Esu developed technology to tame the wild. Every organism bigger than a mite is connected to the world wide lattice network. They're all part of a centrally-controlled, carefully balanced ecosystem, one that's designed for human convenience as much as for the ecological stability of their world. On Eso-La, the spiders never bite people."

The Good Brother looked so astonished that Darian had to laugh.

"Don't believe me? Check with your Familiar part," he said. "The information on lattice technology and its use in managed ecologies should all be there."

Stralasi synchronized his human and Familiar consciousness. Schematics, images, videos, and concepts leaped into his mind. Darian was right. Mammals, birds, fish, reptiles and, yes, insects. All manner of living organisms had had their behavior altered through an integrated micro-lattice.

The various animals lived almost as if humans didn't exist in their world. They ignored the Esu except to skirt around them or skitter into hiding when their paths crossed. Otherwise, they went about their lives separately and in peace, occasionally cleaning up some unsightly plant or cropping grass in a certain pattern, and mating only when directed.

To Stralasi, Eso-La was a kind of Eden, an idyllic world where people lived in synchrony with the rest of nature. He'd never imagined that kind of engineered harmony.

"Oh," he said.

"Definitely, oh," Darian replied. "Adding QUEECH comms to their lattices will allow me to direct them in infiltrating Alum's device. If they can carry a few basic components with them, they should be able to construct an on-site splice of the interface. Alum won't detect a thing and we'll be inside."

"In that case, what are we waiting here for?" Stralasi asked. He pushed his chair back.

"Relax, Brother," Darian said. "The instructions have already been sent, along with shipping directions. We can finish our coffees. It'll take a few days to get what we need."

"Days?"

"Yes, a few days. Patience, my friend. Magic may appear instant, but technology still takes time. The Esu have the required capability, but there's some complex virus vector synthesis involved. A few delicate electronic parts need to be manufactured and tested, the Spyders need to be hatched, and they have to set up the proper transportation."

Stralasi paused. "Can't they just shift everything to us?"

Darian shook his head. "No. Same problem we had getting here. A shipment has to take advantage of official routes. Starstep shifts to the Alumitum become much less frequent once classes start. It'll probably be Friday before the next scheduled jump from Darbiness."

"Friday?" The realization struck Stralasi like a crashing wave, "But we have our first seminar scheduled for Thursday morning!"

"Well, in that case, it looks like your dream has come true," Darian laughed. "You, my friend, are going to teach at the Alumitum!"

A tiny bead of sweat broke out on the Good Brother's forehead.

36

DARAK CAUGHT UP to Darya near So-2, the large bright star that circled the massive black hole at the center of the Milky Way. He watched her work for a few seconds, shifting battle-Cybrids out of the central muster zone. Over the brief time he observed, several thousand attack-groups were randomly selected, deployed, collected, and redeployed.

"You're getting good at this," he said.

"Thanks," Darya replied. "I'm in secondary deployment right now."

She stopped shifting in and out of the region for half a second while they exchanged entangled particles. She used them to open a QUEECH comm channel so she could resume her work and continue talking.

"We've got a little over a million attack teams to disperse within a few dozen light years of Sagittarius A*," she said. "I'm trying to get my time down to a few minutes for a complete dispersal."

"So-2 has been a great staging and training center for that. I've been able to shift entire attack groups in one jump. As soon as they hit their respective battlegrounds, the armies deploy outward, enact the first formation in the pseudorandom sequence, and shoot at the Angel-like drones I set out for them. While one group targets the drones, another maneuvers into position and blasts the simulated array elements. They're doing really well. Most of the practice battles are over within half an hour."

"That's pretty good," Darak admitted. "Anything I can help with?"

"I think we have it mostly under control," she replied. "But I have to say, it has been a little unnerving, carrying out Deplosion Array attack drills right here in the Living God's backyard," she said.

"Yeah, no doubt," Darak commiserated, "but no need to worry. The nearest array element is light years away, and a lot of space lies between here and the nearest detectors. You're as undetectable as if you were still in ESO 461-36. Your blasts won't be visible to any of the detectors for years."

"Logically, I know that. And yet..."

"Yeah, I can almost feel His eyes on us, too." Darak stared out toward the Origin system and Alum's Hall. "Anyway, there's been no Deplosion Array activity and nobody in this locale for ages. They mined this whole system of everything useful long ago and haven't been back."

"I guess practicing so close to the intended battlefield has allowed us to get more familiar with this region," Darya admitted. "Hopefully, the payoff will be worth the risk of detection and the risk from So-2 going nova," she said.

So-2 happened to be nearing periapsis, its closest approach to SagA* in its eccentric sixteen-year orbit, making this a precarious time to be working near the star. This year was particularly dangerous in that the closest star to the black hole, So-102, was coincidentally in its own periapsis, as well.

The two stars had been interacting with each other gravitationally for billions of years. Every time they simultaneously approached closest to SagA*, they ripped great torrents of energetic ejecta from one another, and filled the local sky with dramatic fireworks. Most of the cooling plasma, instead of shrouding or settling on the stars, would eventually be gobbled up by the massive black hole a few light hours away. This activity created an extremely unpleasant neighborhood for several Standard months.

It also suited the rebellion's purposes perfectly.

Had any of Alum's crews still been working in the area, they would have evacuated the neighborhood near both stars by now. But once Alum ramped up construction on the Deplosion Array, nobody bothered to monitor the two roaming stars anymore.

"How's it going? Will you be able to get out of here soon, before things get too dicey?"

"I think we'll be ready to attack the Deplosion Array soon, for sure, long before the stars make it too risky to be near. Just to be safe, we've been monitoring them closely and keeping our visits to the region brief, no more than a few hours at a time. How about you?"

"I've been building a model of the region near SagA* and its two closest companion stars, and overlaying the positions of the simulated array elements. Everything looks good so far."

Darak monitored the distribution until Darya was able to break away, after which they jumped to a few of the simulated battlefields and watched the different approaches play out. They ran in-depth analyses of the various scenarios and Darak offered his suggestions.

"Maybe it's all moot, anyway," Darya said. "No battle plan survives first contact with the enemy."

Darak dug deep into archived memory.

"Aren't you the wise one," he laughed. "Quoting Moltke now, are we?"

"I have you to thank for that," she pointed out. "Not too long ago, I wouldn't have remembered who that was. Thank you for restoring my lost memories. I'm sorry I gave you so much grief over it."

"Thanks for letting me," Darak said. "I know it wasn't an easy decision for you. It took a lot of trust. But enough of that. Now, if we're going to quote great military strategists, how about Dwight D. Eisenhower?"

Darya did her own search.

"That goes back a bit, too. Let's see. My guess is you're referring to this gem: 'In preparing for battle, I have always found that plans are useless, but planning is indispensable.'"

"That's the one. Still fitting after all this time, isn't it?"

They floated for a while, silently contemplating the local battlefield. Powerful energy blasts occasionally speared toward them. They casually shunted the beams into alternative, virtual universes where they could do no harm.

"Earth was a violent place in those days," Darya observed. "I'm afraid we're bringing war back into a Realm that has known peace for over twenty million years."

"Me, too," Darak agreed. "But there would've been no need for this war without Alum's Divine Plan. He didn't leave us much choice."

"It's lucky that the one civilization that threatens the entire universe happened to give rise to more than one active God," Darya said. "Imagine, if we weren't here to challenge Alum's ambition and power, the universe would be reconfigured without a whimper."

Darak grimaced. "It still might be. We humans have always had to reign in our leaders, whether those leaders were Kings, or Emperors, or Presidents, or Gods like Alum."

"Yeah, you've got that right," Darya replied, "We bring it on ourselves, though. We keep clinging to some magical hope that someone better than us, some omnipotent Supreme Being, will come along and rescue us from ourselves. It makes us easy prey for charismatic leaders who can claim any sort of connection to that Supreme Being or, in Alum's case, to set Himself up as that Supreme Being."

"That's because we have a hard time embracing maturity," Darak said. "You know, things like responsibility, accountability, and consequence. Religious belief—unquestioning faith in any leader, really—banks on our desire to offload responsibility for our actions, good or bad.

"I firmly believe that rejection of mature responsibility was one of the things that got Darian killed. He kept pushing humanity to grow up, to take responsibility for its choices and development. Some people don't take kindly to that kind of thing."

"What do you mean, he pushed humanity to grow up?"

"I remember him saying something in his last lecture. 'If as a society—as a species—we can learn to become aware of the behaviors that are good for our species over the long term, we can begin to take steps to select good behaviors from bad ones without needing the threat of eternal punishment. We no longer need the idea of a God or gods to choose good behaviors.' A lot of people, powerful people, took exception to that."

"Considering Alum's Divine Plan, I'm not sure that part about making good decisions and not needing guidance will ever be true," Darya replied. "Who does Alum look to for guidance and judgment?"

"Ha, well, you'll love this! Like all Gods, Alum is an atheist. He assumes full responsibility for what He does. As far as He's concerned, there's no God above Him to judge His actions, unless He still holds some faded concept of the Abrahamic God He modeled Himself after."

"Yov, the Creator-God."

"That's the most recent name they gave Him, yes," Darak said. "Even though, we now know Yov is nothing more than a human fabrication. A story. A stubbornly persistent myth. Our present universe has no need of such concepts."

"If there is no ultimate God, who will judge *us*?" Darya asked quietly.

Darak considered his answer carefully. "As I told Alum, nature is everywhere and always the arbiter of truth. I meant it. *Reality* judges. The universe, or the multiverse if you prefer, judges us all. And continued existence is its only criterion."

"I hear echoes of Darian in that."

"I've created universes," Darak replied. "I've watched them develop and watched them sputter back into the Chaos, and I can say with confidence that continued existence—the continued chance for something surprising or interesting to develop—is all that matters. As much as we'd like to have other criteria to judge good and bad, I've never found any."

"Not even love?"

"Love is powerful, I'll give you that, but it's not always a clear measure of 'good'. If we're not careful, if we let it get out of balance, it can become a destructive force. Over my various lifetimes, versions of me have done many crazy things for love."

"Did you find love again? After me, I mean?" she asked.

Darak overlaid an image of Greg Mahajani onto his physical body that was floating in space with Darya, then transitioned it slowly back to the appearance he'd worn for the past millions of years.

"For many years in this form, I didn't dare allow myself to love without reservation. I was always too close to Alum to let down my guard or be caught in an open and vulnerable state."

He swapped bodies, bringing his Cybrid-self forward from another dimension.

Darya transmitted a gasp of surprise.

"DAR-G!"

"Yeah, surprise! Through the ages, I've been...I *am* Darak, Greg, *and* DAR-G. And then there are my Angel and Aelu identities. But all of my personas—those with human origins—loved you, first as Kathy and then again as DAR-K. I never stopped."

"So many lifetimes ago," Darya whispered.

"Too many, and yet still not enough. That's the problem with perfect memory. I can recall every moment of our lives together. I can remember losing you. Twice. I still have to dampen the pain when I think about it."

"Greg...Darak, I'm so sorry."

Darak changed back into his human form. He shrugged and tried to grin.

"That's okay. I found you again. Even though we may not survive our confrontation with Alum, I've found you again and that makes me happy."

Darya transmitted an image of her human avatar, smiling.

"We could try again. We could run away from all of this."

Darak shook his head.

"I don't know how long we'd survive," he said. "Not long, I imagine. Alum's Deplosion Array is going to alter the multiverse to its core. He's going to rip apart the fabric of reality and make His Heaven the only possible universe. I don't think any of us could survive for long."

"Probably longer than we're going to survive by taking the fight to Him."

Darak stared at his feet, floating on nothing. For a microsecond, he felt torn.

An instinctive reflex. I thought I'd edited those out. In that moment, he realized what Darya had been doing. He burst out laughing.

"What?" she said.

"You always were a good foil," he said. "You know me well enough to know my weaknesses."

She sent an image of innocence.

"I had to know for sure," she said. "Can you fight as hard for the love of a universe as you once did for the love of a woman?"

"'The universe' seems like such a nebulous concept," he said.

"Nothing could be less nebulous than the universe. No pun intended."

"True," he agreed. "I see now why you chose a warrior as your avatar."

Darya conjured an image of her warrior self, standing with her sword in hand at the edge of a city in ruins.

"The persona suited me when I didn't really know who I was. I drew strength from it. Now that I know who I am again, it still fits. Just in a different way."

"Maybe more than ever," Darak agreed. "I'm glad you're here with me. I couldn't imagine anyone else I'd rather have by my side when I confront Alum."

"I'll be out here, though, not at your side."

"There will come a point when this battle, the one out here, will no longer matter. The final battle will be finished in Alum's Hall or in Heaven."

"I'll come to you when you call."

"I know," Darak said, his transmitted voice barely a murmur. "That's why I'm going to spend the next two days with you."

"Oh?"

"Yes. It's time you practiced fighting as a God."

37

THE DEMANDING WEEK was taking a heavy toll on the Good Brother. Bouts of tedious waiting were punctuated by sheer panic every time he contemplated delivering his first lecture at the Alumita. The task was testing Stralasi's fortitude in ways he'd never experienced.

Darian Leigh, as if in intentional contrast, remained the picture of deep internal tranquility and perfect contentment. He was infuriatingly unconcerned by the drawn out days, filling his hours by strolling around the campus, exploring the habitat, and hacking into its InterLat databases. He was unperturbed by Stralasi's wild dashing about in all directions at all hours, frantically compiling research that might be in any way remotely relevant to the course he'd proposed. Indeed, by all outward appearance, Darian seemed impervious to the monk's caterwauling about being "in no way prepared" to lecture to a group of senior students.

"What was I thinking?" the poor Brother wailed from his desk.

Darian pulled his attention from whatever deep internal research he'd been pursuing and cracked open one eye.

Stralasi pushed away from his work and strode over to the window.

"There's so much to cover in a course like this. So many things the Alumit would want me to teach."

"What's the problem, my friend?" Darian asked. "You only have to give one class."

"The material I would have selected a year ago is all Standard theological pedagogy," the Good Brother answered.

"With which I assume you are well acquainted," Darian replied.

"But which I now know to be full of lies!"

"Then adjust the material to fit the truth," Darian suggested.

"Obviously," Stralasi said. "But if I do that, we'd be hauled before the Proctor after the first class."

"Hmm. That could be a problem. Perhaps you could compromise your principles."

Stralasi twisted in his seat and peered over his shoulder. "You do know that we take vows of honesty?"

"I believe we passed that ethical point some time ago," Darian pointed out.

Stralasi turned from the window. The peaceful scenery was distracting. "Any untruths we've told have been necessary to our infiltration; they were needed to save the universe. That greater goal supersedes the obligation to be truthful in all things. Anyway, no one was directly hurt by our tiny lies. But I cannot bring myself to propagate the deceit of the Realm to future generations."

"I'm not suggesting you be deceitful," Darian said, "just choose who you want to be true to."

"What does that mean?"

"For our purposes, that means perhaps it would be better when you lecture on Thursday to be true to the Brother Stralasi you were one year ago, than to the Brother Stralasi you are today."

Stralasi shook his head. "Try again?"

"Deliver the lecture you would have given a year ago. None of this will be relevant a year from now, anyway."

"There is no time limit on the truth," the monk intoned.

Darian laughed. "Normally, I'd agree with you. But, for now, it's much more important that we make it to Friday than you assuage your guilt. It's ironic you chose to teach a course in pragmatics. At the moment, pragmatics would dictate we say whatever we must in order to survive."

Stralasi frowned and returned to his work.

Thursday morning arrived, and the Good Brother stood at the front of a class of two-hundred and fifty senior students feeling utterly terrified and inadequate.

How do I make sure I say only what is safe?—he wondered.

The conflict between the truth he wanted to shout and the lies he had to tell made his stomach hurt.

We are invaders not colonists!—he wanted to say.

We need to respect local life, not adapt everywhere to our needs.

We could build more ringworlds, better suited to our natural biology, and leave other planets to develop as they will. They're not for us anyway.

We pray to a false God to fulfill our needs, when it is actually His Cybrid slaves that do all the work.

He jams us into foreign bodies so we can tolerate environments that would otherwise kill us.

All in the name of growing His Realm.

The treasonous—blasphemous!—thoughts ran through his brain in an uncontrolled torrent. Galaxies away, his Familiar self waved its tentacle manipulators in nervous agitation.

Brother Stralasi tried to calm his jumbled mind by reviewing his notes and class roster while he waited for the bell to sound the start of class.

The resonating *bong* finally sounded directly within their lattices and the class turned their attention to their lecturer.

The Good Brother closed his eyes and took a deep breath. He opened them and put on a confident smile.

"Welcome to Spiritual Pragmatics, 315—Foundations of New Colonizations," Stralasi began.

"This is the first time I've taught this course, so the syllabus might be a bit different from prior years. We're going to cover a lot of material, everything from social dynamics in a Founding Alumston to ecological testing and management. As the course title implies, we will pay as much attention to pragmatic issues as to spiritual—"

A hand shot up in the back of the class. Stralasi's lattice brought up the student's name.

"Yes, Mr. Armundsen," he invited.

Please, please, don't ask if this will be on the test—he thought.

"Professor Stralasi," the young novitiate began.

"Brother Stralasi," the monk interrupted. "I am but a simple Brother in the Alumit. I have no Doctorate degree, simply decades of experience on the front lines, so to speak."

"Uh..okay. *Brother* Stralasi," the student acknowledged.

Stralasi cringed at the smirks and sneers on some of the faces at the back of the class.

"Aren't we going to begin with a prayer?" someone called out.

By the Angels! Stralasi blushed at his rookie mistake. He'd been so focused on the lecture, he'd overlooked basic protocol.

A wave of snickers reached his ears.

He cleared his throat loudly to hide his embarrassment.

"Yes, of course. Of course. Prayer is one of the most essential duties of the Head Brother. Perhaps one day you will be granted the privilege of welcoming a new world into Alum's Realm. It will be your job to ensure the proper litanies make their way into the regular social fabric of the colony. After all, we wouldn't want our worlds to become disconnected from the Lord out of laziness, would we? Or, worse yet, fall into rebellion."

He thought he heard a collective gasp at the notion that new colonies might volunteer to break away from the loving embrace of the Realm. Had he heard it or imagined it? He chided himself for bringing up such a controversial idea on the first day.

More caution in your babblings, Brother!—he reminded himself.

He scrambled to cover his error and bring the class back under control.

"Okay, so what are the most essential prayers for a young Founding Alumston, then?" he asked. "Which shall we recite to open our class, today?"

"The Invocation of Connection, obviously," one of the young men volunteered.

"The Plea for Divine Guidance is more important," suggested another.

"Without the Entreaty for Power, though, a colony would go dark and become disconnected from both the Realm and from Alum," a third pointed out.

The class grew silent as they weighed the choices and wondered if there were any other possibilities.

Stralasi surveyed the room. His silence hinted that they had not yet hit upon the answer he was seeking.

"Any others?" he asked. "Any?"

One hand reached up tentatively from near the front.

Stralasi consulted his class list.

"Yes, Mr. Mathers," he said.

"Um, the Benediction of Gratitude?"

"Why?"

The young man looked uncertain.

"Your answer may be a poor one, Mr. Mathers, or it may be a good one. It may even be the correct one, the one I'm looking for. But if you don't know *why* it is correct, if you have no confidence in its appropriateness, how is one to have any faith in it? How is one to discern it comes from authority and not a lucky guess?"

Mathers slumped further into his seat.

"I.... Uh.... That is,...."

"Because everything is a blessing from Alum," another voice interjected.

Stralasi's attention spun to the other side of the classroom.

"Ah, Mr. Peters. Yes, that's true. The entire Realm is a blessing from Alum. So why would the Benediction of Gratitude be among the most essential prayers for a Founding Alumston?"

Peters sat up straight, emboldened by having had part of the answer.

"Because, how can Alum know if a new world has been seeded properly if that world doesn't think to express its thanks to Him every day?"

Stralasi frowned.

"Are you suggesting that the Living God is limited in His knowledge of His People?" he challenged. "Is Alum not all-knowing and all-powerful?"

Peters sat back, subdued.

Mathers cleared his throat and tried again.

"Our Lord knows all, and sees all," he said. "Alum is perfection, embodied, but we are sinners. We are weak and fallible."

Stralasi smiled encouragingly. "Ah! Now, we are getting somewhere. We humans are sinners, and so...?"

"And so we need to remind ourselves every day to trust in the Lord, God. To remain connected to the Divine Spirit that lives within Alum and guides Him in all things."

"Because, if we don't?" Stralasi prodded.

"If we don't, we might be tempted into apathy, which could lead to abandonment," the young man finished.

"Or rebellion," Stralasi reminded the class.

Mathers nodded in agreement, but his eyes betrayed his barely-suppressed shock at the second mention of that word in such a short time. The young man surveyed the room, as discreetly as he could, to see if anyone else had noticed. Eyes darted to the left and to the right. None would meet the novitiate's gaze.

Stralasi clapped his hands together, a startlingly loud sound in a classroom filled with nervous silence.

"Very well, Mr. Mathers. Why don't you lead us in the Benediction of Gratitude?" he suggested. "I think it's appropriate that we begin this semester by thanking our Lord for granting us the gift of His wisdom."

After Mathers led the class in hushed and reverent prayer, the rest of the hour passed quickly. Stralasi provided an overview of the material they would cover in the months ahead. He was half-surprised to find how easy it was to fall into a teaching cadence, to propagate the myths that formed the foundation of the Realm.

For a moment, he felt a glow of pride for his masterful presentation. As he unveiled the outline of the intended material, he felt a pang of regret that he wouldn't get to teach the entire semester.

It would have been a great course—he thought.

Then he remembered all the things he couldn't say and his wistfulness turned into guilt.

If only I could deliver classes without all of the lies, if I could reveal the truth of Alum's Realm—he wished, knowing full well that it was impossible.

A heavy sigh escaped his lips.

In a different universe....

All of the usual questions one might expect from a first class cropped up, including, "Will this be on the exam?" He managed to navigate them all without diverging from his script.

All, except one.

His slip up began in response to an innocent question.

"How do we choose the site for the Founding Alumston?" Armundsen asked.

"You don't," Stralasi answered. "The Cybrids will have initiated construction of Alumston before you arrive. The Alumita Ceraffice and initial concentrics of the city will have been grown to maturity. Manufacturing and Integration asteroids—"

He stopped mid-sentence when he noticed the blank stares and gaping jaws in his audience.

"What's a...psi-bird?" Mathers asked.

Oh, bother! What have I done?—Stralasi thought.

Regular People know nothing of the machine beings on whom their lives depend, or of the technology that creates their cities and their manufactured goods.

His eyes flicked to Darian, sitting in the Assistant's seat in the front row of the class.

Help!

Darian stood up, drawing all eyes to him.

"Brother Stralasi is referring to the *hybrids*, I believe. The special species of plants Alum develops to Standardize each new world. You may have been led to believe that our Lord simply creates new buildings from air. That is the naive view, one unsuited to a Founding Leader.

"The Lord is both more powerful and more subtle than that. He creates new life to do His bidding on each of our worlds. Much of the work we do on a new world is to help the Living God monitor Standardization of the planet. It is a blessed calling that Alum has given to the People, to join with Him in subduing the wild places and to bring them into the Realm."

The answer was a trivial perversion of Founding technology, bent to fit the theological expectations of the students.

Stralasi mentally braced himself to respond to some deep-thinking student who would recognize the absurdity of Darian's response and issue a challenge.

None came.

The Good Brother worked to collect his thoughts and continue. The students' failure to challenge was as unnerving as any anticipated—and subconsciously hoped-for—challenge they might have thrown at him.

Just one of the advantages of teaching to students trained away from skepticism, I guess. I suppose there are some benefits to being in charge when dealing with people accustomed to accepting whatever they're told.

The class moved onto other issues and Stralasi exercised greater caution in choosing his words.

At the close of class, a few students with additional questions and comments hung back. He was pleased to see they reflected a decent level of enthusiasm for the semester that lay ahead. Much to his relief, his misspoken answer seemed to have been forgotten.

Over lunch, Darian complimented the Good Brother on his preparation and delivery.

"I almost gave us away," Stralasi countered tersely, waving off the legitimately-earned congratulations.

"It was easily corrected, Brother," Darian replied. "You did an excellent job, otherwise. You're a very good teacher."

Stralasi gave in to the gracious comments, picked at his lunch, and dutifully chewed his way through the meal.

Another potentially life-threatening moment survived—he thought. *But this one was of my own doing. Not Darak's and not Darian's.*

He'd been little more than a spectator to events since Darak had chosen him as a travel companion on Gargus 718.5 over a year ago. During that time, others had been responsible for endangering him, for protecting him, for rescuing him, and for planning the next steps.

But this was on me. My words put us and perhaps the whole mission at risk.

The freedom to act, to be one's own agent in life, comes with the responsibility to deal with the consequences.

A lifetime under Alum's protection, secure in the embrace of the Alumit, had meant there was always someone wiser and more powerful to lean on.

Responsibility for one's actions is terrifying.

He drifted through the rest of the day, tugged here and there by Darian as they played out their charade.

That night, Stralasi spent an agitated fifteen minutes trying to sleep until Darian intervened directly and circumvented his relentless replaying of the day's lecture in his mind, allowing the monk a few hours of peace.

* * *

FRIDAY ARRIVED, and Stralasi woke up feeling unexpectedly rested.

"I really enjoyed teaching yesterday," he told Darian over breakfast. "I've missed that kind of interaction with young people, especially with those eager for knowledge. Perhaps I could offer other classes once this is all over. People are going to be hungry for guidance in the new Realm."

At some point, he realized he'd been chattering to an unusually subdued Darian.

"What's wrong?"

Darian pushed his plate aside, took a sip from his coffee, and wiped his lips with a napkin.

"It's happening," he said. "The Spyders are on their way. Darak and Darya are ready at their end." His usual easy smile faltered.

"It's time to put a stop to the Divine Plan."

38

"HMMPH. 'LIKE COORDINATING YOUR HANDS when playing piano,' indeed," Stralasi grumbled.

Sure, if each of those two hands were on completely different worlds, separated by over twenty-five million light years, and one of the hands could be killed at any moment if it were to be discovered. Otherwise, yeah, it felt exactly like he remembered when he was laboring through years of piano lessons.

Arriving to distributed consciousness as late in life as he had, he knew the process was going to require a huge adjustment, but coordinating his consciousness between his human and Familiar parts was proving to be even more challenging than he'd anticipated. And disorienting. At times, disconcerting. Never mind all of the many cultural and social nuances he was struggling to work out.

Until he could spend more time adapting, he'd set his Familiar sensory input to a minimum and positioned it (him!) in a quiet alcove in Crissea's home garden where it (he!) would be able to focus most of its (his!) attention on its (his!) human counterpart.

Stralasi had called on his Familiar's superior processing capacity to prepare for his first class but, aside from that, little else.

The Good Brother was struggling. He let Darian deal with whatever twists the Alumitum Administration presented. Despite access to the heightened processing power of his Familiar's semiconductor lattice, Stralasi could barely keep up with Darian, who'd been working tirelessly on penetrating Administration security. Perhaps owing to years of experience dealing with university bureaucracy, Darian seemed better able to deal with the disturbingly similar Alumit bureaucracy.

The tired, cranky, scared human part of Stralasi trod alongside Darian on their way to rendezvous with the incoming Spyders. They retraced the steps of their first day in the Alumitum, following the river toward the starstep where they'd first arrived. Darian's usual incessant patter fell blessedly silent as the pair made their way toward the plaza.

* * *

BACK ON ESO-LA, Stralasi's Familiar, who'd been faithfully monitoring the pair's progress on the Alumitum, wasn't too distracted to notice Crissea walking into the back of the garden without her Familiar hovering in its customary place behind her right shoulder.

"Where's the rest of you?" Stralasi asked, his voice emanating from his Familiar's speaker.

"We received notification from Darak that it's time," Crissea answered. "Those of us whose Familiars have been modified for battle are gathering outside the system, along with the Aelu soldiers. The rest are preparing to hide Eso-La."

"I wish you'd stay here, hidden with the rest of the world," Stralasi said.

"And I wish you were here with me, Ontro," Crissea replied. "All of you, my love."

"However...," she straightened her back and stood taller, "sometimes hope is just another word for fear. And if wishes were stars, the night sky would shine brightly with our dread."

* * *

LIGHT YEARS AWAY, on a gravel path scratching into the surface of another world, the realization of what they were about to attempt struck Stralasi so hard, it caused his human feet to stumble.

Darian shot out an arm to prevent the monk from falling flat on his face.

A startled Stralasi snapped his attention back to his human part, recovered his balance and composure as best he could, and nodded his thanks.

Neither felt a need to speak.

* * *

ON ESO-LA, Stralasi's Familiar bobbed unsteadily while his human part in the Alumitum worked to regain its balance.

"So, we're going transdimensional, are we?" Stralasi asked through his Familiar, once both of his parts had stabilized.

"That's the plan. The RAF generators are being warmed up right now," Crissea reported.

"Have you done this before?" the Familiar asked.

"Only with a few experimental objects and people. Never with the entire system," Crissea said. "Everything has worked fine so far, though. The theory is sound."

"Theory? Not a great thing to risk an entire world on, especially one with so many people," Stralasi commented.

"If Alum starts searching our galaxy, it would be best to make ourselves hard to find."

"Why not just shift elsewhere? Multiple times, if necessary."

"Because the battle could drag on for days, maybe weeks, or longer. He'd have time to scour the entire galaxy. He'd find us, Ontro."

"But what if the theory isn't quite right? What if it doesn't work on a grander scale? What if Eso-La becomes completely disconnected from this universe?" Stralasi objected.

Crissea smiled. "There is a tiny chance that that could happen, yes. But Darak showed us some ways to prevent that. We'll extend the vast majority of the system into a fourth spatial dimension and touch this dimension at a few hundred different points, each the size of a speck of dust."

"Each the size of a speck of dust," Stralasi echoed.

"All we need is one tiny toehold to find our way back. We'll have plenty," she reassured him. "More than enough."

Stralasi needed to see it for himself. He constructed a representation of the 4D extension in the CPPU of his Familiar part, something his human brain never could have fathomed on its own. He designed and watched a simulation of the transdimensional shifting process play out a few times.

"I imagine a few hundred contact points with this hyperplane increases the risk of discovery." He was amazed he knew what that meant.

"Yes, it does make it a bit riskier," Crissea agreed. "If someone scanned the expected location of Eso-La at high resolution, they might notice specks outlining the arc of our ringworld. I had our best minds randomize the contact points as much as possible. We think it's the best way to manage the risk while maximizing our odds of returning to this dimension."

Stralasi suppressed a shudder.

"If there is anything to return to," he let slip.

"If we lose, we lose in all possible dimensions, in all possible universes. We'll lose more than our location. We'll lose our existence."

She listened to the sound of the leaves gently rustling in the soft breeze. A few birds flitted among the branches with no greater worry than collecting a few tasty berries or bugs. She inhaled the fresh air.

"Once you activate the shift, will we lose touch with our other halves?" Stralasi asked. "Will they be on their own?"

"No, the QUEECH comms operate beneath all of that. The signal goes through the base of virtual particles that underlies reality.

"At least, that's how Darak explains it," she laughed.

The monk soaked up the sound of her laughter.

Will this be the last time I hear her laugh?—he wondered.

"I can follow Darak's explanation on a conceptual basis but the math is a bit beyond me, even with the aid of my Familiar," she confessed.

"So you'll risk your machine part while keeping your human part safe?"

"That's like saying a soldier risks his sword hand while keeping his foot safe. Losing our Familiar part would be worse than dying."

Stralasi's Familiar emitted a hum of embarrassment.

"I'm sorry. I should've realized that. It's a brave thing you're doing."

Crissea's eye glistened. "No more brave than you. Are you almost at the rendezvous point?"

Stralasi looked ahead to his destination.

"Yes, I can see the plaza up ahead. I have no idea what to expect, though."

"I'm sure Darian could tell you, if you asked him."

"I think his mind is elsewhere, right now. I don't want to disturb whatever deep thoughts he may be pursuing."

"Or deep feelings."

"Feelings? He's a God. Sometimes it's irritating, seeing how casually he coasts through difficulties. I'm not sure that he even has any real feelings."

Crissea laid a warm hand on the cool carboceramic carapace of Stralasi's Familiar. Far away, his human face blushed.

"I'm sure he's as frightened as the rest of us, Ontro. Darak says we're all equals in this battle."

"No one is safe this time, I guess," Stralasi said. "You know, I've seen Darak survive such horrific threats that sometimes I forget he's vulnerable, too."

* * *

ON THE ALUMITUM, Darian steered the Good Brother toward a tree on the edge of the starstep plaza. He pretended to engage the monk in conversation, but his attention was elsewhere. His eyes shifted nervously, tracking nearby pedestrians.

A group of five Brothers popped into existence in the middle of the starstep platform. Darian stepped out from behind the broad trunk and stretched lazily.

"Come, Brother," he said, unnecessarily loudly. "We have no classes today. Let's find a café and plan next week's lecture."

He walked toward the monk manning the starstep Prayer Podium. The man sprayed some holy water on the ornately carved pedestal and wiped it reverently with a clean cloth as he mumbled some incantation Stralasi had long since forgotten.

"Pardon me, Brother," Darian called out as he approached the stand. "My companion and I are looking for a quiet place to sit and review our notes. Is there somewhere nearby?"

He stepped onto the starstep platform and looked down on the scowling visage of the monk.

"You shouldn't stand there, Brother," the caretaker of the starstep said. "Unless you're traveling today."

He gently dabbed away a few drops of cleaning solution that threatened to run down the pedestal to the ground.

"Oh, my! You're right, of course," Darian said, looking appropriately flustered. He made to step down, bumped into the podium, tripped, and knocked the spray bottle of holy cleaning solution out of the man's hand.

"Watch out, now!" the Brother cried out. He made a clumsy attempt at catching the bottle but it bounced off the ground and popped open, spilling the precious water onto the pavement.

"Oh dear!" Darian exclaimed.

He rushed forward, keeping his body between the monk and the raised starstep.

"Brother, I am so sorry. Forgive me, please."

He pulled a tissue from the recesses of his robe and crouched as if to soak up the spilled holy water.

"No! Stop! Please, Brother," the other monk shouted, refusing Darian's tissue. "This is *holy* water! You can't just daub it up with any old rag," he exclaimed and stepped around to the far side of the puddle.

Darian maintained his position and insistence on helping.

"Stop!" the caretaker repeated, holding up both hands to deflect any further unwanted assistance. "Really," the exasperated caretaker said. "It's alright. I have this under control. A quiet café, you say? Try Tranquility. It's three blocks that way, turn left, and you'll find it half a block down. I'll take care of this." He forced a polite smile.

From his vantage point a few meters to the side, Stralasi noticed a cluster of dark, wasp-waisted bugs on Darian's lower back, out of sight of the caretaker-monk.

Darian straightened up and looked at the damp tissue in his hands. His eyes searched for a nearby trash receptacle.

The still-flustered caretaker stepped briskly forward. He snatched the tissue from Darian's hand, tossed it in a bin a few steps behind him, and rubbed his hands on his robe.

Stralasi stared at the bugs making their way around Darian's waist and into the front pockets of his robe.

"Uh, Brother," Stralasi said.

The monk's eyes widened as Darian's hands followed the insects halfway into the same pockets.

Darian wheeled around. A bright smile lit up his face.

"Right!" he said. "I'd forgotten all about our meeting."

He wheeled back toward the caretaker, smiled from ear to ear, and bowed.

"Again, my sincere apologies, Brother."

The caretaker waved him off.

"Don't you trouble yourself a moment longer. I'll get more water from the local Alumita. Enjoy Tranquility...or your meeting, whichever," he said, not caring where they were going, so long as they left.

"Thank you, Brother. We'd best be on our way. Good day to you!"

The caretaker grunted in reply.

Darian set off toward the river, hands half-inserted in his pockets, shoulders hunched as if against a cold wind.

"Coming, Brother Stralasi?" he called.

The Good Brother hurried to catch up to his companion. Pressed to his limit to keep up to Darian's brisk pace, he barely managed enough air to beg, "Darian, slow down, please. You'll draw attention."

Darian slowed to a more comfortable pace.

"Sorry, Brother. I wanted to get as far away from there as we could, as fast as possible. We've drawn enough attention.

"I saw something like bees land on you; they crawled into your pocket," Stralasi whispered. "They weren't spiders. I mean, Spyders."

"Transports," Darian said. "The Spyders are tiny, maybe a millimeter across. Walking across the starstep platform is too slow for something so tiny, and there's a high risk of someone stepping on them."

"Those were bees, actual, real bees?"

"Wasps, to be precise. They serve as carriers, primarily, and as protection when needed."

The two men nodded a greeting at a small group walking toward them. As Stralasi dipped his head in greeting, he steepled his fingers over his heart, thumbs together, forming the stylized "A" for Alum. The other group smiled at receiving the blessing of Alum's gratitude for their service.

After they passed, Stralasi asked, "So, what now?" out of the side of his mouth.

"Now, we have an appointment with the Proctor."

"The Proctor? Why?"

"Apparently, someone lodged a complaint about your course. We've been called to review your plans for the semester."

"A complaint!" Stralasi cried. "But we've barely discussed anything, certainly nothing controversial. Except for that one tiny slip, I kept within curriculum guidelines. Who complained?"

Darian turned his face so Stralasi could see his impish grin.

"I did," he answered. "Anonymously, of course. Can you think of a better way to get close to Alum's CPPU and QUEECH comm unit?"

Stralasi's jaw opened and closed, twice, but no sound came out.

"At first, I thought to introduce our friends into the ventilation system from somewhere outside the building. But releasing them at ground level would take too long, and even if they made it to the target, they might not have the energy to complete their mission.

"It looks like you and I will have to serve as the long haul transports on this job. We'll get our friends within striking distance and turn them loose."

Stralasi stopped walking and stared at his companion.

Darian paused and cocked his head to one side.

"What? You didn't think our direct involvement here was done yet, did you? I'm afraid it's just beginning, my friend. Just beginning."

Stralasi didn't like the look of eager anticipation emanating from Darian's face. He didn't like it at all.

39

"IT'S READY, JOHN. The moment I've been building toward for more than ten million years has finally arrived."

Alum and the latest edition of Trillian stood in the small study in Alum's Hall looking at an impressive stylized display of the Deplosion Array hovering in the middle of the room.

A cloud of forty million bright dots clustered near SagA* at the center of the Milky Way. SagA*'s attendant stars, S0-102 and S0-2, were nearing the massive black hole and each other, as they did only once every few million years.

A pity that I won't get to see it play out this time—Alum thought. *My calculations suggest this could be the year they're finally ripped apart by the tidal forces.*

The orbital mechanics of the close approach were wickedly complex even for Alum and, in this case, the result was uncertain. It was a bit of a pity, yes, but there was no point waiting any longer, not when the end of everything was so close at hand.

As was the beginning of a new eternity.

"I've heard reports that the People are grumbling, my Lord," Trillian said. "The absence of resources You've diverted to accelerate the construction of the array has had a considerable impact throughout the Realm. Delays in repair, shortages in certain manufactured goods, allocation problems, food shortages."

"Their discomfort will get regrettably worse before it gets better," Alum replied, "but it won't last long. A few days. Perhaps a week or two."

Trillian's eyes went wide.

"Only days to destroy the entire universe?"

"Yes. Does that surprise you?"

"A little. The Realm spans galaxies millions of light years apart," Trillian said. "The astronomical research stations calculate the size of the *observable* universe to be almost one-hundred billion light years. Their estimate for the entire universe, based on the lack of observable space curvature, suggests it's over one thousand times larger than that. So vast. Vast beyond my comprehension."

"And?" Alum prompted.

"I guess I expected it to take more than a few days to collapse all that matter back into a singularity."

"Mm-hmm, yes, I see how you might have arrived at that conclusion. Incorrectly, of course," Alum replied. "Your understanding is based on science that goes back to humanity's infancy. From that perspective, you'd be quite correct."

"But that's not the way reality works. For starters, you must understand that as vast as the universe is, it's little more than a speck in the infinite Chaos, John.

"All the matter of the universe is connected. At a deep enough level, quarks entangled from the beginning of Creation tie matter together instantaneously across trillions of light years."

Alum moved closer to the hovering display. He swept His hands through the cloud of bright points and stepped back. The display changed to show the local supercluster of galaxies, and pulled back to reveal an extensive map of the observable universe and extrapolations beyond.

"The deplosion field will affect the entire universe almost at once," Alum said. "Expansion of the physics of this universe into the adjacent Chaos was halted a few years ago. I'd have to change either this display or your perception to show this in the required twenty-four dimensional parameter space.

"For the time being, you'll have to take My word for it." He watched the Shard tracking the expanding display.

I've never given Trillian the capacity to understand this—Alum realized. *I wonder if Darak Legsu is capable of comprehending it, whether he has risen as far above those minor Gods that attacked Me as I think he has.*

An ache of something akin to loneliness caught Alum by surprise, a desire for the company of equals.

A little late in the game to be feeling regret. There's only room for one at the pinnacle of Creation—He affirmed, though a little wistfully.

"If everything is instantaneously connected, why would the deplosion take any time at all?" Trillian asked.

"Reality, whether realized or potential, has to be conditioned to accept the new. All forms of matter will be swept away by the deplosion. That will take a small amount of time to propagate. Afterward, the only real matter that any universe will accept will be the matter of Heaven. I've seeded that universe inside Sagittarius A*, within the Schwarzschild radius of the black hole itself.

"From there, Heaven will grow and spread outward eternally. My perfection will never again face any threat from within this universe or any other. All of Creation will be Heaven."

"It will be Your greatest triumph, my Lord," Trillian agreed. "The greatest triumph imaginable. Its perfection will be worth the countless lives lost and the transitory pain caused within the Realm."

Alum flinched.

That sounded a little critical. Is a little adjustment to this newest iteration going to be required?

He cocked an eyebrow at the Shard, but Trillian's face remained placid and accepting.

No, I'm just being paranoid. The attack by the other Gods and the discovery that Darak Legsu still lives must have rattled Me more than I thought—the Living God admitted to Himself.

Will Darak and his allies present themselves and ask to join Me in the re-Creation? Or will they try to stop My Plan?

The Living God had modeled the numerous scenarios.

Yes, the People of His Realm would suffer as deplosion took hold. There were already some minor inconveniences, troubles that would seem large only because the People were accustomed to the Realm running smoothly for the past twenty-five million years.

They've forgotten what it was like during the Aelu Wars.

Among the earliest disturbances brought on by the deplosion field would be things most sensitive to disruption of the laws of nature: power, electronics, starstepping. Crop growth and oxygen production would be affected, too—the delicate quantum mechanisms of photosynthesis would experience significant drops in efficiency. But the re-Creation would be done long before ecosystem failure threatened the People.

As reality dissolved, physics would no longer support any form of life in the universe. Nor would it support the atomic fusion of the stars. People, animals, and plants would die on their many planets, within their asteroid habitats, and on their glorious ringworlds. Shortly after they died by the trillions, stars would begin to destabilize and go nova or supernova. Black holes would fizzle, pop, and evaporate into lengthy streams of ever-weakening energy as they compressed trillions of years of barely-perceptible dissolution into hours.

But long before the universe took any noticeable strides toward homogeneity of light and heat, and long before gravity waves emanated any great distance from disrupted supermassive black holes—limited as that process was by the speed of light—homogeneity of entanglement would spread throughout. Before matter or energy could diffuse far from exploded stars and black holes, it would lose the resonances that made real matter possible, and fall back to a chaotic state.

From this eternal and infinite Chaos, a new universe will arise.

One that springs out from the seed of Heaven I have sown inside SagA.*

One that reflects the eternal perfection I have designed.

No more endless uncertainty; no more endless threat of novelty.

The universe will fulfill My Purpose, rather than its own precarious and haphazard experimentation.

Alum, the Living God, thought on the single universe to come, and He saw that it was good.

40

HOW DO YOU KILL A GOD?—Darak wondered for the millionth time. *Especially such a widely distributed one?* To the best of his knowledge, Alum was the only one who'd ever killed another God. First the Aelu God and then five of the Six.

He reflected on various histories and possibilities as he walked alone along the creek that wound its way from a bubbling spring to a duck pond near the rim of Eso-La.

It was quiet out here. No one lived within a hundred kilometers of the imposing atmosphere-retaining wall that delineated the edge of the ringworld. Not that Eso-La was densely populated. For the most part, solitude was easy to find. But today as they prepared for war, he sought distance from the busy hum of other minds.

He paused to appreciate a tiny waterfall that bubbled and frothed at the end of its two-meter plunge into a small pothole. At the other end of the pool, the little creek continued along a gentle slope toward the ringworld's distant central valleys. A kilometer farther, he crossed a simple but elegant stone-arch bridge spanning the marshy banks of the creek.

Not that the Aelu had any Gods, per se. They'd seen the power to alter the laws of nature for what it was, just another technology to be used, a neutral power that could be used for good or evil. The lack of a supreme being in their history had made them unsuspecting of Alum's megalomaniacal treachery, which led to their ultimate defeat.

But why hadn't the Six fared any better? Surely, they'd been better informed and prepared for Alum's tricks. How had five out of six powerful, battle-ready Gods disappeared without putting up a fight? How had Alum disposed of them?

Darak was stumped. His visit to Depchaun's empire had turned up nothing; there was no sign or sighting of the Neptune-sized God. Glenchax's CPPU hardware sat intact, although empty of everything but a rudimentary concepta.

Could it have been Raytansoh's doing? Was it possible the most xenophobic of the Gods had managed to plant invasive viruses into the others over the ages? If so, why did he not take over their empires himself? Why work through Alum? Had he computed his future and decided he could not succeed against the Living God? Or did Alum develop His own method for killing the other Gods, a little side project while He was destroying the entire universe?

A frown grew on Darak's face. His mind was giving in to the maelstrom of questions.

He tilted his face upward to receive a stray beam of sunlight that had found its way through the leafy canopy. He closed his eyes and took a deep breath. Savoring the nourishing warmth, he focused on the sounds of the forest, the babbling water, and the chirping of birds. Far off, at the edge of his heightened hearing, hooves crunched dried twigs and scratched to expose the delicate, new greenery below.

Another deep breath.

Focus on this moment—he told himself.

Another deep breath.

He opened his eyes and resumed walking.

How will I kill Him?

Ages ago, during his youth, a now-distant time in which the Earth still existed, he'd been a big fan of action-adventure science fiction. Many of the books and movies he devoured depicted so-called gods that pummeled each other with fists, cast bolts of lightning, and hurled balls of energy.

How ridiculous!

While both he and Alum were capable of harnessing plasma from intensely hot, young universes and using it to hurl spectacularly devastating energy blasts at one another, that was all for show.

It played well on the movie screens of his youth, but it was nonsense. Unless their attention strayed during battle, there was no energy beam powerful enough to touch Darak or Alum.

They were, after all, Gods.

The real battle would be fought on a playing field different from any that the favorite storytellers of his youth had imagined.

We'll hurl Chaos at each other; that's where the real danger will come from.

Darak had put the quark-spin lattice of DAR-G's expanded mind to work for weeks, modeling fields he could cast against Alum, and fields he expected Alum to project onto him.

If it came to violence—and he could see no way to avoid it—they would bring on a kind of battle unlike any the universe had ever seen. They would tear into each other with fields that changed the laws of physics upon which each relied for existence. They would try to disrupt the base matter and energy of which the other was composed. They would rend apart time, and space, and information.

At the same time, Darak planned to employ more subtle attacks to undermine Alum's strengths. Small changes to electron conductivity of the Living God's silicene lattice would make Him a little slower to respond in defense. A flood of soltronic energy would poison His particle analyzers, making it harder to follow the rapid changes in the laws of physics that maintained His integrity.

No doubt, Alum would attempt the same on him.

There will be concepta attacks. He'll try to invade my mind while I try to invade His.

Only some of the attacks would be physical, such as by nanite robots designed to interface with CPPU circuitry. Others would be attempted by signal. Each would try to penetrate the anti-virus security of the other, and break the code that made up their opponents mind.

Luckily, I have the quark-spin lattice at my disposal, thanks to the engineering ingenuity that passed from Kathy to Darya.

As far as any of them knew, Alum had not yet cracked the secret of the Cybrid's unique computational substrate. On the other hand, they couldn't assume Alum's own lattice design had remained static over millions of years, either.

It wasn't going to be easy to infiltrate the Living God's CPPU while fending off attacks on his own mind and person but on some deep, primal level, the challenge excited him.

Would he be able to hold his own and keep Stralasi's Familiar safe and connected to the judges throughout the battle?

The billions of judges whom Darak had been secretly equipping with enhanced lattices and appropriate background knowledge would be the key. One final infusion of data, a complete history and explanation of the economic sociopolitics of the Realm, would activate them.

It was crucial that Alum hear the voice of His People and feel the weight of their judgment of His Divine Plan.

Otherwise, what's the point?

He and Alum held mutually incompatible philosophies and visions of what constituted a desirable universe. How could either God feel justified in deciding which was best for all inhabitants?

To be fair, Alum is experienced, and He is brilliant—Darak allowed.

Maybe the Living God's vision of the perfect universe is best. But I am not going to let either one of us make that decision alone. It has to be a shared decision among all who call the Realm home.

He was acutely aware that five of the six other known Gods had already demonstrated their disapproval.

And lost.

Five powerful Gods, gone forever.

Which brought to mind the problem of how to deal with Alum's distributed nature. There were millions of Him scattered throughout the universe, at least one for each world.

At some point near the end, the Living God would have to either pull all of His scattered nodes together or abandon the majority of them forever.

Heaven will be where He gathers whatever nodes of His consciousness He wishes to keep—Darak thought. *So our plan has to include a confrontation in Alum's Heaven. There's no way around that. All I have to do is get the Living God to take me there. More precisely, take me there with all of my capabilities intact.*

Which was far from an easy thing.

If Alum allowed Darak to shift into Heaven by his own power, He would have to share the definition of the physics of Perfection. Would the Living God risk exposing His perfect universe to an outside God?

That will depend on how confident Alum is in His strength and abilities, and how much He fears mine.

Such latitude was unlikely, but that didn't stop the man-God from thinking up ways to steer the conversation toward such an invitation.

If that doesn't pan out, there's still Darian and the Spyders.

His former mentor and Stralasi had already received the creatures. In a few hours, they'd be ready to start infiltration.

Truth be told, Darak didn't put a lot of stock in their chances of hacking into Alum's QUEECH comm network at all, never mind undetected. Still, with everything else going on, anything was possible. He'd maintain an open channel with Darian, and was prepared to take advantage should they manage to break in.

Darak approached the quiet pond where the creek ended. He could hear the soft quacking of the ducks and caught glints of sunlight reflecting off the water. A bright sparkle of light struck his eyes, and he squinted.

A wave of nausea passed over him. He hardly had time to take note before his RAF generators reconfigured their fields to reassert the specific reality around him.

Darya's QUEECH call arrived less than a millisecond behind the mysterious wave of dizziness.

"What was that?"

"Are you alright?" Darak answered.

"I'm okay, now," she said. "Are we under attack?"

Darak choked out a laugh as his equilibrium settled.

"Not us, specifically. In fact, except for you, me, and Darian, I doubt anybody noticed anything out of the ordinary."

"How could they not?"

"Because they can't feel reality. They don't know what it's made of and what holds it together."

"I almost envy them in their ignorance," Darya replied. "Almost. Do you think that was Alum activating the full Deplosion Array?"

"That would be my guess. The dizziness would be our reality analyzers trying to interpret the disruption from the array. If you shift into the Chaos, it feels a lot like that."

"Is that how it'll feel to fight against Alum?" she asked.

"No, it'll feel much worse. Of that we can be sure."

"Those who die instantly won't feel a thing, will they?"

"No, they shouldn't. The reality disruption will wash over them so quickly their sensory systems won't have a chance to process the pain."

"Just as well, I suppose."

"Enough have suffered in Alum's name," Darak growled.

"And in the names of Gods who've gone before Him," Darya added.

"Yeah," Darak muttered under his breath.

"Is everything ready?" Darya asked.

"Getting close; I just activated the last download to the judges."

"That should stir things up in the Realm," she laughed.

"It should," Darak agreed. "At the end of the data transmission, I'll introduce myself and call on the judges to join me in confronting Alum."

"Will anyone answer the call to judge?" Her voice conveyed more doubt than question.

"Some won't respond out of fear of Alum's retribution," Darak replied. "Others, out of reverence or misguided loyalty for their Living God. A few won't see themselves as worthy of passing judgment on Him. But I'm counting on the majority to at least show up. Whether out of curiosity, duty, or responsibility to the future, I don't really care. I just hope they come. We need every one we can get. Right now, though, I have to go collect Stralasi's Familiar."

"And I have an attack to initiate. Will Eso-La be safe?"

"As safe as we can make it. The Esu are ready to go transdimensional."

"That'll hide them?"

"I hope so. If Alum destroys Eso-La, we lose a billion fighters right away. The Esu Familiars would be out of the battle."

"I could retreat back here and engage Alum if He finds them," Darya offered.

"No, best stick to the plan. If the Deplosion Array isn't stopped, nothing will matter."

"So, you're going to visit Heaven?"

"If I can talk Alum into it."

"You could stay there. You could join Him."

"I can't imagine a worse fate," Darak said.

Darya transmitted an image. It began as her warrior persona, drawn from the fierceness inside her, the one she summoned when she needed courage. The edges softened as the image transformed into a smiling Kathy Liang, exactly the way she'd looked when Darak had first seen her, back when he was still Greg Mahajani.

"Thank you," he said.

The image emitted a sigh. "I know we're different people now than when we first met," she said. "But I want you to know, I remember the love we shared."

"Maybe," Darak said, "when this is all over—"

"And if we survive—," Darya added.

Darak smiled, happy that she knew what he was thinking.

"Then, we'd better survive," he said. "I think we've been battling the Reality Assertion Field in one way or another as long as we've known each other. It'll be nice to have some time together, without that hanging over us."

"Yes, that would be refreshing, wouldn't it?"

Darak gave her one last smile.

"To battle," he announced in his best approximation of a superhero's voice.

Darya's image returned to that of fierce warrior holding her sword aloft.

"To battle!"

41

DARAK LEGSU AND STRALASI'S FAMILIAR materialized on Starstep One, the gateway to Alum's Hall.

Ages ago, Darak had added his own personal entangled particles to the standard store held within the reserve. He'd never used them for fear someone might trace them back to him and so there they sat, undetected, for ages.

"You finally decided to join Me," Alum's voice boomed in the tiny reception chamber.

"I've decided to talk to You," Darak answered.

He wasn't surprised that his presence had been immediately detected. Starstep One didn't employ autonomous workers; not a single Cybrid, human, or Angel monitored the traffic. Alum alone controlled maintenance functions and He saw all.

"I see you've brought a friend."

"A former Brother of the Alumita," Darak replied. "Your records will recognize the name of Brother Ontro nem Stralasi, most recently from Alumston on Gargus 718.5."

The air shimmered near the window and a middle-aged man materialized.

Stralasi's Familiar bobbed politely, "My Lord," he said to the man.

"I guess old habits die hard," Darak commented on seeing the Familiar's unquestioning deference.

Witnessing this exchange from far away, Stralasi was touched to hear the man-God's voice tinged with a mix of amusement and sadness. He was also thankful that, contrary to his own inclination, his Familiar had no protocols for kneeling in abject fear.

"You are free of all Lords now, Brother," Darak said to the Familiar.

"You address this Cybrid as Brother," the man said, "but no machine has ever attended the Alumitum," Alum said. "And I have records from the Angel Mika, reporting the death of Ontro nem Stralasi on Gargus. Did you transfer his concepta to this machine?"

"Those reports were premature," Darak replied. "Brother Stralasi is very much alive. His biological body is on Eso-La and he's linked to this machine, his Familiar, by QUEECH comms."

Stralasi decided not to correct Darak's tiny lie about the physical location of his human self. *A little misdirection might be prudent right now*—he thought.

"Eso-La?" Alum said. "So the rebels in the ESO 461-36 system live?"

"Yes, and not merely alive, they're thriving. They're marvels of success and as strong and independent-minded as ever."

"Thanks to you, I presume."

"An old story. Perhaps I'll share it with You some day."

"Don't tell me, you decided to continue the integration experiment?"

Darak shook his head. "No, the Esu decided. It's amazing how competent a group of intelligent, well-informed people are at making decisions for themselves."

"Democracy!" Alum spat. "Puhh! Humans tried it for thousands of years and it led to nothing but conflict."

"And to progress," Darak pointed out, "the kind of progress that made You and me possible."

"We've enjoyed over a hundred million years of peace," Alum countered. "The so-called progress you laud resulted in the destruction of Earth and, quite nearly, all of humanity."

"If I remember correctly, You had a large role in Earth's destruction. And it seems to me that You're now on the verge of destroying the entire universe."

"Re-birthing the universe is the ultimate act of Creation."

"That's up for interpretation, I think," Darak replied. "In any case, Brother Stralasi is now distributed, not unlike You, actually."

"Ha!" Alum roared. "My presence spans many worlds across multiple galaxies. Soon it will span all of Creation."

"A somewhat reduced Creation, really." The sardonic smile on Darak's face broadcast his contempt, in case there had been any doubt.

"It's a perfect version of Creation, one that will fill eternity."

Darak stepped toward the viewing port in the rocky wall of the chamber. Distant Sol was a sparkling beacon in the black of space.

In his mind, Darak overlaid the orbits of Alum's Hall and myriad other asteroids that had long ago been converted to CPPUs for Alum's enormous mind.

"Such a perfect Creation must be glorious to contemplate," he said.

Alum stepped over to the window and stood beside Darak. He looked out at the sun. "The vast emptiness of space does have its own beauty," He admitted. "But I've always found it such a waste."

"Only from the perspective of life."

"What other purpose could there be to Creation?" Alum asked. "If the universe is to praise the glories of its Creator, why would so much of it be filled with empty silence?"

"Verification that this universe never had a Creator," Darak answered, "or none that desired praise."

"Physicalism, Darak? Really? Still going with that, are you?"

The man-God eyed Alum patiently, levelly, and took his time to answer. "You knew me so well and yet You never knew me at all."

"You were always so distant from the faith," Alum agreed. "I figured it was because you spent too much time creating your own imaginary worlds."

"Oh! Now, that's rich! *You*, worried *I* was developing a God complex?"

"You were plotting to replace Me, were you not?"

"Is that what you think? That I lusted after Your throne?" Darak asked.

"If you're not here to challenge Me, are you here to join Me? To accept your righteous place at My left hand while Trillian sits at My right?"

He almost sounds hopeful. Sad, really. It's time I set him straight—Darak thought.

"You never recognized me? Not once?" Darak asked.

"What do you mean? When?"

"You never saw any hint of the man I was before I was Darak Legsu? You never suspected? Think back. You knew me long before You ever met me as Darak Legsu."

To help jog Alum's memory, Darak blinked and his face transformed. His hair and complexion darkened, his lips thinned, and the hook in his nose returned.

"What's this?"

Darak smiled.

"This is me. The original me. The face I was born with. Don't you recognize me?"

Alum's brows furrowed in concentration and, gradually, recognition washed over his face.

"Greg Mahajani!"

Darak/Greg smiled and bowed.

"At your service."

"You escaped."

"I escaped it all. Your attempt to murder me. The destruction of Earth by the Eater that You unleashed. Your sabotage of the original starsteps. The loss of the shifting devices that You stole from me. I made it to Vesta on my own. I hid. I survived."

Alum's eyes went wide with sudden realization.

"*You!* You killed Me!" Alum bellowed.

Darak/Greg shrugged, "I tried. I would've succeeded, except for Trillian."

Alum glared at him, and Darak felt reality shimmer. He brushed it off with a thought and returned to his current appearance.

"Since that particular version of me seems to be irritating You," Darak said, "let's stick to this one."

He gave Alum a casual smile. "Oh, You thought I could be removed from this universe so easily? A small adjustment to local reality and I would just melt away?"

Alum frowned.

"Apparently, I was mistaken. It won't happen again," Alum assured him.

Darak turned his head and flicked his chin toward Stralasi's Familiar. The machine had been silently hovering near the centre of the reception chamber.

"Stralasi's not only QUEECH connected to his own body," Darak teased.

"Okay, so you can still surprise Me," the Living God said. "What else is he connected to?"

"He's connected to billions of Your People," Darak answered casually. "They're here to listen to You. To judge You."

"Ha!" Alum roared. "Judge ME? My People worship Me. They follow Me. They do not judge Me."

"Well, now, they do," Darak said.

Alum whirled on him. "What have you done?"

"I've opened their eyes," Darak replied. "Given them minds to understand, and restored the context and history that You denied them."

"All those strange reports. The proposals. The innovation. I should have known you were at the bottom of that."

Darak dropped his hands to his side and smiled, a tacit admission of his role and his guilt.

"It was impossible not to have some premature effect when I enhanced their lattices. Intelligence. Curiosity. Distrust of authority. Independence of thought. Loss of blind faith."

"Discontent, unhappiness, misery," Alum finished. "Were you jealous that the People had found peace and you had not?"

It was Darak's turn to glare. "The peace of mindless sheep has little value. It comes at the price of potential. It replaces the curiosity of the human mind with the contentment of the well-fed cud chewer. And now, You are leading Your flock to slaughter."

"You're baiting Me, trying to make Me angry. Stop it," Alum warned. "It's pointless. You can't pervert how the People see Me. I am their Savior. I bring perfection. I bring Heaven."

"But they won't get to enjoy it."

"Pah! Technicalities. In the eternal joy of Heaven, all possible minds will be resurrected. Death is truly defeated in Heaven."

"Except for theirs. Their death is going to be very real for them. How do You think they're going to feel about that? If Your Divine Plan to re-Create the universe as Heaven is so perfect," Darak said, "such perfection should be obvious to all People, not only to a God."

Alum nodded. "Indeed. Anyone should be able to judge it perfect for themselves. Yes, yes. I see where your argument leads. But God does not ask His Creation to approve His design."

"In the previous instance, there was no one to ask," Darak countered. "Not that we know of. This universe arose naturally without the intent of any Creator."

"That's blasphemy!" Alum replied.

"It is the truth," Darak replied. "You know the evidence and the arguments as well as I do."

Alum smiled. "It is possible to twist the Book of Yov into a story of the natural evolution of this universe. I will grant you that. Such an interpretation is sufficient explanation for the imperfection we see in this universe.

"Fortunately, a consciousness with an improved vision has arisen, one that can lead to a perfect Creation."

"And that consciousness would be Yours, I presume," Darak stated, knowing full well what Alum had meant.

It was Alum's turn for a gracious bow.

"I am at the service of the People."

"And Heaven is Your gift to them?"

"You see the Truth, as well."

Darak frowned.

"I see *Your* narrow version, but is Your take on Heaven a gift people want or need?"

Alum waved an invitation for Stralasi's Familiar to approach.

"A fair question," He said to Darak. "Let's find out. I'll take you and Brother Stralasi on a tour. Through his QUEECH connection, billions of My People can experience the glory that awaits them in the next life."

Darak suppressed a smile.

Bingo! And it was His own idea.

"I'd be happy to accompany You," Darak replied. "Just send me the parameters and I'll join You there."

"Oh, ho!" Alum said. "And open all of Heaven to your manipulation and perversion? Not likely! Why don't you permit Me to transport you there, instead?"

"And open myself to Your RAF generators?" Darak countered. "I don't think that would be wise until after the People have judged."

Alum held His hands up in a gesture of helplessness.

"Your unwillingness puts us at an impasse, I'd say."

"Likewise," Darak said, and pretended to consider alternatives. "How about this? If Brother Stralasi agrees, You can take his Familiar there and I'll follow one of his tracking particles."

Alum's brow twitched and then rested. He smiled broadly.

"You'll remain apart, separate from Heaven?"

"For the most part, yes. It will suffice for me to see it," Darak said. "I can give You the parameters for a sensory interface, if You'd like. You can provide the rest."

Theoretically, that would give Darak enough information to complete the physical specifications for Heaven, if he could get the time to compute them. Then he'd be able to confront Alum in His new home.

But that wasn't his only goal.

Distraction is also part of the game—he thought. *Keep Alum focused on this and buy Darya and Darian time to do their work.*

"Agreed!" Alum said.

The Living God and Stralasi disappeared. He left behind the minimal set of parameters that Darak would need to follow.

Darak integrated the data with his own interface, took a quick breath, and sent two QUEECH messages.

To Darian, he sent, "Whenever you're ready."

"More than ready," Darian responded; he was already on his way to the Alumitum Administration tower.

And to Darya, "On my way to Heaven. Begin your attack."

"Godspeed," Darya replied, and sent an image of a teapot in solar orbit somewhere between Earth and Mars.

Darak laughed. *Russell's teapot! You couldn't resist a touch of irony. Godspeed, indeed, along with other things that don't exist, like teapots in solar orbit somewhere between Earth and Mars.*

In his long life, the best laughs and the best therapeutic moments had been those shared in the most dire and often least appropriate moments.

He shook his head at her wry humor and shifted.

42

"QUITE AN ACCOMPLISHMENT, BROTHERS!" said the Angel guarding the entrance to the Administration building. He did not mean it in a good way.

The deep, rich voice startled Stralasi, even though he'd expected it. What he hadn't expected was humor. He dropped to one knee.

Rather uncharacteristically, Darian took a knee beside him.

"Merely a misunderstanding, my Lord," he explained.

The Angel smiled a coldly beautiful and threatening smile.

"You seem to attract them," he said. "Misunderstandings, that is."

"In this particular case, it was no more than an unfortunate byproduct of Brother Stralasi's zeal," Darian answered. "The other instances were simply misfortune and misadventure."

He stood up and pulled a reluctant Stralasi upright alongside him.

"It wasn't my fault," the sagging monk whimpered.

Darian glanced at his companion. "As I said, my Lord, a simple misunderstanding."

"It seems your associate's inexperience may have led him into some sort of impropriety of doctrine," the Angel suggested.

"Oh, no, my Lord!" Darian feigned being aghast. "I'm sure there was no impropriety involved. My friend may have uttered an ill-chosen word or two but nothing more, I'm sure."

Stralasi felt nauseated, which was an understandable, natural fear response triggered by watching Darian engage in a life-threatening argument with an Angel.

No, something else niggled at his mind. He checked in on his Familiar self.

That's odd.

His Familiar was no longer in Eso-La. It would seem that—this couldn't be right—Nem had left the universe entirely. Taken to Heaven by Alum?

The Good Brother focused his attention fully into his Familiar's perspective. Yes, Nem was now alone with the Living God in another universe, and presently looking out on Perfection.

Darak Legsu wavered into partially-synchronized existence beside the Familiar's body.

Back in the other universe, next to Darian Leigh, a very human sigh escaped Stralasi's human body.

Darian eyed the Good Brother.

"Are you okay, Brother?" he asked, genuinely worried.

Stralasi waved off the concern. He forced himself to shut out the incredible live feed that was streaming into his integrated consciousness from his Familiar part and focus on the pressing business at hand. He could synchronize with the Familiar's experience later.

"A summons to meet with the Proctor is not what I desired after my first week here," he managed to answer.

He pushed back his shoulders and smiled his bravest smile.

"But, as you say, I'm sure it's all a simple misunderstanding that can be easily cleared up."

Stralasi turned back to the Angel and gave a deep bow.

"My Lord," he said. "I hope to return to preparing this week's lesson soon but, right now, I suspect we are about to be late for our meeting. I don't imagine the Proctor would look favorably on that."

"I suspect not," the Angel said and turned his impassive face forward again.

Dismissed, Stralasi and Darian hurried through the main doors and up to the floor of Proctor's Office.

The receptionist stood waiting for them as they stepped off the elevator. The silent judgment that narrowed his eyes to horizontal slits replaced the usual courtesies. Without a word, he turned and ushered them down the hallway toward the appointed room.

Stralasi bowed his head and followed obediently.

Darian, apparently equally oblivious to the social cues and to the weight of the meeting they'd been summoned to attend, casually regaled them with his usual stream of incessant chatter.

While chattering on and on without pause about nothing of import, he gently released the transport wasps, one by one, from out of his sleeve.

When the trio arrived at the threshold of the office, the receptionist stepped aside to let the two men enter, softly closed the door behind them, and abandoned them to their fate.

The bald, shiny head presenting itself to them from the other side of the desk only emphasized the severe look on the man's face that eventually deemed to look up and acknowledge them. A brusque twitching of the man's hand indicated the visitors should sit.

They sat.

Images of all the times he'd summoned members of his community for a "corrective consultation" whirled unbidden and unwanted through Stralasi's imagination.

The Proctor clasped his hands together and leaned forward. He peered into Darian's and Stralasi's eyes, each for a few seconds, without a word.

When Stralasi could stand it no longer and looked away, the Proctor glanced at his notes and began the interview.

"Brothers, we're less than a full week into classes and already you have a complaint against you," he stated as a matter of fact. "Usually, our students allow a little more leeway before deciding an instructor is unbearable."

He read the complaint, which was now floating in a prominent display on his desktop, out loud and in full for the benefit of the visitors. At the end of the message, he swiped the document to the side and turned his stern stare to the two men opposite him.

"So, tell me, what do you have to say for yourselves?"

"Uh...uh," Stralasi stuttered.

"We are at a bit of a loss, Proctor," Darian answered. "I, for one, can't agree that those particulars form a reasonable basis for a complaint." He blinked innocently.

"At a loss, are you?" The Proctor answered.

"No idea," Darian answered.

"Hm. I'm sure! Well, let's examine them point by point," the Proctor said as he leaned over his desk and drew the window with the anonymous complaint a little closer.

"This Lecturer was intensely dull," the Proctor began. "Not that that's a crime," he noted, looking up briefly. He didn't smile.

"It goes on to say, 'He used words I've never heard in any Alumitum lecture. Words like integration asteroids and Cybrids. And rebellion.'"

The Proctor pinched the bridge of his nose and looked up at Stralasi.

"Now, I realize things are different on the Frontier and this is your first time teaching in the Alumitum," he said, "but must you stir up fear of rebellion in your first class?"

"That was spoken only as a warning, Proctor," Stralasi sputtered. "As cautionary counsel that one must never disregard one's duty to mindful prayer."

"Ah, yes. Prayer," the Proctor replied. "The missive also states that you failed to begin class with a suitable prayer until reminded by your students. Again, I realize this is your first assignment but surely you are not so long or far away on the edges of the Realm that you forgot your own training, here at this very Alumitum. We don't need to recommend a refresher semester or two, do we?"

Stralasi's eyes darted anxiously about the room while he sought an appropriate response.

A refresher? After centuries of indoctrination and training? The stigma of being ordered to a retraining semester at the Alumitum would destroy any hope of a career on Founding worlds.

The Proctor walked over and looked out the window. He rocked back and forth on the balls of his feet, hands clasped loosely behind his back, humming.

Confused, Stralasi turned to Darian, who sat suspiciously quiet, eyes closed and in apparent concentration.

Stralasi gave him a nudge with his elbow.

"Eh? He's not done yet, is he?"

Darian opened one eye.

"Pay attention," Stralasi hissed.

"I am."

Stralasi waved his chin toward the Proctor, still humming by the window.

"He threatened to send me for retraining!"

"Yes, and..?" Darian prompted.

"It'll end my career!"

"Proctor," Darian raised his voice to catch the head administrator's attention.

The man turned slowly, as if in a daze.

"Yes?"

"Is anyone's career in danger today?"

"No," the Proctor answered, "only the universe."

He turned back to the view.

Jaw agape, Stralasi's eyes moved back and forth between the other two men. Darian was sporting a silly grin.

"What have you done?" the monk demanded.

"Only what was necessary," Darian answered. "I set up a little loop in his lattice to keep him occupied while I work."

"Loop?" the Proctor asked.

"No matter how long he stares out that window, he'll think he's only been there a second or two," Darian explained.

Stralasi stared at the Proctor.

"Do you mean to say you have control over his mind?"

"I do," Darian answered. "I control his perception, his thinking, and what he does."

"I don't like the sound of that," Stralasi said.

How many times has he done that to me?—the Good Brother wondered. *How often have I been in his power?*

It didn't seem right. It wasn't ethical. He'd watched Darak control Angels and Cybrids but that was different. Angels and Cybrids were, basically, machines. The Proctor was a human being. But what did that say about his own integration with his Familiar? Wasn't his Familiar a machine as well? Yet, as a part of his integral self, wasn't that as much a part of his human identity as his biological self? He wasn't sure he could identify any difference.

Darian shrugged.

"Don't get yourself worked up. For the moment, it's nothing but a convenient trick that allows me to concentrate on penetrating Alum's node without the distraction of keeping up this charade."

Stralasi's eyes blinked rapidly.

Charade?

He'd been so caught up in their act that he'd almost forgotten it was all fake. He rubbed his eyes, let his head flop back, and looked at the ceiling. He exhaled gently but fully, counted to two, and let his lungs refill.

"So what do we—"

Darian held up a finger, silencing the monk.

"If you don't mind, Brother. This next bit I'm working on is a little tricky."

Stralasi's mouth clapped shut. He walked over and stood beside the Proctor, peered into the man's vacant expression, and felt lost and useless. Again.

* * *

THE TRANSPORT WASPS LEFT THE SHELTER of Darian's sleeve one by one and lit out on their own. They knew where they were headed and would find their own best route.

Days earlier, the memories Darian had studied in the neural traces of Trillian's brain provided a clear picture of the floor plan of the Alumitum Administration Tower. More importantly, there was a blueprint of the ventilation ductwork shared between the Proctor's floor and the one above that was occupied by Alum's local CPPU and support machinery.

Darian programmed relevant information into the bugs' brains. After that, all he had to do was set them loose and track their progress over the

QUEECH comm channel while they navigated their way up to the top floor of the tower. Child's play, but he devoted all of his attention to it just in case his direct intervention was needed.

The wasps made their way to a return air grill near the floor of the machine room that housed Alum's local node, the closest point they could convene as a group without risking detection. The target device sat at the edge of a pure cube of nanostructured silicene the size of a small floater vehicle.

In every one of Alum's other nodes throughout the realm, the QUEECH comm device was internal to the node. Except this one. Trillian had selected and isolated this particular device himself, and had personally managed its maintenance in order to avoid integration directly into the silicene lattice of Alum's node.

Trillian, the original Trillian, had needed to keep this device accessible from outside. His escape plan, should he ever need one, was to make an excuse to visit the node and leave a specific program with the maintenance Cybrid for the next routine cycle. The program would prime the Cybrid to act as a conduit for the Shard to access this comm device, a direct link to Alum's node. To guarantee accessibility, he'd installed one of his own maintenance Partials with a back channel command and a control module to remain in place with the device.

Darian's wasp transports and their cargo of QUEECH-hacking Spyders were now within a few meters of that very same Cybrid.

An admirable plan, Trillian, but it's not going to be fast enough for us—Darian thought. *We can't wait for the next maintenance cycle. We need immediate access.*

He sent one of the wasps through the ventilation grill to survey the room. It flew along the floorboard, passed behind the Cybrid, and landed on top of the Cybrid's spherical shell.

The Cybrid didn't raise any alarms. If it had noticed the bug, it wasn't acknowledging the fact.

Through the wasp's feed, Darian saw Alum's silicene node sitting about fifteen meters away in the center of the room. Optical cables snaked along the floor from nearby cabinets and into the device.

*Cables that connect it to cameras and microphones all over the habitat—*Darian remembered.

Trillian's memories, not mine.

Many of the cables led to sub-processors that ran the habitat machinery. From there, Alum's sub-mind could coordinate the power supplies of all six habitat tunnels that ran the length of Vesta. Lights could be turned on and off, heaters or coolers could be activated, air and water circulating pumps could be sped up or slowed down. Everything, from systems that affected the ecosystem to automated personal transportation vehicles, could be controlled from this node.

This local node is the brain, and Vesta is the body—Darian mused. *I wonder how much of the lattice is devoted to conscious thought and how much to autonomic functions.*

Trillian's memories provided no direct insight on that topic.

From the outside, the unassuming node looked harmless, like any other piece of innocuous machinery. Looks, in this case, were deceiving.

From here, Alum could cast complex local RAF fields as big as the entire asteroid of Vesta. And the RAF generators that studded the exterior of the asteroid were capable of much more.

From here, He could tear reality apart, from one end of the solar system to the other. We have to get in, but we have to do it carefully.

He checked Trillian's memories and found nothing more about local defenses protecting the node.

Surely, Alum wouldn't leave a node unprotected. Rather careless of Him.

Then again, what need would Alum have for high-level defenses within the religious center of the Realm? Macroscopic attacks would be easily detected and defended against. With two Angels on duty outside the Tower, any conceivable internal threat could be dispensed within seconds. Anything that got past the Angels would be dealt with directly by the Living God.

That left the microscopic and nanoscopic.

The room looked spotlessly clean, aside from the normal traces of dust in the air. Did the Cybrid Partial clean daily or weekly? Luckily, the room lacked HEPA filters on the return air ducts.

If we'd had to get past Class 100 conditions, that would've been a problem!

He initiated an approach program in the exploratory wasp and highlighted the top of the QUEECH comm device as the landing zone.

Might as well try the simplest approach, first—he thought. *Maybe we'll get lucky.*

The wasp, carrying its tiny Spyder passenger, lifted from the top of the maintenance Cybrid and headed toward the node in what Darian hoped was a natural-looking, slightly erratic pattern.

It buzzed across the chamber, unhindered.

Five, ten, twelve meters.

Could it be this easy?—Darian wondered.

The feed from the bug disappeared.

Darian switched his attention to one of the wasps waiting in the ventilation duct and reviewed its observations.

The explorer wasp had approached the target. The maintenance Cybrid stationed at the edge of the room didn't move. Darian half-expected the Cybrid to snap out a small butterfly net on the end of a specialized tentacle or whip out a can of insecticide. But it didn't. Instead, a green laser light pierced the air from a corner of the room. The wasp and its QUEECH-hacking Spyder passenger were vaporized instantly. In the Proctor's office one floor below, Darian jumped.

I guess that explains why there are no bug carcasses lying around—he thought. *There's nothing left of them to litter the floor.*

The laser defense system hadn't struck right away. If he sent another wasp, how close could it get to the node before a laser zapped it? Was the defense system adaptive? Would it respond sooner next time? One real wasp finding its way into this room per day would be highly unlikely. Two appearing on the same day would be so improbable, it was sure to be noticed.

But he couldn't have the tiny Spyders crawl the whole fifteen meters from the vent to the comm device. That was about fifteen thousand times their body length, the equivalent of asking a human to walk thirty klicks and then climb a three-kilometer high sheer vertical wall at the end.

If he were to send a transport wasp to within a few meters and have the Spyders parachute to the floor on a silk thread, how many tries would he get before triggering another alarm?

Could I get away with dropping them right over the node? They could crawl down from there, no problem. And if I let the wasps fly into the room using a Gaussian distribution, it'll look like a hive wandered into the ventilation system by mistake. That'll provide a plausible reason for more than one wasp in the room on the same day.

He had eleven wasps and Spyders left. He modeled how a natural distribution and movement might look; he'd only have one chance to get it right.

At the last second, he decided to hold one insect back to record the operation and serve as a fallback plan. Should the swarm-pattern idea not work out, he'd be ready with one last, less than ideal option that would be guaranteed to put a Spyder in position, but also guaranteed to alert Alum to a God-level intrusion.

Very, very much less than ideal. He hoped it didn't come to that.

Darian released ten wasps into the room in a carefully timed pattern. They infiltrated slowly, flying in all directions. Most explored to the right and left along the wall, some climbed up to the ceiling, and two spread out across the floor. The invasion looked completely natural, like a small nest had been disturbed and the inhabitants had spread out, seeking safety or enemies.

When the first of the wasps got within three meters of the silicene cube, a bolt of green lanced out and vaporized it.

Damn!—Darian thought. *Just as I'd feared, the defense system has become more sensitive.*

A second wasp circled lazily within five meters. He instructed its Spyder to parachute to the floor on a thread. It would take at least an hour for it to wander across the open tiles to the QUEECH device but it could end up being the only chance. Darian watched it descend gracefully to the floor and noted its trajectory before turning his attention to the others.

As he'd feared, the other nine wasps and Spyders approaching the node were being vaporized outside a wider and wider defense perimeter. All of them but the solitary walker.

Darian watched his single soldier inch across the tiled expanse, hoping its insignificant size would protect it. After an hour of painstakingly slow progress, the Spyder made it within a few dozen centimeters of the target.

It had almost reached the base of the device when a green flash put an end to that hope.

In the Proctor's office, Darian exhaled noisily. He stood up from the chair he'd been glued to for the past sixty minutes, and stretched. Stralasi stopped his incessant pacing.

"Success?" he asked, eyebrows raised high in hope of a positive reply.

Darian shook his head.

"The opposite," he muttered.

Stralasi's shoulders slumped.

"I have one Spyder left," Darian said. "One final chance to get inside."

Stralasi grunted. "If you couldn't get to the device with the other eleven, what good will this one do?"

"Oh, I can get it there," Darian answered. "Guaranteed."

Stralasi frowned. "Okay, so why didn't you just do that, first?"

"There's no way to do it secretly," Darian replied. "Alum will know I'm here."

"Oh! Well, then, don't do that!" Stralasi said.

Darian continued, "He'll activate His defenses, call in the Angels, throw up the shift-blocking field."

Stralasi blanched.

"I see," he said.

"Yeah, you'll be trapped."

Stralasi pursed his lips and exhaled loudly. "Again."

Darian gave him a lopsided grin.

"But not all of you," he added brightly.

"My Familiar is in Heaven. With Alum."

"Darak will protect you there," Darian said. "And I'll protect you here."

"Until the end of the universe?" Stralasi scoffed.

Darian nodded solemnly. "For as long as we can."

The Good Brother had nothing to say.

Darian gave him a moment to get used to the idea before pressing.

"It's our only chance."

"I see no other option," said the Good Brother. "You have to do it" He held his hands, palms up, in front of him as if about to make a point. He let them drop to his side. "It's just...hard."

"I know," Darian said. "The eternal plight of humanity, being at the mercy of the Gods."

His eyes caught Stralasi's. The Brother's were filled with despair, whereas his twinkled with humor and determination.

"Yes, so it would seem," Stralasi agreed.

Darian shifted the last Spyder from its perch atop the back of the transport wasp in the return-air duct to the top of the QUEECH comm device.

"Here we go," he announced.

As the tiny Spyder made its way through a gap in the metal housing and toward the heart of the device, alarms started sounding throughout the Alumitum.

Darian reached out all over the Alumitum Administration and its neighborhood, shifting people and things as random decoys. Lastly, he shifted one of the guarding Angels into the office and released the Proctor from his consciousness loop.

"...and so, you really must be more careful," the Proctor continued, mid-sermon.

On hearing the alarms, he snapped his mouth shut and whirled away from the window. He froze in place as he beheld the imposing figure of the Angel standing inside his office door.

The Angel's drawn sword crackled with barely-restrained energy along the length of the blade.

Darian felt the shift-blocking fields snap into place around Vesta. They wouldn't hold him, but he couldn't leave without breaking his promise to the monk.

The Proctor's face contorted with fear and confusion.

"Wha...What's happening?" he stammered.

43

MIRLY STEPPED DAINTILY between the sparse ferns of the old-growth forest. Plants sprang up from the damp floor wherever Alum's light shone through the thick canopy to the ground below. Enormous coniferous trees rose up, branchless for the first ten meters or more before their generous limbs spread out and their highest tips brushed the bottoms of wispy clouds to feed on Alum's Glory.

Earlier, when she'd been at the fringe of the First Forest, Mirly had been able to make out the slight curvature of the ceiling that was under a kilometer away. But here this close to the center of Heaven, the thin clouds made it hard to judge how low the sky was.

This is the last layer—she thought. *Or the first, I guess, counting from the center, outward.* The ceiling above was the floor of Heaven's Core, where Alum resided and possibly where she'd find a doorway to the "greater universe" outside.

From her position near the edge of Heaven, Mirly had been able to shift this close to the Core because she'd once visited the lush jungle of the First Forest during a hummingbird phase. That was before she'd extended roots and spent a few years as an orchid, growing between the always moist branches of a sheltering forsythia.

A peaceful, beautiful time—she recalled. Then again, all of her time in Heaven had been peaceful and beautiful. Right up until she'd made that horrible mandala. Since then, she'd shifted and trudged through much of the only universe she'd ever known, seeking a way to redeem herself for being the source of the disappointment she'd seen in Alum's eyes.

The visit to the outer edge of Heaven—where the fires of Creation pulled the firmament of Heaven from the great nothing—had proven fruitless. Having found no way past the flames, she'd turned back toward the life-giving Core.

For weeks now, she'd pushed ever inward from the rainforest of her youth, trying to track the gentle curvature of the sky, walking endlessly with barely any rest, ever closer to the center of the universe.

Life guided her. The closer Mirly came to the center, the larger and more magnificent life grew. Older and wiser beings migrated nearer to the center to be closer to Alum in their final millennia. The closer they got to the Core, the bigger they grew. In the veg state, they put down roots for centuries at a time. In their final anima state, they turned into great, lumbering beasts that sang hauntingly beautiful odes to their Creator.

Now, the gigantic trees of the First Forest told her she was nearing her journey's end. The woods were silent, save for whispering leaves, creaking trunks, and branches rocked by the gentle breeze.

There were seldom any animals here. Those in their vibrant anima phases preferred the faster life of the less majestic areas. They left the ancient trees to their slow, sage thoughts.

One of the trees she passed was near to shaking off its last sleepy ponderings and changing into the anima state for its final journey to the Core, where it would join Alum in eternal bliss.

Its leaves and branches were already fully re-absorbed, and its trunk had shortened and become swollen. The body of the beast was forming as its massive head slumbered. The base of the trunk was dividing into four stocky legs, though they remained deeply rooted in the ground.

I could wait for it to finish its transition and follow it to the Core—Mirly thought. In their ultimate anima phase, all Alum's people had an intuitive knowledge of how to reach the Center of Heaven. But such an enormous transition could take months or more, and she found it hard to imagine having the patience to sit there and watch the entire time.

She took note of the area, paying particular attention to any differentiating features in the woodland. It was hard; the trees looked the same in every direction. The pond she'd passed a few days earlier was easily the most distinctive place she could remember. Calling its image to mind would allow her to return here if she made no progress by walking.

Satisfied, she set off in search of any discernible route that might have been left by an earlier mammoth on their final journey to join Alum.

She hoped her own path had been spiraling closer to the center, however slowly.

Legend said there was only a single Gateway to the Center of Heaven, though there were infinite approaches. She suspected everyone on their final journey wound their own way to the Gateway from wherever they happened to transition into their ultimate anima form. The transitions took place rarely. It would be a great stroke of fortune to happen upon anything she could recognize as the movements of one of the behemoths.

Deep in thought about her travels, Mirly stumbled into a shallow depression hidden beneath the plants and composting leaves on the forest floor. Her front-right leg dropped a little lower than expected, upset her balance, and caused her full weight to come down hard onto the errant hoof.

Ow! That was clumsy—she chastised herself and rubbed her leg with one hand.

Mirly looked back to see what she'd tripped on. She cleared away some leaves and a few dead branches. There in the dried mud was a huge footprint about a meter long and deep enough to have made her lose her footing.

It must have walked through here after a rainfall.

Wait! What must have walked?—she asked herself. Clearly, this was an anima person on their final journey.

A path!

She craned her neck left and right, following the length-wise axis of the footprint. The spacing of the trees was wide in every direction.

Is that a broken branch?

Her eyes sought confirmation in the distance.

Yes, there! And again, over there!

She could make it out now, a trail of bent and occasionally broken low-hanging branches, and subtle shadows cast in compressed detritus on the ground.

Hints of other footprints?

She set off to follow them.

Mirly walked at a brisk pace until impatience drove her into a trot and, soon after, into a full-out gallop. The path seemed to go on forever and as she grew tired she slowed to a patient walk. A few hours later, she grew bored and distracted.

She'd been trudging on in a straight line for a quite a few minutes before she realized she'd lost the trail. The endless forest of towering trunks, light fog, constant mist, and lack of light finding its way from Alum's Glory above to the forest floor all conspired to make it nearly impossible to determine if she were moving in the right direction.

Exasperated, she backtracked until she again found signs that the elephantine person had passed by.

Hours passed. Whole days went by. Her alertness diminished and she felt the pull of the rich earth beneath her feet more than once, as her internal energy stores decreased dangerously.

If I plant roots here to recharge, it would be ages before I could transition to the anima state again—she thought. *So little light reaches the forest floor that it would take forever to replenish my stores. I just can't wait that long; Alum needs my help, now!*

She pushed on, determined not to waste her last, best hope.

Finally, the light ahead grew stronger and the forest thinned.

Have I come to the end?—she wondered. *Or have I retraced my way back to the beginning?* She couldn't imagine why anyone would have walked out of the First Forest on their journey to the Core.

Then again, what do I know? Hope—even my last, best one—has not guided me especially well so far.

Click. Click.

In her exhausted, trance-like state, she didn't notice stepping out from under the final tree and onto a marble terrace until the soft click, click of her hooves reached her fading consciousness and sparked her attention.

Click. Click.

Fifteen meters away, stood a wide garden gate. It didn't look like much, the sort of ornamental iron gate one might use to set off one part of a clearing from another.

Surely, this can't be "the" gate. The entrance to the Core of Heaven should be more beautiful than any other gate—she thought.

I suppose that it's here at all makes it special. Metal gates aren't all that common in Heaven. Stones with fairly pure iron were hard to find, and metal forging was an unusual hobby. Still, this particular one was a little...underwhelming. She'd seen one or two gates at least as fancy as this one in her lifetime.

Her efforts to reconcile reality bumping up against her expectations this way made her laugh out loud.

Oh, Mirly!—she chided herself. *What need did the Living God have of decoration, when the entire universe was His to make as intricate and beautiful as He desired? What would be the point of trying to inspire more awe in His people, when they already admire Him, love Him, and worship Him with every fiber of their being?*

Silly me. That must be why Alum's always so casual and relaxed when He visits—she realized. *All of Heaven rejoices in Him and praises His glory. All of Heaven is His home. He doesn't value any one part of it more than any other.*

She wondered if this setting looked any different to a person on their final journey, on their way to becoming one with their Creator. She'd always imagined a soul-warming, brilliant light spilling out from the open gate as Alum welcomed one of His children home.

Home! A chance to speak privately with her Lord!

A chance to seek a way to help Him in the "greater universe" outside!

She stepped forward tentatively and put one hand on the gate. It felt cool to the touch but not uncomfortably so. She pushed it forward a crack and saw that the marble tiles carried right through to the other side.

No soul-warming, brilliant light.

Mirly opened the gate enough to squeeze through, entered, and closed it gently behind her. She closed her eyes and faced inward again, barely daring to examine the Core.

"Ah! You've made it!"

Her eyes flew open at Alum's voice.

God stood at the far end of a large clearing—she didn't have the words for such a place. It had barren floor and walls, and a ceiling visible only a few meters above. A dull sphere, slightly smaller in diameter than her Lord was tall, floated behind Him.

A second being with the same upright bipedal aspect as Alum shimmered uncertainly in a haze between Alum and the sphere.

Another God?—Mirly wondered. *How could that be?*

While Heaven boasted an amazing variety of life in a wealth of forms, there were none, absolutely none, in the image of their Lord. Only Alum stood on two legs, with hands hanging at His side.

Mirly felt her knees go weak, and she started to tremble.

Alum rushed forward. He took the quivering doe-centaur's hand and steadied her. She gave Him a weak smile of gratitude, and He led her back to where the other God stood with the hovering globe.

"Mirly, My dear," Alum began. "I'd like to introduce you to some of My friends from the universe outside of Heaven."

He indicated the other bipedal form with one hand.

"This is Darak Legsu, an old friend and comrade," He said through a broad smile. "You'll have to pardon his rather insubstantial appearance. A small matter of mutual distrust, I'm afraid." He waved His hand dismissively. "Temporary, I'm sure."

He gestured toward the dull-grey sphere.

"And this, I'm told, is the Familiar of Brother Stralasi, the machine embodiment of a man who, until only last year, was a monk of the Alumita, the spiritual home of My People in that other universe. At present, Brother Stralasi himself is apparently a citizen of a colony I once founded; sadly, it turned to rebellion some years ago. Nothing to do with our dedicated Good Brother, of course. Perhaps he was visiting to see if he could bring them back into the fold. Wouldn't that be lovely?"

So many unfamiliar words and concepts! Mirly struggled to make sense of Alum's introduction. Uncertain of the etiquette of her situation, Mirly gave a low formal bow. The other God—Darak—returned the bow graciously, and the metal sphere gave a little bob.

"In addition to these two, who are more or less physically present,"

Alum continued, "we are blessed with the presence of several billion People viewing remotely from My external Realm."

She bowed to the sphere. "Welcome, all," she said, though it came out a little more tired-sounding than she'd intended.

The four stood still, exchanging stares, equally uncertain of how to proceed.

Alum broke the silence, addressing His words to Mirly.

"We were nearly finished our tour of Heaven. But you've been on quite the tour, yourself, haven't you? I've followed your progress with some interest. Perhaps you would share some of your experiences with us?"

Share my travels and my thoughts with two Gods, a floating ball, and billions of strangers who are somehow listening, even though they aren't really here?—Mirly fretted.

"My Lord, I am hardly worthy to contribute anything useful in such company," she protested.

"Nonsense," He replied. "We are all just people, here. All just trying to come to a conclusion about the fate of our two universes. Your story is as valuable as any of ours. I have been blessed with your art before and found it joyful. Bless us all, now, with your tale. Please."

Joyful? That wasn't how she remembered His reaction to her last mandala, the one that had set her on her arduous journey. But if that was how Alum wanted to represent her art, He had to have His reasons.

A cushion-stone appeared to one side of the four of them. Alum motioned for Mirly to be seated. She delicately walked to the stone and rested her haunches on it. It felt good to be in a more restful pose.

"Ah, my dear. I beg your pardon. You've traveled far with little rest," Alum said. "Your energy stores must be depleted."

He flourished a hand and Mirly felt instantly refreshed and revived.

"A gift," He said, "for sharing your stories and perspective."

"Thank you, Lord," Mirly replied. "I haven't been as careful of my energy levels as I should have been during my travels."

Alum waved away her apology.

"No need for regrets. You had much to see, and needed great determination to see it all. Tell us about the structure and function of Heaven, of its beauty, of its people. Tell us of the good, the imperfect, and the confusing. The others can ask their questions, and the outside universe can learn of our world."

Mirly shifted on her seat and tried to compose her thoughts. So much had happened to her. She had traveled far, through a great variety of terrain from the edge of Heaven to its Core. She'd also collected centuries of memories—almost all happy—of her life as one of God's creatures.

She began.

44

"LIFE IN HEAVEN is nothing but pure joy and continuous blessing," Mirly said.

"I have lived many long lives, happy to be growing, learning, and improving. I was filled with love for our Lord and dedicated myself, as we all do, to singing His praises. My gifts in my current anima form run toward music and the visual arts."

She smiled. "I like to arrange musical notes in unusual combinations and compositions. And I like to arrange pretty stones and colored sands into complex shapes."

"Ah, yes," Alum said. "Let's examine your last work. The one that set you on your journey. The one you believe I disapprove of."

How could He know that?—Mirly wondered. Then she remembered God truly did know all. Had she needed more proof, this would be it.

The Living God shifted all four of them to the top of the gigantic boulder, looking down on the very same mandala Mirly had created, the one that had started her misery. Somehow, Alum had magically caused the mandala to reappear in all of its glorious, swirling colors!

Mirly smiled on hearing her composition for the variable flute playing in the background. The pleasing notes floated over them; she couldn't tell from where.

Are we really here, again?—she wondered. *Or is this a shared dream?*

Darak grunted. "Earth, from high above the North Pole."

Mirly looked down. The colors and design still pleased her but much less so now, knowing that Alum had been less than happy with it.

Alum walked to one edge of the boulder and pointed to a section of the picture.

"You can see, here, where some of My less pleasant memories crept into this universe from outside."

Darak followed His outstretched arm and laughed.

"Oh, my! Yes, I can see why this might not have been completely pleasing to You, but how could this poor creature have known?"

Stralasi's Familiar floated forward.

"What am I looking at?" he asked.

"You know it as Origin," Darak answered, "Ancient Earth. Humanity's birthplace, shortly before its destruction."

He glowered at Alum and his chin pointed to the same gray blob that Alum had indicated. "Perhaps You would like to tell them how *that* was released."

"Perhaps you would like to tell them how it was *created*," Alum replied.

Stralasi heard the challenge in His voice. In both voices. *Extraordinary!*

"I didn't know at the time," Darak said, "but I do, now. A colleague used something he didn't fully understand to kill our mentor."

"Your mentor—you mean, Dr. Darian Leigh?"

Darak nodded. "Yes, that's right. Our lab mate, Larry Rusalov, became unwell, pathologically jealous, paranoid. He couldn't tolerate that Darian's nanotech-lattice—an abomination of nature—gave him enhanced intelligence, or that Darian wanted to share his gift with the world. He was insanely envious and yet at the same time he rejected Darian's offer to receive the enhancement himself. He rejected the research in its entirety and came to see Darian as a dangerous enemy that had to be eliminated.

"In Larry's defense, he had no idea that Darian's attempt to protect himself would produce the Eater. I don't imagine even Darian realized what effect his attempts to survive would bring about."

"*That's* the Eater? But it's so small," Stralasi exclaimed.

This insignificant gray blob depicted in the mandala looked nothing like the solar-system sized monstrosity he and Darak had hunted.

"In the beginning, it was, yes," Darak answered.

"We tried to contain it and slow its growth. That worked for a short while. We were on the verge of moving it into deep space when *somebody*—I believe that was you, Alum—destroyed the enclosure. With nothing to curb its appetite, the Eater grew rapidly. In less than a few days, it went from the size of a small house to something capable of absorbing several cities. A week later, the entire planet was gone.

"It was a nightmare come true. Over time, the legends we created in Alum's Realm changed its name from the Eater to the Da'arkness, a perversion of Darian's name. They made it out to be even more terrifying than it ever was, originally, I mean. It became the new bogeyman, the infinite blackness of empty, hungry space. It became something to frighten little children and their parents. A tool used to turn people away from science, and research, and anything unknown."

"I named the Da'arkness for the horror that it truly was," Alum answered.

"And, coincidentally, precisely the right horror to aim at Eso-La?" Darak countered.

"What do you mean?" the Living God asked in a manner so convincing that everyone listening in believed Alum sincerely had no idea what Darak was talking about.

Darak didn't let the ploy pique his anger.

"I found the Eater on its new trajectory about a light year away from the ESO colony and closing in. Oh, no need to worry. I found a safe place to send it. Thanks for lending me three of Your element arrays; they came in handy."

Alum's face darkened. "The Eater was an appropriate gift for those rebels. Not that it matters anymore. The universe would not have endured long enough to see it reach Eso-La."

"Did You know that Darian Leigh was still inside it?" Darak asked in a casual tone. "Well, more or less inside. I pulled him out and rebuilt him, as much as I could."

"You rescued Darian, the high priest of the Da'arkness, himself? Can we surmise that your own assumed name is some perversion of his?" Alum asked.

"I chose my name to honor my mentor," Darak said quietly. "Just like Kathy Liang did."

Alum flinched.

"Ah, yes. I see You remember her," Darak noted. "Kathy Liang used the DAR prefix to identify the Cybrids she constructed from our minds. That was before You killed her, the human her, anyway. Kathy lives on in her Cybrid self. You'll recognize that name too. It's Darya."

Alum's eyes widened.

Darak smiled back, pleased with himself at having surprised the Living God.

"Ancient history," Alum sniffed. "It has little meaning or significance today."

Darak shadowed Him as He strolled across the boulder.

"It still reverberates," Darak said. "But now, it's not only *our* history."

He waved a hand at Stralasi's floating Familiar.

"Now, it's *humanity's* history. The billions of people listening in know our story. How we all came to be who we are. How we got to this point."

Alum ignored him. "Tell me, little one," he said to Mirly, "Where did you find your inspiration for this particular piece?"

"I..I don't know, Lord," the doe-centaur stammered.

"It came from Me!" Alum cried triumphantly.

"All things in Heaven flow from its Creator. My Glory shines upon all, bringing life to inanimate clay. My Fires burn at the edge of Heaven, drawing new matter from the endless Chaos that surrounds us. My Thoughts inspire creativity in My children."

"Your own thoughts displease You, then?" Darak asked.

Alum wheeled on him.

"The thoughts that led to this abomination? Yes, those ones do. They are the result of the imperfections and uncertainty in the outside universe. An uncertainty brought on by its very nature and by *your* meddling."

"I was looking around," Darak shrugged. "Taking stock of what the Realm has become. Trying to understand why You were so willing to throw our entire universe away—all universes—away."

"All but this one, My one truly good Creation."

"Why are You willing to sacrifice everything, including all of us, for this version of Heaven?"

"Are you blind? Can you not see? Heaven is perfection!" Alum roared. He turned to Mirly.

"Isn't that right, Mirly? Mirly has seen its almost endless beauty, its pleasing variety, its joyous celebration of the cycle of life without suffering. She has traveled much of this world. Tell Me, child, have you seen suffering anywhere in Heaven?"

Mirly thought back over her travels across great plains, over rolling hills, through lush forests, and along the shores of lakes, rivers, and streams. Indeed, it was all beautiful, peaceful, loving, and glorious. Even when she'd approached the stark edge of Heaven, she'd found the vast proliferation of microscopic life to be wonderful.

Except for me, it was all perfect—she realized.

Mirly hung her head low.

"I am the only imperfection I saw in all of Heaven, Lord."

Alum placed His hand on her shoulder.

"No, child," He said. "The imperfection came from outside, through Me. Through My concerns about this unholy rebellion. When the outside is gone, all will return to the way I intended it. Soon, you will be as pure as you once were."

"I'd like that." She smiled hopefully.

"Or you could leave here," Darak suggested.

Leave? The only reason Mirly had wanted to visit outside of Heaven was to combat Alum's concerns in the outside universe. What reason would she have to leave if those concerns were removed?

Sensing her doubt, Darak explained.

"Even if all other possible universes were destroyed, Alum will still carry the memory of our universe. Heaven is a dream. A myth. You think you have perfection but all you have here is stasis and stagnation. Beautiful things may happen here, but *interesting* things never will. He will never allow it."

Darak searched Mirly's eyes.

"You've tasted what *interesting* feels like," he said. "You've journeyed well outside of your comfort zone, mentally and physically. You've come to understand something of conflict, hardship, and danger. But you also understand adventure, curiosity, and possibility."

"I...," Mirly began.

She didn't know how to finish that sentence. Would she like to see outside? Did she want more adventure and new things? Or did she yearn for the peaceful certitude of the life she'd once known?

Darak left her with her thoughts. She had to decide for herself. He turned away and, through Stralasi's Familiar, addressed the gathered billions.

"Alum can have His Heaven. It's a universe He's created according to His own ideas and, yes, they have a certain beauty. We have no need or desire to deny Heaven its right to exist. But Alum would deny all other possible universes *their* right to exist, so that His version of Heaven alone can thrive, and no other universes will ever intrude on this one.

"When I first sensed our universe had stopped expanding, I returned to this universe from the Chaos. I wanted to understand what caused the beginning of the end of possibility.

"What I discovered was that Alum has gone beyond stopping our universe or any other universes from growing in the Chaos. He has begun the process of reversing Creation. Soon, the laws of nature that hold the stable, real matter of our universe, or of any other universe besides Alum's so-called Heaven, will become untenable.

"I say, let Alum have His Heaven, but not at the price of all other possibilities for the rest of eternity."

"Judges, Witnesses, People of the Realm, I have given you the knowledge you need to understand this pressing situation and its context, along with the intelligence to evaluate it. Now, I ask you to vote, and let us hope that this man who views Himself as the Living God will heed the guidance of your collective wisdom."

"I ask you all now, will you submit to Alum's vision or will you remain open to unimaginable possibility?"

After no more than a few tense seconds, the results were complete.

A little over half voted to keep the universe as it was, not to allow

Alum's vision to become the only one, to allow the multiverse to continue flourishing.

Darak's shoulders slumped in relief.

Even Stralasi chuckled nervously to himself in disbelief.

Only a tiny fraction of a percent more than half had made the difference. A few thousand votes, at most, had swung the Realm to reject Alum's offer.

That's it? It's all over?—he wondered.

Now what?

Alum's disdainful laughter shook the boulder on which they stood. Suddenly, all four were back at the Core of Heaven.

"Puh! Barely a majority," He said. "Even with all of your influence and meddling with the minds of My People, you could hardly convince half of your 'judges' to follow your vision."

"Nonetheless, it was a majority," Darak replied quietly. "After living years under Your all-pervasive rule, more than half of these representatives—people who have only just now learned the true history of Your Realm and Your Divine Plan—voted against You."

"Voted?" Alum spat. "Did you really think I would listen to your *vote*? I, who dreamed of Paradise for tens of millions of years, who planned and experimented, whose wisdom exceeds yours as much as yours exceeds that of the smallest insect?

"Fools! I have given you millions of years of peace and prosperity. Now, I offer Perfection and you would reject it? For what? For adventure?"

"You know Your idea of perfection puts an end to surprise and unanticipated possibilities," said Darak. "Even Your own People, those who've worshipped You for ages, can see the value in potential for innovation over this perfect, bland sameness."

"My Will be done!" Alum shouted.

He waved a hand and Stralasi's Familiar shimmered and faded.

Darak didn't look away from the Living God, but Stralasi's Familiar re-solidified.

"I had hoped You would listen to Your own People," the man-God said. "But I was prepared for the possibility that You might not."

"You will not stop Me," Alum replied. "All you've done is sow discord among My People. Your meddling has been inconsequential. As one might have predicted, most of My flock remain loyal, unconvinced by your plea. The few who voted with you will stand alone against the might of the Realm."

Darak shook his head.

"You still don't get it, do You? Let me set You straight. We don't fear Your might," he said. "And we are not alone."

DAR-G's analysis of the interface shell had been complete for some minutes. He'd acquired the complete physical parameters of Heaven. Darak's presence in the Core solidified as he merged with the local reality, and brought all four of his physical forms into Heaven. The Angel Gabriel stood on Darak's right and the Aelu leader, Fal sek Troal, stood on his left. The floating Cybrid form of DAR-G rapidly computed aggressive fields from a spot behind the three.

"What the...," Alum gasped. Without completing the question, He shifted several large silicene nodes and the God, Raytansoh, into the Core of Heaven.

DAR-G cast the first RAF fields, permeating Raytansoh with three incompatible sets of physical laws.

The octopoid God wavered and screamed in pain, solidified briefly, and was shredded by changes too fast for him to follow. What little was left of him in Heaven fell to the floor, dead.

The battle was only a second old, and its first victim had already been claimed.

Fury disfigured Alum's face. He flourished His hands and cast ornate fields of rapidly-fluctuating physics. Enormous energies accumulated in His palms, awaiting release.

Alum attacked.

45

"WHERE..? HOW..? WHO SUMMONED ME?" the Angelic Alumitum guard demanded, as he struggled to make sense of his sudden and unexpected relocation.

Obviously, it couldn't have been Alum who'd shifted him to the Proctor's Office. The Living God's shifts were always preceded by a terse but clear edict.

The Angel looked to the Proctor, the next highest authority in the room, but the man looked equally nonplussed. Clearly, he hadn't summoned the Angel, either.

The Angel's scrutiny moved to the already too-familiar faces of Darian Leigh and Brother Stralasi. The former's oddly calm demeanor and the latter's barely contained terror provided no clues.

There was no one else in the room to consider.

"I brought you here," Darian said indifferently, addressing the Angel as if speaking of mundane matters of little consequence to anyone present.

The Angel faced the man he'd intuitively tagged as a troublemaker the first time he'd laid sensors on him. Yes, his instincts had been proven correct; they almost always were. As to what particular brand of trouble the fellow was instigating, the Angel was less sure. But he would find out.

Contrary to what most would consider common sense under the circumstances, Darian spoke up, unbidden.

"I thought your Lord Alum might prefer speaking through you, His humble Angelic servant, rather than convey His message as a disembodied voice," he explained. "I hope that's okay."

The Angel moved faster than Stralasi's lightly-enhanced human brain could process. After a millisecond lag while his perception caught up, the Good Brother correctly interpolated that the Angel had shifted, unsheathed his mighty sword and swept it through the air in a single decisive arc, cleaving Darian's chair in two. The supersonic shockwave left in the wake of the slashing blade blew out the nearest window.

Stralasi watched broken glass fly outward in what felt like slow motion. Apparently, the Angel was not okay with Darian's suggestion.

Darian? Where did Darian go?

As if reading his mind, Darian placed a protective hand on the Good Brother's shoulder.

Stralasi looked back and, sure enough, there was Darian. He'd somehow shifted away ahead of the fierce slash and now stood relaxed and entirely unscathed off to the monk's back quarter.

"You won't be able to harm us," Darian informed the Angel, gently but firmly stating a plain truth to someone who might be thinking otherwise.

Flummoxed, the Angel shifted directly behind the two men and plunged his sword forward with enough force to skewer them.

"This is going to get tiresome rather quickly," Darian commented from across the room. Stralasi and the Proctor stood beside him in front of the blown-out window. The fresh breeze at their backs ruffled the folds of the monk's robe.

"My friend, if you insist on playing this game, I can avoid you all day," Darian assured the Angel. "Perhaps, I should just shut you down until you can restrain yourself or until Alum deigns to join us," he said.

The Angel went limp and crumpled to the floor. Darian gave the lifeless form a sad smile, waved a finger, and reactivated the winged defender of the Living God.

"Are we good?" Darian asked.

The Angel sprang to his feet, pointed its sword at the trio, and unleashed a blinding bolt of energy.

A sharp crack of thunder shook the chamber but the accompanying energy stream splashed off the protective shield that had sprung up instantly around the three. The men were unhurt but the Proctor's desk burst into flame.

"You'll hurt the building and the habitat more than us, that way," Darian informed the Angel. He waved a hand and extinguished the flaming desk.

"HOLD!"

The energy stream snapped off at the sound of Alum's voice.

The Angel sheathed his sword and stood silently, head bowed, arms at his side. When he looked up again, it was Alum's own fire that burned in his eyes.

* * *

ONE FLOOR ABOVE, THE LAST TINY SPYDER pushed through a gap in the metal housing of the QUEECH device. A centimeter beyond, microchips and other electronic components crowded a printed circuit board. The Spyder jumped onto a cylindrical resistor and slid down to a section of the board below. It carefully avoided contact with the protruding metal posts and copper strips, keeping the conductive pads on its legs a safe distance from any active electronics that snaked underneath.

Darian had designed the Spyder to guide itself and set up the hack into Alum's backbone network autonomously. Following its programmed memory and instincts, it made its way past warm microchips toward the optoelectronic components at the far edge of the circuit.

With single-minded purpose, the tiny spy neared its goal, the interface chip that connected the entangled particles to Alum's silicene node. Neither the excitement of a dangerous task nor the fear of losing its own life along the way clouded its arachnid brain. It was a biomachine, a smart, independent, adaptive agent programmed to achieve a single intention: to reach and subvert its target.

It was almost there.

* * *

"WHO ARE YOU?"

The voice projected by the Angel was overlaid with the unmistakable power and confidence of the Living God.

"Alum, I presume," Darian replied. "A pleasure to finally make Your acquaintance. I've heard so much about You."

"I don't recognize your face but your voice reminds me of Shard Trillian," the Living God replied in a more relaxed tone. "Ah, yes, I see traces of cosmetic surgery," He noted. "But you're not Shard Trillian, are you?"

Darian took one step forward and gave a shallow bow.

"You're astute, and correct. I wear Shard Trillian's body, though his mind had already vacated by the time I first inhabited this shell."

"Are you one of the Six? Did one of you escape My wrath?"

"One of Darak's group? No," Darian replied.

The Angel tipped his head.

Darian smiled enigmatically. "It surprises You that others know of Darak and his Gods? Oh, don't worry. I'm not one of them. Do you like riddles? Here's one for you. I go back further than any of them and yet I am younger than all."

"Riddles do not amuse Me," Alum replied. "Neither does your presence here at this time amuse Me. Be gone."

He made the Angel's right hand sweep outward and cast a field to shift Darian and Brother Stralasi into the oblivion that was the Chaos.

Darian stepped further into the room, away from the broken window. He pulled Stralasi with him, but left the Proctor standing against the wall, stunned and speechless.

"Banishment to Hell? Or should I say, dematerialization into the Chaos? Either way, simple RAF tricks like that have no effect on the likes of us, do they?"

"I sense *what* you are," Alum replied. "I asked you, *who*."

"Hasn't Darak told You?" Darian taunted. "I'm sure he must have mentioned me by now. Sorry I couldn't join You and Your chosen few in Your 'Heavenly' little universe." He drew air quotes around the word Heavenly as he spoke it. "Darak thought I might be more useful speaking to You here."

"Ah, the infamous Darian Leigh," Alum guessed, "risen from the dead?"

Darian grinned. "Rescued from within the Eater, in any case," he said.

"You are but a distraction and not much of that," Alum said. "Tell me what you came here to say and be on your way. I have other matters to attend to."

Darian laughed. "Yes, I'm sure You must. Darak's been keeping You rather busy, has he? I guarantee You that, very soon, You'll be even busier."

"None of that matters. By now, you must be feeling the weakening of forces that hold this universe together."

"Yes, yes, I'm aware, we are all aware, that Your Deplosion Array has been activated."

"Then, what do you want?" Alum demanded. "More of your useless demands for democracy? Another worthless evaluation of My Divine Plan?"

A sly smile grew on the Angel's beautiful face. "Or have you realized the futility of resisting Me? Perhaps you'd like to join Me?"

"No, thanks. I'm fine," Darian replied, as indifferently as if he'd been offered a stale cookie.

"THEN, SPEAK OR I WILL DESTROY YOU! What is the purpose behind all this shifting activity?"

Darian shrugged.

"Honestly, I just wanted to talk to You, to have Your full and undivided attention for a few moments. I suppose I could have been more subtle about it."

"Have My attention...?" Alum said. "You mean, *distract* My attention."

He calculated some cursory probabilities.

"The wasps near My node, they didn't venture in there by accident or random coincidence, did they?"

"Wasps? What wasps? I have no idea what you're talking," Darian feigned innocence.

He imagined Alum analyzing the countless possibilities of an attack on His node, and tried to guess the likely progression of His thoughts. The all too coincidental presence of wasps up there would point to a microscale or nanoscale invasion. No doubt, Alum would be examining conditions in the machine room at the moment. Darian sensed the maintenance Cybrid's float fields activating.

He needed another distraction.

Darian directed hundreds of nanoscopic particles to the security Angel's sword hand. Before Alum could reassert control, the hand pulled the sword from its sheath, aimed it straight overhead, and let loose a blast targeted at the machine room.

The Angel's face registered Alum's shock at losing control over its body. In any being slower than an Angel endowed with nanoelectric muscles, the Living God could've prevented the blast. Milliseconds too late, Alum shifted the Angel's the offending sword, and the hand that held it, outside the habitat where they would do less harm.

It was no accident that Darian had aimed the energy beam dangerously close to Alum's silicene node, but a meter to one side.

We need to keep that node intact.

With Alum briefly distracted, Darian threw a shifting field around himself and Brother Stralasi. He jumped them both to a quiet side street near the far north end of the habitat. He grabbed the stunned monk's arm and steered him casually toward a small café.

By the time Alum returned His attention to the Proctor's Office, Darian and Stralasi were gone.

* * *

DARIAN PULLED OUT A CHAIR and motioned for the monk to sit. Stralasi stared at him without comprehension. Darian applied gentle pressure to the Brother's shoulder and Stralasi crumpled into the seat.

While Stralasi looked on blankly, Darian ordered coffee for both of them, pulled out his tablet, and connected it to the bigger tabletop display. Lesson plans, reference materials, and videos swarmed across its surface, moving out from under the cups and saucers.

They looked like any other pair of instructors discussing their teaching plans for the upcoming week.

Darian shuffled some random file icons around on the tabletop.

"We'll wait here," he said.

Stralasi noticed the cappuccino on the table in front of him. *When did that arrive? Have we been here long?*

He picked up his cup and took a sip, barely tasting it. His trembling hand set the cup back down on the saucer. He let out a ragged exhalation.

"Wait here?" he asked. "Wait for what?"

"Our friend has almost reached its destination."

"Our friend? Oh, the Spyder."

"Yes. The end is nearing."

"Which end?" Stralasi asked. "The end of Alum or the end of the universe?"

"Ha!" Darian barked a quick laugh. "Yes, that *is* the question."

* * *

MINUTE VIBRATIONS TICKLED the sensitive hairs on the Spyder's feet. The little spy stopped. It hesitated to change course, now that it was almost at the interface chip.

Something above clicked, sending the Spyder scurrying under the cover of a large buffer chip. Light streamed in as the maintenance Cybrid removed the external cover of the QUEECH comm device.

The Spyder lifted it legs and tucked its body up into a shallow depression on the underside of the chip. It stayed perfectly still.

A roaming tentacle tipped with an optical sensor appeared through the opening above, casting a shadow on the printed circuit board near the little spy's hiding place.

The camera scanned horizontally across the circuit board, performing a thorough visual inspection above, around, and beneath the electronics. It spotted nothing unusual. When it reached the far end, the tentacle pulled back a little to allow its hair-thin digital probe appendages clear access to the device components.

Several of the whiskers examined the Spyder's target, testing it for any sign of incursion or compromise. After a few tenths of a second, they disengaged and worked their way outward to the support circuitry. They passed within a hair's breadth of the inert Spyder and paused at the conductive posts of the buffer chip beneath which it hid.

The Spyder didn't move.

The probes passed by the intruder and contacted the conductive metal pegs of the microchip. They maintained contact for half-a-dozen seconds before slipping away to the next test site.

Satisfied that the comm device was uncompromised, the Cybrid retracted its various appendages and reattached the housing of the node.

The Spyder waited for the previous stillness, darkness, and silence to return to the room, counted out an additional sixty seconds, carefully unfurled its tiny legs, and continued on toward its destination.

46

DARYA DROPPED A MILLION ATTACK SQUADS into position around randomly-selected elements of the Deplosion Array. Each squad comprised two thousand soldiers, a combination of battle Cybrids, converted Familiars, and Aelu.

Overpowering force, surprise, and unpredictability. Will that be enough?

The first squads met practically no resistance. They overwhelmed the comparatively meager defense mounted by the local groups of Alum's Angels and quickly destroyed thousands of array elements.

Monitoring progress from the muster point near So-2, Mary and Timothy received the troops' initial reports with a mixture of relief and triumph. It was already looking like their new grand-scale maneuvers using over two billion troops might succeed where their smaller attacks had failed.

The sense of triumph was short lived.

Even as they prematurely cheered their victories, Alum adapted to the changed format and forced the rebels to pull back.

Wherever Darya dropped in troops to attack a new asteroid base, ten thousand Angels would instantly spring into place between her squads and their targets.

Where are they all coming from?—she wondered. *How many Angels does Alum have?*

"Go dark!" she transmitted. Her troops deactivated transponders and shifted into the midst of the enemy formations.

Darya fought against disappointment, as reports of destroyed asteroids slowed.

Be patient—she thought. *Mary and Timothy's plan is a good one. Take the slow victory, if that's all we can have.*

The pair had projected this very outcome; they knew they were only going to get a few unimpeded seconds at most before Alum's defenses fully engaged. Still, Darya couldn't help but feel disheartened as reports of destroyed bases slowed to a trickle while her troops' losses grew significantly.

Not just losses—she reminded herself. *Lives. Real people, not statistics.*

Friends are dying. Cybrids are dying. Aelu are dying. And I can't even imagine what it feels like for the Esu to lose their Familiars.

She forced the unproductive thoughts aside and focused on comparing the incoming battle results with those predicted by their models.

To a casual observer, the combat looked sterile and unexciting, devoid of the horrifying sounds and action of ancient land-based battlefields. In space, the rebel troops shifted, listened to transponder signals from the enemy for a few hundred milliseconds, computed optimal firing trajectories, let loose a blast of energy, and shifted again. Energy beams and kinetic weapon assaults were silent, invisible, and harmless unless one were directly in the line of fire, in which case, they were visible and brutally lethal.

Mary, Timothy, and Darya watched the number of enemy transponder signals decrease by one or two at each battlefield every few seconds. They stood by helplessly whenever, less frequently than the Angels, one of Darya's soldiers got caught in the middle of their opponents' disorganized crossfire and was killed.

Darya tried to focus on the numbers and strategies and ignore how many of her people were dying. She relayed Mary and Timothy's fine-tuning adjustments to her soldiers and tweaked individual formations to optimize their effectiveness.

Five minutes into battle, Alum's Archangels joined in. Their weapons discharged violent plasma bolts from the heart of a black hole, cutting through the battlefields indiscriminately and destroying both friend and foe.

Darya followed Mary and Timothy's suggestion to spread out her troop formations and increase their already rapid rate of shifting.

"Trust us on this. Our kill rate will drop off, but our casualties will decline even more," Mary had explained. "The Archangels will do a lot of the work for us, destroying more on their own side than ours."

Frustrated at not achieving their expected level of devastation, the Archangels pulled back from the offensive and formed close-knit, protective rings around the array elements.

"What do we do now?" one of Mary's attack leaders asked.

"Same pattern, but we'll offset you into the middle of the Archangel formations," Mary replied. She transmitted new shifting coordinates and sequences to their teams.

Now that they were closer to the asteroids, the continuous radar pulses from the array elements illuminated the rebel soldiers, stripping them of the protective cloak of deep-space darkness and leaving them exposed and vulnerable. As expected, the odds shifted quickly in favor of the Archangels.

Darya watched her teams being picked off. She doubled the rate of pattern shifting. It slowed the decimation, but it wouldn't be long until the enemy gutted them.

I have to get in there and help—she thought. *The Archangels are too powerful. They're destroying us. We need to change the attack parameters. Quickly.* There had to be something she could use from her recent elevation to godhood.

She hadn't had time to familiarize herself with her toolbox of godhood tricks. The ability to control the laws of physics brought all sorts of possibilities to her vastly expanded mind. Too many. It was overwhelming to think about.

She focused on what she knew from her own experience. Most of the Deplosion Array elements housed limited, specialized nodes of Alum. The deplosion fields were so complex that the individual CPPUs were dedicated to the required math. That left little processing power to house any of the Living God's consciousness. Once activated, the field generators were set to run on automatic. Alum had never seriously considered the possibility of attack by someone with RAF capabilities. He never thought He'd need to be personally present to defend His Deplosion Array.

Okay, that gives me something to work with—she thought.

"Mary," she sent via QUEECH comms, "which element has resisted attack the longest?" *Best start with our most difficult target*—she thought.

"Easy. That would be SagA* 129.564.992. We're twenty minutes in and the asteroid's practically unscathed. Both sides are taking heavy losses and nobody's been able to gain a consistent advantage. I suggest we move that team to a different target."

"Hold off on that," Darya replied. She jumped to the well-defended asteroid and examined the battle.

Her fighters were following the modified attack plan. They were executing blind shifts reliably and accurately. Alum was losing a lot of Angels but kept bolstering their ranks with a small number of Archangels—not enough to win the battle but they were holding their own.

What's it going to take to tip the scales?—Darya wondered.

She watched through several shifting cycles. Each time her attack group got within range of the asteroid, they met with heavy resistance from the Archangels, and were repelled before inflicting much damage.

Repelled? Why are they leaving without completing their firing sequence?

"Mary, Timothy, this team's energy blasts are being cut short by about a hundred milliseconds. Only half the projected energy is released on each volley. What's going on?"

They watched as another group fired a few shots and left prematurely.

"I have no idea," Mary replied.

Darya shifted five of her attackers a few light minutes away from the battle.

"Why did you leave without completing your full attack sequence?" she demanded.

Confused, the battle-Cybrids hesitated. They compared their data among themselves.

"We didn't," they answered together and sent their recordings of the half-second they'd spent near the asteroid before shifting. All five showed a synchronized jump into their pre-assigned positions, followed by 300 milliseconds of target acquisition, and a 200 millisecond burst of fire.

"Except you only fired for a quarter of that time," Darya said, "which did nothing to the asteroid, and then you left early."

Her assertion was met with stunned silence.

"What time do you have?" she asked.

They compared chronometers. All five were 225 milliseconds slow.

"I know what's going on," Darya said. "Alum's messing with local time."

It's my own fault for not anticipating this. I have to start thinking like a God— she realized. Her fighters were attacking the asteroids from within a thin shell outside of its jump-blocking fields, as close as they could possibly get without conventional rockets.

Alum must have used the Deplosion generators to produce a localized time dilation effect, a tweak so small we didn't notice it.

She sent a message to Mary and Timothy.

"We need to mix it up a little. Vary the distances from which we shoot at the array elements. It's too predictable and Alum's taking advantage of that."

"But it'll weaken the blasts," Mary protested. "It'll add fifty percent to the number of hits needed to kill one asteroid."

"I know," Darya replied. "But I need the time it'll buy us."

She returned the five Cybrids to their next assigned positions.

*One God's direct intervention deserves another—*she thought, and shifted herself directly inside the asteroid.

As she passed through the asteroid's RAF field, she felt a wave of nausea but nothing she couldn't handle. She materialized next to the main CPPU.

Let's see, what do we have here? Standard asteroid layout, power and computational support near the core, massive arrays of RAF generating antennae spread just under the surface.

"WELCOME!" a booming voice greeted her. "DARYA, I PRESUME?"

Alum?

The shock of hearing that voice, His voice, here inside this particular asteroid sent her mind reeling. Was it a trap? Why would the Living God house any portion of His consciousness inside this array element?

"I guess I shouldn't be surprised to find You here," she answered, feigning more calm than she felt.

"Nor I, you," Alum replied.

And just how much of You is here?—she wondered as she bobbed politely.

"Sometimes, direct involvement is required in an engagement," she said aloud. "As I'm sure you know."

"Do you really think your direct involvement here will make any difference?" the Living God challenged.

Darya heard the arrogance and disdain, born of millions of years of unchallenged supremacy. She yearned to rip that haughtiness from His throat, to teach Him that even Gods have responsibilities—to Their own people, at least, but also to the universes.

He has no right to eliminate this and all other universes. Whether natural or created, a universe has the right to an existence that doesn't depend on the capriciousness of a single Being, however supreme.

But can I convince Him of that? If not, am I prepared to enforce my belief?

Here, deep inside Alum's lair, surrounded by RAF generators that can cast fields across the whole universe and into the Chaos, what hope do I have? Is there anything at all that I, a newbie to godhood, can do against a Living God with eons of experience?

Now that she was beginning to understand the kind of power that came with the ability to shape the laws of nature, she was also beginning to see the limitations of that power and the responsibilities.

I've fought against Alum for millions of years. Ever since I learned what the Deplosion Array was for, what His Divine Plan meant for the universe, I've plotted and resisted. And I've made no headway. I am never going to win like this. We are going to die, every last one of us, and Alum is going to live on.

She caught herself wanting to give up, and laughed. She refused to lose this battle over her own uncertainties and fears. If she was going to lose, she was not going to make it easy for Him. She conjured up the image of herself as rebellious warrior princess and held it firmly in her mind.

Am I going to quit now?—she asked herself.

Hell, no!—came her instant reply. *I've fought Him for ages as a Cybrid. Now, I'm here as a God, an equal. And I am a force to be reckoned with.*

She threw out fields to shift Alum's CPPU into space, disrupted His power supply, and transferred bits of the entangled interior of the M87 supermassive black hole into His local RAF processor.

Alum brushed away the troublesome fields.

"I'm happy to see your new capabilities," He said. "It will make destroying you all the more pleasing."

He launched a massive, rapid-fire assault that directly altered the physics of her CPPU substrate in twenty different ways across several different parts of her brain, and shifted three Archangels into the chamber with her.

The Archangels fired beams of unrestrained black-hole energy.

Had she still been a mere Cybrid, such an attack would have finished her. Thankfully, she was no longer that person. She hadn't been able to explore her whole god-level toolbox yet but, when Darak had shown her how he isolated other manifestations of himself in hidden dimensions, she'd immediately supplemented her lattice with four Familiar CPPUs from the Esu, all modified to her special substrate, and hidden them in different dimensional extensions.

While part of her screamed in agony at the changes Alum had imposed on her physical presence, three other parts quickly analyzed His projections and cast their own fields to neutralize the effect.

Her fourth hidden mind added yet another field, diverting the Archangel blasts harmlessly into the Chaos, and reached out with its own fields to shut down the Archangels.

"Interesting," Alum said as His fighting constructs toppled. "And impressive. You have resources beyond what I expected. But are your abilities up to this challenge?"

She could hear the sneer in Alum's voice. He did not like to be surprised and, most certainly, never bested. At anything.

The Archangels disappeared.

Four more CPPU nodes, adorned with complex electronic antennae and exotic matter transmitters appeared alongside His existing node. Altogether, they took up half the empty floor space. Their combined processing power provided Alum with the capability to generate more RAF fields and fields of greater complexity than Darya could hope to keep up with.

Time to abort—Darya decided.

She tried to shift back to her team but was unable to leave.

She extended her range to various locations light years across the universe. Again, no luck.

Desperate, she tried to escape to entirely different universes of her own conception. Alum brought her back each time.

She attacked. She threw dozens of different realities at Him. She altered the matter around the chamber to explode in a fiery fusion reaction. As soon as the unleashed energies settled, the room appeared again as it had been. Nothing had changed. There was no damage to the chamber, and the five "Alum" nodes chugged away as if it were any other ordinary day.

Darya felt the deplosion field from the asteroid temporarily shut down as more copies of Alum poured into the local processors.

Before she could take advantage of the minor blip, she felt Alum shifting her nearby soldiers into the oblivion of the Chaos.

"Noooooo!" she cried.

Despite eons of training and conditioning, panic seeped in. Then, anger. The anger became fury.

She threw everything she could at Him to stop what He was doing but it was too late. Her soldiers were gone.

In Heaven, the biological Alum smiled and shifted more processing nodes to the asteroid.

Darya found herself encased in a world under Alum's control. His pervasive consciousness instantly analyzed her projected fields, no matter how complex, and used the asteroid's massive RAF antenna to neutralize whatever she tried to do.

She clenched her virtual jaw. Her resolve was indestructible. She didn't get to such an advanced age without learning a few tricks, and she'd had plenty of time to hone her perseverance along the way. No matter how unlikely survival appeared, she was not going to give up.

She waited for the next lull in Alum's onslaught and disabled one of His nodes. A tiny victory! Renewed confidence surged through her lattice.

"HOW DARE YOU!" Alum roared.

He shifted out the disabled CPPU and brought in two replacements.

The brutality of His attack was surging with His ire, and Darya felt the desperation of imminent defeat.

She screamed in rage and defiance.

47

IN THE CORE OF HEAVEN, THE BATTLE between the Gods intensified.

From their vantage point only a few meters away, it didn't look like much of a battle at all to Brother Stralasi and Mirly. The pair looked on with little understanding as the manifestations of Darak and Alum materialized in the Core of Heaven and joined in combat.

The human incarnations of the two Gods appeared to do little more than stand and glare at each other in intense concentration. At a level far above what the two observers could sense or understand, the two Gods fought ferociously, projecting enormous energies and complex, reality-altering fields.

To external observers, their cast fields had limited effect. One of the Gods projected some alteration to the basic laws of physics. The air around their opponent shimmered a little and returned to normal as the field was neutralized. The opponent launched a counter-offensive field with equally little apparent effect.

Internally, the battle was more like a combination of deep math, 3-D chess, and mental martial arts as the two probed each other for weakness.

To supplement His human form, Alum shifted in a dozen refrigerator-sized nodes from the outside universe.

Darak's manifestation of the Angel Gabriel, his most fierce persona, took up position alongside the man-God. His wings spread high, and his face settled into a fixed, fierce mask. His sword answered Alum's energy blasts but it was his RAF fields that held the most potential to hurt the Living God.

Stralasi could read no emotions from the gesticulating upper appendages and smooth elliptical body of Darak's Aelu persona, Fal sek

Troal, standing to the man-God's left. The creature's three arms waved rapidly overhead, throwing out reality-altering fields. Aside from that, the Aelo didn't move at all.

The hovering matte-gray sphere of DAR-G that floated behind Darak's three other manifestations was entirely inscrutable to the monk, as were Alum's machine CPPUs.

Alum's human personification, a distinguished-looking middle-aged man with a tidy goatee, stood before a neatly-grouted brick wall. He looked critically outnumbered facing off alone against Darak's several manifestations.

"But appearances," Stralasi told Mirly, "are often deceptive. That brick wall, for instance, hides the most powerful of foes, the enormous RAF machinery that comprises Alum's central node in Heaven."

Stralasi eyed the wall with reverence and fear.

What might one expect of a fighting wall?—he wondered. *No fierce anger. No panicked evasion of flying bullets or beams. No deflection of slashing swords. Such weapons were for lesser beings.*

"The Gods fight with the substance and basis of reality itself," Stralasi explained. "They pull exotic matter from other universes and weave complex mathematical mysteries to hurl at each other. They seek to overwhelm their opponents' essence in both obvious and subtle ways."

Intense beams crisscrossed the space between the opposing sides only to be silently dissipated, diverted, or harmlessly absorbed by unseen shields. Most of the beams were in energy ranges invisible to Stralasi and Mirly, though they caught flashes of visible light from the ionized atmosphere.

A gaping hole into another universe opened up next to Darak and his manifestations, threatening to swallow them whole or spill strange and deadly matter onto them. DAR-G closed the hole and cast a field of his own.

The air around Alum shimmered as the light of Heaven tried to make sense of physical laws that didn't include it, that didn't permit the photons of visible light. The Living God waved and the flickering ceased.

Mirly and Stralasi huddled together near the entrance gate to the Core, lost in their own thoughts. Shaking uncontrollably, Mirly leaned against the folds of the Good Brother's robe for support and comfort.

"Don't worry, Mirly," the monk reassured her. The young centaur-doe's quaking muscles and rapid breathing concerned him. "Stay close to me until they're done. I'm scared, too, but I've been in several similarly terrifying situations during my travels with Darak. I've learned to accept that this is beyond us mere mortals; let the Gods sort it out. It won't take long. We'll be okay."

He didn't worry her needlessly with the information that this battle, though it looked only slightly more fierce than a chess tournament fought under strobe lights, was probably deadlier than any other ever fought throughout the long history of humanity.

If Darak or Alum felt any pain from one another's attacks, let alone from sheer exertion of battle, neither showed it. The Gods bore their injuries, if any, in grim silence.

"No matter the outcome," Stralasi added, "you'll be free to stay here in Heaven if Alum wins, or to leave with us if Darak prevails."

Leave?—Mirly wondered. *Why would I leave? Leave Heaven? Leave my home? Leave Alum's Perfection?*

She felt both drawn to the idea of further travels and adventure, and repulsed. Overall, she supposed the notion appealed to her, now that she no longer suffered the worrisome starvation of energy that had plagued her journey these past few days.

On the other hand, having had a taste of adventure and the wider world, how could she ignore her fear of a vast unknown universe, one that was more foreign to her than the Edge of Heaven? Would the strange God, Darak, protect her in that other universe? Would he guide her or abandon her even more horribly than Alum had abandoned her here?

She didn't know what she wished for, or who she wanted to emerge victorious from the battle. It was both confusing and distressing.

Stralasi was far less conflicted. Though he'd spent the majority of his life, hundreds of years, in service to Alum and the Alumita, he'd come to agree with most of Darak's views. The siren call of security was hard to resist for one who'd grown up immersed in certainty, but it was a universe of limitless possibility that had led him to Gargus 718.5, to meeting Darak, to Eso-La, and to Crissea. It was hard to ignore that.

His attention flicked rapidly back and forth between his Familiar's consciousness that was bearing witness in the Core of Heaven, and his human consciousness that was sitting with Darian Leigh outside a café on the Alumitum.

Both of his selves shared a common sense of frustration and powerlessness.

I can't do anything but watch and wait. That seems to have been my fate ever since I met Darak. Would I have been better off never knowing the universe is filled with things beyond my paltry education, knowledge that I'll never grasp? Would I have felt more secure had I never witnessed the power of the Almighty? Correction, the Almighties? Oh, to go back to simpler times when my biggest worry was ensuring proper obeisance to the proscribed prayers!

He was tired of being little more than a footnote, a plaything, an insignificant speck of dust caught in a hurricane of Godly intent. He made a sour face as the image rose in his mind.

There are too many Gods in the universe—he thought as he watched the battle progress. *Even one God is too many.*

The blasphemous conclusion startled him.

Less than a year ago, I never would've conceived of such a thought. I've changed a lot—grown a lot—since my early days as a monk.

His easy acceptance of that growth scared and excited him.

What must the billions of Alum's People be thinking right now as they watch this battle of Gods in Heaven play out? Through my Familiar, no less, another foreign concept to most of them! How are they interpreting what they see? What meaning will they ascribe? How will they be changed by all of this?

Based on what he'd seen and knew, he guessed half of the People would view this battle as a brave attempt to fulfill the promise of freedom and novelty that they'd only recently begun to experience. The other half would see it as a heretical leap into a state of uncertainty that they'd never desired.

They're as much motes as I am—Stralasi thought. *Insignificant specks. Their own God—my own God—announced that their votes were meaningless. That has to hurt. But why should a God listen to the bleating of His sheep? In the end, a God has the power to impose His will on His People. Alum's Divine Plan and the way He ignored the voice of the People proved that.*

What will happen to the People if Darak wins? If Alum no longer governs the Realm? Though he had the power of a God, Darak never chose to rule, at least, not in this universe.

Was it possible to be a God and not desire a Realm or worshippers?

Possible, yes. But not common. One in eight, maybe. Out of Darak, Alum, and every one of the Gods that Darak called "the Six," only Darak had chosen a path that didn't place him at the top of a personal empire.

What if there were no lesser beings to cajole, extort, or force into worship?—he wondered. *What if we were all equal?*

What if there aren't too many Gods, but too few?

He tried to imagine a universe in which everyone was a God.

He attached a feed directly into the QUEECH comm channel that linked him with the billions of spectators in the Realm.

"Question: If you could be a God yourself, would you?" he broadcast. "Not to rule over others but to live freely, to associate freely with others, to share, to guide, to travel, to learn, and so on. Would you wish to be elevated?"

Millions of questions flooded back from the observers, seeking clarification of the parameters of his poll. He wrote himself a quick subroutine to classify the queries.

"Would it be open to all? Would I become immortal? Would I have to fight or compete with other Gods? How many Gods could there be? Would I have to/get to have my own universe?"

Even with the classification program, Stralasi felt overwhelmed by the questions.

I don't know what it's like to be a God, only to travel with one—he thought.

Sipping on a coffee in the climate-controlled comfort of the Alumitum habitat, he decided to forward the question to one who would know.

"Uh, Darian?" he said.

Darian looked up from pretending to play with icons on the tabletop, while he monitored his Spyder's progress inside Alum's QUEECH device.

"Yes?"

"I know you're busy with the Spyders but do you have a sec?"

"Sure. I'm just waiting for the last one to report in."

"I sent a poll to Darak's observers, the judges, and I need some insight to respond to some of their questions."

"A poll? What kind of poll?"

"I asked if they'd like to be Gods, all of them, if they could."

"What? If anything, I'd think this fight with Alum would convince you godhood is dangerous."

"That's an understatement. But wasn't it more dangerous when Alum was the only God? When He did whatever He pleased, unopposed? Wasn't that what allowed Him to activate His Divine Plan in the first place?"

Darian frowned. "Yeah, okay. You have a point."

"Okay, so what's the optimal number of Gods to have in the universe?"

"Oh, ho! We're into impossible questions, now, are we?" Darian laughed.

"Seriously," Stralasi replied. "Obviously, one is not enough. No restraints. Two sounds like a recipe for constant competition and battle for supremacy. Eight or ten doesn't seem much better."

He gulped noisily then continued.

"So what about trillions? I mean, it's just a question. A thought experiment, really. But...what do you think? Does it sound utterly absurd? Imagine trillions and trillions of beings, all with the power to create their own universes and alter the laws of reality. How would that look?"

Darian ran his hand through his hair.

"Wow. Well, there's certainly something to be said for safety in numbers. Primitive humans armed with nothing but a sword and their skill were more or less equal. Until someone with greater tools or skills came along."

"That's what I'd be worried about," Stralasi said. "The Gods I've known all seemed hungry for competition. They wanted to be the only one in charge."

"You're discounting the tens of millions of years of peace they brought before Alum went crazy," Darian pointed out. "Had He not desired to rule everything and, later, to remake everything, there would've been no conflict."

"Do you think conflict is inevitable?" Stralasi asked.

"I think the root of conflict is competition," Darian suggested. "Historically, at least for humans, that meant competition for resources, land, food, water, energy, minerals, cheap labor, and that sort of thing. On Eso-La, they developed a society that has no real need for competition. Look at the Esu. They're more or less all equal, and they're peaceful and cooperative."

"Alum's Realm had little need for competition," Stralasi pointed out. "Except for fun, of course. But can a free people also be free of the drive to compete?"

"Free *people*? Maybe not," Darian replied. "Free *Gods*, though, possibly. If you could rule out the kind of megalomania we saw in Alum, why not? Nothing restricts us from the resources we need. There's no real need to rule over others to ensure our own security. We can go wherever we want, and we can do whatever we want. We can make our own reality if the present one doesn't suit us."

"How would we restrain unbridled ambition? The kind with singular purpose like Alum has?"

Darian raised an eyebrow. "The kind that's incompatible with everything else in existence in this universe? Or in the multiverse, for that matter?"

"Yes. If the universe were filled with trillions and trillions of Alums, how could it ever be safe?"

"Safe?" Darian laughed. "Be careful you don't fall into that trap. That drive for everything to feel safe is Alum's biggest flaw. He focuses on what's safe and predictable for Him, not for everyone else. He craves certainty and security—to a fault. He's willing to sacrifice everything in pursuit of it. He sees no problem squandering the endless, chaotic, probabilistic possibilities of an unrestrained universe to achieve His dream."

"Hmm," Stralasi replied. "How can He be so smart and not see that *safe* is just a perception, and an unreliable one at that?"

Instead of answering, Darian stood up and paced the length of the fenced-off patio, some dozen paces, and back. Deep in thought, he repeated the action, once with his hands clasped at his chin and index fingers steepled to his lips, and a couple more times with his hands clasped behind his back.

While he silently paced, Stralasi polled the observers among the

People. They'd been listening to his conversation with Darian. The few remaining questions were ones Stralasi could easily field himself.

Darian stopped abruptly. A mischievous smile lit up his face.

"Brother, you've surprised me," he said. "If I had time to consult with Darak, I'm sure he'd echo that sentiment. Your proposal is impossible to model. It's impossible to predict. And that, my friend, is why it could be the best answer of all."

"What proposal? I made no proposal," Stralasi grumbled.

"That's why it's so perfect," Darian said. "Don't you see?"

"No, I don't. Not at all," Stralasi answered, shifting from confusion to mounting irritation. "Have you lost your mind?"

"Only once, but that's an old story now. Look, hear me out. Your proposal begins with an open-ended question, whose answer leads to an explosion of possibilities; it's the perfect counter-solution to Alum's vision.

"Imagine endless novelty, endless possibility," Darian held open his arms as if holding the wondrous explosion of potential between them. "And it's all available with a single stroke. A gift, easily given."

"What do you mean?" Stralasi asked.

"This," Darian said.

He opened his mind and poured knowledge through Stralasi's link and out into the Realm. The knowledge of reality, of how and why the multiverse was as it was, flew outward into the prepared minds of the billions of listening judges throughout Human and Cybrid space.

As it passed through the monk, it filled him as well and, in that moment, he finally understood *everything*: the laws of physics, chemistry, biology, mathematics, all kinds of information.

With it came the knowledge of how to weave and project reality-altering RAF fields directly from their minds.

Oh!—Stralasi thought. *That's what makes nature work.* And he saw the infinite possibilities of other natures, of other universes latent in the probabilities of the Chaos.

"How will we use this?" they cried. "How can we defeat Alum's Divine Plan with this?"

"Kill Him!" some answered. "Imprison Him," others said. "Destroy His Deplosion Array! Banish Him to His Heaven!"

As Darian listened to the clamor relayed back to him through Stralasi, an image came to mind. It was an ancient image, one from his youth.

He remembered watching Greg and Kathy perform an exercise in a stone-floored courtyard surrounded by white cement walls, bamboo, and water-shaped rocks. The smooth motions of their hands traced a symbol in the air, a symbol of the good inherent in evil, and the evil inherent in good, of dark transitioning into light and vice versa, of potential becoming reality.

Yin and Yang—he remembered. *The ultimate symbol of potential and reality.* A symbol of meeting hard with soft, of engaging push with pull, of diffusing aggression with tranquility or retreat.

And the answer revealed itself to him.

* * *

THE SPYDER FINALLY REACHED the optoelectronic chip at the far end of the printed circuit board. The interface circuitry that enabled Alum's distributed consciousness to function as an integral being lay exposed.

The Spyder's eight delicate legs wrapped themselves around a set of predetermined conductive posts that made the connections between the QUEECH comm chip and other circuitry. Five legs went to metallic posts on the chip and three shunted signals to bypass an encryption integrity detector.

It brought all eight of its conductive pads in contact with the targets, loaded the handshake virus, and ended its own brief life by fusing internal breakers to complete the circuit, essentially soldering its microscopic QUEECH comm unit into place between the local node and Alum's greater intergalactic mind.

Sitting across from Brother Stralasi at a table outside of the café, Darian received the first of Alum's thoughts through the Spyder's QUEECH and smiled.

"We're in," he said.

48

IT HAD BEEN A LONG TIME since the Living God felt fear. Not since the Aelu Wars had He considered that He might not prevail in a conflict. But Darak, Darya, and Darian were proving to be annoyingly formidable opponents.

Attacking Me on three fronts as the Deplosion Array is on the verge of fulfilling the Divine Plan! Such a daring strategy that I can't help but admire it, even in the hands of an enemy—He thought with a tiny bit of His vastly distributed mind.

The clumsy frontal attack by the five Gods had been nowhere near as elegant or as threatening as what He now faced. The Five had naively brought the battle to His territory, His long-held stronghold in the cradle of humanity.

His thousands of nodes in the Origin system had set numerous reality-distorting mines in the paths of the Gods. Thinking they were the ones springing the surprise attack, the Five had been ill-prepared to deal with the surprises that greeted them in the space near Sol. They died within seconds of beginning their battle.

Thanks to Raytansoh. He gave a moment of thought to the God, now dead, who had betrayed his five allies and warned Alum of their imminent attack.

Allies? What a thought! Raytansoh should've known that true alliances are impossible among Gods.

He didn't regret that Darak had killed Raytansoh.

It saves Me from having to deal with that nuisance at some later time.

And it made coordinating His own defense and counterattacks that much simpler. Not that there was anything simple about this battle or the rest of this long war.

Darya's Cybrid forces, coupled with the Esu Familiars and those remnants of the cursed Aelu, were having alarming success against the Angel and Archangel defenses.

Two-point-seven percent of the array gone! Not significant to the deplosion rate but worrisome, nonetheless.

After previous losses to the array—an unfortunate result of Darya's scheming—He'd reengineered the structure with twenty-percent overcapacity. Small losses wouldn't slow His schedule for altering all of reality. He only had to keep eighty percent of the array functioning for five more days and victory would be His.

In just five more days, deplosion will be irreversible.

My defense forces should be able to hold off the rebels for that long, especially with a little help from My subtle interventions.

He'd equipped many of the newest array elements with minor nodes capable of projecting simple RAF fields to distort time dilation in their vicinity. It was just enough to give the Archangels a defensive advantage against direct attacks on the elements. That tweak alone had hindered the enemy's destructive successes for many minutes.

And it had been working fine until Darya decided to get directly involved.

Foolish Cybrid, if only she'd been content to just interfere with the Archangels, that actually would've worked better against me. I would've had a much harder time countering her strength out there.

But she just couldn't contain her curiosity. She had to investigate, and that would be her undoing.

When Darya materialized inside one of His array element asteroids, He'd been elated. He'd thrown a complex attack at her, expecting a quick victory. To His surprise, the Cybrid had not only parried but managed to incapacitate one of His nodes. He'd howled at the pain of losing even a single mind, shifted out the useless node, and replaced it with two more. Infuriated, He'd redoubled His attacks, and pushed with deadly determination against her defenses.

Back in Heaven, the four-fold being that was Darak had figured out the reality parameters of Alum's unique Creation and was threatening His very heart, the Core of Heaven.

Despite being only four relatively insubstantial minds against Alum's behemoth Heavenly CPPU—a mind that filled the center of that universe—Darak was proving to be a capable adversary. Alum supplemented His Heavenly strength by shifting in nodes from the outside universe.

He threw everything He had at Darak's four manifestations: the man-

God, the rebel Angel, the unexpected Aelu, and the mysterious Cybrid. The four fought as one being, deflecting or absorbing Alum's attacks, and unleashing their own damage on the Living God.

No matter what, Heaven must not fall. I've moved too much of Me into Heaven's Core in preparation for the end of the external multiverse.

One by one, they destroyed Alum's imported nodes or made them useless by combined projected RAF fields and blasts from strange realities. The Living God tossed His spent nodes into the Chaos and replaced them with new ones.

As He did, entire planets in the universe outside of Heaven found themselves suddenly cut off from communication with their God. Starsteps failed, prayers went unanswered, and cities went dark as Alum's nodes disconnected from local resource coordination and joined the war in Heaven.

Despite the intensity of the other attacks, there was one other issue, seemingly minor but puzzling, that troubled the Living God. He diverted a tiny fraction of His attention for a closer look at what Darian Leigh was doing in the Alumitum. Had Darian's appearance in the home of Alum's own Church been intended as a distraction from the battles in Heaven and near the Deplosion Array?

Had the sudden blast from the Angel's sword been a deliberate near-miss or a serious attempt to disrupt Alum's node network?

Disabling My Alumitum node would have no greater impact than any other single node—Alum thought. *Did they not know this? How could they not?*

Wheels within wheels within wheels. Overlapping complexities.

He'd checked on His Alumitum node and its QUEECH comm machinery. Everything had been normal. There'd been no incursion, aside from the interesting coincidence of the wasps.

Darian was still somewhere in the Alumitum, though He couldn't find him at the moment. *No matter*—He thought. *I'll set Alumitum Angels to look for him.*

Perhaps that part of their strategy failed outright and Darian simply fled in defeat.

The thought inspired Him. He accelerated His attacks against Darak in Heaven and against Darya on the array element.

He threw even more of His consciousness into computing ever-stranger RAF fields to project against Darya and all four of Darak's manifestations.

He all but ignored His own defenses, shifting replacement nodes into the battlegrounds as soon as an existing one showed any signs of damage.

Days passed in ever-intensifying battle.

His losses grew but such losses were to be expected and, besides, the tipping point toward victory was getting close. He could sense it. His enemies were retreating under the might of His righteous attacks.

His mind felt as great as all of Creation, as powerful and unfettered as the Chaos itself. He connected to the deplosion field and His awareness penetrated to the limits of reality and beyond.

He was one with the multiverse, now, with extant and latent realities. He suffused Himself with all possibilities and He crushed them all, forcing everything that was, everything that ever could be, into His Divine Vision.

His minds raced faster and faster, grew greater and greater, until He was everything and everywhere. He pulled His will from the Chaos and hurled it at His foes. Time itself slipped.

And, then, the fighting was over.

The distortions of reality that had been hurled against Him came to an abrupt end. With no fields to counter, no energies to neutralize, His defenses went silent. His RAF casts fell, unchallenged, upon empty space.

His enemies were vanquished!

Darak, Gabriel, the Aelu, and the strange Cybrid, were all gone from Heaven. Darya and her armies of battle-Cybrids, the Aelu, and the Esu Familiars had all been destroyed or had fled. Darian had escaped or was still trapped on the Alumitum. It didn't matter which; he would die when reality collapsed.

Creation became quiet.

Peaceful.

No one was left to oppose His might.

Is it really done?—He wondered.

Have I won?

He reigned in His reality-altering fields and listened with all of His senses in case Darya and Darak had only retreated to regroup.

Nothing.

Their attacks were done. They were gone. Whether dead or escaped, He couldn't tell. The fog of blindingly-fast shifts in reality and spacetime-distorting blasts of energy hid exactly when and how the fighting had ended.

I am victorious; that is all that matters.

The Gods who'd fought against Him had been vanquished. It didn't matter whether they were dead or had fled.

Nothing would escape the deplosion field.

Nothing was left to oppose Him.

In the anticlimax of uncontested silence, an unaccustomed twinge of disappointment crept up on Him. It was then He realized Mirly and the part of Brother Stralasi that was his Familiar were no longer in Heaven's Core, either.

He extended His senses throughout Heaven. They were nowhere to be found. Whether they'd been caught in the intense crossfire or pulled from Heaven by Darak, He didn't know. He couldn't remember.

No matter.

He realized His own People had also grown silent in the outside universe.

He surveyed the Realm and found the deplosion field had already strengthened to such an extent that starsteps, Cybrids, Angels, and power generators everywhere had failed, likely, hours earlier.

His People were dying, as the physical and chemical reality on which their own biology relied fell into disarray.

No matter.

He would repopulate Heaven with infinitely many more People than the universe had ever supported.

Over the following days, stars grew unstable as the forces of gravity weakened and atomic fusion fizzled. Black holes, even those massive ones in the centers of galaxies, shook with unrestrained energies as the laws of physics changed within them. Across the width of the universe, ultra-novas blossomed brighter than any light since the Big Bang.

As the Chaos flooded back into the universe, into all possible universes, matter fell apart in brilliant showers of photons. The universe flared and fell dark. Soon, all that was left was a single black hole floating in the middle of Nothing.

Sagittarius A*, once the center of the Milky Way, now stood at the center of Creation, alone except for the Deplosion Array that surrounded it like pearls on a necklace.

From outside of that to the end of eternity was infinite Nothing. The deplosion field had even forced the Chaos into quiescence. No more zero-point energy to feed virtual particles popping in and out of existence. No more struggle for new kinds of interactions, new kinds of matter, to evolve. Possibility was dead.

I am Supreme!—Alum rejoiced as He looked out on the nothingness that surrounded His Creation.

He turned off the Deplosion Array and let the Nothing wash up against the edge of Sagittarius A*.

The event horizon fell away, revealing Heaven.

As the vacuum of Nothing lapped against the Edge of Heaven, the Fires of Creation began forming new matter from the tamed energy of the Chaos.

Alum's perfect universe grew.

His Creation was now the only Creation possible.
For now and forever, I will fill the cosmos with My Heaven.
He looked out upon the universe He had made.
And He saw that it was good.

49

"DOES HE BELIEVE IT?"

"Completely."

"I'm still not sure I agree that it was the proper solution."

"You think we should have killed Him?"

"I think we could have."

"But that would have left the Realm in disarray. And it would have left Heaven and its multitude of creatures alone."

"No more alone than we are in this universe."

"Sure, but unlike our universe, Alum's Heaven was created; it was *engineered*. We evolved naturally through generation of trial and error. We can adapt. Could *they* have survived without His continued guidance?"

"Maybe. Maybe not," Darak answered.

Mirly watched in stunned amazement as Darak, Darya, and Darian, along with Stralasi in both human and Familiar form, bantered over the fate of her former home and the only Supreme Being she'd ever known.

Before today—she realized. Could any God ever be called Supreme again when there were so many of them?

Billions—Brother Stralasi had said. *In another month, there will be trillions.*

Mirly stood in a pressurized chamber in Primus, the oldest Deplosion Array element, now lying quiescent like all the rest, and listened to the four Gods (*I'm in a chamber with four Gods!*) argue.

She was having trouble following the conversation. Her mind kept following her eyes as they peered out the window to the stars outside.

I made it!—she realized. *I made it outside of Heaven to the Greater Universe!*

It wasn't perfect like Heaven but it had its own stark beauty. And Stralasi had told her how big it was, how far away the nearest star really was.

"If you could shift a thousand kilometers every second of every day", the Good Brother, now a God himself, had said. "It would still take you over a thousand years to go from here to there."

Mirly thought she'd covered great distances during her journey from the Edge of Heaven to its Core but the size of the Greater Universe staggered her imagination.

Her journey had been grueling; she almost hadn't survived the first part of it, let alone the fierce fighting between Alum and Darak at the end. The RAF fields and energy blasts had splashed off defensive shields and come dangerously close to where she and Stralasi had huddled in fear. Without even meaning to, she'd pulled him outside the walls and into the First Forest, where they'd waited for the end of the conflict.

When she'd realized Darak's defeat might mean Stralasi's death, she'd thought to hide him among the trees. In turn, Stralasi had pledged to remove her to the safety of the outside universe should Darak be victorious.

She'd surprised herself by accepting.

She still didn't understand how Stralasi could be simultaneously a man and a hovering matte-gray sphere, but he said everything would become clear in a few days. He'd set an enhanced lattice growing in her brain, promising her the gift of knowledge equal to her former Lord's. The idea of that much understanding, and that much responsibility, terrified her.

"Well, I think it was the ideal solution," Darian was saying. "Thank you, Brother Stralasi, for coming up with it."

"Don't look at me," Stralasi protested. "I didn't even recognize it as a suggestion at the time. It was just a question."

"What would a universe with trillions of Gods look like?" Darak recalled. "A dangerous question, Brother."

"Call me Ontro. I no longer feel like a monk of the Alumita."

Darak cocked an eyebrow at the new God.

"Ha! Is that what we have to look forward to? Trillions upon trillions of new Gods with identity issues?"

"Alum was a multitude in and of Himself," Darian answered. "We needed greater numbers to defeat Him."

"But we didn't defeat Him," Darya pointed out. "We only jailed Him."

"He jailed Himself," Darian corrected. "Everything He expected to happen, happened."

"Virtually," Darak said.

"Sure," Darian agreed. "It's amazing what a billion or two God-minds all working together can accomplish. Feeding a completely convincing-looking deplosion of the multiverse into Alum's mind through the hacked Alumitum link was a clean solution."

"Alum withdrew into His very real Heaven voluntarily," Stralasi added.

"We were monitoring His thoughts. He was completely convinced of His victory."

"And He will remain that way," Darian said. "Forever."

"Forever is a long time to promise," Darak warned.

"It is. But in this case, I think it might hold," Darian replied. "We pulled Heaven out of Sag A* and embedded it in the thinfinity of the Chaos."

"Thinfinity?" Darya asked. "Your word?"

"An appropriate word," Darian answered. "Heaven has a thin layer of the Chaos around it, but distance measurements are impossible without material reference and so it is, simultaneously, essentially infinite." He smiled, pleased with his ingenuity. "Thinfinity."

"All surrounded by a filter of our devising," Stralasi added. "Alum expects the Chaos around Heaven to have the potential to create only more Heavenly matter. The filter makes the Chaos appear only as He expects it."

"An eternal virtual jail, then?" Darak asked.

"Alum would have to guess at His imprisonment," Darian said. "And He would have to do that without any evidence. There will be no clues coming from the walls of His jail. Heaven, floating in the infinite Chaos, will look exactly how He expects it to look. A perfect simulation, lasting forever."

Darak relaxed. It was hard to believe the battle was over. The threat to all of existence had been defeated. He bowed his head, thinking of the millions of lives—Human, Cybrid, Aelu, Esu, Angel, Archangel—that had been lost in the battle with the Living God.

And the untold trillions more we saved.

When Alum withdrew His consciousness into Heaven, He'd left behind vacant CPPU machinery across the Realm. The billions of freshly-minted Gods quickly established new Partial AIs to continue basic maintenance functions on the ringworlds, planetary colonies, and asteroid habitats of the Realm.

They were offering to all citizens of the Realm, and to the peoples of the Six, the very same choice Darian had given them. The civilizations of the other known Gods had come as a surprise to the Realm but it didn't take the new Gods long to decide to grant them full rights. They could decide their own fates and societal development.

Daily life and society was undergoing rapid change in the Realm. Freedom and knowledge, once won, was not easily contained. It desired to spread, to flourish.

The new Gods of the Realm agreed they would not restrict it artificially, believing that heavy handed restriction would be more irresponsible than opening themselves up to the possible dangers that came with their abilities.

The universe was infinite and the multiverse even more so. There was potential, and room enough, for an unlimited number of Gods.

Across the Realm, trillions upon trillions assented and began the process of enhancing their lattices to God-like capability. Trillions of others decided to remain as unenhanced humans or Cybrids or Angels or Aelu for the moment, preferring a simpler life and the stability of a familiar culture.

Some expected that each of the Gods would immediately lay claim to their own worlds or even to their own universes. The ancient assumption that with infinite power would come infinite greed and infinite ambition was a stubborn one.

But that sentiment lasted less than a second in the hearts and minds of the new Gods. Their power brought contentment and altruism. No longer needing anything for themselves, they turned to making their worlds better places for all life, including those who rejected godhood.

The universe lay before them, an infinite playground of possibility to be molded into beauty and astonishment. Even with what they knew, and they knew a great deal, there was still much to be learned and many places to be visited. They had life and new experience to be enjoyed.

"How will it all work out?" Stralasi asked.

"That, my dear friend, is unpredictable," Darak answered.

—The End—

Thank you for reading this book. If you enjoyed it, I hope you'll leave a review. For independent authors like me, reviews are the best way of telling others a book is worth reading.

Books by Paul Anlee

The Deplosion Series

The Reality Thief
Buy on Amazon at:
https://www.amazon.com/dp/B06XSML7V5

The Reality Incursion
Buy on Amazon at:
https://www.amazon.com/dp/B074FH1J44

The Reality Rebellions
Buy on Amazon at:
https://www.amazon.com/dp/B078Q84W9G

The Reality Assertion

Other Publications

Friends in Foreign Places Omnibus Edition
(contains the Paul Anlee short story: Illegal Alien)
Buy on Amazon at:
https://www.amazon.com/Omnibus-Friends-Places-Complete-Anthology-ebook/dp/B01LBDPVC6

Access these books through your local library or bookstore. Ask your librarian or retailer to order them through IngramSpark!

Points to Ponder
Book Club & Study Questions

THE DEPLOSION SERIES IS INTENDED to be more than just a story. I hope it inspires thinking and exchange on a variety of philosophical, religious, scientific, and social issues. The following questions will help get you started. Additional discussion can be found on the Paul Anlee Facebook page, and on my science and philosophy blog at www.paulanlee.com. I encourage you to visit and to contribute your thoughts.

1) Darya is shocked to learn that her own Kathy Liang alter ego once decided to keep the laws of the Reality Assertion Field from her, even going so far as to alter her natural interests so she'd avoid the subject despite her interest in all other aspects of science. Is there any knowledge that is simply too dangerous for humans to explore? What about genetic engineering, nuclear technologies or artificial intelligence (in particular, super general artificial intelligence—SGAI)? Should scientists be free to follow their curiosity, providing their methods receive ethical oversight?

2) "Godhood" (the ability to create universes) could be a technology to which humans might one day aspire. Could you ever view a living being as a God? Why or why not? What capabilities or characteristics would you need to see in a being who claimed to be "God" before you considered them worthy of your worship?

3) In writing this series, I made a serious attempt to create a "Heavenly" universe that would be close to perfection for all life in it. What is your idea of Heaven or a Heavenly universe? Do you believe that Heaven would be like Earth but a little bit better, or a place where every one of your idyllic wishes is fulfilled? How can a Heaven populated with other people fulfill everyone's every wish?

Is there any distinction between common conceptions of Heaven and some video games where one (real) player gets to live out their every fantasy among an infinite number of (simulated/non-real) other players?

Prior to this book, I blogged about some of the strange (to me) ideas held by different religions about Heaven (https://www.paulanlee.com/2017/09/21/whats-your-idea-of-heaven/).

"One of the strangest things I've ever read was written after the death of actor James Arness, famous for playing Marshal Matt Dillon on "Gunsmoke" for 20 years. 'Heaven's a little safer now,' the headline in The Daily Quarterly proclaimed." I've heard similar pronouncements following the death of firemen, law enforcers, and soldiers. In your version of Heaven, is there any crime or danger, any need for law enforcement, fire, or other emergency rescue workers?

4) Compare and contrast Mirly's view of Alum, the Living God, needing help with His concerns in the greater universe, with the Christian idea that "God is omniscient, omnipotent, and has a plan for us." Does it make sense that an omnipotent force could need human help in a "war against evil"? If God is omniscient, omnipotent and has a Plan, why would anyone pray, and why would He respond to prayer?

5) Science fiction authors have been depicting different versions of battles in space since the beginning of the genre. Most such battles tend to be centered on ideas about ships in three-dimensional space and extrapolate largely from naval battles. In the Deplosion series, I tried to present a view that doesn't rely on hulking monstrosities with large, easily-recognizable human crews. Do you think humans will ever make significant journeys into space with enormous, crewed vessels? Will we ever fight wars there?

6) What would a battle between Gods look like? While they could conceivably unleash huge energies at each other, it always seemed more likely to me that they would try to distort each other's reality. Can you imagine other ways in which beings with the ability to alter the underlying physics of their opponent's world might fight? What kinds of plausible defenses would you engage, if you were a God?

7) How did you feel at the end of the second last chapter when you realized the Living God had won? Did that seem like a proper outcome for the series? After all, though I may have focused on the side of the rebels, Alum was just trying to create a perfect Heaven for everyone to live in forever. What's so bad about that? If the Creator of our universe (if you believe in such a being) were to turn the entire universe into such a Heaven, would that be a good thing?

8) There has been a fair bit of discussion on the web about the opportunities and perils of general artificial intelligence (GAI) and of the ability of such a machine to rapidly self-evolve into a super GAI

(SGAI). I wrote about Brother Stralasi deciding to become like other Esu (by accepting to be connected to his own Cybrid "Familiar") to show one possible way in which humans could avoid a conflict with a machine intelligence. Do you think machine GAIs will be forever beyond our reach? Does biology have anything to offer an SGAI machine-based being? Is conflict inevitable if we continue developing the field of artificial intelligence? <u>If you care to discuss this particular question with others, please note,</u> **<u>this chapter can be downloaded for free</u>** <u>from my website as the short story, *Distributed.*</u>

9) Darak unleashed a virus for lattice development in humans and Cybrids without consulting anyone. Similarly, Darian decided to promote the billions of judges to Gods. Were Darak and Darian "right" to do that without asking? Does the outcome outweigh their ethical transgressions? Given the time restraints and pending danger, could the results have been achieved any other way? How do their decisions compare to the respect that Darak showed Darya in not tampering with her mind until she gave permission? Is it consistent thinking, or how does that thinking or scenario differ?

10) At one point, Brother Stalasi says, "At the risk of an even greater headache, what do you mean?" How did you feel about the many "deep science" and high concept passages in this series? How do you deal with complex information in your own life, do you try to balance curiosity and the effort required to learn new or complex concepts? How do you feel about the presence or absence, and the depth and breadth of scientific information in mainstream and social media?

11) Upon meeting Darak Legsu, Brother Stralasi dealt with a steep learning curve, and he does so again in his relationship with his Esu love interest, Crissea. The monk's worldview and perception of reality were challenged as he traveled, and he had to rebuild it and adapt. Multiple times. How would you respond to such paradigm-shifting information if you were in his shoes?

Has your worldview ever been seriously challenged, either as a child or as an adult? Have you travelled outside of your comfort zone, say for example, outside of your home country to a place where people did not speak your language or perhaps held different worldviews? How did you find the experience? Was it challenging, exciting, tiring, energizing, scary, rewarding, easy, difficult? Did your experience change how you viewed yourself, your home country and culture, or did it solidify the view you held before you left?

12) To his credit, the Good Brother maintains his curiosity, his drive to know and understand the truth, to understand the people and universe around him, and how things work. He asks questions, even though he anticipates that the answers will be challenging to digest. He frequently struggles but pushes through moments of feeling exhausted, confused, shocked, overwhelmed, and resentful, and tries to keep an open mind. Where do you think this character might go from here, from the end of this story? Could he ever go back to being a monk, a leader of the people on his home planet? Being a man with a long history as a caring, compassionate leader of his people, would he ever be able to abandon them? Now that his people have enhanced lattice-assisted intelligence and archives of knowledge, how would Brother Stralasi's role change?

13) Alum is a murderer, perhaps the most horrendous the universe has ever known. When He conspired to release the Eater on Earth, He knowingly caused the death of billions. Now, His Divine Plan will destroy all life in the universe. And yet, He also treasures life. His Heaven has no carnivores or prey; every being passes between vegetative and animal states and gets energy directly from Heaven's Divine Light. He has very carefully set up the physics of Heaven to avoid death and suffering. His two perspectives of life—that it is both precious and inconsequential—seem contradictory. How could He rationalize this? How can He not be bothered by this? Is this a sign of cognitive dissonance, compartmentalization, or is His perspective less paradoxical than it might appear? How does society reconcile this same contradiction?

Further Reading

THIS SERIES CONTAINS A LOT OF REAL SCIENCE and speculates heavily on possible advances in several fields. If you're interested in learning more about some of the areas discussed in this book, I suggest the following:

Lawrence Krauss, A Universe From Nothing.
An excellent review of cosmology and the possible origins of the universe.

Andrew Thomas, Hidden In Plain Sight.
A great series of eleven books (and growing) covering everything from gravity, relativity, quantum mechanics, time, space, consciousness and the particles that comprise all matter.

Richard Dawkins, The God Delusion.
A powerful analytic indictment of religious belief that applies logic and reason to spirit and faith.

Francis Collins, The Language of God.
A famous scientist's perspective on reconciling belief in God with scientific studies of evolution.

Jerry Coyne, Why Evolution is True.
A fact-filled romp through the scientific evidence in support of evolution.

George M. Church and Ed Regis, Regenesis.
Inside the mind of one of the world's leading synthetic biologists. Includes the origins of the field, current practices, and stunning visions of the future.

James Rickards, The Death of Money.
Analysis of how modern currency wars will be fought among major countries of the world, resulting in the collapse of the international monetary system.

Matt Strassler (https://profmattstrassler.com/), Of Particular Significance.
Insightful and informative website from a theoretical physicist with essays on a variety of topics in physics.

http://igem.org/Main_Page
iGEM is the International Genetically Engineered Machines annual competition. This is *the* place to go to learn about the exciting research done every year by university undergrads from around the world.

Acknowledgements

THANKS TO LEE for being the most patient editor imaginable, and to my great team of ARC readers and reviewers. This is a much better series thanks to your invaluable and insightful feedback.

A special thanks to the members of *Cuenca: Writing Our World* for your support.

Science fiction writers owe a debt to the giants who have gone before us, many of whom still produce prolifically. I have been influenced by many of the best, though none bear the responsibility for any of my errors. Isaac Asimov, Iain M. Banks, Greg Bear, Gregory Benford, Ray Bradbury, David Brin, Arthur C. Clarke, Peter F. Hamilton, Robert A. Heinlein, Ursula K. Le Guin, Larry Niven, Jerry Pournelle, Sheri S. Tepper, and John C. Wright, you have all been great inspirations.

The scientific community crosses many borders and intellectual boundaries. My career in biology has been guided by great scientists like David Baillie, David Pilgrim, and David Wishart. No, I don't know why I always worked for guys named David. My love of developmental biology, molecular biology, and genetics was inspired by Bruce P. Brandhorst during my undergraduate years at Simon Fraser University. I also owe a deep debt of gratitude for the exciting and inspiring researchers in synthetic biology including: Drew Endy, George Church, Tom Knight, Pam Silver, Chris Voigt, and Jay Keasling.

In coming up with the speculative science, philosophies, and sociopolitical economics in the Deplosion series, I built upon the ideas of many great thinkers. The following have all been sources for ideas, but none of them can be blamed for any misinterpretation or where I may have gone astray with the inspiration: Lawrence Krauss, Richard Dawkins, Andrew Thomas, Matt Strassler, John Mauldin, John Hussman, James Rickards, and Thom Hartmann.

About the Author

CANADIAN AUTHOR PAUL ANLEE writes provocative, epic sci-fi in the style of Asimov, Heinlein, Asher, and Reynolds, stories that challenge our assumptions and stretch our imagination. Literary, fact-based, and fast-paced, the Deplosion series explores themes in philosophy, politics, religion, economics, AI (artificial intelligence, VR (virtual reality), nanotech, synbio (synthetic biology), quantum reality, and beyond.

"When I was young, a teacher asked our class to write about what we wanted to be when we grew up. My story was entitled 'Me, The Everything!' I've been fortunate to come close to fulfilling that dream in my life, at least intellectually. Computer programming, molecular biology, nanotechnology, systems biology, synthetic biology, business consulting, and photocopy repair, I've worked in many fields. I've spent way too much of my life in school, eventually earning degrees in computing science (BSc) and in molecular biology and genetics (PhD). I've even had the chance to work with some of the best researchers in the world at The National Institute for Nanotechnology in Edmonton, Canada.

"After decades of reading almost nothing but high-tech science fiction and thirsting for more, I decided to take a shot at writing some. I aim for stories that are true to the best available science while pushing my imagination beyond the edge of what we know today. I love biology, particle physics, cosmology, artificial intelligence, cognitive psychology, politics, and economics. My personal philosophy is empirical physicalism and I blog regularly about the science and ideas found in my novels. I believe fiction should educate and stimulate, as much as it entertains."

Paul and his wife currently live in Cuenca, Ecuador, where they study Spanish and Chen-style Tai Chi when they're not working on exciting and provocative new stories.

Follow Paul Anlee on Facebook or write me at: paul.anlee.author@gmail.com. Even better, visit me at my website, https://www.paulanlee.com/, read the blog, leave a comment, and sign-up on my email list to be the first to hear about new books, new posts, and special announcements. That's the best way to hear about FREE offers and special deals.

Darian Publishing House (DarianPublishingHouse@gmail.com)
Chatham, Ontario, Canada

Book Layout & Design ©2013 - BookDesignTemplates.com
Design Cover - Elizabeth Mackey Graphic Design
Author Photo - John Keeble
Background image on cover art - Copyright Jean-Michel ALIMI, DEUS Consortium

The author thanks **Jean-Michel ALIMI, Scientific Director of DEUS Consortium (deus-consortium.org)** and **Director of DEUS Consortium** for making available the background cover image obtained through DEUS numerical simulations. This image reproduces the distribution of dark matter in a universe with a cosmological constant.

Visit the author's website at: www.paulanlee.com
Follow the author on Facebook at: Paul Anlee or Paul Anlee Fans
Email the author at: paul.anlee.author@gmail.com

The Reality Assertion / Paul Anlee - 1st ed.

ISBN ebook: 978-0-9958442-9-2

ISBN Paperback: 978-1-9991812-0-8